Tales from Gr

Memories from Acorn Hill

MELODY CARLSON

New York, New York

Memories from Acorn Hill

ISBN-10: 0-8249-4906-4
ISBN-13: 978-0-8249-4906-8

Published by Guideposts
16 East 34ᵗʰ Street
New York, New York 10016
www.guideposts.org

Distributed by Ideals Publications, a Guideposts company
2630 Elm Hill Pike, Suite 100
Nashville, TN 37214

Library of Congress Cataloging-in-Publication Data for *All in the Timing* and *Ready to Wed* on file.

Cover by Deborah Chabrian
Interior design by Marisa Jackson
Typeset by Aptara

Printed and bound in the United States of America
10 9 8 7 6 5 4 3 2 1

All in the
Timing

Chapter One

Alice paused to admire the vibrant flowerbeds that lined the walk up to Grace Chapel Inn. Bursting with sassy pinks, sunny yellows and rich hues of purple, the spring bulbs that Jane had planted last fall were now a glorious rainbow of color. Springtime was definitely here, with Easter just over a week away.

"Alice," called a voice from the front porch. Alice looked up to see her younger sister Jane garbed in her gardening overalls, tending a large terra-cotta pot of tulips, hyacinths and daffodils. Alice marveled at how her fifty-year-old sister looked years younger with her dark hair gathered in a ponytail.

"Everything looks so beautiful," Alice said as she headed up the stairs. "You've done a fantastic job with the flowers this year, Jane."

"It just keeps getting better, doesn't it?" Jane looked out over her workmanship and smiled.

Alice nodded. "Wouldn't Mother be pleased?"

"It is lovely," said Louise, their older sister, as she stepped out the door and greeted Alice. In her hands was a tray with three tumblers and a crystal pitcher of what appeared to be freshly made lemonade. "It reminds me of how it looked when we were little girls."

"It really does," agreed Alice. "I think Mother's gardening genes are fast at work in our little sister."

Jane smiled, but there was a touch of sadness in her blue eyes. Madeleine Howard had died giving birth to Jane when Alice was twelve and Louise, fifteen.

Louise noticed Jane's expression, for she frowned dramatically at the hole in the knee of Jane's faded overalls and said, "I don't think our mother ever would have worn those kinds of 'gardening jeans.'"

Jane laughed. "Hey, Louise made a pun."

"That's not all I made," said Louise as she held out the pitcher and smiled. "It's such a warm day that I couldn't resist. Do you girls have time?"

"Are you kidding?" said Alice. "Some lemonade would be heavenly. The hospital was so busy that I barely had a moment for a break today. I would love to sit out here and put my feet up for a spell."

"Me too," said Jane. "I'll run inside and wash my hands first. And maybe I'll bring back some oatmeal raisin cookies that I made this morning."

"*Mmm . . .*," said Alice as she eased herself into the porch swing and ran a hand through her reddish-brown bob. "Don't you just love springtime, Louise?"

Louise nodded as she carefully filled the three glasses, then handed one to Alice. "It is such a time of renewal," she said as she made herself comfortable in the wicker rocker, "as if God is giving all of creation a fresh new start."

Alice sipped the icy lemonade and sighed happily.

Jane rejoined them, setting a plate holding a generous number of cookies on the wicker coffee table. "Did you tell Alice the news yet, Louise?"

Alice reached down for a cookie, then studied Jane's face. She could tell by her sister's expression that something was up.

Louise pushed a strand of her short silver hair from her forehead and cleared her throat. "Mark Graves sent an e-mail to the inn today," she began, waiting, it seemed, for Alice to react. The three sisters had run Grace Chapel Inn in their Victorian home since the death of their father.

Alice took a bite of the cookie and simply nodded. Mark, her college sweetheart, had recently come back into her life. They saw each other occasionally when he was not traveling with his job as chief veterinarian for the Philadelphia Zoo.

"As you know, Mark has a reservation for all next week, from this Saturday through Easter."

Alice nodded again, waiting for Louise to continue, her curiosity beginning to escalate.

"Well, his e-mail today was to request a second room."

"A second room?" echoed Alice.

"Yes," said Jane with raised eyebrows. "What do you think that means?"

"I don't know," admitted Alice.

"He hasn't mentioned anything?" asked Jane.

"No, not a thing," Alice said, turning her attention to Wendell, who was now rubbing himself against her legs. "Does it really matter?"

"Well, isn't Mark coming here to see you?" said Jane. "Why would he suddenly bring someone else along? Does that make any sense?"

"Oh, Jane," said Alice. "I think you're working your brain overtime on this. If Mark requested a second room, I'm sure he has a good reason." She looked at Louise. "Do we have another room? I thought we were all booked."

Louise smiled. "Fortunately for Mark, I had just received a cancellation. Mark and his mysterious friend will be occupying both the Sunset and the Sunrise rooms."

Of course, this inspired Jane to begin singing, rather badly, "Sunrise, sunset . . . sunrise, sunset, quickly flow the years . . . ."

Louise cleared her throat loudly this time. "Please, Jane."

Jane grinned. "It just seemed appropriate. I mean since Mark is coming to see Alice and they might be—"

"I hate to disappoint you, Jane," interrupted Alice, "but it's just a friendly visit. We're certainly not planning to run away and get married, if that's what you're thinking."

"Goodness," said Louise. "I certainly hope not."

Jane smiled as she plucked up another cookie. "Well, that's a relief. Imagine running this inn with only two sisters. It just wouldn't seem right."

"Don't worry," said Alice, winking at Louise. "I'm afraid that, for better or for worse, you two are stuck with me."

Even so, Alice wondered about this mystery guest whom her old beau was bringing to the inn next week. Despite her confident answer to Jane, she was not entirely certain that Mark Graves had the intention of being just friends. But, then, sisters do not have to tell each other absolutely everything.

Chapter Two

*F*riday was Alice's day off, but she got up early as usual and walked with her friend Vera Humbert, a fifth-grade teacher. Alice spent the rest of the morning working on a quilt that she had been too busy to give attention to the last few months. She planned to take the quilt to Peggy Sanders' baby shower next month, but the busywork was also a good distraction from thoughts of Mark Graves's arrival tomorrow.

"That's looking beautiful," said Jane as she poked her head into Alice's room. "Peggy is going to love it."

"I hope so," said Alice. "Peach and pale green are the colors she chose for the nursery. They work for a boy or a girl."

Jane picked up a section of blocks and admired them. "You're getting really good at this. Sylvia's quilting class must've really helped you."

Alice turned back to her sewing machine to cut a thread. "I'm afraid I've made a few mistakes on it, but the baby won't notice."

"Well, we all have to start somewhere."

Alice nodded. "I've wanted to do a quilting project for a while. It's nice to finally have the time."

"So does it feel good to be on vacation now?"

Alice smiled. "It's wonderful, Jane. I'm so glad you suggested that I take Easter week off."

"You work too hard anyway. Everyone needs to take a break sometimes."

Alice straightened her back, stretching her shoulders. "Perhaps I should take a break now."

"Good idea. I'll see you later," said Jane as she headed off to her room.

Alice went downstairs to the kitchen, then decided to get the mail. She went out the kitchen door and walked to the end of the driveway and the mailbox. She knew that there probably wouldn't be a letter from Mark today, but on the days she wasn't working, she liked to be the first one to get the mail. That way, if there was a letter, she wouldn't have to go through her sisters' questions when they gave it to her later. Sneaky perhaps, but just simpler, she told herself. As expected, there was no letter from him today.

"Hello, Alice." Ethel Buckley waved from her porch as Alice walked back from the mailbox. Ethel, the sisters' aunt, had lived in the inn's carriage house for the past ten years.

"Morning, Auntie," called Alice. "Lovely day, isn't it?"

"Simply beautiful," Ethel called back.

When Alice opened the front door, she saw that Louise had just finished registering new guests.

"I'd like you to meet the Winstons," said Louise. Alice smiled as she was introduced to the attractive middle-aged couple and their pretty teenaged daughter.

"How nice to meet you all," Alice said. "Laura, you must be about sixteen?"

"Laura is seventeen," said the mother, "and a senior."

"What an exciting time of life," said Alice as she studied the girl. Laura's long, chestnut hair was pulled back into a ponytail, and her khaki skirt and navy-and-white striped top were casual but stylish. Although they were indoors, Laura wore a pair of big sunglasses with lime-green frames. More striking than the glasses was the unhappy scowl on her face. It seemed that Laura Winston would rather be anyplace but there.

Alice turned her attention back to the parents. "Will you be in Acorn Hill for long?"

"Laura is on Easter break all next week, so we plan to stay here until next Sunday," said Mrs. Winston. "My parents used to live in Acorn Hill, and I've always wanted Laura to see—" She stopped herself and glanced uncomfortably at her daughter. "I mean I've always wanted Laura to experience her grandparents' hometown—"

"Give it a break, Mom," snapped the teen as she tightly folded her arms across her chest.

Alice decided to change the subject. "What was your mother's maiden name, Mrs. Winston? Perhaps we knew your parents."

"Campbell," said Mrs. Winston.

"Eleanor and Roland Campbell?" asked Louise with interest.

"Yes." Mrs. Winston nodded with enthusiasm. "That's right."

"Eleanor and I went to school together," said Louise. "I always liked her. How is she doing?"

"She's fine," said Mrs. Winston.

"Didn't they move to Florida?" asked Alice.

"Yes. That was about fifteen years ago," said Mrs. Winston. "My father had some serious health problems that forced him to retire early. He passed away shortly after they settled down there, but my mother made lots of friends and loves the sunshine. She decided to stay down there. Her condo is near Orlando. In a recent letter, she mentioned relatives still living near Acorn Hill."

Mr. Winston picked up the suitcases in an obvious attempt to end this conversation. Just then, the phone rang. Louise excused herself and went to the office to answer it.

"May I show you up to your room?" offered Alice, feeling sorry for Mr. Winston. "I'm sure you'd like to get settled."

"Yes, thank you," said Mr. Winston.

Mrs. Winston nodded as she took her daughter's arm. "Your sister said that the roll-away is all set up in there."

Laura made a groaning sound. "Great, I get to spend a whole week sleeping on a cot in my parents' room. What a fun spring break."

Alice laughed as she led them up the stairs. "Yes, I'm sure it will seem rather tame around here, Laura. The teens from our church are having a get-together on Saturday night. Maybe you'd like to—"

"No thanks," said Laura.

"Well, perhaps you'll enjoy getting to know the town," said Alice optimistically, "becoming familiar with the history and whatnot."

"Yes," said Mrs. Winston eagerly. "That's just what I was hoping."

"I'm guessing you're staying in the Garden Room," said Alice when they reached the landing at the top of the stairs. "Since that's the largest room."

"Yes," said Mr. Winston as he waited for Alice to lead the way, "that's what your sister told us."

Alice took them into the spacious room and smiled to see that Jane, as usual, had placed fresh flowers on the bureau as well as in the bathroom. Foil-wrapped home-made chocolates were on the bed pillows, including the one on the roll-away bed that was set up by a window.

"I hope you'll all be very comfortable here," she said as the three of them entered the room. "Please, let us know if you need anything."

"Thank you," said Mr. Winston as he set a bag on the suitcase stand. He started to reach for his wallet as if to get a tip.

Alice laughed and held up her hand. "You don't need to tip me, Mr. Winston."

He nodded. "Oh, sorry. *Um,* thanks."

Alice was on her way out the door when Mrs. Winston called out. "Oh yes, now that I think of it, there is something I need . . . if you have a minute?"

"Yes?" said Alice, turning.

Mrs. Winston nodded to the door. "I'll go downstairs with you." Once they were downstairs, Mrs. Winston told Alice she had a problem.

"Why don't we go to the parlor?" Alice suggested.

After they were seated, Mrs. Winston began to explain. "I really hate to trouble you, Alice," she began, "but, well, you see, Laura is having a very difficult time."

Alice nodded. "Yes, that's not uncommon with teenagers, is it?"

"Yes, well, it's a bit more than just adolescent angst," she continued. "You see, Laura has grown up with juvenile diabetes. Actually, diabetes runs in my side of the family. That's what my father died from, or rather complications from the disease."

"Oh, I'm sorry," said Alice. "I'm a nurse and I know how debilitating diabetes can be. But with proper care and nutrition, most diabetics can lead a normal life. I hope that is the case with Laura."

"Up until this year, Laura was doing just fine. She had been diligent with her diet and insulin shots and exercise and, well, everything. In fact, she was such an excellent soccer player that she was even being considered for an athletic scholarship from the local college. We thought that everything was perfectly under control." Mrs. Winston sighed and reached into her pocket for a tissue. "And then it all just fell apart." She dabbed at a stray tear that was streaking down her cheek now.

"I'm so sorry," said Alice as she placed her hand on Mrs. Winston's shoulder. She truly was sorry for this poor woman, but even so, she wondered what she could possibly do to help. "You can be sure I'll tell my sister Jane to have the right kinds of foods on hand for Laura's condition," she added. "Don't worry, Jane knows a lot about nutrition and I will confer with her."

"Thank you," said Mrs. Winston.

"We have several kinds of fruit juice in the refrigerator, in case Laura's blood sugar drops. Please feel free to help yourself to whatever you need from the kitchen. I'll let Jane know about this too."

"Yes," said Mrs. Winston. "I do appreciate that. But what I really wanted to tell you and your sisters is that Laura is blind." She paused to blow her nose.

"Oh my," said Alice. "I am so sorry. I noticed that you held on to her arm, but I thought perhaps that you were steadying yourself. Is her blindness connected to the diabetes? I believe that it's quite rare for anyone to suffer retinopathy at such a young age."

"Yes, you're right, it is. Unfortunately, Laura spent a long weekend at a soccer camp in February, and the schedule was rather demanding. I think Laura was a bit forgetful about her health." She shook her head. "I probably never should've let her go."

"You couldn't know that something would go wrong."

"Perhaps not. Laura overexerted herself and didn't have her insulin when she needed it, and, of course, with all these kids bringing treats from home, well, Laura ate the wrong kinds of things as well." Mrs. Winston just shook her head.

"Oh dear," said Alice. "That can be very dangerous."

"Yes. It was. Laura ended up in the emergency room. We nearly lost her. She was in a coma for several days and when she came out of it, well . . . her vision was almost completely gone. It has steadily degenerated since then. She can still see shadows sometimes, or so she says, but she is legally blind. Naturally, she won't be playing any soccer now."

"Poor thing," said Alice. "No wonder she's so unhappy."

Mrs. Winston nodded. "Yes, I just thought you and your sisters should know how her condition came about. Oh, I suppose it's silly, but I didn't want you to assume that Laura was simply a spoiled brat. She can be quite difficult, but she's still trying to adjust to all that she has lost."

"We wouldn't have thought that, but I am glad you told me."

"And, of course, there's the difficulty in getting around," said Mrs. Winston. "Laura refuses to get a cane or a dog or even to do the most basic training that's been offered to her. I think she's in denial right now. All her friends have been very helpful to her at school. Naturally, her grades have gone down and we may have to consider a special school, which she refuses even to discuss with us."

"Oh, it must be a difficult time for everyone."

"Yes. I suppose I hoped this trip might give us all a break and maybe that something would change. Of course, my husband thinks I'm crazy. He can't understand why I insisted on bringing our blind daughter to a strange place. . . ." She paused and looked close to tears again. "Maybe he's right."

"Oh no," said Alice as she patted Mrs. Winston's hand. "I think it's a wonderful idea to come to Acorn Hill. Who knows what might happen here? I usually work part-time as a nurse at the hospital in Potterston, but I've taken the week off, so I hope you'll feel free to call on me if you need anything. I will try to do whatever I can to help Laura feel right at home."

"Thank you, Alice."

"I'll let my sisters know about everything," she assured her.

"Well, I feel much better now." Mrs. Winston smiled. "Perhaps you're right. Who knows what might happen?"

"Yes," said Alice. "I believe that God really does work in mysterious ways. I think that by the time you leave next week, things will be looking up."

"Oh, I hope so."

After the two women parted, Alice went off in search of her sisters. She found them on the back porch, with their backs to her. They were discussing whether to plant the geraniums that Jane had started in the sunroom.

"I think it is far too soon," said Louise with authority. "We might still get frost."

"I can watch the weather forecast," said Jane in a slightly irritated voice. "I'll cover them if necessary. I'm just so tired of looking at those empty flower boxes outside the kitchen and I—"

"Excuse me," said Alice.

"Oh, I didn't hear you," said Jane as she pushed a dark strand of hair from her face. "We were just trying to decide about—"

"Yes, I heard your discussion." Alice suppressed a grin. "And just for your information, I will not act as a tie-breaker in this little dispute."

Jane laughed. Louise smiled, then said, "Thank you for taking care of the Winstons for me. That was a very aggravating phone call. A gentleman from Pittsburgh wanted to make reservations for Easter weekend, and even though I told him we were booked full, he just would not give up. Then he asked about Memorial Day weekend, and once again I had to tell him we were full. Well, he started getting quite irate with me."

"You should've told him that we'll never have room for him," said Jane.

"I tried to keep my patience," said Louise. "Finally he asked about a weekend in August that was open, but, to be perfectly honest, I wanted to tell him that it was booked too."

Alice chuckled. "So did you go ahead and make his reservation?"

Louise nodded.

"So when exactly is Mr. Sourpuss coming?" asked Jane. "I think I'll make sure to be out of town that weekend."

Louise gave her youngest sister the look—the look that she had been giving Jane since she was a little girl—the look that meant "don't even think about it."

"Well, maybe we should just put up a sign," suggested Jane. "You know, like they have in restaurants: 'We have the right to refuse service.'"

"That certainly wouldn't be hospitable," said Louise.

"Especially for an inn that's called Grace Chapel," added Alice.

"I suppose you're right," said Jane.

"Speaking of disgruntled guests," said Alice as she closed the door between the porch and the kitchen. "I need to tell you about Laura Winston."

"My goodness," said Louise. "I don't think that I have ever seen such an unfriendly teenager. If I were her mother I would—"

"You don't understand," said Alice, then she quickly explained the situation in detail.

"Oh, the poor thing," said Jane. "That's so sad. To become blind at any age is a tragedy, but at seventeen? Just when life is beginning to unfold."

Louise shook her head. "I had no idea. Goodness, I feel so bad having judged her."

"I did the exact same thing myself," admitted Alice.

"Well, we must do everything we can to make her stay here as pleasant as possible," said Jane.

"Yes," said Alice. "I told Mrs. Winston that Laura would be in good hands here."

"How about the teen thing?" asked Jane. "Laura might enjoy meeting some new—"

"I already mentioned it to her," said Alice. "She wasn't interested."

"Oh."

"I suppose someone else could invite her again," said Alice. "It might be the kind of situation where we need to be persistent to get—"

"Yoo-hoo," called a familiar voice.

"Hi, Aunt Ethel," said Jane.

"What's going on here?" asked Ethel. "Some kind of secret sister meeting?"

"No," said Louise. "Alice was just giving us some information about a guest."

Ethel's eyebrows lifted. "Oh my. Certainly my nieces are not gossiping, are you?"

"Not gossip," said Alice, then Louise explained the situation with Laura.

"Dear me," said Ethel. "That's too bad."

"So, we've decided that we should try to reach out to her," said Alice. "Maybe one of us can break through to her before the week is up."

"Speaking of guests," said Ethel, turning her attention to Alice, "when is that handsome animal doctor showing up here?"

Alice felt her cheeks growing warm. "Not until tomorrow," she told Ethel. "His last letter said he expects to be here late Saturday night." She suddenly turned to Louise. "That is, unless that has changed too. Did he mention—"

"I don't recall him mentioning a change in his arrival time," said Louise.

"So what else has changed?" asked Ethel.

"Why don't we go inside," suggested Jane as she opened the door into her kitchen. "It's getting a little crowded out here."

As soon as they were in the kitchen, Louise told Ethel about Mark's mystery guest and once again all attention was back on Alice.

"Who do you think it is?" asked Ethel.

Alice just shrugged. "I don't have a clue."

Just then, they heard the bell in the foyer ding, and Louise excused herself. "That's probably the Langleys," she said as she hurried out.

"A full house this week?" asked Ethel.

"That's right," said Jane as she put on the teakettle. "Tea, anyone?"

"Do you have any of those delicious ginger biscotti left?" asked Ethel hopefully.

Jane grinned as she produced the cookie jar and peeked inside. "Lucky for you, there are just enough left for a little tea party."

Chapter Three

*A*lice had offered to put away the tea things while Jane made a quick run to the grocery store and Louise went off to search for a heating pad for Mr. Langley. The poor man had strained his back loading his wife's luggage into the trunk of their car and had been in pain the whole three hours that it took them to drive to Acorn Hill. Alice had promptly prescribed treatments of alternate hot and cold packs, along with ibuprofen and rest.

"Send me your bill later," the elderly man had teased her as Louise and his wife helped him to make his way slowly up the stairs.

"Just remember, I'm not a doctor," said Alice. "I hope that I won't wish that I had malpractice insurance."

"I don't put much stock in doctors anyway," said Mr. Langley.

"Well, I'm sure that you'll be feeling much better by tomorrow," Alice assured him.

Now Alice hummed to herself as she puttered about Jane's cheerful kitchen. A real departure from the antiques and the more formal feeling of the rest of the house, Jane's bright, paprika-colored cabinets, perky curtains, and black and white checkerboard tile floors always made Alice happy. Just as she was hanging up the dishtowel, she heard the familiar ding of the bell in the foyer.

She removed her apron and patted her hair in place. It was still a day early for Mark and his friend to be arriving, but, on the other hand, no other guests were expected at the inn. When she entered the foyer, she saw a young man looking up at the high ceiling. He seemed out of place. In fact, he was a rather untidy young man with shaggy blond hair and oversized pants that appeared to be almost falling off his narrow hips.

"May I help you?" she asked with a smile.

"Yeah," he said, looking over his shoulder uncomfortably. "I think I'm supposed to be here, at this inn, you know. I mean I'm supposed to be meeting someone here."

"Are you here with Dr. Mark Graves?" she asked.

He nodded. "Yeah, sort of. I mean he told me to meet him here. Is he here yet?"

"No. I don't believe he is arriving until tomorrow evening." She held out her hand. "I'm Alice Howard. My sisters and I run this inn."

He shook her hand, then quickly pulled his away. "Yeah, right. I'm Adam. Adam Peterson."

She could tell that he did not recognize her name. *But then,* she thought, *why should he? Why would Mark have bothered to tell this young man about me?* "So are you going to be staying here?" she asked. "In the inn, I mean. I was told that Dr. Graves was bringing a friend and—"

"Yeah, I guess so," he said quickly. "Mark told me to meet him here and I was going to spend time with him next week. I thought he said to come today. Am I too early or something?"

"No, no," she said. "You're fine. Your room is all ready for you. Would you like me to show you up now?" she offered.

"Yeah," he said. "That'd be cool."

"Do you have any bags?" she asked.

He hoisted a dusty black backpack over his shoulder. "This is it."

"Okay, then I'll take you up."

"That's all right," he said, after glancing up the stairs. "You can just give me the key and tell me where it is. You don't have to go up there or anything."

"Oh, it's no trouble," she said as she headed up the stairs ahead of him. She hated to admit it to herself, but something about this young man bothered her. She did not want to judge him, but his manner made her uncomfortable.

"How long have you known Dr. Graves?" she asked him after they reached the top of the stairs.

He shrugged, then turned his attention to Wendell, who was happily warming himself in a shaft of sunshine. "Oh, like forever, you know. He's been around since I was a baby." He set aside his backpack as he knelt to pet the cat.

Alice smiled. "Friend of the family?"

"Yeah, I guess you could say that." His back remained to her as he continued to stroke Wendell.

It seemed fairly clear that Adam was not about to divulge any unnecessary information, so Alice opened the door to the Sunset Room and simply said, "This is your room." She had already decided that Mark should have the Sunrise Room, since it was the room that she had decorated . . . with some help from Jane. It seemed logical that his friend should have the room just across the hall.

"This is nice," Adam said as he looked around.

"I hope you'll be comfortable." Alice went through the information about when they served breakfast, that there were restaurants in town for other meals, but that he and Mark were invited to have dinners with the sisters.

"Where's the TV?" he asked as he dropped his backpack to the floor with a loud thump.

"I'm sorry," she said. "We don't have televisions in the inn. We like to provide a quiet place for our guests to relax and unwind. We do have a library downstairs from which you are free to borrow books, and my sister Louise occasionally plays piano in the evenings. . . ." She could tell by his expression that this did not impress him in the least.

"Yeah, okay," he said. "Whatever."

She forced another smile as she made her way to the door. "Well, make yourself at home and let us know if you need anything."

He nodded, but just continued to stand there in the middle of the room as if he had no idea how he had gotten there or why he had come. It was, in fact, a mystery to Alice too. She asked herself, *Who is this young man and what does he have to do with Mark Graves?* She tried to push these questions from her mind as she made her way downstairs.

"Hello, Alice," said Mrs. Winston as she and her husband met Alice at the bottom of the stairs. "We're going out for a walk just now."

Alice looked at the couple as they headed toward the door. "Laura's not joining you?" she asked.

Mrs. Winston sadly shook her head. "She said she wants to take a nap."

"She sleeps too much," said Mr. Winston as he opened the door. "Some fresh air would probably do her good."

"Well, we can't very well force her, dear," said Mrs. Winston.

"Have a nice walk," said Alice, feeling sorry about the stress that this couple seemed to be experiencing.

"I'm back," called Jane from the kitchen.

Alice went in and offered to help unload groceries.

"Thanks," said Jane.

"How about if I bring them in from the car and you can start putting them away," said Alice, "since you do a better job at fitting everything in place than I do."

"Sounds like a plan," said Jane as she put a jug of milk into the refrigerator.

Alice finally brought the last bag from the car and then sat down at the table to watch as Jane continued to put things away. "We got a new guest while you were out," said Alice as Jane filled a large ceramic bowl with apples.

"Really?" Jane turned and looked at her. "Is it Mark?"

Alice shook her head. "Guess again."

"Mark's mysterious friend?" Jane balanced the last apple on top.

"What is this about Mark's friend?" asked Louise as she came into the kitchen. "Have they arrived already?"

"Not *they*," said Alice. "Mark's friend is here. At least I think he's Mark's friend. To be honest, I felt a bit confused."

"Why is that?" asked Louise.

"I'm not sure. But something about him seemed, well, a bit odd." Alice shook her head. "Perhaps I'm just imagining things. I don't know."

"*Who* is Mark's friend?" demanded Jane.

"He's a young man named Adam Peterson," said Alice.

"A *young* man?" Louise frowned. "How young?"

"I didn't ask, but I'm guessing maybe college age. I'm not sure."

"Do you know what his relationship is to Mark?" asked Louise.

Alice took an apple from the bowl and went to the sink to wash it off. "He said he's known Mark his whole life. His sister doesn't have a son named Adam. So he's not Mark's nephew."

"No, that's right," Alice said, then took a bite of the apple.

Jane's eyebrows shot up. "Maybe he's Mark's long-lost son!"

"Son? How can that be?" Louise asked. "Mark Graves has never been married."

"Well, you don't—"

"Jane," said Alice. "Mark has never mentioned any son."

"Well, I'm reading a novel about a young man who is searching for his birth father and he's—"

"That is exactly why you should read something besides fiction," Louise said. "Goodness knows how it fills your head with strange ideas."

Alice chuckled. "Well, I'm reading a murder mystery, Louise. Do you think I might become dangerous?"

"Harrumph," Louise said, giving Alice an exasperated look.

"Well, what was this young man like?" asked Jane. "You said his name was Adam?"

"Yes," said Alice. "To be honest, he seemed unhappy."

"Well, that is about right," said Louise. "We already have a depressed teenager and a guest who is suffering with a bad back. Why should we not have an unhappy young man as well?"

"Won't we be the jolly bunch for Easter week," said Jane as she put several pounds of butter into the refrigerator.

"Remember," said Alice. "Part of our mission in this inn has always been to help people. Maybe that's what this week will be about."

"You are absolutely right," said Louise.

"I'm still curious," said Jane. "I'd like to know what Adam has to do with Mark Graves. And why it was so important for them to spend this week together when everyone knows that the only reason Mark is coming back to Acorn Hill is to see Alice."

"Oh, Jane," said Alice. "Mark is coming here because he really likes our town and wants to—"

"Go on, Alice," said Jane, waving a hand at her older sister as she took a bite out of her own apple. "You can go ahead and act as if there's nothing between you and Mark if you like. But I'm not buying it."

Alice dropped her apple core into the trash and just shrugged. "I guess only time will tell."

Jane nodded as she chewed and finally said, "Yep, Alice. That's exactly what I'm counting on."

Just then they heard a loud crash from the direction of the foyer.

"Oh dear!" cried Louise.

The three sisters hurried out to see what was wrong.

"Oh, Laura," exclaimed Alice when she found the girl squatting in front of the shattered pieces of a broken ceramic vase that had held a flower arrangement. She took Laura's hand in her own. "You've cut yourself."

"I'm sorry," said Laura, pulling her hand away. "I shouldn't have come down by myself. I just thought that—"

"Don't worry," said Alice as she gently helped the girl to her feet. "Be careful of the wet floor, I'm sure it's slippery."

She moved the girl out of harm's way. "I'm a nurse and I can take care of that cut for—"

"That's right," Jane assured her. "I'm Alice's sister Jane, and speaking from experience, there's no one better than Alice to bandage a cut."

Laura turned her head toward the sound of Jane's voice. "I—I'm sorry if I made a mess," she muttered. "I ran into something, I think a table maybe. I'd just come downstairs. I was trying to pick it up and—"

"Hey, no problem," said Jane. "I never really liked that vase anyway."

"That's true enough," said Louise with a frown since it had been her vase. "I'm Louise, dear. Don't worry, Jane and I will have it cleaned up before you know it."

"Come on," Alice urged Laura. "Let's go to the bathroom and wash out your cut. I don't think you need stitches, but I want to be sure."

As Alice attended to the cut, which did not need stitches, she said, "It must be hard getting used to not having your sight."

Laura sighed loudly, but said nothing.

Alice continued to talk as she cleaned the wound. "When someone loses the ability to do something they once loved, it seems they must go through a period of grieving."

"Grieving?"

"Yes, as if someone you loved had died. You have to work through the stages. For instance, you might've felt some denial at first."

Laura nodded.

"You tell yourself that it's not really happening."

"Yeah."

"And then you feel guilt." Alice began to wrap Laura's hand in gauze.

"Like it was my fault that I lost my vision?"

"That's right."

"Yeah, well, I guess I felt that too. Like if I'd been more careful with my insulin and stuff, things might've gone differently. But it's still not fair. I mean other kids don't have to put up with this kind of crud!"

"And then you get angry—"

"That's right!" snapped Laura. "And that's how I feel right now." She held up her bandaged hand. "Like this! This never would've happened before. It's just so stupid and senseless! I don't see why God allows stuff like this to happen to anyone."

"That's a natural reaction," said Alice as she finished with the last bit of tape.

"Really?" Laura seemed somewhat soothed.

"Yes." Alice snapped the first-aid box closed. "But you just don't want to stay in that angry stage for too long, Laura. You want to move on."

"What if I can't?"

Alice pushed a strand of hair from Laura's eyes. "You must ask God to help you."

Laura stood up, looking unconvinced. She thanked Alice for her help and fumbled to find the door.

"Let me get that," said Alice.

Just as they emerged from the bathroom, Mr. and Mrs. Winston were entering the inn.

"Oh no!" exclaimed Mrs. Winston when she saw the white bandage. "What happened to your hand, Laura?"

After Alice quickly explained, Laura asked her mother to help take her back to their room.

"I thought you were going to take a nap, Laura," said Mr. Winston as the three of them went upstairs. "If you had wanted to walk around, you should've come with us."

"Oh, don't pick on her," said Mrs. Winston. "It's plain to see she changed her mind. Does it hurt much, honey?"

"No, it's fine," said Laura in an irritated tone. "I wish you wouldn't freak every time something happens, Mom."

Alice paused in the parlor to say a silent prayer for the Winstons before she headed back into the kitchen to help Jane with dinner. Suddenly, she suspected this week was not going to be easy for anyone at Grace Chapel Inn.

Chapter Four

Alice dropped the last pieces of pared potato into a pot of water and then rinsed off the peeler. "Anything else?" she asked her sister.

"No, that should do it." Jane grinned. "It's so nice that you don't mind doing things like peeling potatoes or chopping vegetables. It's very helpful to have a good prep cook."

Alice laughed. "Is that what I am?"

"Sure. If you ever get tired of nursing and still need a job, I'll be happy to give you a good recommendation. Good prep cooks can be hard to come by."

"I'll keep that in mind."

"Have you seen anything of Mark's young friend this afternoon?" asked Jane as she measured the seasoning mix that she had made for her special roast chicken. Jane's roast chicken was so tender and flavorful that Alice and Louise looked forward to the occasions when Jane served this homey dish.

"I don't think he's come downstairs at all," said Alice as she put the lid on the seasoning and returned it to the spice cupboard. "I was hoping that he would. I wanted to talk to him some more. He seems so somber. I thought that I might interest him in reading something. Perhaps that book about hiking the Appalachian Trail that Mr. Stefan left for our library. Adam looks as if he might like the outdoors and he certainly could use some laughs. I remember Mr. Stefan saying that it was a very funny book. I must admit that I felt bad when I saw how disturbed Adam was by our not having televisions for the guests."

Jane chuckled. "Well, to the younger generation, it is fairly disturbing." She glanced up at her small black-and-white TV, which was tucked into the cabinet. "Sometimes I think I might get a little loopy if I couldn't catch up on the latest news."

"But you hardly ever turn it on," observed Alice.

"Yes, but I know that I can, and that makes all the difference."

"Perhaps we should have another TV somewhere in the inn, one that doesn't actually work. Then maybe our young guests would feel reassured just to see it."

"Ha," said Jane. "You could be onto something."

"Hello," said Louise as she joined them. "Oh, good, roast chicken."

Jane smiled as she basted the golden meat and a delicious aroma filled the kitchen. "It's not fancy, but it's good."

"Alice," said Louise in a lowered voice, "I thought you should know that your young man is wandering about the inn."

Alice felt her eyebrows lifting. "My young man?"

"Oh, you know what I mean." Louise frowned. "I realize that he is a guest, but he looks rather, well, unkempt."

Jane laughed. "That's just the way kids dress, Louie."

"Have you seen him?" demanded Louise.

"Well, no . . ."

Alice cleared her throat. "Louise is right, Jane. Adam carries the sloppy look to an extreme."

"Yes," agreed Louise. "I think you should go and check on him, Alice."

"*Check* on him?" Even though Alice agreed with Louise about Adam's appearance, she did not care for the insinuation. "Why exactly do you think I should check on him, Louise?"

"Maybe she's afraid he's going to steal the family silver," teased Jane as she adjusted the low flame under the covered pot holding the potatoes.

"No," said Louise. "I don't think he is a thief, but as I said, there is something about him, Alice. Something doesn't feel right to me. It occurs to me that we have allowed him into our house without knowing a single thing about him. Goodness, it could turn out that he is not even associated with Mark Graves. You told me that you had mentioned Mark's name to him when he arrived. Adam could have just picked up on what you were assuming."

"Oh, I don't think . . ."

"But you don't know either," finished Louise. "And I, for one, would appreciate it if someone kept an eye on him. At least until Mark arrives."

"Oh, Louise," said Jane. "Surely, you don't expect Alice to keep him under surveillance. Seriously, what do you think he's going to do?"

"I don't know. All I know is that he makes me uncomfortable in my own home."

"All right," said Alice. "Don't worry about it any-more, Louise. I shall go and keep our young man com-pany." Alice left the kitchen, feeling glad to get away from Louise's suspicions. The truth was, however, that Alice found Adam to be unsettling, and she was very eager to learn what his connection could possibly be to Mark. Despite herself, she had considered the possibility that Jane had suggested. What if Adam was indeed Mark's son? It was possible, but she sincerely hoped that it was not true.

Alice discovered Adam in the library. *Handy*, she thought, since she wanted to recommend some books. "Hello, Adam," she said as she entered the room.

He quickly replaced a small bronze statue that a parishioner had given her father many years ago and turned around without saying anything.

"I thought I could suggest some books for you," she said, ignoring the young man's lack of manners.

He shrugged and looked away.

"I thought that you might be bored without television and I recalled a book—"

"I'm not interested in reading," he said quickly. "I did enough of that in school."

"So you're not in school now?" she asked.

He just shook his head and moved over to where her father's old chess set was sitting on a side table.

"I assume that you must be out of high school," she continued as she fluffed a sofa cushion.

"Yeah," he said as he picked up the black king and examined it more closely.

"Do you play chess?" she asked.

He just shrugged again. "A little."

"I enjoy playing chess," she told him. "Would you like to—"

"Look, lady . . ." He set the chess piece back in its place and turned to her. "I don't expect you to entertain me or anything. I'm mostly just killing time until Mark gets here. I might not even stay, you know. I just have some business to take care of with him. So, don't worry about me, okay? I can take care of myself." Then, before she could respond, he walked out of the room.

She followed him out to the foyer, wishing for something kind and gracious to say to him in response to his rudeness, but all she could think was that this young man needed a course in manners and etiquette. If he was any relation to Mark Graves, she would be very surprised. In fact, she was beginning to understand Louise's concern. What if this young man was a complete stranger and he had simply taken advantage of her assumption that he was a friend of Mark's?

She decided to ask him now about the specifics of his relationship with Mark, but it was too late. He was already out the front door. She looked out the window in time to see him getting into the dilapidated old Nissan that was parked on the street in front of the inn. With a squeal of tires, he took off.

"Oh my!" she said aloud.

"You see," said Louise as she came out of the living room and joined Alice. "Something is not right with that young man."

"I'll admit that his manners could use improving," said Alice, "but I think it's unfair to judge him. I'm sure that Mark will make things clear when he arrives tomorrow."

"Well," said Louise. "I just hope he doesn't kill us in the middle of the night."

"Louise!" said Alice.

"I'm not serious, sister," said Louise with a twinkle in her blue eyes. "On the other hand, I may ask Jane to hide the family silver."

Alice just shook her head; it was too late to respond since the Winstons were just coming down the stairs.

"We're off to dinner," said Mrs. Winston. "We have reservations at that nice-looking restaurant downtown."

"Oh, you must mean Zachary's."

"Yes, that's it."

"Have a lovely evening," said Louise.

Alice noticed that Laura had on a pair of hot pink sunglasses that matched her sweater top. "How's your hand, Laura?"

Laura held up the bandaged hand and shrugged. "It throbs a little, but I guess it's okay."

"Maybe you should let me check it when you get back from dinner," suggested Alice. "We wouldn't want any infection to set in."

"That's a good idea," said Mrs. Winston.

"Enjoy your dinner," said Alice as she closed the front door behind them.

"Poor child," said Louise. "Her blindness must be so hard on her."

Alice nodded. "I'm really praying for a breakthrough for her."

"I had better go help Jane," said Louise. "I'm going to take some dinner up to the Langleys since he is still laid up with his back."

"That's nice of Jane to offer them dinner," said Alice. "Let me help you with it."

It was not long before the Langleys were all set, and it turned out that Mr. Langley absolutely adored roast chicken. "Guess it's not so bad being laid up," he said as Alice arranged the tray on his bed for him.

"Well, you certainly picked the right place to recover," said Louise as she handed him a cloth napkin. "Between my sister the gourmet cook and my sister the registered nurse, you could hardly be in better hands."

"Bless all three of you," said Mrs. Langley as she sat down at the small table on which Louise had set her tray. "This looks delicious."

By the time they got downstairs, Jane had the kitchen table set and ready for dinner. "I was about to ring the dinner bell," she said as they came and sat down.

"Well, the guests are all taken care of," said Louise after a short blessing had been said. "So, I guess we can just relax for a while."

"All the guests?" asked Jane as she passed the mashed potatoes to Alice. "What is our young man doing for dinner tonight?"

"I have no idea," said Alice. "When he arrived, I told him that he and Mark were invited to dinner, but he didn't indicate if he'd join us."

"Well, he certainly took off in a huff," said Louise. "I'm sure that half of Acorn Hill heard his tires squealing down the street."

Jane laughed. "That's what that noise was?"

"He's not a very thoughtful young man," said Louise as she buttered her roll. "I will be very interested to hear what his relationship is to Mark Graves. If you ask me, those two are as different as night and day. I am almost positive that they are of no relation whatsoever."

"He seems troubled," said Alice as she took a portion of cooked carrots with butter and dill sauce.

"Humph," said Louise. "At least he has his sight."

"There's an idea," said Alice suddenly. "Maybe I should introduce Adam to Laura and see if—"

"No, Alice!" said Louise vehemently.

"Why not?" asked Jane.

"Really," said Louise, "it would be wrong to introduce that young girl to the influence of that surly, not to mention unkempt, young man. I won't hear of it. We have a responsibility to our guests, Alice. We cannot simply hand Laura over to Adam because we assume that he is an acquaintance of Mark's."

Alice frowned. Louise sometimes took her role as the eldest a bit too seriously. "But, Louise," Alice said. "It might be good for both of them."

"I think it's a bad idea," Louise insisted, "a very bad idea. For one thing, consider Laura's parents . . . how would they feel if we exposed their daughter to a questionable young man like that?"

"How do we know he's questionable?" asked Alice.

"I know that we shouldn't judge people on appearances, but just look at him and you must admit that all is not right," said Louise. "Then there is the way he talks to you. Good grief, he won't look anyone directly in the eye."

"Louise may be right," said Jane. "I hate to judge him, but until Mark gets here, we really don't know much about him. It might be a mistake to encourage a friendship with Laura. Think about it, Alice. She is very vulnerable right now, and it's clear that she has her own issues to deal with. We don't want to create any unnecessary problems for her or her parents."

Alice nodded. "I suppose you could be right."

"She *is* right," said Louise. "It just would not be prudent."

Jane suddenly pointed her fork at Alice. "I'm just dying to know what Adam has to do with Mark. Does Mark have a cell phone or some way that we could reach him, Alice? Do you think he's checking his e-mail?"

Alice shrugged. "He has a cell phone, but I don't have the number. I use his work or his home number. I don't know how often he checks his e-mail."

"Well," said Louise, "I think I would sleep better tonight if I knew that Adam really is a trustworthy young man."

"Oh, Louise." Alice was feeling unusually exasperated tonight. "Do you honestly think Mark would send some criminal to stay in our inn?"

"Not at all," said Louise. "I am only concerned that Adam may have nothing to do with Mark at all."

Jane laughed. "Yes, perhaps he's an impostor. Maybe he got rid of the real Adam Peterson and has taken his identity."

"I'm not joking," said Louise. "Until we know for sure who this young man is, we should exercise caution."

"Oh." Alice could think of no other response to that. The more she considered it, the more she wondered if her sisters' scenarios could have merit. *But,* she thought, *even if Adam isn't who he says he is, what can I do about it now?*

Chapter Five

After the Winstons had returned from dinner, Alice examined Laura's wound and put on another sterile bandage. Then she decided to retire to her room to work on her quilt. She tinkered at it for a couple of hours, but the results seemed paltry compared to the efforts. After sewing the downside of the fabric up and having to pick apart the seam, she decided to set the project aside.

She put on her cozy blue pajamas, then made herself comfortable in her easy chair. She had recently purchased a new paperback book from Nine Lives Bookstore. It was a newly released mystery from one of her favorite writers, but after just a few pages, she found herself, once again, distracted and unable to focus. She finally closed the book and sighed.

Was this strange uneasiness due to Mark's impending visit to the inn? Goodness, it had not been that long since she had last seen him, and they had kept in touch in the meantime. Why should she feel so unsettled now? Perhaps she was just worried about the young man, whom both her sisters seemed to dislike. To be honest, Alice was not fond of Adam herself. If he was a friend of Mark's, should she try to think of him as a friend of hers? She picked up her book again, telling herself to just let these things go for the night, but she could not.

Finally, she gave up and decided to go downstairs to fix some cocoa. A mug of warm cocoa usually helped her to relax and, eventually, to sleep. She had made the cocoa and was tiptoeing with it back through the darkened inn when she heard voices coming from the library. Curious about who was in there at that hour, she decided to investigate.

As she approached the door to the library, she determined that the voices belonged to Laura Winston and Adam Peterson. Despite her earlier idea about getting these two young people together, she felt seriously alarmed now. Questions ran through her mind. *What are they doing down here? Are they alone? Do Laura's parents know where she is? How did Laura find her way down here in the first place?*

"So how long have you been blind?" Alice heard Adam ask.

"A couple of months," she said.

"And you can't see *anything?* "

"Shadows, sometimes."

"And it's not going to get better?"

"I don't know. . . ."

"Well, that's a bummer, all right."

"Yeah, tell me about it."

"Laura?" a woman's voice called out in a whisper, yet Alice could hear the sound of worry in it. It came from upstairs, and Alice knew it was Mrs. Winston calling. She hurried to the foot of the stairs to reassure the woman.

"Down here," called Alice quietly.

Mrs. Winston, wearing a pink satin robe, peered over the railing with a troubled expression. "Pardon?"

"Laura's down here," Alice mouthed the words, pointing in the direction of the library.

Within seconds, Mrs. Winston was at Alice's side. "Is she all right?"

"Yes," whispered Alice. "She's fine."

"But how did she get down here?"

"I don't know. She's talking to another guest in the library just now."

"We had fallen asleep, but when I got up for a drink of water, I saw that Laura was gone." She still looked frightened. "I didn't know what to think."

"Mom?" Just then Laura came out of the library, using the hallway wall to guide her. "Is that you?"

"Yes, dear." Mrs. Winston went over and took Laura's arm. "What are you doing down here?"

"I couldn't sleep," she said. "I didn't want to disturb you, so I went out on the landing and Adam was out there. And, well, we just started talking and stuff and he thought it'd be better to go downstairs so we wouldn't wake anyone."

"I see." Mrs. Winston nodded, but her expression was troubled. "Well, it's late, Laura. I think both you and, uh, Adam should call it a night." She glanced in the direction of the library, but Adam did not seem to wish to make an appearance.

"Good night," said Alice. "Sleep well."

"Thank you," said Mrs. Winston. "I'm sorry if we disturbed you."

"Not at all," she assured them. "I was still up." Then, as they went upstairs, she went to the library to check on Adam. "It's rather late," she told him, hoping it did not sound too much like a scolding, although it was meant to be a hint.

"Yeah, I couldn't sleep."

"Yes, I heard that, but Laura's mother was quite worried about her. You probably should check with the Winstons before you, uh, well, before you spend any time with Laura."

"Why's that?" he asked in a belligerent voice.

"Because they're both very concerned for Laura. She has only been blind a short while and—"

"I know all about that," he said.

"She doesn't really have the skills to get around yet," continued Alice, no longer caring if she sounded like she was scolding or not. "In fact, she ran into a table earlier today and actually cut her—"

"I know about that too." He stood now and, without even looking at her, headed for the door.

"I'm just saying you should check with her parents before—"

"Yeah, yeah," he said as he exited. "I heard what you said."

"Well, good night, Adam."

He just kept on walking down the hall and then up the stairs without bothering to say good night to her. *Well!* she thought, as she turned off the light in the library and headed back up to her room. By the time she got there, her cocoa was tepid and unappealing. She took a few sips of the lukewarm liquid, then decided to go to bed.

Before she fell asleep, she prayed for both Adam and Laura. Surely they both had problems and needed some divine help. Then she prayed for herself.

Please, heavenly Father, she prayed. *Give me an extra-large dose of patience for that young man. Because the truth is, I would like to wring his neck. I'm sorry about that. Please, forgive me, and help me to be gracious and kind. Amen.*

To her surprise, she slept relatively well that night, though she felt nervous and unsettled the following morning. Just the same, she adhered to her regular Saturday routine, putting on her jeans, sweatshirt and walking shoes, then heading over to Vera Humbert's for their morning walk.

"You seem troubled," said Vera after they had barely gone one block. "What's the problem?" Vera and Alice had been friends for years and were very sensitive to each other's moods.

Alice frowned. "I'm not entirely sure."

"Worried about Mark coming today?" Vera asked gently.

"Yes," she admitted. "I guess I'm not certain . . ."

"About what?"

"Oh, you know," said Alice. "About us, I suppose. I'm not sure what our relationship is going to be . . . what it should be."

"What do you think Mark expects?"

"I don't know. The idea of marriage came up once, but we haven't discussed it seriously."

"What does he talk about in his letters?"

"He mostly writes about his work, and if he says anything concerning us and our relationship, it's more about our friendship and how much he appreciates it. Oh, and a few other things, I suppose." Alice was not sure that she wanted to tell even her best friend *everything*.

"And how does that make you feel?"

Alice shrugged.

"Well, what do you want from the relationship, Alice?" Vera had stopped walking now and was looking right into her eyes.

"I don't know, Vera. I really don't." Alice sighed. "And there's a complication."

"A complication?"

"Yes." Alice told her about Adam and even confessed that she disliked the young man. "And that's just not like me," she continued. "You know me, Vera, I try to see the good in everyone. But there's something about Adam that just sets my teeth on edge. Louise can barely tolerate him. And, Jane, well, she's trying to be patient, but I can tell that even she's feeling concerned."

"Oh my." Vera shook her head, then they continued walking. "That is quite a complication. But, tell me, what exactly is Adam's relationship to Mark?"

"I have no idea. All I know is that Adam has known Mark all his life."

"Maybe Adam's a relative. A nephew perhaps?"

"I know Mark's only sister, and Adam is not her child."

Vera considered this. "Do you think Adam could be . . ." Then she stopped herself. "No, that's ridiculous."

"If you were wondering if he might be Mark's son, you're not alone. Jane has already suggested that possibility. As far as I know, Mark has never been married," Alice paused, "but Mark and I have only been reacquainted for such a short time . . . after so many years. It's possible that I don't know everything about him."

"No, I think we're on the wrong track there," said Vera quickly. "Sorry, Alice. I shouldn't have suggested such a thing."

Alice nodded. "Yes, it does seem rather unlikely."

"Well," said Vera as they paused on the curb for the morning traffic to move along. "You do have your work cut out for you this week, my friend."

Alice sighed. "Yes, that's what I'm thinking too."

They spent the rest of their walk making final plans for the annual Easter egg hunt that Grace Chapel had scheduled for next Saturday. As usual, it would be held in the city park. Vera had already placed the notice in the newspaper that all residents of Acorn Hill were invited to attend. By the time they reached the inn, their parting place, they had just about covered everything.

"Whose car is that?" asked Vera as they paused on the sidewalk to say good-bye.

Alice followed Vera's gaze over to where Adam's dilapidated Nissan was parked. Sporting three different colors of paint, the small vehicle had a dented front fender and a missing taillight, and duct tape appeared to be the only thing keeping the trunk closed. "That's Adam's car," she told Vera.

"Looks like this young man is a little down on his luck." Vera peered into the car and then turned to Alice and made a funny face. "It appears that he's been living out of his car," she said in a lowered voice, as if someone else might hear.

Alice hesitated, hating to be so nosy, but finally walked over and peeked into the car herself. It was filled with piles of what appeared to be dirty or at least very wrinkled clothes, a sleeping bag, blankets, pillows, lots of fast food containers and miscellaneous pieces of debris. "Goodness," said Alice quietly. "One could only imagine what it must smell like in there."

"Well, as I said, it appears that you have your work cut out for you this week." Vera laughed. "Enjoy your little vacation, Alice."

"Thanks a lot."

"See you tomorrow," called Vera. "If not sooner, and I'll want a complete update."

Alice waved, then went into the house and through to the kitchen.

"Morning, Alice," said Jane as Alice came into the room. "Good walk?"

"Yes," said Alice, noticing Jane's damp hair. "Have you already done your jogging and showered?"

Jane nodded as she cracked an egg into a small mixing bowl. "It was so nice and sunny out that I couldn't resist getting an early start on the day."

"Impressive." Alice peeked into the oven to see what was the source of the delicious aroma that was perfuming the room. "Ah, cinnamon rolls."

"And omelets," said Jane.

"Sounds good."

"I had planned to make waffles," said Jane as she cracked another egg. "But I got to thinking about Laura's diabetes and all that maple syrup."

Alice nodded. "Good for you. Protein is a great way to go. Now, I'm going to run on up and get showered so that I can hurry back down to help you."

Alice tried not to think about Mark as she hurriedly showered and then dressed carefully. Oh, she knew that she was putting more effort than usual into her appearance, especially for a Saturday. Still, she could not help herself. Besides, she knew that if she didn't, Jane would probably give her a lecture.

As she gave her hair a final pat in front of the mirror, she prayed a quick, but heartfelt prayer. *Your will be done, Father. Amen.* Then she went back downstairs.

Chapter Six

"Don't you look pretty," said Jane as Alice returned to the kitchen.

Alice looked down at her sage green sweater set and olive-colored trousers. "I thought Louise might be glad to see that I'm wearing the set she got me for Christmas. She's mentioned that I hardly ever wear it, but it's just that it's so nice I don't want to spoil it."

"That color is great on you," said Jane as she handed Alice an apron. "Would you please grate this cheese while I run upstairs to get something?"

"Of course."

Alice put on an apron, then hummed to herself as she grated first cheddar cheese, then Monterey Jack. She was just finishing up when Jane returned.

"Close your eyes and hold out your hand," said Jane.

"What?"

"Just do it," said Jane.

Alice complied, expecting Jane to put something into her upturned palm, but instead she felt Jane putting something around her wrist.

"Okay, open your eyes."

Alice opened her eyes to see that Jane had clasped a lovely beaded bracelet around her wrist. It had several shades of green beads along with some pretty amber and coral colors.

"That's beautiful, Jane!"

"Thanks. I made it for you for Easter, but when I saw your sweater set, I decided you needed to have it today."

Alice hugged her sister. "The colors are absolutely perfect. I love it."

"Good." Jane grinned. "Now do you want to chop some mushrooms and green onions?"

"Your wish is my command."

Alice had just finished her chopping and was washing the knife and cutting board when someone knocked on the back door. "I'll get it," she called to Jane, who was taking the cinnamon rolls from the oven.

Before she got there, Ethel was letting herself in. *"Yoo-hoo,"* she called in her familiar greeting.

"Hey, Aunt Ethel," said Jane as she set the fragrant rolls on the butcher-block countertop. "What's up?"

"I'm all out of coffee," said Ethel as she stood in the doorway with a childish pouting expression. "And I thought maybe I could borrow a bit—"

"Come in, and pour yourself a cup," said Alice as she gave her sister a knowing grin.

Jane winked at Alice. It was their little joke that Ethel always ran out of something if she was hungry, lonely or just wanted to know what was going on at the inn. "Yes, Auntie, do come in," said Jane. "We have plenty of coffee. We have freshly brewed, freshly ground or even still in the bean form. Take your pick. I suspect you haven't had your breakfast yet."

Ethel's eyebrows lifted hopefully as she leaned over to sniff the cinnamon rolls. "No, as a matter of fact, I haven't."

"Maybe you'd like to join us," said Alice.

Ethel smiled as she helped herself to a cup of coffee. "That sounds perfectly lovely."

"Is Lloyd going to dress up like Mr. Easter Rabbit again this year?" asked Jane.

Acorn Hill's mayor, Lloyd Tynan, was a tireless promoter of town functions and was Ethel's beau.

"Of course, dear," said Ethel sitting down at the kitchen table. "I've already steamed his costume and fluffed his tail."

"Fluffed whose tail?" asked Louise as she came into the kitchen and poured herself a cup of coffee.

"Lloyd's," said Ethel in a matter-of-fact voice.

"I beg your pardon?" Louise turned around and stared at her aunt.

"Mr. Easter Rabbit," explained Ethel.

"Oh," Louise said, looking relieved. "Goodness, one can certainly get confused when hearing only part of a conversation."

"Speaking of conversations," said Jane, "what was going on down here last night, Alice? I heard voices, including yours. Mrs. Winston sounded a bit upset."

Alice explained how Mrs. Winston had thought that Laura had gone missing. She tried not to sound critical of Adam, but Louise was already on that tack.

"That boy," said Louise. "I don't think he is a good influence on Laura. I will be most relieved when Mark arrives and sets things straight."

"Sets things straight?" echoed Jane. "Just how is Mark supposed to do that?"

"Well, if he knows Adam, then he can explain to us his relationship to the young man and he can exert some influence over his behavior."

"You mean teach him some manners?" said Jane in a teasing voice.

"Perhaps."

"I haven't seen him yet," said Ethel, "but I've seen that horrid-looking little car in front of the inn. What an eyesore. Don't you think you could get him to park it in back?"

"I already suggested that to him," said Louise, "but he apparently didn't take me seriously. I'm hoping that Mark will get through to him."

"I wonder why he's so moody," said Jane as she began mixing some cream cheese frosting for the cinnamon rolls. "He's got a great big chip on his shoulder."

Alice went to the dining room to set the table. It was not that she wanted to avoid the conversation about Adam so much as it was that she felt responsible for the young man's behavior. She knew that this was ridiculous since she had nothing to do with him. He was here because of Mark and, well, Mark was going to be here because of her. *Or was he?* She shook her head at the thought.

"Good morning," said Mr. Winston as he came into the dining room.

Alice smiled. "Good morning." She nodded to a side table where a small selection of newspapers was neatly arranged. "Help yourself to a paper, if you like. I'm sure that breakfast will soon be ready."

"Thank you." He picked up the Philadelphia paper and scanned the headlines.

"Did you sleep well?" she asked.

He nodded as he moved to the table. "Surprisingly well. To be honest, I hadn't expected to be this comfortable in a bed-and-breakfast."

"Oh, good," she said with one hand on the kitchen door. "Would you like some coffee or tea?"

"Coffee," he said. "I don't know when the rest of my family will be down. My wife was primping in the bathroom, and Laura was still asleep."

Alice smiled. "Perhaps that roll-away wasn't too bad after all."

"If you ask me, kids can sleep anywhere. It's only when you get to be old and achy that a good bed becomes imperative."

"True enough," said Alice as she left to get his coffee.

It was not long before the Langleys and Mrs. Winston were also in the dining room. Louise and Ethel joined them, Louise playing the role of hostess and Ethel adding some local spice and flavor to the conversation. Meanwhile, Alice helped Jane with the made-to-order omelets.

"Mr. Winston wants cheese and mushrooms," she told Jane. "Mrs. Winston wants mushrooms and onions. The Langleys both want the works. They've already become great fans of the chef."

Jane laughed. "How's Mr. Langley's back?"

"He said it was much better, but I warned him to keep taking the ibuprofen anyway. Too many people stop taking the medicine as soon as they feel better. The next thing you know, they're in pain again."

Jane expertly flipped the omelet over, then out of the pan, and Alice carried the plate to the dining room.

"Will your sister mind making an omelet for Laura?" asked Mrs. Winston as Alice set the plate before her. "If she doesn't get up in time, that is. I thought I could take breakfast up to her in a bit—"

"If Laura wants breakfast," her husband interrupted, "she should come down here like the rest of us and get it herself."

"I know, dear," said Mrs. Winston in a low voice, "but you know what happens if she doesn't eat regularly."

"It's no problem," Alice assured them both. "Just let us know how Laura likes her omelet when you're ready to go back—" She stopped in mid-sentence when she saw both Laura and Adam coming into the dining room. "Good morning," she said to them, and the others turned to see. Laura had on pale blue sweats, and her hair was pulled back into a slightly messy ponytail. Today's sunglasses were square-shaped with tangerine rims. Adam's hair looked even worse than yesterday, and Alice suspected that he had actually slept in his clothes. She wondered if she should offer to let him use their laundry facilities or if that would sound too pushy.

"Laura!" exclaimed Mrs. Winston. "How did you get downstairs—"

"Adam helped me," said Laura in a somewhat irritated voice. "It's no big deal, Mom."

"Come sit down," said Alice as she went over to Laura and guided her to an empty chair next to her mother.

Mrs. Winston gave Alice a grateful smile. "Well, I'm glad you could join us. Jane's omelets are divine."

"And her cinnamon rolls are excellent," said Mr. Winston. "I think I'll have another."

Alice took Laura's and Adam's orders for their omelets and then returned to the kitchen. Before long, everyone, except Alice and Jane, had been served.

"Shall we join them?" asked Jane as she slid Alice's omelet onto a plate.

Alice shrugged. "If you want to, but I don't think they'll miss us. It's a full table and Aunt Ethel has been doing a good job of keeping them entertained. She's filling them in on all this week's activities, including a detailed description of Mr. Easter Rabbit's breakfast next Saturday before the big egg hunt."

Jane laughed. "I vote to eat in here."

Soon, they were both seated at the kitchen table, and Alice voiced her concerns about Adam spending time with Laura. "I don't know what to do about it," she finally admitted.

"I don't see why you should do anything," said Jane as she peeled off a section of her cinnamon roll. "It's not as if Adam is your personal responsibility, Alice."

"I know . . . it's just that I feel as if it's my fault that he's here and possibly spoiling things for the Winstons."

"I don't see how his help in getting Laura downstairs should be perceived as spoiling anything."

"But you should see their faces, Jane. I can tell they're concerned about his appearance, not to mention his manners. Of course, they're too polite to say anything." Alice lowered her voice, although she knew they could not be heard in the dining room. "Honestly, Jane, I am seriously considering telling him that he should do his laundry while he's here. I'm almost certain he slept in his clothes, and I think he may have even been living in his car."

Jane laughed. "That's not such a big deal for a kid. I saw a lot of that when I lived in San Francisco."

"It's not exactly the norm for Acorn Hill," said Alice.

"Not exactly."

"Oh, I'll be so relieved when Mark gets here."

"What if?" said Jane in her teasing voice. "What if Mark has never met this kid before? What if he doesn't know him from—from Adam?" Then she started giggling. "What if Mark's real friend is some dignified professor from Harvard and this kid has been sleeping in his bed and—" She burst out laughing now.

Despite herself, Alice laughed too. "Oh dear," she finally muttered. "Wouldn't Louise be furious at me."

"Furious at what?" said Louise as she carried a small stack of dishes into the kitchen.

Alice giggled. "Oh nothing, big sister. I was just being silly."

Louise set the dishes by the sink and then came over to the table. "I am getting quite concerned over your young man," she said in a lowered voice.

Alice nodded. "I know. If it makes you feel any better, I am too."

"But he's not *Alice's* young man," Jane defended.

Louise held one finger in the air. "I say he is. At least until Mark arrives." She looked at Alice now. "I think you should keep tabs on him until then."

"Yes," agreed Alice. "I think you're right."

Jane shrugged as she forked her last bite. "Well, I'll leave all that to you two. As for me, I plan to spend most of my day gardening in this beautiful spring sunshine."

Alice was surprised to see that Adam was still in the dining room when she went to clear the table. He seemed to be trapped in a conversation with Ethel. Alice tried not to appear to be eavesdropping as she slowly gathered up things from the table.

"Do you plan to return to school next year then?" asked Ethel.

He shrugged and looked down at the table. "I don't know."

"But don't you think it would be wise?"

"I don't know."

"My goodness, son!" she exclaimed. "You don't seem to know much, now, do you?"

He stood up and gave her an exasperated look. "I guess not."

"Well, you should work on that," she said. "Folks who don't know much hardly ever amount to much. And I think that—"

"I gotta go," he said, which was more of a good-bye than Alice had heard from him before. Then he hurried out of the dining room.

"Well," said Ethel, clearly insulted. "What a rude young man."

"At least he spoke to you," said Alice as she picked up the last coffee cup. "That's more than I've gotten."

"Really?" Ethel smiled in a coquettish fashion. "Well, I've always had a way with young men."

Alice tried not to giggle as she pushed the door open into the kitchen. Too bad she could not pawn off Adam onto her aunt today. Ethel followed Alice into the kitchen, chattering at her as she went.

"Thank you, girls, for the lovely breakfast," she told them. "I think I'll head off to the store for some coffee. Anything I can pick up for you, Jane?"

"No thanks," said Jane.

"How about you, Alice?" she offered.

"Nothing that I can think of."

"And when is the handsome vet arriving?" asked Ethel.

"I'm not sure," said Alice. "I think it'll be later this afternoon."

"Well, I can't wait to see him," said her aunt as she patted her bright red hair. "And I can't wait to get to the bottom of this Adam mystery."

"You and everyone else," said Alice. Suddenly, even though it was still morning, she felt very, very tired.

"Toodles," Ethel called out as she exited by the back door.

Chapter Seven

*E*xcuse me," said Alice as she caught Adam coming down the stairs. "I wanted to let you know that you're welcome to use the laundry facilities if you'd like. I can show you how everything works—"

"I don't want to do laundry," he told her in a voice that seemed to be saying "butt out."

"But I've noticed that . . ." Alice paused. "Well, perhaps you'd like me to do some laundry for you. I don't mind."

He studied her for a moment. "Look, you're probably just trying to be nice, but I don't need it, okay? I'm not going to be here for long, so maybe you should just pretend like I'm not here at all."

"But I—"

"Just chill," he said in an irritated tone.

She nodded as she watched him heading toward the front door. Then, remembering Louise's warning, she decided to persist. "Adam," she said in her most authoritative voice.

He turned and looked at her.

"My sister would appreciate it if you parked your car in the parking area reserved for the inn. We try to keep the street clear of vehicles." She cleared her throat. "City ordinances, you know."

He rolled his eyes. "Yeah, whatever."

"And," she continued, "are you going out?"

He exhaled loudly, shoved his hands into his pockets, but did not answer.

"I just wondered," she said. "In case Mark arrives and you're not here. When shall I tell him that you'll be back?"

"I'm not gonna be gone long," he said, reaching for the doorknob.

Just then the door opened, and Mrs. Winston and Laura came in. "Oh, hello," said Mrs. Winston when she nearly ran into Adam. "We just took a little walk around town."

"Hey," he said, looking at Laura.

"Adam?" asked Laura eagerly.

"Yeah," he answered. "I'm just heading out."

"Where are you going?" she asked.

"Just to town, you know."

"Need any company?" she asked.

Alice noticed the look of alarm in Mrs. Winston's eyes. "Uh, Laura," she said quickly. "You told me you were tired and we just went—"

"Not as much tired as bored," said Laura.

"You can come if you want," said Adam.

"Oh, I don't know," began Mrs. Winston.

"It's just to town, Mom," said Laura. "It's not like he's going to kidnap me or anything." She almost smiled now, and Alice realized how pretty she would be if she smiled more. "Are you, Adam?"

He shook his head, then remembering that she couldn't see him, quickly said, "Nah, I wasn't planning on it."

"Great," said Laura as she reached out for him.

"Uh, okay," he said as he took her hand.

"But, I'm not sure that it's—"

"Both you and Dad keep telling me to get out and do something," Laura said as Adam guided her out the still-open door.

"But when will you be back?" implored her worried mother.

Laura shrugged, but continued going.

"Adam said he wouldn't be gone long," offered Alice, certain that she felt as concerned as Mrs. Winston did. "After all, Acorn Hill's not a very big town."

"Yes, I realize that." Mrs. Winston stood looking out the door as Adam and Laura walked over to his car. "Oh dear," said Mrs. Winston. "I didn't know they would be driving."

Alice went over to see. Laura was waiting on the sidewalk as Adam opened a rear door to his car, then dug around as if looking for something. Finally, he emerged with a gray sweatshirt that he pulled over his head. "Oh," said Alice in relief. "Maybe he's not going to drive after all."

To her dismay, he then opened the front passenger door, threw some things in the back and helped Laura get in.

"Oh no," said Mrs. Winston.

Alice watched helplessly as Adam then stooped over and helped Laura find the seatbelt. "At least he's being safe," she offered.

Mrs. Winston just nodded, but her expression was one of complete hopelessness.

"I'm sure they'll be just fine." The truth was, Alice was not so sure. She did not trust Adam any farther than she could throw him. Oh, if only Mark would get here. Soon!

Alice tried to look busy during the next hour, puttering about but really accomplishing little more than keeping a wary eye on the street in front of the inn, hoping and even praying that the two young guests would return soon.

Finally, she heard voices coming in the back door and hurried toward the kitchen to see Adam and Laura being led in by Jane. "Feel free to help yourself if you want a snack," Jane said, as she removed her gardening gloves and stuffed them into a pocket of her overalls. "There's fresh fruit and some oatmeal cookies."

"I'm cool," said Adam.

"Do you have any apples?" asked Laura.

As Jane was getting Laura an apple, Adam walked past Alice without saying a word in response to her greeting.

"Did you have a good time?" asked Alice.

"It was okay," said Laura. She took a bite of the apple. "Adam?" she said, unaware that he had left the room.

"He's gone," said Alice.

"Oh." Now Laura looked troubled.

"Do you want me to help you find your mom?" offered Alice.

"Yeah, I guess."

Alice took Laura's arm and led her through the inn. "I didn't see Adam's car," she said as they came to the staircase.

"He said you told him to park it off the street," said Laura.

"Oh yes," said Alice. "That's right."

"Laura!" exclaimed Mrs. Winston as she came down the hallway that led to the library. "You're back."

"I told you I'd be back," said Laura in a flat voice.

"Good," said Mr. Winston from behind his wife. "I want to take my favorite ladies out for a little ride and then some lunch." He held up a map and travel brochure. "I've discovered some places of local interest that I think we should investigate."

Laura sighed. "Not me, Dad, I'm tired. I think I'll just rest."

"But what about—"

She cut him off. "Seriously, Dad. I just want to listen to my new CD and maybe take a nap. You and Mom go on ahead. I'll be fine."

"Oh, I don't think—"

"Laura's right," Mr. Winston said to his wife. "I think you and I should go ahead as planned. And Laura can rest. Then maybe we can all do something together this afternoon. Is that agreeable to you, Laura?"

She shrugged. "Yeah, whatever."

"But will you be okay by yourself, honey?" asked her mother.

"I'll be here all day," said Alice. "If Laura needs any—"

"I'll be fine," said Laura. "I'll just stay in the room and rest. Okay?"

"Well . . ." her mother did not look convinced.

"She'll be fine," said Mr. Winston as he took his wife's arm and led her to the front door.

"Have a good time," said Alice. She turned to Laura. "Do you want me to help you to your room now?"

"Yeah, I guess so."

After Laura was safely in her room, Alice went upstairs to get her new mystery. She had decided that she would stay nearby, at least within shouting distance, just in case Laura needed something. She settled herself in the parlor, choosing an upright chair that was close to the door, as she attempted to focus her mind on the sentences before her. Some time passed, and she glanced at her watch and was surprised to see that it was almost noon. She knew that Laura's diabetes and medication made it important for her to eat at regular intervals, so she decided to go and check on the girl. By the time she reached the second floor, Laura and Adam were on the landing discussing the possibility of going out to lunch.

"My treat," insisted Laura.

Adam shrugged. "Yeah, like, whatever."

"Are you going out again?" asked Alice.

"We're going to get some lunch in town," said Laura.

"Oh." Then, thinking that she might head this off, she said, "But there's plenty to eat here and Jane said to—"

"I thought this was a bed-and-*breakfast,*" said Laura.

"Well, it is—"

"We already had breakfast." She reached out for Adam and he took her hand. "So we want to go out and get some lunch."

Alice had nothing else to say that she thought would dissuade these two young people. She watched as they slowly headed downstairs, praying that Laura would be safe in Adam's care.

Finally, they were gone, and Alice went into the kitchen. She was not actually hungry. Mostly, she was nervous and hoped that perhaps Jane would be taking a lunch break.

"Hey, you," said Jane when Alice came in. "I just saw the odd couple leaving."

Despite her worries, Alice had to laugh. "That just about describes them, doesn't it?"

"I think so. I mean, here we have Laura, a cute little preppy that any parent would be proud of—well, other than her attitude, which is excusable under the circumstances— and then you have Adam, the kid who looks like he's been living on the streets or maybe rooming with Oscar the Grouch."

"Oscar the Grouch? Do you mean the one who played the slob in *The Odd Couple?*"

Jane laughed. "No, I mean Oscar the Grouch, the puppet who lives in a trash can. Didn't you ever watch *Sesame Street?*"

"Oh, I've seen bits of it on the children's ward at the hospital."

Jane took out a loaf of bread. "I used to watch it with kids when I was babysitting. Oscar the Grouch was always messy and grumbling. Adam reminds me of him a little."

Alice chuckled. "Well, let's keep that to ourselves."

"I'm making a grilled cheese sandwich," said Jane. "Want one?"

"Yes, please." Alice went to the refrigerator for the cheese and pickles. "I offered to do Adam's laundry," she told Jane as she set the items on the counter.

"And he didn't take you up on it?" She picked up a knife. "That kid's not only rude, but dumb too."

"Too bad," said Alice as she got plates. "Where's Louise?"

"She walked to town. She's meeting Viola for lunch."

"Oh, good," said Alice. "Maybe she'll see Adam and Laura and keep an eye on them. Or call me if it looks like anything is amiss."

"If Louise sees Adam out with Laura, she'll probably call the police."

"Oh, I don't think . . ."

Jane laughed. "She'll probably assume that he's abducted her and planning on holding her hostage or something."

Alice sighed. "Okay, in that case, let's hope that Louise does not see them at lunch." She shook her head. "I feel so bad about all this."

"Just remember," said Jane. "No matter what happens, it's *not* your fault. Neither of those kids is your responsibility."

"So you say . . ."

After lunch, Alice resumed her post. She knew that Jane was right, that these kids were not her responsibility, but she could not help feeling concern for Laura, and more than anything, she wished that Adam had never shown up at their inn. It was clear that he did not want to be here and was only here to see Mark. Or so she assumed. What a relief it would be to find out that Mark did not even know Adam and that this was all simply a silly mistake. They would kindly send Adam on his way to who knew where, and then they could all get on with life.

Chapter Eight

*I*t was nearly three when Adam and Laura returned. Alice was a nervous wreck. It probably didn't help the state of her mind that she was reading a mystery that involved an abducted woman. Maybe Louise was correct about her taste in books. She set the novel aside and rose to greet them.

"Did you have a nice lunch?" she asked.

"Yeah," said Laura. "Considering the size of this town, I suppose it was okay."

"I'm going to my room," said Adam, and without offering to take Laura upstairs, he disappeared.

Laura looked somewhat dismayed and, once again, Alice felt sorry for her. "What would you like to do?" asked Alice.

Laura shrugged. "I'm kind of tired."

"Want me to help you to your room?"

"Yeah, please."

With Laura safely in her room, Alice resisted the urge to barricade the door and went upstairs to her own room.

There, she attempted to work on the baby quilt, leaving her door open and trying to keep her ears tuned in case Laura needed something or attempted to make another foray from her room. Alice could not stop her, of course, but at least she would know where Laura was if the Winstons came home and wondered where their daughter had wandered off to. Alice sincerely hoped that they would get home before Laura and Adam decided on some new excursion.

Alice had been relieved to see that the Langleys had decided to walk to town this afternoon. She had told them about the Coffee Shop's delicious blackberry pie and had assured Mr. Langley that the walk to town was a mild form of exercise that would probably be therapeutic for his back. And now, she told herself, she should enjoy this peaceful time during which it seemed that nothing much was going on at the inn. She considered taking a nap herself so that she would be refreshed and energetic by the time Mark arrived. She felt a current of nervous energy running through her, however, and suspected that even if she were to lie down, she would not be able to sleep. And so, she carefully pinned and then checked each quilt piece to be sure the right side was up, then meticulously sewed, pausing now and then to listen to the silence of the inn.

Concentrating on her sewing diverted her thoughts from Mark, and she was surprised when she looked up at the clock to discover it was nearly five. Concerned about Laura, Alice went down to the second floor to look around. All was quiet, but this did not reassure her. Deciding that she could use Laura's health and her need to have regular snacks to balance out her insulin shots to excuse the interruption, Alice knocked on Laura's door. When no one answered, Alice grew even more concerned. *What if Laura has had a seizure?* She hated to intrude, but she felt that she had to check on the girl. Alice quietly opened the door and glanced around the room. "Laura?" she called. No answer. Alice tiptoed over to the open bathroom door, but she saw that the room was empty.

She stood in the middle of the room gathering her thoughts, then she decided to check on Adam. She didn't care if he was insulted by her doing so. She knocked on his door and, when he didn't answer, she took the liberty of peeking into his room. To her surprise, it was completely devoid of any personal items, as if he had checked out. Alice closed the door and headed downstairs. Maybe her sisters would know what was up.

Jane was putting away her gardening tools when Alice came out into the backyard and asked her about Laura and Adam.

"I haven't seen them," said Jane. "But Adam's car isn't in the parking area and it's not out front."

"Oh dear." Alice held the shed door open for Jane. "I don't suppose you've seen the Winstons?"

"Sorry. But I've been back here all afternoon." Jane hung up her hoe and closed the door. "I did see the Langleys coming back from their walk. They said they were going to have a little nap and then perhaps try going out for dinner if Mr. Langley's back continued to hold up."

Alice nodded. "Oh, good for them."

"Don't worry about Laura," said Jane. "She's seventeen and responsible for herself. And, keep in mind, even her parents can't seem to control her. Who knows? Maybe this is a good thing for her. After all, her parents have been concerned about her lack of independence."

"That's true. It's funny, isn't it? Sometimes you want something so badly, and then you get it and you're not sure that you want it anymore."

Jane looked at her sister, her eyebrows arching slightly. "Are we still talking about Laura?"

Alice gave a rueful little laugh. "I don't know. Anything I can do to help in the kitchen while you're cleaning up?" She pulled a twig out of Jane's hair.

Jane looked at her overalls and held up her dirty hands. "You really think I need to clean up?"

Alice smiled. "Not if you're trying to impress Adam."

"Yeah, right. If you could go ahead and start a green salad that would be great. Do you think Mark will be here in time for dinner?"

"I have no idea. It was Louise who took his reservation."

"Well, I put a roast in the oven, just in case. Although he may want to take you out tonight, Alice."

"I doubt it," said Alice. "Remember we still have the Adam factor."

"That's true. So does that mean you don't think he ran off with Laura?"

"Well, let's hope not permanently."

As Alice shredded lettuce and peeled carrots and cucumbers, she wondered where Laura's parents were and how they would react if they came home to discover that Laura and Adam were gone and that no one knew where they went. Once again, she prayed. This time she prayed primarily for Laura. Alice could not imagine how it would feel to be blind. She knew that God could bring good out of what seemed like a terrible situation, but Alice could not imagine what good thing that might be. Under the surface of her worry for Laura was annoyance with Adam. She had specifically told him that he should not take Laura anywhere without her parents' permission. He could have at least informed Alice that they were going out.

"Hello in there?" called a familiar male voice.

Alice dropped the vegetable peeler and listened.

"Mark!" she heard Louise say. Alice attempted to compose herself, but already her heart was beating so hard that she felt like she had just run a footrace.

"I am so glad to see you," said Louise. Hearing her, Alice felt that the primary reason her sister was glad had to do with Adam. "Alice?" Louise called out. "Are you down here?"

"I'm in the kitchen," she called back as she hurriedly took off her apron and rinsed her hands. "I'll be out in a minute." Before she finished drying her hands, however, Louise had brought Mark in.

"Look who's here," said Louise, proudly showing off Mark as if she had produced him herself.

Alice smiled and extended her hand. "Oh, it's so good to see you again." She examined him more closely. "You look wonderful—a little thinner perhaps, and there's a bit more white in your beard. Very distinguished."

He looked into her eyes as he continued to hold her hand in a warm grasp. "You look even more lovely than the last time I saw you," he finally proclaimed.

"Oh, Mark . . ."

"As does your sister and this inn and the entire charming town of Acorn Hill." He released her hand and turned to Louise with a smile. "Am I just getting old or is life getting sweeter?"

She laughed. "Well, since you're asking me, I must admit that age does sweeten a few things."

"Mark!" cried Jane as she entered the room. "You're finally here."

"In the flesh," he said. "And as I was telling your sisters, everything about this town looks lovelier than the last time I saw it. As do you, Jane."

"Thank you, kind sir." She laughed. "We need more charming gentlemen around here."

"Speaking of gentlemen," said Mark, turning back to Alice, "has my guest arrived yet?"

The sisters exchanged a quick look, then Alice asked, "Adam?" holding on to the hope that Adam had nothing to do with Mark.

He smiled. "Oh, good, he's here. Kids sometimes have different ideas about schedules."

"Yes," said Alice. "He actually arrived yesterday." She thought, *Was it really only a day ago that he came? Goodness, so much has happened.*

"Is he in his room?" asked Mark.

"Well, to be honest, I'm not sure where he is," she admitted with a frown.

He noticed Alice's expression and asked, "Is something wrong?"

Alice glanced uneasily at her sisters, unsure of how best to proceed. "Perhaps we should talk," she said to him.

"Maybe we could take a walk," he suggested. "I'd like to stretch my legs after that drive."

"That's an excellent idea."

Soon they were outside, and Mark was admiring Jane's handiwork in the garden. "I'm not exaggerating, Alice. Everything looks so lovely to me in this town. Maybe it's the springtime or maybe I'm just glad to be here."

"It's a lovely time of year."

He looked at her. "Or maybe it's you."

She felt herself blushing. Unprepared to be moving in this direction so quickly, she decided it was best simply to express her concerns about Adam openly. "Mark, we need to talk about Adam," she said in a serious voice.

"Certainly." He nodded as they continued to walk. "I didn't realize he'd get here before me or I would've explained his situation. I'm sorry."

"His situation?"

"Yes, he's going through a rough time, and I feel it's my responsibility to help see him through. I thought if he met me here in Acorn Hill, we could discuss his future."

She cleared her throat. "Uh, what exactly is your relationship to Adam?"

"Didn't I tell you?"

"No, not that I recall."

Mark slapped his forehead. "I'm getting forgetful in my old age."

Alice felt as if she was holding her breath now, waiting for Mark to answer.

"Adam is my godson," he said as they neared the house where Vera and her husband, Fred, lived. "His father Gregory Peterson was my best friend from grammar school and throughout college. He was the best."

"Was?"

Mark nodded sadly. "Evidently, I didn't tell you about this either. I suspect it was because I was so depressed by the news myself, I probably didn't want to burden you with it."

"What happened?"

"Gregory and his wife Amy were killed in a car wreck."

"Oh dear, how tragic."

"Adam had just started his second year of college. An only child, he was shattered by the loss."

"Of course." Now Alice felt bad for not having been kinder to the boy.

"His grandmother, who is quite elderly, wrote me that Adam was having some problems and that she was concerned. Apparently, he has dropped out of college to travel, he told her. She thought that he was just going through a phase, grieving or something."

"That is entirely possible."

"Yes, but months passed, and he continued living in what she describes as his 'dead-end' lifestyle. She was very frustrated and hoped that I could help. That's why I invited him to meet me here."

"I see."

He paused and gave her a concerned look. "I hope it hasn't been an inconvenience."

Alice decided simply to tell him what had been going on and how it had been disturbing to her and her sisters. Even as she related those things, she felt guilty for the pettiness of their assumptions. "I feel so bad now," she admitted. "I mean, if I'd known what Adam was going through, well, I'm sure I would've been more patient, as would have Louise and Jane. But we just weren't aware. And then there is the situation with Laura and her parents. The Winstons are so worried about her blindness and how she's adjusting and, well, Adam has just seemed to exacerbate things. And now with them both missing—"

"Missing?" Mark sounded alarmed now. "What do you mean?"

She held up her hands. "I'm not sure what I mean. All I know is that they're both gone. And judging by Adam's room, he could be gone for good."

"Oh, I don't think—"

"No, Mark. I'm sorry. I shouldn't have said that. I have no reason to think such a thing. I guess it's just that I've been worried. . . ."

"No, I'm the one to apologize. I'm so sorry that having Adam here has been troubling to you." He sighed deeply.

"Well, I feel better about everything now. But to be honest, I am worried about him, Mark. After what you've told me, I would guess that he is depressed. That would certainly explain his lack of care about his personal hygiene and—"

"His personal hygiene?"

"You'll understand what I mean when you see him. He's been living in his car. Well, it all makes sense now. When I offered to do his laundry, he said no, but of course, if he's depressed, he probably really doesn't care." She realized that she was almost talking to herself. "I'm sorry to go on and on."

"No, it's good to know these things. It helps me to evaluate the situation before I speak to him. I haven't been around him that much since he grew up. I used to see him a lot when he was a little kid and his parents still lived in Philadelphia. We had some great times together, and I thought he was the greatest. I used to take him on small veterinary assignments with me, and he was actually quite helpful with the animals. Then the family moved a few hours away and my practice grew increasingly busy, and I rarely saw them after that. To be honest, those few times I did see the teenaged Adam, I thought that he had become selfish and spoiled. He never seemed to treat his parents with much respect, and I guess I didn't really enjoy being around him."

"Mark!" Alice pointed to the car coming down the street.

"That's him! That's Adam's car."

They both waved from where they were standing on the opposite side of the street, but Adam did not appear to notice.

"Oh dear," said Alice, clapping her hand over her mouth.

"What?"

"He's alone! Where is Laura?"

They both turned around and quickly began walking back toward the inn. "Trust me," said Mark, "we'll soon find out."

Chapter Nine

They were both slightly out of breath when they finally reached the inn. They discovered Adam near his car, which to Alice's dismay was parked once again on the street in front of the inn. Adam was standing slightly hunched, lighting a cigarette.

"Adam!" called Mark as they hurried over.

Adam looked up from his lighter. "Hey," he said in a casual voice, as if he saw Mark every day. He snapped his lighter closed, dropped it into one of the pockets on his baggy pants and took a long drag from his cigarette.

For a moment, it looked as if Mark was going to hug Adam, but the young man shifted away and Mark shook his hand while lightly patting him on the back.

"You smoke now?" said Mark in a surprisingly parental tone.

Adam shrugged and slowly exhaled the smoke from his nostrils as he studied Mark and Alice.

"I suppose you've heard all the lectures about how that stuff can kill you?"

Adam shrugged again, then took another drag. "We're all going to die anyway, Mark. That's the unavoidable human condition."

Mark frowned but said nothing.

"I'm wondering about Laura," began Alice, "I—uh—I thought maybe she was with you."

"Well, you can see that she's not."

"Do you know where she is?" asked Mark.

Adam shrugged. "Why should I know?"

"Haven't you been with her?" asked Mark. "Alice said that you—"

"What?" snapped Adam. "That I abducted her?"

"No, not at all," said Alice. "I only said that you two had been spending time together. Laura is not at the inn, and I don't know where she has gone. And, well, her mother had asked me to keep an eye on her. I'm just worried."

"Understandable," said Mark, patting Alice on the back. "A missing blind girl is a serious problem."

Hearing it put like that only proved to be more upsetting to Alice. She felt her eyes tearing and she reached in her trouser pocket for a tissue. "Oh dear," she said.

"So, are you saying that you don't know where she is?" Mark asked Adam again, this time in a very firm voice.

"Man, what is it with you people?" snapped Adam as he dropped his cigarette and snuffed it out beneath his grimy tennis shoe. "Say Adam, how are you doing? How's life treating you, Adam? Just questions and accusations like you actually think I did something to Laura. It figures!" He shook his head and walked around to the other side of his car, climbed in, started the engine, gunned it and took off.

"Oh dear," said Alice. "He is upset."

"I didn't handle that well," admitted Mark as he rubbed his beard.

"I'm afraid that's my fault," said Alice. "I shouldn't have dumped all that information on you before you'd had a chance to speak to Adam."

"Your concern for the girl was legitimate." He sighed. "I wonder if this is how it would feel to be parents."

"Oh dear," said Alice. "In that case, we should be thankful that we're not."

Mark laughed. "Well, I'm sure that Adam will cool off. If not, I may go out to look for him and see if we can iron this thing out. I have to admit that I don't much care for his attitude, and you're right about his appearance."

"Don't forget that he's probably depressed," Alice reminded him. "That could explain everything."

"I know that's true, but you just have to deal with grief and keep on keeping on."

"Maybe that works for some people," said Alice, "but it's not like that for everyone. Some people need professional help."

Just then she noticed another familiar car approaching the inn. *"Oh no!"*

"Who is it?"

"Laura's parents," gasped Alice. "Oh dear, what on earth am I going to tell them?"

As the car drew closer, Alice felt her knees growing weaker. "This is so awful, Mark." She stared down at the ground, almost afraid to even see the Winstons face to face. *Oh, what will I say?* she thought.

"Don't worry," he said. "I'm here with you. Somehow we'll—" he paused. "Say, do they have two daughters, Alice?"

"No." She looked up in time to see Mrs. Winston happily waving from the front seat and Laura, glum as usual, sitting in the back. "That's her," said Alice. "That's Laura!"

Mark smiled. "So, all's well that ends well."

"What about Adam?" she asked in a meek voice, wondering which was worse, a missing blind girl or a broken-hearted, depressed boy. *God help me,* she prayed silently as they walked back to the house. *And help Adam too.*

Louise showed Mark to his room while Alice returned to the kitchen to help Jane. While they worked, she told

Jane the whole story about Adam and, finally, how she and Mark had practically accused him of kidnapping Laura. "I feel so bad about it," she confessed. "Adam must despise me."

"Sounds like that kid needs some help," said Jane as she seasoned the gravy.

"That's what I told Mark." Alice unwrapped a stick of butter and set it in the butter dish. "Even so, I wish I had handled the Laura situation better." She shook her head. "I don't know how the Winstons came in and got Laura and left the inn without my hearing."

"Well, you said that you were sewing. It's possible they came while your machine was running."

"I suppose."

"With both the Langleys and the Winstons going out for dinner tonight, we could eat in the dining room," said Jane.

"Do you want me to set it up in there?"

"It's up to you, Alice." Jane checked on the oven. "Oh, by the way, I got conned into inviting Aunt Ethel for dinner tonight."

Alice sighed. "Why does that not surprise me?"

"Yes, she can't wait to get her hands on your 'young man' as she calls Mark. She wants to hear all about his veterinary adventures."

"How did she persuade you?"

"She has the most beautiful daylilies in her side yard, and I've been begging her to share some with me. They're an old-fashioned variety that's hard to find. So this afternoon, she traipsed over and announced that she was just dividing the clump and asked if I would like some. Well, I jumped up from planting onions and ran over to her house, and while I was putting my lilies into a box, she mentioned how she hoped she'd get to see Mark when he arrived and was I planning some special dinner?"

"So she bribed you with daylilies."

"Basically."

"Leave it to Aunt Ethel."

"At least she's bringing dessert."

"Let me guess," said Alice.

"Peach tarts," they said simultaneously.

"Mark will be pleased," said Alice. "He loves Auntie's tarts."

It was not long before they were all seated around the dining room table. "Isn't this nice?" said Mark as he looked at the women surrounding him. He offered to say the blessing. "For dear friends and good food and fine fellowship, dear Lord, we give You thanks. Amen."

Alice looked up and glanced at the one empty place. "I wish Adam could've joined us."

"No luck in your search for him?" said Jane as she passed the rolls.

"I scoured the town," said Mark as he ladled some gravy onto his meat. "If he was in Acorn Hill, I'm sure I would've found him."

"Do you think he went home?" asked Louise.

Alice glanced uncomfortably at Mark. Louise and Ethel had yet to hear all the details about their young guest. Perhaps they didn't need to. Certainly, it wasn't Alice's place to inform them. Not, at least, while Mark was here.

"As far as I know," began Mark, "Adam has been living in his car." Then he went on to explain about the death of Adam's parents and his grandmother's recent worries. "His parents left insurance money for him, but it's tied up in a trust fund controlled by the grandmother. She told me that the money is only to be used for college and living expenses until he's twenty-five, but when Adam dropped out of college, she froze all funds. And now Adam is on his own."

"Oh, what a terrible thing, losing his parents and so suddenly," said Louise. "The poor boy must be suffering."

"My parents died when I was young," said Ethel. "If it hadn't been for my brother, these girls' dear father, well, I don't know what would've become of me. He and his sweet wife took me right into their home. Do you girls remember that?" she asked. "I mean Alice and Louise. Of course, Jane hadn't been born yet."

Louise and Alice nodded. Ethel took a bite of her Yorkshire pudding, then continued. "I did what I could to help with the girls. And then after Madeleine died, well, I was glad to be there to help Daniel and his three mother-less girls through their time of need."

"You really do need family at a time like that," said Alice. "Unfortunately for Adam, he only has his grand-mother for family. Amy's only sister died quite young from leukemia and Gregory was an only child."

"It is good that he has you," said Louise.

"That's right," said Ethel. "His parents were wise to pick such a responsible person for their son's godfather."

Mark laughed. "I'm not so sure about that. At the time, even though I was in my forties, I would not have described myself as anything that resembled responsible. But Gregory and I had always been good friends. We'd been as close as brothers growing up. Been rowdy college boys together. I had even been the best man at their wedding about ten years before Adam was born."

"Wow," said Jane, "that was a long wait for a baby."

"Yes," said Mark, "there was some problem about get-ting pregnant, and they were ecstatic when Adam came along. I still remember the christening. You never saw prouder parents. But honestly, I think their choice of me as godfather had more to do with friendship than anything else. I certainly had no experience with kids. To be perfectly honest, I didn't even know what the role of a godparent was. I'm not sure that I do now. Oh, I went to Adam's christening, and I always send him gifts for birthdays, Christmas, special occasions. But other than that? I'm really not sure."

"Well, when Father did baptisms," began Alice, "he would always point out that godparents were to be responsible for a child's spiritual upbringing should a parent be unable to perform that duty."

Mark's eyes grew wide. "Seriously?"

"My father took it very seriously," said Alice. "He would question the godparent to discern if they were really willing to commit to this important role. He would remind them that, while it was an honor to be chosen for a godparent, it was also a big responsibility that should last a lifetime."

Mark nodded. "That's a big commitment."

"Well," said Ethel in a time-to-change-the-subject tone, "did I tell you girls about Lloyd's latest idea to have a barbecue this year?" She launched into a long-winded story about how Lloyd Tynan had met this Southern gentleman at a mayor's conference, and the man had the most wonderful recipe for ribs. "And Lloyd has invited him up here so that he can teach Lloyd how to make it, and then Lloyd is going to put on a barbecue that not one of his guests will ever forget."

Jane and Alice had just begun clearing the table when Adam walked in. Alice went over to him. "Oh, Adam," she said, "we're so glad you made it." She pointed to the unused place setting. "There's still lots of roast beef and I can reheat the gravy and the Yorkshire pudding and—"

"You don't have to be nice to me just because Mark is here."

Alice felt her eyes growing large. "Well, that's not it. I just feel very sorry for the way I assumed that Laura would be with you. I hope that you'll forgive me."

"So she showed up?"

Alice thought she saw the slightest flicker of interest in his eyes. As small as it was, it gave her hope. "Yes. It turned out that she'd been with her parents."

"Come and join us," said Mark. "Jane is an excellent cook."

"Yes," said Ethel, and she launched into a history of Jane's culinary achievements as a chef in San Francisco.

Jane chuckled as she turned on the stove to reheat the gravy. "Aunt Ethel's tales get better with every telling, don't they? To hear her talk, you'd think that Wolfgang Puck would be knocking down my door."

"Next thing we know, you'll be a featured chef on a cooking show." Alice turned away from Jane as she put the pudding into the microwave to warm. She did not want to admit it, but Adam's comment that she was being nice because of Mark still stung.

Jane chuckled. The microwave dinged, and Alice got a potholder to remove the dish.

"He's getting to you, isn't he?" said Jane as she refilled the gravy boat with hot gravy.

"Who?"

"Adam." Jane came over to Alice. "He may have lost his parents, Alice, but that doesn't mean he had to lose his manners too. I wouldn't let him talk to me like that."

"But I couldn't . . ."

"I realize that you and Mark have some things to figure out," she continued, "and while it's none of my business, you better figure out this thing with Adam too. A kid like that could drive a real wedge into any relationship."

Alice did not respond since they were already heading back into the dining room with the reheated food. Now Mark was regaling everyone with an exciting story about piranhas and how an Amazon River guide had lost some fingers to the feisty fish. Alice felt relieved that Adam seemed mildly interested in the graphic tale, but she noticed the chilly look he gave her when she set the warmed Yorkshire pudding before him.

She told herself that Adam was still irked about her assumption that he had something to do with Laura's disappearance. And she could not blame him. Even so, she felt it might be deeper than that. She wondered if he resented her relationship with Mark. Perhaps he felt that this was a time when he needed someone like Mark in his life, but then there was Alice just getting in the way.

Chapter Ten

S hall we have dessert in the living room?" suggested Louise. "Then perhaps Mark would show us some of his photos of his recent trip."

"Don't twist my arm," teased Mark.

"That's an excellent idea," said Alice as she picked up a serving dish. "Why don't all of you head on in there while I take care of these—"

"Nothing doing." Jane grabbed the dish from Alice. "I've got everything under control."

"And I can help Jane," said Ethel as she picked up Mark's dinner plate and headed toward the kitchen.

Alice knew her sister would not be pleased by this offer, since Ethel had a tendency to talk more than help, but Jane simply smiled and continued to clear the table. Alice suspected that her loquacious aunt would rather be in the center of the limelight than share it with something as mundane as travel photos.

They began working their way through the photos, which Mark had nicely arranged in albums with notations explaining them. Alice was pleased to see that Adam actually seemed to be interested. He even asked Mark several rather intelligent questions that began to give her hope for this young man.

"If you ever give up veterinary work," said Alice as she studied a particularly lovely shot of a sunset on a river, "you could consider photography, Mark. Some of these are worthy of framing."

"Well, thank you," said Mark. "I was afraid that I took too many photos. But I figured I might never get back there again."

"Why not?" asked Adam.

Mark smiled. "I guess because I'm getting old."

"Aren't you about the same age as my dad was?"

"That's right."

"Well, that's not that old. Old is my grandma's age. She's like ninety, I think."

"Yes," said Mark. "I'm not as old as your grandmother, though sometimes I feel like it."

"Here comes dessert," sang out Ethel as she and Jane came in bearing trays laden with small peach tarts buried under miniature mountains of whipped cream.

"I hope everyone wanted whipped cream," said Jane, "since Aunt Ethel got a bit carried away."

Ethel laughed. "Well, Jane has all the best toys in her kitchen. Her fancy whipped cream maker was so much fun that I just couldn't stop myself."

After everyone had been served, Ethel sat next to Mark and told him in explicit detail about her latest ailment, a bad bunion on her left foot. Apparently, she thought an animal doctor should know about human medicine as well. The others brought Jane up to date on the photos, and Adam even explained a few things to her.

"Wow, Adam," she said. "You seem to know a lot about faraway places. Have you traveled a lot?"

"No. But I've read a lot about travel and I used to think I'd like to go around the world."

"Used to?" asked Jane.

He shrugged and looked down at his empty dessert plate. "Yeah, back when I was a little kid."

"But don't you still think it would be exciting as a grownup?" she asked.

He seemed to consider this. "Maybe."

"Maybe if you finished college," suggested Alice, "then perhaps you could get a job that—"

"Look," Adam pointed his finger at Alice, and the room grew suddenly quiet. "I don't need you telling me what to do, okay?"

Alice actually started, then nodded. "That's fine." She quickly stood and busily gathered several empty plates as if that was just what she had intended to do. Then she headed for the door, but not soon enough to miss Mark's attempt at correcting his discourteous godson.

"That's not a very respectful way to speak to an elder," he began in a quiet voice.

Fortunately, she was down the hall before Adam could respond. One thing was clear to her, painfully clear: Adam disliked her. She knew it was not her imagination. Furthermore, despite her good intentions, she did not like him. Perhaps that was the most disturbing discovery of the evening.

She heard someone behind her and, worried Mark might be coming to apologize for Adam's impolite behavior, she hastened her step. She did not want him to see her like this, not with these hot tears running down her flushed cheeks, but her hands were full and all she could do was hurry to the kitchen and hope to dry her face on a tissue before he noticed.

She was relieved to discover it was Jane who had followed.

"Oh, Alice," Jane said when she saw the tears. She set aside Alice's stack of plates and gave her sister a big hug.

"I feel so silly," muttered Alice as they stepped apart.

"That Adam," Jane shook her head. "He was just making me start to like him and then he goes and says something as dimwitted as that."

"Oh, he's just unhappy," said Alice as she reached for a tissue to dry her tears.

"And he wants you to be unhappy with him? Misery loves company?"

Alice shrugged. "I think he may resent me."

"Of course he does," said Jane. "He probably sees Mark as someone who was going to rescue him and you as someone who might mess things up."

Alice nodded. "Yes, that's what I was thinking too."

"Just be patient with him."

"I'm trying."

Jane gently rubbed Alice's back. "I know you are, sweetie. You're doing far better than I would be under the same circumstances."

Jane's sympathy only made Alice cry harder. "Goodness," she said as she used another tissue to dry her eyes, "I don't know what's wrong with me tonight. I feel as if I'm falling apart."

"I know what's wrong," said Jane. "And I'm going to give you the same remedy that you once gave me."

Alice soon found herself excused from the evening's gathering. Before she could protest, Jane had escorted her up the back stairway to her room where the door was quickly closed to shut out the sounds of piano music coming from down below.

"Don't worry about a single thing," promised Jane as she filled Alice's tub with hot, lavender-scented water. "I will tell everyone that you've come down with a migraine or perhaps something even more exotic. What was that disease that Mark was telling us about?"

"Oh no!" Alice certainly hoped that Jane would not lie on her behalf. Then she touched her forehead. "Actually, my head is throbbing a bit."

"See," said Jane as she lit a scented candle, then reached into her pocket to produce several homemade truffles, which she artistically arranged along the side of the tub. "Take these and call me in the morning."

Despite her misery, Alice laughed. "You're an angel."

"Hey, I learned from the best." She handed Alice her bathrobe. "Now, I want you to just relax and totally empty your head. Hey, do you have a good book?"

Soon, Alice was steeping in bubbles, munching on chocolates and slowly erasing the day's worries as she got lost in her mystery. When she finally climbed into bed, she realized that sometimes the best way to deal with a bad situation was simply to escape from it—at least temporarily, for she was no fool and she knew that she would not be able to escape forever. She would deal with those challenges tomorrow, but for tonight, she would simply pray and go to sleep.

∞

When Alice awoke early the next morning, she decided to give Vera a call even though it was Sunday. She and Vera usually did not walk on Sundays because they were often busy with last-minute preparations for Sunday school or whatnot.

"Of course I want to walk," said Vera without missing a beat. "How else will I ever hear what's going on over there? I saw you and Mark walk by my house yesterday. You were so immersed in your conversation with him that you didn't even see me wave. Then the next thing I knew, you were practically running back home. I've got to hear what on earth has happened."

So they met and walked, and Alice talked. Although she could not make complete sense of her troubles with Adam and Mark, she did feel better when she had finished. Vera had raised two children of her own and had some sage advice about young adults to offer.

"Sure, they think they're all grown up," she told Alice, "or they want you to think they are, but underneath they are scared to death."

"Scared?"

"You know, of failing. They're old enough to realize that getting from where they are now to where they want to be may not be as easy as they had hoped. And it scares them. Overwhelms lots of them. Haven't you heard of the throngs of twenty-something kids that have returned to the nest?"

"Yes, but I guess I never thought about why that is. To be honest, I don't remember feeling like that. I just wanted to come home to help take care of my father. It had nothing to do with being scared."

"Well, maybe you're just different," teased Vera.

"Thanks a lot."

"I'm guessing that Adam is scared about a lot of things. I mean big things like life and death."

"I'm sure you're right," she told Vera when they reached the inn. "Now that I've had my therapy session, what do I owe you?"

"Hey, you've already paid me by telling me what's going on," said Vera. "Now I don't have to mug you after services to get the scoop."

Well, one thing Alice could trust about Vera was that even if she did "get the scoop," she was very discreet about keeping it to herself. Alice knew that her story was safe with her friend.

"Good morning," said Mark as Alice came into the inn. "Been walking?"

"Yes, as a matter of fact."

"Feeling better?"

"Oh yes," she told him. "I feel much better. Jane insisted I go right to bed last night. At the time, I felt bad about doing so, but I think she was right."

"Well, you'd had quite a day." He lowered his voice. "What with the missing girl and Adam's shenanigans."

She smiled at the use of that old-fashioned word. "I better go get cleaned up so that I can help Jane with breakfast."

He nodded. "And I am about to take a walk myself." He peered out the window. "What a great morning for it too."

As she hurried up the stairs, she wondered if she should have asked him about Adam and whether they should invite him to church or not. Well, that was Mark's concern, she told herself as she hurried to shower. After all, Sunday was a day of rest. Perhaps that is just what she needed today. No more "babysitting" teenaged girls or willful young adults. Today, she would enjoy church, family and friends, and let someone else take care of the problems.

"How are you feeling?" asked Jane when Alice came into the kitchen.

"Great," said Alice. "Thanks for the remedy."

Jane giggled. "I guess that's what we'll have to call it from now on. Whenever a sister is ready to lose it, we'll just recommend 'the remedy' and we'll all know what we mean."

Alice went to work slicing fresh strawberries and bananas. It was not long until Louise joined them and was put to work supervising the waffle iron.

"I couldn't resist," said Jane. "I'll make Laura whatever she would like, but I thought the other guests shouldn't be deprived."

Louise poured a ladle full of batter onto the hot iron. "I saw the Langleys on my way down. Mr. Langley looked fit as a fiddle. He said he had never felt better."

Alice smiled. "Perhaps this will be a good day for everyone."

"I certainly hope so." Louise gave Alice a funny look, almost as if she wanted to ask her about what was going on, but Alice was thankful that she did not.

Alice was tempted to eat breakfast in the kitchen, something they all felt comfortable doing when there was a full house and the table was filled with guests. But knowing that Mark would wonder at her absence, she decided it would be better to simply go out and sit down. She reminded herself to hold her tongue, especially when it came to Adam.

To her relief, all went well at breakfast. When Louise offered the general invitation to the chapel that was always given guests on Sunday mornings, Alice was surprised that Mark spoke for both himself and Adam. "We plan to be there, don't we, Adam?"

Adam frowned, but nodded as if this had been previously arranged and not open to debate, and Alice began to clear the table.

"So far, so good," said Jane as she joined her in the kitchen. "Maybe Mark's little speech got through to our young man."

"Little speech?" Alice cringed at the thought of Adam being lectured because of her hurt feelings. That certainly wouldn't help anything.

"Yes," said Jane. "I missed it, but Louise filled me in last night. Apparently, Mark really laid into his godson."

"Oh dear."

"Now, don't worry about it. Louise thought it was quite appropriate, as did Aunt Ethel. And they're the only ones in this family who've actually raised kids, so maybe they know a thing or two."

"Maybe," said Alice, but she wasn't so sure. If anything, she anticipated that Adam would dislike her more than ever now. And, honestly, who could blame him? *Oh dear, she thought, I am in serious need of divine help on this problem.*

Chapter Eleven

Alice and Louise walked over to the chapel early. Louise wanted to warm up on the organ, and Alice was meeting with her middle school girls church group before the service. Called "the ANGELs," an acronym for something only Alice and the girls knew, the group was in charge of dispensing the palms since this was Palm Sunday. Alice had planned a little talk for the girls because, last year, they had discovered that the palms were useful in whacking the heads of boys in the congregation. Alice wanted to ensure that no head-whacking occurred today.

It was a lovely service. Alice never grew tired of hearing the Easter story, of Jesus' triumphal ride into Jerusalem and the way the people heralded Him as King.

As she left the chapel, Alice realized she was feeling better than she had in days. Perhaps her problems with Adam would be resolved. Then she caught the look Adam gave her as she made her way toward the sidewalk, and the ache in her heart returned. She could see the obvious dislike in his eyes and, even more upsetting, she was afraid that her eyes reflected the feeling right back at him. No matter that she knew he was hurting and that he needed unconditional acceptance, she could not control her feelings. For the first time in her adult life, she felt almost as if she were the same emotional age as one of her ANGELs; for a moment, she longed to grab one of those palms and whack Adam on the head.

She had complimented Rev. Kenneth Thompson on his fine sermon, visited with all her friends and was finally ready to go home when Mark came over and took her hand. "I hope that you have time in your busy schedule to join me for lunch," he said with a bright smile.

"Well, of course." She returned his smile, relieved that he had finally been able to break away from Ethel, who had taken him around to show off to all her friends.

"I thought we'd drive into the hills a bit. Are you up for a drive?"

"Certainly." She smiled.

"Good. Can you be ready to go soon?"

"Shall I change?" she asked. "Is this a formal or informal lunch?"

"Informal," he said. "I told Adam we'd try to get in a little hiking. I think it would be good for him."

She nodded slowly as the realization sunk in. This was

not a date. This was a group outing. Still, it was too late to back out gracefully and, besides, she told herself, why should she?

She hurried up to her room and put on jeans and a denim shirt with a tan sweatshirt over it, just in case there was a chill in the air, and then her walking shoes. *I can do this,* she told herself. *I can do this.*

"Where are you going?" asked Jane as she saw Alice emerging from her room with a determined look in her eye.

"With Mark and Adam," she said. "For lunch and a hike."

Jane stifled a giggle. "You sound like a Marine sergeant, Alice."

"That's because I'm trying to convince myself that *I can do this,*" she said in a hup-two-three kind of voice. " *I can do this.*"

"Well, I hope you're right. If not, there's always 'the remedy.'"

Alice smiled. "You know, that's quite consoling, little sister."

Jane nodded. "Hey, get your comfort where you can. In the meantime, have fun and don't let him get to you."

"Mark?" asked Alice in an innocent voice.

"Yeah, you bet." Jane gently thumped her sister on the head. "You know who I mean."

"Right." Alice nodded. "I can do this."

Like a mantra, Alice mentally repeated that phrase as they got into Mark's Range Rover. *I can do this—I can do this—I can do this.* She was surprised that these were not the first words out of her mouth when Mark offered her a stick of gum.

"Uh, yes, thanks," she muttered, feeling somewhat dimwitted as he held the pack before her with a questioning expression.

"You okay?" he asked.

She smiled and nodded. "Yes, just thinking about something else."

"You all set back there?" he asked Adam as he started the engine.

Alice heard Adam muttering something back but could not quite make it out. Probably, it made no difference since he was not talking to her anyway.

"Is that so?" said Mark.

Now her ears perked up a bit. What had she missed? Mark was looking at her with an expression that suggested he expected some kind of response on her part.

"Did I miss something?" she asked.

"Adam just mentioned that he gets carsick in the backseat," said Mark.

"Oh." Alice turned to look at Adam and noticed that he seemed to be smirking. "Well, I don't mind sitting in back," she said.

Mark looked torn. "You don't get carsick, do you?"

She smiled. "Never have before." She was already opening the door. They quickly switched seats, and although she knew it was foolish, she felt as if she had been one-upped by Adam. Once she had taken her place in the back seat, it seemed as if their roles had been reversed, and she was suddenly the youth and the two adults were sitting up front.

Mark tried to include her in his comments, mostly about the region and various hiking trails and sites, but every time she attempted to engage in the conversation, it seemed that she was either cut off or frozen out by Adam. Finally, she decided to focus her attention on the scenery that was flashing by the window. The ride reminded her of when she was a child before Mother had passed away, and her family would take day trips to the mountains.

She smiled to herself as she remembered how her prim and proper older sister never wanted to get dirty or muss her hair, whereas Alice had been a bit of a tomboy. She had not minded baiting a hook or gathering firewood or wading through a creek to catch crawdads. Even the bugs and snakes had not worried her. She just thought they were interesting.

Her father appreciated these qualities, but Louise would sometimes tease her by calling her Al, and Mother would get concerned if Alice carried the dungarees and flannel shirts too far. "Don't forget you are a lady," Mother would counsel her, "and a pretty one at that." Of course, Alice had never considered herself pretty, with her red hair and freckles. Oh, her eyes were nice and people always told her she had a sweet, pleasant face, but pretty? No, she wouldn't go that far. Now Jane and Mother, they were the pretty ones—beauties really, and Louise had always possessed rather handsome good looks.

Alice wondered why she was thinking about all of this now. It was not the sort of thing that normally occupied her thoughts. Perhaps it was because she was supposed to be on something of a date. But was it really? Here she was, sitting in the backseat, for the most part overlooked. She wondered now if it would have made any difference if she had not come at all. Furthermore, she wished that she had not. She would have been happier at home with her sisters than riding in the backseat with a surly young man taking her place up front. Suddenly, she wondered if she might too get carsick and actually had to suppress the urge to say, "Are we almost there?"

She looked back out the window, reminding herself that she was an adult, and then hummed hymns quietly, harmonizing with the sound of the tires on the curving mountain road.

"First stop, Cutter's Pass," said Mark as he parked the Range Rover in a small parking area. "I thought we could have a little hike to work up our appetites and then there's a café down the way where we can have lunch."

Adam climbed out of the car and stretched lazily. "I haven't hiked since Boy Scouts," he said to Mark. "Not sure if I'll be able to keep up." He looked longingly at the front seat. "Maybe I should just wait here."

"Nothing doing," said Mark. "We came to hike, and hike we will."

"Surely you can keep up with two old fogies like us," said Alice, instantly wishing she had not spoken when she noticed the frown shadowing Adam's face.

Mark laughed. "That's right, Adam. We're three times as old as you. I think that definitely gives you the advantage."

"Yeah, whatever."

"It's a beautiful day." Not taking any chances, Alice directed this comment to Mark. "Unseasonably warm for April."

Mark nodded. Soon they were off, and although Adam complained a bit at the start, he had no problem keeping up, and it was not long before Alice noticed that not only was he keeping up, but he also seemed to be driving them faster. They were going up a steady incline when she paused to catch her breath and remove her sweatshirt. It was much warmer than she had expected.

"You okay?" Mark called back to her. Adam was ahead of Mark, standing at the top of the rise now with his hands on his hips as if he was becoming impatient. From where he stood, looking down on Alice, it almost seemed a set up to show off his physical stamina and superiority. Maybe that was just her imagination. She wondered if fatigue could possibly give way to paranoia.

"I'm fine," she called up the hill as she tied the arms of the sweatshirt around her waist. "Just a bit too warm." She considered telling them to go on ahead without her, but that might suggest defeat or that she was too old and feeble to keep up with them. For whatever reason, maybe the competitive tomboy still residing within her older woman's body, she was simply not willing to give in.

"I can do this," she muttered aloud as she continued walking uphill. But as she said it, she could hear her breaths coming out in short quick gasps and she knew her feet were dragging. Even though she had on her best walking shoes, she was getting a hot spot on her big right toe, which would probably become a blister if she didn't take care.

When she reached the top of the second rise, she paused in the shade to catch her breath and wipe the perspiration from her brow. That is when she noticed that Mark had on some sort of a safari hat and Adam was wearing his ball cap, actually facing forward now. They were both somewhat shielded from the noonday sun. She wished she had thought to bring along a hat or at least apply some sunscreen. Why hadn't she planned better?

"How are you holding up?"

She forced a smile to her lips. "Not as well as you two."

Mark pulled a handkerchief from his pocket and wiped a stream of sweat from his face. "Maybe we should slow down a little." He turned to Adam. "What do you think?"

Adam made a disappointed face. "I was just starting to enjoy this."

"That's okay," said Alice. "I'll be fine. How about if we just go at our own pace. If I get tired, I'll sit down and wait for you guys to come back for me."

"Are you sure?" asked Mark.

She nodded. "Yes, it's lovely out here. I would be happy to go at a more leisurely pace and simply enjoy all this natural beauty. I've barely had time to admire the wildflowers yet."

He smiled. "Okay, then."

It was not long before Mark and Adam were out of sight, but this did not bother Alice in the least. In fact, she was relieved. She stopped by a stream and removed her shoes, allowing her hot, tired feet a refreshing soak in the icy water. She splashed some on her face and even considered drinking, but she knew that would not be wise. Too bad she hadn't thought to bring a water bottle.

Finally, her feet felt like ice cubes and even the hotspot seemed a bit better. She looked around until she spotted a nice big log that could serve as a handy bench. She had just put her socks back on when she heard a buzzing sound around her head. When she looked up, she saw a number of yellow jackets diving right at her. She grabbed her shoes and leapt to her feet, swinging her arms like a windmill as she attempted to fend off the angry little beasts. But it was too late. She suddenly felt a hot stinging sensation on her left forearm and then another on her right hand. She saw one wasp coming straight at her face. Panicking, she actually threw a shoe at it. Of course, that did no good. She missed the insect, but it did not miss her, and the flying shoe landed right in the stream where it began floating away like a little white raft.

With her remaining shoe in hand and yellow jackets still coming at her, Alice began to run along the stream, hoping to catch the wayward shoe, but after about fifty feet, she realized she was running a losing race. She gave up and just shook her head sadly. She wanted to cry, but would not give in to her emotions. "You are a registered nurse," she told herself. "You know how to handle emergencies." Her hand, arm and cheek were all throbbing from the stings.

She looked about for anything that might help her and noticed the mud along the edge of the stream. She remembered that Native Americans had used mud poultices for healing. She scooped up some mud and applied it to the welts. The cool sticky substance, she found, was somewhat soothing. Now, she wondered, what could she do about the missing shoe? First, she knew that she should get back to the trail in case Mark and Adam had already turned back. She suspected that was unlikely since Adam had been so miraculously transformed into a mountain goat, but she did not want to miss them on the trail.

As she walked in her soggy socks toward the trail, she chided herself for being critical of Adam. What was wrong with her that she would feel like this toward an unfortunate young man who had lost both parents and was probably suffering from genuine depression? Just what kind of person was she anyway? Once she reached the trail, she found a rock and carefully examined it for wildlife. Finding it clear of danger, she sat down, looked at her remaining shoe and just sighed. One shoe is not good for anything. She thought that she probably should have thrown it into the stream too, then perhaps it would meet its mate and someone might find a pair of shoes. But that seemed like littering. She wished she had thought to make fresh poultices before she came back to the trail. The old ones were getting warm and dry now, but she left them on with the hope that the drying mud would absorb some of the yellow jacket venom. Fortunately, she was not allergic to stings. She would have been in trouble if that were the case; she had treated a boy in the hospital who almost died of anaphylactic shock from being stung just once. Alice was grateful that the yellow jackets had not gone into a full-scale rampage and swarmed her. She knew that even people who were not allergic could die from multiple stings. She paused to say a prayer of thanks. She knew that, despite her somewhat regrettable straits, He was still watching out for her.

She wondered why things had gone the way they had today. Was it Adam's fault? No, she knew it was not fair to blame the boy for her own carelessness. One should look before one sits—especially in the woods. Nevertheless, it did annoy her that Adam had been pushing them too hard. Even Mark had appeared exhausted when he paused to catch his breath. Still, Alice knew he would do what he could to keep up, especially if he felt that this was helping

Adam—perhaps just the sort of connection Adam needed right now.

All that was fine and good, but why, she wondered, had she come along today? So far, it only seemed to be a lesson in pain and misery for her. And, of course, a blow to her pride. Tomboy indeed! She would much rather be at home, putting her feet up and having a nice cool lemonade on the front porch and visiting with guests. "Alice!" called Mark from up the trail.

She waved her one walking shoe from where she was seated. She felt pitiful and embarrassed for her sorry condition. Mark was actually jogging toward her now. Adam merely walked. "What's happened? Are you okay? What's on your face?"

She attempted a smile and then related her encounter with the yellow jackets, the loss of the shoe, and finally why she was slathered in mud. She could tell that Mark was caught between feeling concern and wanting to laugh.

"Go ahead and laugh," she told him. "I'm sure that I must be a sight."

By now, Adam had joined them, and he just stared at Alice as if she had two heads. But when Mark started laughing, Alice could not help herself and she began laughing too. Then she described how it had felt to see her walking shoe floating down the stream, and the two

of them were laughing so hard that she had tears streaming down her cheeks.

"Old people," said Adam. Then, rolling his eyes, he
turned and continued going down the trail.

First, Alice felt somewhat stunned by Adam's complete
lack of compassion. Then she saw Mark's perplexed face,
and she just threw back her head and laughed even harder.

"Young people," she said, but not loud enough for Adam,
who had already walked quite a way down the trail, to hear.

Mark nodded. "You said it." Then he helped her to her
feet. "Do you think you can walk in your socks?" he asked
with concern.

"Fortunately, I wore a thick pair," she said. "At least it's
mostly downhill."

"I could go back to the car and drive ahead to see if I
could find you some shoes," he said.

She smiled. "Now where do you think you would find a
pair of size eight shoes out here? I'll be fine."

So they took the hike back slowly, pausing to allow
Alice to rest her feet, which truly were feeling worse for
wear. It was nearly three o'clock when they reached the
Range Rover. Alice slid thankfully into the backseat and
removed her ruined socks.

"How are your feet?" asked Mark as he started the
engine.

"They've been better."

"That took you guys forever," complained Adam. "I thought I was going to have to call out the search and rescue."

"Well, that would have added another dimension to the adventure," said Alice with a tired smile.

"Man, I can't believe you actually threw your shoe in the creek," said Adam in a disgusted tone that sounded as if he were addressing a three-year-old. "That's like so totally lame."

"Yes," said Alice, "and that's how I feel too—lame."

"Are you hungry?" asked Mark.

"I'm starving," said Adam.

"How about you, Alice?"

"I'm hungry, but I don't think any respectable restaurant will let me in. Not in this condition."

"That's right," said Adam. "No shirts, no shoes, no service."

Alice sighed.

"Well, the place I'm taking you is at a lodge," said Mark. "They have a little gift shop. Maybe you can clean up and find some sort of footwear there."

As it turned out, the lodge had everything Alice needed. She purchased a pair of flip-flops, the kind that teens wear, with little palm trees on the sole, a periwinkle T-shirt with the logo of the lodge and a small packet of Advil, which she hoped would reduce the swelling of her bites and ease the pain in her feet. She even found some peach-scented lotion to soothe her irritated skin. And after about ten minutes in the ladies room, she emerged looking somewhat civilized, except for the big red welt on her cheek. *A battle scar,* she told herself.

"There you are," said Mark as he met her in the lobby. "I just talked the manager of the restaurant into staying open long enough for us to get something to eat. They normally close at three until the dinner hour, but I explained your circumstances and he took pity on us."

"Yeah," said Adam. "And I told him that I was starving."

Alice nodded without speaking. Maybe that is how she would get through the rest of their "outdoor adventure" trip. Just smile and nod, like those silly little bobble-head car ornaments that she had just seen in the gift shop.

Chapter Twelve

W hat on earth happened to you?" cried Jane when Alice walked into the inn later that afternoon. "You look absolutely awful."

Alice forced a smile. "Thanks a lot."

Jane peered at the stings on Alice's swollen cheek and arm and then frowned. "Seriously, Alice, you're a mess."

"Yes, well, it's been an interesting day."

"She's a trooper," said Mark as he came in behind her. Adam pushed his way past the two of them, then headed straight up the stairs without saying a word of greeting to anyone.

Jane put her arm around Alice's shoulders. "Looks like you're in need of 'the remedy.'"

"The what?" Mark looked confused.

"Never mind," said Jane as she began ushering Alice upstairs.

"I'm sorry about everything," called Mark from behind her.

"That's okay," said Alice. "As I said, it was my own silly fault."

Alice gave Jane the shortened version of her disastrous hike, and by the time they reached the third floor, Jane was in stitches. "You really threw a shoe?"

"They were my favorite walking shoes too," Alice sighed as she reached for her doorknob.

"Hey, that's pretty cool footwear you're sporting right now," said Jane as she noticed Alice's colorful flip-flops.

Alice chuckled. "Actually, they're starting to grow on me. Honestly, with the shape my feet are in, I probably couldn't fit into regular shoes anyway. I think I should soak my feet in ice water."

"I'll bring some up for you," said Jane. "And some cortisone cream while I'm at it. We have some in the first aid kit downstairs."

"Thanks."

Alice felt like an eight-year-old again, as if she were incapable of caring for herself and was in need of special attention. Maybe she was. Anyway, she was not about to argue with Jane. Just going up the two flights of stairs had made her tender feet throb even more than the last leg of that ill-fated hike.

By the time she emerged from her shower, Jane had already set out a pan of ice water right in front of Alice's easy chair. The cortisone cream was on the little side table, along with a note instructing Alice to remain in her room and have dinner up there. *Unless you insist on coming down,* stated the final sentence.

Alice laughed. *Not on your life.*

She applied the cream to her stings and was instantly reminded of the year that she and Louise had gone to summer camp. She had been ten at the time and not happy about being away from home for two weeks. Once there, Alice had almost immediately broken out in a rash from contact with poison ivy. At first, she thought it the perfect excuse to return to Acorn Hill since she was desperately homesick already, but the camp nurse assured her that they had treated many a case of poison ivy and had not lost a camper yet. The nurse was very nice. Funny, Alice hadn't thought about that incident for years.

Just as Alice leaned back into her easy chair, Wendell pushed open the door, which had been ajar, and with tail held high, strutted into her room. She smiled at him as she patted her lap, and he jumped up and quickly made himself comfortable. There she sat, soaking her feet in the cold water for nearly an hour, dozing off and on, as the cat purred happily in her lap.

"Ready for some supper?" asked Louise, coming in with a tray.

Alice opened her eyes and smiled. "Yes, thank you. That's very thoughtful of you and Jane. I honestly don't know if I could have made it back down the stairs and then up again. I think I've done enough climbing for one day."

Louise chuckled. "Yes, Jane filled me in. Aren't you a bit old for that sort of nonsense?" She cleared the side table next to Alice, then set the tray on it.

"Actually, I had been thinking I was in pretty good shape," admitted Alice. "That is, until today. Now I feel as if I'm a hundred years old."

"I heard that Adam gave you and Mark a run for your money." Louise sat down on the bed, folding her arms across her front as she waited for Alice to taste the soup.

"*Mmm,* Jane's tomato bisque is the best."

Louise cleared her throat. "Adam is downstairs right now. He is telling Laura about how you slowed them down on their hike this afternoon and how they almost missed lunch because of you."

Alice sighed. "That figures."

"He is the rudest young man."

"I shouldn't have gone with them today," said Alice. "It should've just been a special time for Mark and Adam, a guys' trip, you know. Adam is right. I did ruin the day for them."

"*Humph.* It sounds more like Adam ruined the day for you."

"I'm just not sure how I fit in," said Alice as she set her spoon down.

"What do you mean?"

"Oh, with Mark, I guess."

"But how could you possibly know? It seems that all this trouble with Adam is quite a distraction for you and Mark. That is, if your plan was to spend time with him. By the way, did you know that Mark has an appointment with Richard Watson this week?"

Alice's eyes grew wide—Richard Watson was a local real estate agent. "Seriously?"

Louise nodded. "Richard told me as much himself at church this morning."

"Mark is planning to do some real estate shopping?"

"So it seems. Richard said that Mark set it up with him soon after he got into town. Apparently, he saw a for sale sign in front of the old Olsen house as he was driving by and thought it looked like a worthwhile investment."

"That is a darling house," said Alice as she pictured the small white cottage in her mind's eye. "Of course, it's a bit run down, but it could be very sweet if fixed up properly. And the rose garden was always lovely. I suspect that there might still be some bushes surviving amongst the weeds."

Louise nodded as she stood. "Well, I should get back down to help Jane with dinner. Mark and Adam are going to join us again tonight."

Alice frowned as she looked down at her puffy red feet. "I feel like a naughty child who's been banished to her room for the evening."

Louise laughed as she paused in the doorway. "That's not too far from the truth. But that's only because you failed to remember your age today, my dear."

"I don't think I'll do that again."

"I certainly hope not."

"Please make my apologies to Mark, and uh, Adam too."

"*Humph.* I will tell Mark, but I don't think I will be making any apologies to Adam."

Louise went back downstairs, and Alice was left to her quiet dinner and continued foot-soaking. She actually welcomed this bit of solitude. Too much had been going on these past few days, and now, more than ever, she felt the need for some quiet time. Lounging in pajamas, reading her mystery and going to bed early sounded like the perfect prescription for her. Maybe Louise was right. Maybe she was getting old.

Fortunately, Alice felt more like herself the following morning. She awoke earlier than usual and was surprised that she was actually able to get her feet into her loafers. They were still a bit sore, but much better than yesterday. Even so, she was not sure that she wanted to walk with Vera today. She decided to give her good friend a call. Alice slowly made her way downstairs to the phone at the reception desk, feeling each step in her sore muscles and feet.

"I hope you're not seriously injured," said Vera after Alice had briefly explained her condition.

Alice laughed. "My only serious injury was to my pride, Vera. It is painfully clear that I'm no spring chicken."

"Who wants to be?"

"Well, I'd just be glad not to feel like I'm a hundred and three today."

"So when will we be walking again?"

"I'll let you know. Maybe tomorrow if we take it easy. But first I'll have to get some new walking shoes."

Vera laughed. "And no more using them as projectiles."

After hanging up the phone, Alice went into the kitchen where she discovered Jane already puttering about.

"Smells good," said Alice as she eyed the nicely browned loaf that was cooling on the butcher-block countertop. "Banana nut loaf?"

"I thought it would be nice to have it warm for breakfast." Jane regarded Alice closely. "How're you feeling?"

"Better, I think."

"I stopped by your room last night, but you were sound asleep."

"I was pretty worn out."

Jane rolled her eyes. "Imagine that."

"Yes, I know," said Alice. "Louise already gave me the lecture."

"You mean to start acting your age instead of your shoe size?"

Alice nodded as she poured herself a cup of tea. "Funny thing is that I've been feeling about the same age as my shoe size lately."

"Oh well," said Jane, "no harm in being young at heart."

"*Yoo-hoo,*" sang out Ethel as she opened the back door.

"Hello, Auntie," called Jane.

"I had to pop in and see how Alice's date with Mark went yesterday."

"Date?" Alice frowned. "It wasn't exactly a date."

"Well, whatever you young people call it."

Alice had to laugh. *"Young people!"*

Ethel went for a cup of coffee. "Well, younger than some of us." She sat down across from Alice. "Go ahead," she said. "Tell Auntie everything."

So for the third time, Alice told about the unfortunate hiking trip, trying to do a condensed version, but when she failed to embellish it properly, Jane took over and very dramatically reenacted the whole thing, until all three of them were laughing so hard, they had tears running down their faces.

"Is that what *really* happened?" asked Ethel as she wiped her eyes.

"Well, Jane *is* given to exaggeration," said Alice.

"Creative license," said Jane.

"Oh my." Ethel just shook her head. "I don't think I'd call that a date either, dear."

"No, I'd call it a catastrophe." Alice reconsidered this. "Although, our late lunch was actually rather nice. And I have to say that Mark was entirely gracious and kind throughout everything."

"How about the boy?" Ethel peered at Alice with undisguised curiosity.

"Well . . ."

"He was a complete brat," said Jane, "and he wasn't much better last night either."

"Oh dear," said Alice. "What did he do?"

"Well, for starters, he took Laura off without even talking to her parents—just whisked her away after dinner without telling anyone. Needless to say, they were quite upset."

"Oh my."

"And then he and Mark got into an argument about it."

"Poor Mark."

"Yes," agreed Jane. "I have to give it to Mark. He was surprisingly patient with that surly young man, but I could tell that he wanted to throttle him."

"Someone *should* throttle him," said Ethel.

"Are you volunteering?" Jane pointed a wooden spoon at her aunt.

Ethel chuckled. "Wouldn't be the first time I set a young person in his rightful place."

"I can vouch for that," said Alice.

"Morning, girls," called Louise as she came into the kitchen. "I see the party has already begun."

"Isn't it nice having Alice home this week?" said Jane.

"It's a good thing too," said Alice, "Since I'm sure I would've been completely useless at the hospital right now."

"So what are your plans today?" asked Louise as she poured herself a cup of coffee and sat down across from Ethel.

Alice shrugged. "I'm not sure—well, other than that I won't be taking any hikes. I would like to get to Potterston to shop for a new pair of walking shoes."

"Hello?" called a masculine voice. Mark pushed open the door to the kitchen. "Are males allowed in here?"

Jane laughed. "Only you, Mark. Come on in."

"That is correct," said Louise. "You are special."

"Thanks." He smiled at Alice. "How are you doing today?"

"Much better, thanks."

"Coffee?" offered Jane.

He nodded and took a chair across from Alice. "I am so sorry for every—"

"As I said," she told him, "it wasn't your fault. I brought it on myself."

"I shouldn't have let Adam push us so much," he said, then groaned as he rubbed the top of his legs. "Believe me, I'm paying for it too."

Alice felt selfishly relieved at this admission. "Well, I suppose we're not as young as we used to be."

"You're telling me." He shook his head. "I could barely make it down the stairs without screaming in pain just now."

Alice laughed. "Well, I would recommend some ibuprofen for starters. And then perhaps a hot soak in the tub might help."

"And that's your professional opinion?"

"Well, that and don't let Adam push you around so much."

The other women actually gave a little applause for this.

"I know," said Mark. "It's awful, isn't it? I feel so terrible about how things went last night with Laura. I'm considering giving Adam his walking papers today."

"Oh, Mark," began Alice. "You don't really want to—"

"I don't see why not. He doesn't seem to appreciate anything, and it's clear that he doesn't want to be here. All he does is stir up trouble."

"But it's only because he's feeling so—"

"I don't buy that, Alice," he said in a firm voice. "I mean, I realize that he's hurting about his parents, but that certainly doesn't give him the right to make everyone else miserable."

"That's true," said Louise.

"We're all mature adults," said Jane. "We ought to be able to come up with something that will get through to this young man."

"You mean besides my throttling him?" said Ethel.

Alice made an apologetic smile to Mark. "She offered."

"Not a bad idea."

"Can't you just give him a little more time?" asked Alice, surprised that she was actually feeling sorry for Adam now. The idea of Mark asking him to leave the inn was unsettling.

"Maybe I can give him a warning," said Mark, "that he can either shape up or ship out."

"Yes," agreed Alice. "That sounds fair."

"Now, not to change the subject," said Jane, "but, Alice, would you mind picking up a couple of things for me if you go to Potterston today?"

"Not at all."

"You're going to Potterston?" asked Mark.

"To purchase some new walking shoes." She grinned at him. "For some reason I find myself in need."

"Want some company?"

"Sure."

"Though I do have an appointment this morning," he said. "Do you mind waiting until after that? I should be back by eleven."

"That's fine."

"And, considering that you may still be recovering from that horrible hike yesterday, perhaps I should drive you."

"That would be great." Then she considered something worrisome, but hated to ask.

"Something wrong?" he asked.

"Well, I was just wondering . . . uh, do you plan to invite Adam to join us today?"

He laughed. "Ah, not this time."

"Oh." She hated that she felt so relieved.

"I'll give you my list after breakfast," said Jane. "Most of all, I want you to go by Gierson's and get lots of eggs.

They're having a great special and you know we need a bunch for the egg hunt."

"You use real eggs?" asked Mark.

"Of course," said Louise, "and everyone at the inn is invited to an egg-dyeing party on Friday afternoon."

"Sounds like fun," said Mark. "Count me in."

Chapter Thirteen

*A*lice had to admit that she enjoyed riding in the front seat this time. It felt nice to be a grownup sitting next to Mark as he drove them to Potterston. Their conversation was light and comfortable, carried mainly by Mark as he related several exciting stories about his practice at the zoo.

"You are quite a storyteller," she said. She wanted to ask him about his appointment with Richard Watson and whether he liked the Olsen house, but since he did not mention anything about it, she thought perhaps he would prefer that she didn't know. Still, she was curious about what he was planning.

"I spoke to Adam this morning," said Mark.

"How did it go?"

He shook his head. "Not too well. Adam immediately got quite defensive. He said that if I didn't want him around that he might as well just clear out."

"Oh dear."

"I assured him that I wanted him around, but that I wanted him to be more courteous to others."

"Could he understand that?"

"I'm not sure. He acted as if he hadn't done much wrong. It's almost as if he wanted to push me, to see what I'd do about it." He scratched his beard. "If I didn't know better, I'd say that Adam is testing me, but that seems ridiculous. Good grief, he's almost twenty years old. It's not as if I plan to act like a father to him. I just want to help him."

"I know you do, Mark."

"The thing is, Alice . . ." He paused to glance at her, then put his eyes back on the road. "I hate to admit this, but I really don't like Adam very much."

Alice did not know what to say. The truth was that she didn't either.

"I know that sounds horrible. It's certainly not a very Christian way to feel about someone, especially about the only son of your deceased best friend, as well as your own godson. But that's how I feel. If I were to meet Adam on the street after all he's put me through, well, I probably wouldn't give him the time of day. Except that I feel responsible for him, you know?"

"I know."

"But I have to ask myself, just what exactly is my responsibility to him?"

"I'm not sure, Mark."

"I'm not sure either. I've considered what your father used to teach, that a godfather was responsible for a child's spiritual upbringing should the parents be unable. And while I agree with this, at least in theory, I have to wonder what I can possibly do to influence Adam now that he's all grown up. And do you know what really bugs me, Alice?"

"What?"

"I'm feeling angry at Gregory now. I feel that he must not have done a good job raising Adam. It feels horrible to think that, especially considering how much I loved Gregory." Mark sighed deeply.

"I can see that it's complicated."

"You said it."

Alice was relieved that they had arrived in Potterston now. Otherwise, she might have felt compelled to confess that she, too, disliked Adam. Somehow, she just did not want to admit that to Mark. It was bad enough that he was having problems with his feelings. At least Alice should try to appear to like the young man. As they walked into the shoe store, Alice decided to look for the good qualities in Adam. Surely, he must have some.

Alice found an excellent pair of walking shoes after only trying on a few pairs. "These are so comfortable," she said as she walked around the store, "I don't want to take them off."

"You don't have to," said the pleased salesman. "I can ring them up for you and put your other shoes in the box."

"Perfect," said Alice.

After that, Mark insisted on treating Alice to lunch. "I know I can't make up for yesterday," he said after they were seated at a window table at a nice restaurant, "but I can try."

She waved her hand. "I think that the sooner we forget about all that the better we'll feel."

He nodded and looked down at the menu. Alice studied him from the other side of the table. He was such a kind and gracious man, and he treated her so well. What more could anyone hope for? Yet she was not sure—not only about her own feelings, but also about his. Perhaps it was better just to go on the way they were and be content that they were simply friends. They both decided to try out the special, a salmon soufflé with sautéed asparagus, and neither of them was disappointed.

"That was excellent," said Alice to Mark as the waiter removed their empty dishes.

"Dessert?" he asked.

"Oh, I shouldn't—" began Alice.

"Why not?" said Mark.

She smiled as she considered all the calories that she must have burned off yesterday. "Yes, why not?" They both ordered the crème caramel, which turned out to be delicious.

"We have similar tastes," observed Mark as they were leaving.

Alice nodded. "Except that you had coffee with your dessert and I had tea."

"Well, we wouldn't want the waiter to think we were boring." He smiled as he held the door for her.

"Thank you," she told him. "Lunch was just lovely."

Mark dropped off Alice at the grocery store. "Do you mind if I run some errands," he asked, "while you shop?"

"Not at all."

They agreed on how long it should take, and Alice took Jane's short list and went into the store. She piled her cart high with eggs, relieved to see that there was no limit on the special price. Then she gathered the other items and made her way to the checkout stand.

"Alice Howard?"

Alice turned to see a vaguely familiar face behind her. She smiled at the attractive woman in the periwinkle-blue jogging suit but still could not quite place her. "Yes?"

"Oh, I thought that was you." The woman smiled brightly. "Matilda Singleton," she said. "Or at least I used to be."

"Matilda Singleton?" Alice struggled to put this vaguely familiar face with the vaguely familiar name.

"We went to college together."

Alice nodded and smiled. "Oh yes, Matilda, of course. I remember you now."

The woman patted her platinum-colored hair and stood straighter. "Well, I have to admit that I've changed some. And I go by Mattie now."

"You look great," said Alice. It was true. Matilda, or Mattie, almost looked better now than she had back in college.

"Well, I finally lost that weight." Mattie patted her chin with the back of her hand, causing her assortment of gold bangle bracelets to jangle. "And then I got a little work done here and there. Just small things, you know. But every little bit helps when we get to be this age. Right?"

Alice nodded uncertainly as she moved her cart forward in the line. "Do you live around here, Mattie?"

"I just moved to Potterston last year," said Mattie. "My late husband Arnold grew up here and he'd always dreamed of retiring in his hometown. We'd barely moved into our condo when he suffered a cardiac arrest."

"Oh, I'm sorry."

Mattie did not look particularly upset. "Well, between you and me and the lamppost, I was about to divorce him anyway."

Unsure of how she should respond to that, Alice continued unloading her cart, placing carton after carton of eggs on the moving belt.

Mattie continued chattering at her as the cashier rang up Alice's groceries.

"Lotta eggs," said the young man. "You planning to make a giant omelet or something?"

Alice laughed. "Actually, we're going to boil and dye them for an Easter egg hunt."

"You're serious?" He blinked, then totaled the cost. "I didn't know people did stuff like that anymore."

"They do where I live." Alice gave him her money and waited.

"And where's that?" he asked as he gave her the change.

"Acorn Hill," she told him.

"Oh, you live in Acorn Hill," said Mattie as she began to unload her groceries onto the belt. "That's such a sweet little town. I tried to talk Arnold into settling down there but, oh no, he would have nothing to do with it. Potterston or nothing."

Alice noticed Mark coming in the store's entrance. "Need a hand?" he called as he got closer.

Alice smiled and waved him over. "Do you remember Mark Graves?" she asked Mattie as she returned her wallet to her purse.

"Is *that* Mark Graves?" cooed Mattie with obvious appreciation. "Well, he's still just as handsome as ever." Then she lowered her voice. "So you actually nabbed him after all. And here I'd heard that you two had broken up."

"Actually, we're just—"

"Mark Graves," called Mattie cheerfully. "I'll bet you don't remember me."

Mark and Alice waited for Mattie to complete her purchases, then the three of them chatted briefly near the exit. Finally, Mattie suggested that they should stow their groceries and meet at the coffee shop next to the grocery store. "We can keep talking about old times," she told them. "My treat."

Mark wheeled Alice's cart to the Range Rover and then opened the trunk. They decided the weather was cool enough that the eggs would be safe for a short visit.

"Do you remember her from when we were dating in college?" Alice asked as she handed Mark a bag to be placed in the back. "She was a casual friend of mine."

"Not exactly," he admitted. "The name sounds a bit familiar, but I don't really recall her face."

"Well, she's lost some weight and even admitted that she's had some, uh, work done."

Mark nodded knowingly as he closed the back of his car with a thud. "Went under the knife to look younger, eh? It's got to make you wonder."

"What?" Alice peered at him as they walked across the parking lot.

"Whether it's worth all that pain, money and danger. Any surgery has its risks. Why take the chance?"

"But she does look good, doesn't she?"

He shrugged, and suddenly Alice remembered something.

"I didn't get a chance to straighten her out," she said quickly as they walked toward the coffee shop. "Mattie, uh, well, she thinks we're married."

Mark chuckled. "She does, does she?"

"I was about to explain to her that we're not, but then she began chatting with you and I didn't get the—"

"Hello, you two," called Mattie as she joined them.

As Mark went to the counter to order, Alice filled Mattie in on her marital status.

"Oh, I see." Mattie's carefully penciled eyebrows lifted. "Well, isn't that something. Alice Howard never married and Mattie Singleton has been through four husbands already."

Alice felt her eyes growing wide. *"Four?"*

Mattie laughed. "That's right. I have to admit that those alimony checks came in handy, and then, of course, the insurance."

"Oh my."

"Now don't act as if it's so scandalous," said Mattie. "It's not as if all of the divorces were my fault. Well, other than the fact that I have the worst luck imaginable when it comes to picking good men and just marriage in general."

Alice noticed her large diamond rings, one on each hand, and her glittering earrings. Mattie may have had bad luck with men, but it appeared that alimony and insurance money had paid off. Still, Alice did not believe that baubles were worth the heartache of failed relationships.

"There you go," said Mark as he set down the tray of coffee and tea on the small table and joined them.

"Mark Graves," said Mattie in an interested, if not slightly flirtatious, tone. "So, tell me, what have you been doing with yourself all these years?"

Mark smiled and then pleasantly indulged her with a short but impressive synopsis of his forty-year career in animal medicine, including mentions of his various travels.

"Fascinating," said Mattie. "I've traveled quite a bit myself. Two of my husbands were avid globetrotters. About ten years ago, I even went down the Amazon. My husband Richard booked us a cruise right down that river. I wasn't too sure about it. Fortunately, the cruise ship turned out to be quite luxurious, and I never even had to get off it if I didn't want to."

"A cruise ship on the Amazon?" Alice thought this sounded rather strange.

Mattie laughed. "Yes, it does seem a bit incongruous since the people who live down there are so primitive and impoverished. I suppose it was an interesting study in contrasts."

"And what have you been doing since college, Mattie?" asked Mark. "Well, other than cruising down the Amazon?"

Mattie smiled and launched into a descriptive tale about all the various places she had lived and all the unusual things she had done. Apparently, Mattie had only married rich men.

By the time Mattie finished, Alice felt exhausted. Of course, Mattie had not gone into too much detail about the careers or personalities of the four husbands or their financial contribution to her affluent and exciting lifestyle, Alice noted. "Wow," said Mark. "That's quite impressive."

"Oh, it's not much compared to all that you've done," said Mattie in a flattering tone. "How fulfilling it must be for you to go around the world saving endangered animals. I feel rather selfish not to have pursued a career."

"Careers aren't everything," Mark assured her.

"Well, I guess I can't complain," she said. "At least I've seen and done a lot in my lifetime. I always tell my daughter whenever she complains that I'm traveling too much, you only live once and you might as well do it with flair."

"You've certainly done that," said Alice.

"How about you?" Mattie turned her attention to Alice now. "What have you been up to all these years?"

Alice felt that her life would sound dull and boring compared to what she had just heard, but she had no reason to make it seem bigger than it was. It was not as if she was ashamed of her life.

"Don't let Alice fool you," said Mark. "Acorn Hill is a delightful place to live. And, believe me, that so-called quiet little town of hers is full of all kinds of funny adventures and excitement."

"Oh, I don't know . . ."

"We do have our share of adventures," admitted Alice. "And it's rather nice living in a town where everyone knows you."

"And were you serious about what you said in the grocery store?" asked Mattie. "Do you really intend to boil all those dozens of eggs and then dye them for an Easter egg hunt?"

"That's right," said Alice. "My mother started doing this when Louise and I were just little girls, and I started it up again when I moved back to Acorn Hill. We've been doing it ever since. It has grown and has become a local tradition."

"Well, it sounds like fun. I might have to come over and see all this for myself," said Mattie.

"You're most welcome," said Alice.

"And then I can see your little inn too." Mattie nodded. "In fact, that's just what I think I'll do. I'll drive over next Saturday."

"Good," said Alice. "Perhaps you'd like to join us for dinner at the inn that night."

"Now that would be nice."

"Alice's sister Jane used to be a professional chef in San Francisco," said Mark. "You won't be disappointed."

"Well, this just gets better and better." Mattie smiled. "Please, count me in."

They visited a bit more, then Alice grew concerned about the eggs in the back of Mark's Range Rover. "We probably should get those groceries home," she said to Mark.

He nodded. "Yes, we sure don't want to take the chance of making anyone ill."

"See you on Saturday," called out Mattie.

Alice was not sure why she felt slightly down as Mark drove them back to Acorn Hill. It was not as if she was jealous of the exciting life that Mattie had led, and yet something about their conversation did trouble her.

"That Mattie is quite a gal," said Mark in a voice that sounded as if he was not so sure.

"She certainly has led an interesting life," agreed Alice.

"Although she doesn't really seem happy," he observed.

"You don't think so?" Alice considered this. "She puts on a good show of it. She's done and seen so much."

"Lots of people are like that, Alice. They try to make things seem bigger and brighter than they actually are. I guess it makes them feel better, even if it's only briefly."

"That is an interesting observation."

"That's what I like about you, Alice."

She turned and looked at him. "What?"

"You're the real deal."

She smiled. "The real deal?"

He nodded. "If you ask me, that's worth a whole lot more than all the diamonds and cruises in the world."

Chapter Fourteen

O h, good," said Jane as Alice and Mark brought in the groceries. "It looks as though you bought the eggs at the special price too. Goodness, I hope I cleared enough space in the refrigerator for them." She turned to Mark. "By the way, Adam's been asking when you were getting back."

He nodded. "Yes, I told him we'd do something together this afternoon. I better go find him now."

After he left, Jane told Alice that the Winstons had taken a day trip to the Amish country. "I think they were trying to get Laura away from Adam today," she admitted as she put away the last carton of eggs.

"Oh dear," said Alice. "I feel so bad when it seems that guests aren't feeling comfortable at the inn."

"Don't worry about it," said Jane. "It's not as if it's your fault."

Alice nodded. "I know you're right, but I just feel responsible. How did Laura seem?"

"Quiet." Jane checked her oven. "I felt sorry for her as her parents hauled her away. I mean, she's seventeen going on eighteen, in her last year of high school, and here she is stuck spending spring break with her parents in a town where the most lively activities include choir practice and quilting bees."

Alice frowned. "Poor Laura."

"It's no wonder that she likes hanging with Adam. At least he's closer to her age, and they certainly seem to get along well."

"Although he's perhaps not the best influence."

"Maybe not." Jane pointed to Alice's new shoes. "Nice. How are your feet feeling?"

"Better. But I think I'll go upstairs and give them a rest." She glanced around the kitchen. "That is, unless, you need help with anything?"

"Nah, not much going right now. You go put your feet up."

"I was hoping to work on my quilt."

"Sounds like a plan."

Alice became so absorbed working on the baby quilt that she actually lost track of the passing hours. When she finally glanced at her clock, she saw that it was time for her to go down and help Jane with dinner preparations. She stood up and stretched. She wondered if Mark and

Adam were back yet. Mark had hoped to join them for the evening meal. She freshened up and changed into an outfit she usually reserved for church. Jane thought that the caramel-colored sweater looked nice on Alice. She paused in front of her bureau mirror and remembered Mattie's words earlier today: "Every little bit helps when we get to be this age."

Alice's goal had always been to grow old gracefully, which, to her, meant allowing nature to take its course. She looked at her graying hair and slightly sagging chin and sighed. Under normal circumstances, these signs of aging did not trouble her in the least, but tonight they seemed more noticeable. She looked closer, wondering what had happened to the red-haired girl who used to be able to keep up with the boys. Then she smiled, knowing that the girl was still in there. After all, Alice's spirit had not aged at all. That was what really counted.

Alice headed down the stairs with a bit more bounce in her step.

"Oh, there you are," said Jane when they met on the second landing. "I was just doing a quick turndown and truffle drop."

"The old turndown and truffle drop," teased Alice. "Sounds like something an acrobat in the circus might do."

"Yes," said Jane. "I am quite spry for my age."

"Age . . ." Alice sighed. "I'm trying not to think about it too much. Isn't it just a number anyway?"

Jane laughed. "I should think you'd be feeling like a young girl these days, Alice, with Mark paying you all this special attention."

Alice was just about to tell Jane about Mattie when they reached the foyer, and Jane paused to look at a large vase of yellow roses. "Where did these come from?"

Alice looked more closely at the roses. "They are beautiful, aren't they?"

"I'll say." Jane spotted a small white envelope tucked into the back of the arrangement. "They're from Wild Things. Oh, that must've been why I saw Craig Tracy's van on the street this afternoon. I was working in my herb bed." She handed Alice the card. "They're for you."

Alice recognized the handwriting on the envelope. The bouquet was from Mark. She pulled out a card and read the simple message.

Dear Alice,

> *Sorry about yesterday's horrible hike.*

> > *Warmly,*

> > *Mark*

"So what is it?" demanded Jane. "A proclamation of undying love? A proposal? An invitation to a secret marriage ceremony?"

Alice laughed. "Hardly." She handed Jane the note. "Just a sweet apology. Goodness, he didn't need to go to such trouble." Then she bent down to smell the flowers. "Although I do love yellow roses."

"Look," said Jane pointing to a single red rose. "There's one red one too." She thought a minute. "You know, Alice, yellow roses are symbolic of friendship, but red is supposed to be for true love. Do you think this bouquet is meant to have some sort of message?" Jane counted the roses. "Eleven yellows, and one red. *Hmmm?*"

"Maybe Craig was short on yellow roses," suggested Alice. "So he stuck in a red one to make a full dozen."

"That's unlikely. Roses usually come in to shops by the dozen. No, Alice, here's what I think," said Jane as they walked toward the kitchen. "I think that Mark is assuring you of his friendship, and that's important, but the single red rose is meant to be like a question mark—as if he's asking whether or not you still love him."

"Oh, I don't think . . ."

"Just consider it, Alice. It makes perfect sense."

They were in the kitchen now, and Alice turned to the sink to wash her hands, her regular practice before she helped Jane, but perhaps she was doing a bit more thorough job than usual. She knew it was an attempt to avoid Jane's prying questions. She truly didn't know the answers to Jane's questions. Did she love Mark as she did in college before they broke up to go their separate ways, he to his career and she to Acorn Hill and her father? She was very fond of Mark, but . . .

"Come on, Alice," said Jane as she pulled some things from the refrigerator. "Don't pretend to ignore me."

Alice turned around and looked at her younger sister. "I just really don't know, Jane. Mark and I haven't even talked about, well, us."

"That's because he's been so distracted by Adam."

Alice nodded. "That's true enough."

"Adam isn't exactly helping matters."

"Especially since it seems he can barely stand to be around me."

"Who can't stand to be around you?" asked Louise as she came into the kitchen. "Mercy, Alice, I'm sure that you must be imagining things. I don't believe I can think of a single person in Acorn Hill who doesn't love you."

"I'm speaking of Adam," said Alice.

"Oh." Louise nodded and sighed. "Yes, you may be right about that. I've tried to put that young man out of my head. He is certainly a troublemaker."

"Better watch ourselves," warned Jane. "I hear someone coming in the front door just now, and I'm expecting Mark and Adam to join us for dinner tonight."

The sisters started chatting about the latest goings on in town as they worked together to prepare a meal of ham and Jane's special recipe for herbed scalloped potatoes.

"Hello in there," called Mark a few minutes later as he peered in the kitchen door, as if he was afraid to enter.

"You're back," said Alice. "Come on in. I love the beautiful roses, Mark. Thank you."

"It was the least that I could do after your ordeal."

"Come sit down," said Jane. "Tell us about your afternoon."

"I just made a fresh pot of decaf," offered Louise. "Would you like some?"

Mark sighed as he eased himself into a chair. "That would be delightful."

"You sound tired," noted Alice.

"Exhausted," admitted Mark. "I'm too old to be trying to keep up with someone Adam's age."

"Then why are you?" asked Alice.

Mark thought about this as he stirred some cream into his coffee. "I'm not exactly sure. I guess I'm hoping that I'll make a connection with him somehow."

"So what did you do this afternoon?" asked Jane.

Mark laughed. "Believe it or not, we went go-cart racing. We drove past a place on the outskirts of Potterston where they have—"

"Crazy Jack's Racetrack?" exclaimed Jane. "You went there?"

Mark nodded. "Well, it seemed to spark something in Adam when he saw it. Suddenly, he remembered the time when his dad and I took him racing about ten years ago. And so I decided to just take a chance. Of course, when I suggested it, his immediate response was that it was silly. Then I stupidly talked him into it." Mark exhaled loudly. "We ended up spending three hours there. I could barely pry myself out of the little car when we were done."

"But Adam enjoyed it?" asked Alice.

"Yes, sort of. As we were leaving, Adam noticed this scrawny kitten that kept meowing. The owner, Crazy Jack, I guess, said it was a stray that he was going to take to the pound. Adam was all over that kitten, saying that the people at the pound would kill it. I assured him that they would probably just give it some shots and some good food and find it a good home, but Adam wouldn't believe me."

"And?" Louise peered over her glasses at Mark.

"And . . . well . . . I hope it's okay, but Adam brought the kitten home. I mean to the inn."

"Oh, that's perfectly fine," said Alice.

"Yes, just tell him to watch out for Wendell," warned Jane.

"Maybe he should introduce them so Wendell doesn't do anything mean to the kitten," suggested Alice. "Wendell does seem to think he rules the house."

"We stopped by the pet store where we got all the necessary accessories: a collar, a bed and kitty litter. I can easily give him the shots and whatnot myself, although it was too late to stop by a vet clinic to get the serums." Mark set down his cup. "I know it isn't a good idea. I told Adam it made no sense for him to adopt a pet when he can barely take care of himself."

"That's true," said Louise.

"Naturally, that ended up in a big fight," said Mark. "Adam is probably in his room pouting now."

"Goodness," said Louise, "he really needs to get a grip on his emotions."

"It's really not that easy when you're depressed," said Alice.

"Maybe the kitten will help," suggested Jane.

Mark just shook his head. "I don't know. I actually feel sorry for the kitten. He might've gotten a good home if he'd been taken to the pound. He's rather cute, really, all black with four white paws. I can't quite imagine him enjoying living in Adam's car."

"Well, it's a step up from living on the street," said Jane.

"Is living in his car what Adam plans to continue doing?" asked Alice as she finished making the sauce for the brandied peaches to go with the ham.

"That's what he says."

"He doesn't want to continue his education?" asked Louise.

"No interest at all. He says it's a waste of time."

"Yeah," said Jane, removing the foil from the scalloped potatoes and slipping the pan back into the oven, "like living in your car's a great way to spend your days."

"Try to tell him that," said Mark.

When dinner was ready, the three sisters, Mark and Adam gathered around the table. Alice made a polite inquiry about Adam's new kitten, but his reply was so chilly that Alice was warned against further conversation with him.

"What's his name?" asked Jane as she passed Adam the breadbasket.

"Boots," said Adam. "At least for now. It's not the greatest name."

"I think it's cute," said Jane. "Mark told us that he has white feet."

Adam brightened. "He does. Maybe you'd like to see him after dinner."

Alice tried not to feel put out by the way Adam seemed to warm up to Jane. *At least he's engaging with someone,* she assured herself. *Even if it isn't me.*

"Is he eating well?" asked Louise. "We heard he was quite skinny."

"Mark said to only feed him small amounts at first," explained Adam, "and to feed him every couple of hours."

"How's it going?" asked Mark.

"He ate every bite," said Adam. "I think he wanted more, but I didn't give him any."

"Good," said Mark. "Too much could really make him sick."

Alice wanted to ask if Boots knew how to use the litter box, but knew she would not get much of a response. Instead, she asked Louise, "Do you remember the kitten we had as girls? Oliver?"

"Yes." Louise nodded. "Wasn't he black and white too?"

"That's what I recall," said Alice. "I think he had three white feet and a white nose."

"I remember him!" exclaimed Jane.

"Oh, I think not," said Louise. "You weren't born when we got him."

"I remember a big, old cat named Oliver," insisted Jane. "Then one day he was gone, and when I asked Father where he went, he told me that he'd gone away, but he would be fine."

"Oh dear," said Louise. "Maybe you do remember Oliver."

"What happened to him?" demanded Jane.

"Well, he died, of course," said Louise.

"Old age," added Alice. "Goodness, he must've been about fifteen."

"So I did know Oliver," said Jane with satisfaction. She turned to Mark and Adam. "Those two are always remembering something that happened before I was born, but I got them this time."

"You certainly did," admitted Louise. "Now that you mention it, I do remember that Father was unsure about how much to tell you at the time. You were quite young and probably would not have really comprehended that Oliver had died."

"Maybe," agreed Jane, "but it was upsetting, even to my child's mind, that Oliver had simply *gone away*. I imagined that he had packed his little kitty bag and taken off down the street to live with some other family. I think I even blamed myself, as if I'd been nicer to him he might've stayed."

Everyone laughed—everyone except Adam. Without even finishing his dinner, he excused himself and left the table.

"Oh dear," said Alice after they heard him go upstairs, "I think we came too close to his feelings about his parents."

Jane sighed. "It's really hard to predict what will upset him. I thought cats were a safe topic. Well, we are making some progress. At least he said 'excuse me' this time."

Mark just rolled his eyes and sighed deeply, then said, "My most sincere apologies, ladies."

Chapter Fifteen

"Poor Mark," said Jane as she and Alice finished up in the kitchen. "I think this thing with Adam is making him old before his time."

"I know how he feels," admitted Alice. "Adam does that to me too."

"He's not very subtle, is he?"

"What do you mean?"

"I mean he is so obviously ignoring you, Alice. It's almost humorous."

Alice hung up the dishtowel. "I guess I missed the funny part."

"Mark didn't want dessert?" asked Louise as she joined them.

"No," said Alice. "He said he just wanted to turn in early. Sounds like he and Adam are planning another full day tomorrow."

"Maybe it will help," said Louise as she put on the kettle. "At least it will keep him away from Laura." She lowered her voice. "I'm certain the Winstons will appreciate that."

"Are they back?" asked Alice.

"They just came in."

"I wonder if they'd like some dessert?" suggested Jane. "There's plenty of cherry cheesecake. I already offered some to the Langleys. I told them I'd set it up in the dining room, and it would be self-serve."

"I'll go and ask them," offered Alice.

"Yes, and perhaps I will play for a bit," said Louise as she stretched her fingers. "I could use a little practice."

Alice found the Winstons still in the foyer, discussing whether they would turn in for the night. "Jane has made a lovely dessert," she told them. "Cherry cheesecake. We're setting it up in the dining room. If you'd care for any, just help yourselves. And Louise is going to play the piano tonight."

"Oh, that sounds wonderful," said Mrs. Winston.

Mr. Winston looked at his watch. "Not for me, thanks. I've got a good book I'd like to finish."

Laura just yawned and looked bored.

"Well, as always," said Alice, "just make yourselves at home." Then she returned to the kitchen.

Before long, the Langleys, Mrs. Winston, Laura and the three sisters were all settled into the parlor with dessert and tea. Louise began playing. Laura was seated by herself near the door, and Alice was not surprised when the teen, unnoticed by her mother, made a getaway. Alice had to give Laura credit; she was doing much better at finding her way around than when she had first arrived. Alice waited a couple of minutes, then carefully picked up a few of the empty dishes and made a quiet exit too. She was curious about where Laura had gone, but did not see her in the foyer or on the stairs. After depositing the dishes in the dishwasher, Alice went out to the reception desk and paused to tidy up the paperwork and brochures there. It was then she heard quiet voices coming from behind the closed door to the library. She did not intend to eavesdrop, but Louise had stopped playing and the conversation in the library carried quite clearly to where Alice was working.

"He's so soft," cooed Laura.

"His name is Boots, because he's black with four white feet," said Adam. "Do you think that's lame? I mean like Puss in Boots."

"Oh, that sounds so cute. No, seriously, I think Boots is a cool name."

"Can you feel how skinny he is?"

"Yeah, he seems really bony."

"I think he was starving. He's not very old. Mark said he was probably too young to be weaned. I think maybe the mother cat died, and he was left on his own."

"Kind of like you?"

"Yeah, I guess, sort of."

Then Louise began playing again, and the rest of their conversation was lost in the music. Still, what little she heard made her heart soften toward Adam. She suspected that Adam's hard veneer was just a protective coating that kept him from getting hurt. Alice couldn't understand why he was so wary of her. She had no intention of hurting the boy. Of course, he could not know that. Goodness, he barely knew her. She would just have to be very patient.

She returned to the parlor and stood by the door. Jane was comfortably seated in an easy chair, flipping through a magazine as she listened to Louise. Mrs. Winston was sitting next to Mrs. Langley, and both women were leaning back into the sofa with closed eyes, as if the calming music was transporting them to another time and place. Alice felt sure that Mrs. Winston had yet to notice her daughter's absence, and Alice did not feel the need to inform her. Mrs. Winston looked so peaceful and relaxed, and Laura was perfectly fine and just a few feet away down the hallway.

Without being observed, Alice went back out of the room and then upstairs. It was not that she was physically tired, but she was weary of all the comings and goings. On top of that, there was Adam and his strong dislike of her. Alice thought that was enough to make anyone weary.

She picked up the quilt but set it aside almost immediately. She had made good progress on it earlier today, and to work on it at night, when she was not her clearest, might be inviting trouble. Alice detested picking apart seams. She took off her shoes and put on slippers, then picked up her mystery book. She was about halfway through it. Although it was not her favorite type of mystery, it had finally gotten her hooked. She wondered what had become of the missing curator of the museum, kind old Mr. Beacon with the wooden leg. She hoped that he was all right. He didn't deserve to come to harm.

It was after ten o'clock when Alice paused in her reading. Her eyes were getting blurry, and she knew she should go to bed. Oddly enough, she did not feel the least bit sleepy. It must be a cocoa night, she told herself, as she slipped out of her room and quietly began down the stairs. All was silent in the house now. She was careful on the fifth stair down since she knew it had a squeak in it. She hurried past the second floor and on down into the darkened kitchen, and before long, her cocoa was nice and hot. She turned off the lights in the kitchen, then moved toward the stairs. A sliver of light coming from under the door to the library stopped her. *Had Adam and Laura forgotten to turn off the light?* she wondered. Of course, it wasn't a big deal, but living all those years with her father had taught her to be conservative when it came to electricity—especially about turning off lights. So she walked over to the library. She was just reaching for the knob when she heard voices again. Adam and Laura. Now this surprised Alice.

"Pssst," came a quiet whisper from the parlor.

Alice tiptoed down the hallway to the darkened parlor.

"It's Steph Winston, Alice," whispered a woman's voice.

"Mrs. Winston?" Alice whispered back. She paused in the doorway, her eyes slowly adjusting to the darkness until she saw a figure sitting in the easy chair.

"Yes. I'm being something of a chaperone," she explained. "Or perhaps an overprotective and snoopy mother."

Alice smiled. "I understand completely."

"I hadn't really meant to listen," she admitted, "but when I did, it was oddly reassuring."

"I know what you mean." Alice partially closed the door. Just in case. "I overheard a bit of their conversation earlier this evening."

"As crazy as it sounds, I'm beginning to think that boy is good medicine for my daughter."

"I had the same thought. In fact, I think maybe your daughter is good medicine for Adam too."

"They are both rather needy."

"I know," said Alice, "and they seem to understand each other."

"Perhaps it's one of those blessings in disguise," said Mrs. Winston.

"I think you are right."

"But even so . . . well, I just feel a little uneasy about leaving them down here all alone."

"I don't blame you."

"I certainly don't want him taking her off in the middle of the night," said Mrs. Winston. "But I'm getting very sleepy."

Alice sat down in the chair by the door, careful not to spill her cocoa. "How about if I take over for you?"

"Oh, I couldn't—"

"No, it's all right," said Alice. "I came down because I couldn't sleep anyway. If they carry on for too long, I'll simply play housemother and tell them it's time to call it a night."

"Oh, that would be so much better coming from you," said Mrs. Winston gratefully.

"I think so too."

Mrs. Winston stood. "Well, thank you then. I really do appreciate it."

"I'll make sure they wrap it up by eleven," said Alice.

After Mrs. Winston left, Alice leaned back into the

chair and sipped cocoa. Although she wasn't trying to, she could hear the voices of the two young people next door.

"You can't give up," Adam was saying. "I mean, look at you, Laura. You've got everything going for you."

"Like what?"

"You're smart and pretty, you've got both your parents, and they really seem to care about you."

"They suffocate me."

"They love you, Laura."

"Yeah, I guess."

"You know what I would give to have my parents back?"

Now there was a long silence.

"No, what?"

"Everything."

"I'm sorry, Adam."

"I wasn't trying to hold a pity party," he said quickly. "I just wanted to remind you that you're lucky. In fact, I would gladly give up my eyesight if it would bring my parents back."

"Yeah, I know . . ."

"And I'm not trying to make it seem like it's no big deal, Laura. I mean I can't imagine what it feels like to be blind, but I think you can make things work for you. You can take those classes your parents keep pushing and—"

"Just give in to it, you mean?"

"It's not like you have a choice, you know."

There was a long pause, and Alice wondered what she should do. Were they finished talking now? Was it time for her to go in, play the chaperone and help them to call it a night?

"What about you, Adam?" said Laura finally. "Are *you* ever going to just give in to it?"

"What do you mean?"

"Well, look at you. I mean everyone can see it, even me and I'm blind."

Adam gave a little laugh. "What do you mean? What can you see?"

"That you're pushing everyone away from you. I mean the ones who probably care the most anyway. Like Dr. Graves and, well, Alice too. My mom says it's because they're a couple and that it probably bugs you or something."

"That's not it. I don't care if they're a couple or not. What difference does it make to me anyway?"

"So then why are you so mean to her?"

"I don't know . . ."

"She's really nice, Adam. You should get to know her."

"Why?" he said in a louder voice. "Why should I bother? I mean what if I do get to know her? And even Mark too?

What difference does it make if they're just going to leave me anyway?"

"You don't know that."

"Everybody leaves," he said in a bitter voice. "Even my grandma is talking about going into a home now. I know she's old and everything, and she can't stick around forever. Everyone just leaves eventually—" his voice broke.

"You don't know that, Adam."

"It's how life is," he said. "Even if it's all wrong. It's the way things are, you know."

"Things can change," she told him.

"Yeah, they can get worse. It's just not fair."

Alice could hear Adam crying now. She could also hear Laura trying to say things to comfort him—quiet, soothing things. It was sweet, but Alice suspected by his response that he was feeling embarrassed. It sounded as if he was trying to push Laura away.

"It's no big deal," he said in a gruff voice. "I don't know why I even said all that stuff. Just forget about it, okay."

"But it's—"

"Look, it's really late, Laura. I'm sure your parents will be down here with a shotgun before long."

"No, that's okay—"

"It's late," he insisted. "Come on, let's get you upstairs before someone's down here reading me the riot act."

Just like that, without Alice having to play housemother or even say a word, the two young people took themselves upstairs, and soon the inn was completely quiet.

Alice wiped away a tear as she stood. More than ever, she felt sorry for Adam. So that was what he was doing— pushing people away to avoid being hurt. It was a wonder he was allowing Mark into his life. Even then it seemed like two steps forward and one step back, but at least it made some sense now.

She longed to tell Mark about what she had heard. She knew how discouraged he had been when he went to his room earlier this evening. She returned her empty cocoa cup to the kitchen sink, then tiptoed up the stairs, pausing at Mark's door. Dare she knock? If she did, how would it look? At least she was still in her daytime clothes. But still . . .

As much as she wanted to let Mark know what she had heard, she knew it would have to wait until morning. Besides, there was not any light coming from under his door. He was probably fast asleep. On the other hand, she could see light beneath Adam's door. She did not dare chance his overhearing her tell Mark that she had been eavesdropping on him and Laura. No, that would not do at all.

Alice continued on up to her room, knowing that this news had to keep until the morning. Before she went to sleep, she said a special prayer for Adam. She asked that

God would somehow soften him, so that he might allow people back into his life. He was far too young to be trapped into a life of bitterness and seclusion. He needed to get rid of the bitterness before the bitterness took hold of him. Perhaps she would not be able to speak to him directly, but she could talk to Mark.

Even better than that, she could pray. *And pray,* she decided, *I will.*

Chapter Sixteen

So how goes it at the inn?" asked Vera when Alice showed up at the Humberts' house for their walk early the following morning.

"I'm feeling hopeful," said Alice. "As well as a little guilty."

"Guilty?"

"Well, for eavesdropping . . . sort of." Then she explained the bits of Adam and Laura's conversation that she had overheard last night.

"Oh, that's not exactly eavesdropping," said Vera. "That was more like chaperoning. You had promised Laura's mother to watch out for her. I don't think there's anything wrong with that."

"And at least it was a positive conversation. Mark had been so down on Adam last night. He was so discouraged that he even went to bed early. I felt bad for him."

"Did you tell him about the conversation?"

"Not yet. I was the only one up this morning. I'll tell him when I get back. It should make him feel better."

"Well, it can't be easy for Adam to feel as if he's alone in the world at such a young age. I just saw a news show about twenty-something kids and how so many of them feel so lost.

Even after they graduate from college, they don't know where they fit into the world."

"That's too bad, but at least they have finished college. Adam keeps telling everyone he has no interest in continuing his education."

"Oh," said Vera with a frown. "As a teacher, I can't understand that attitude. Well, if anyone can talk sense into that boy, it'll be Mark."

"I hope so."

"Are we going too far?" asked Vera. "Are your feet okay?"

"I'm okay," said Alice.

They walked and chatted and, before Alice knew it, they were back at the inn. "Wow, that seemed to go fast," she said.

Vera nodded. "I better run. I just remembered that it's my turn to take treats to the teachers' lounge today. I still have to stop by the bakery."

Alice waved to her friend and then walked toward the inn. "Hey there, Wendell," she said as the cat ambled up to her and rubbed himself against her legs. "Have you met the new kitten yet?" Wendell just purred in that self-satisfied way of his, and Alice obligingly bent down to pet him.

"You're a good old cat," she finally told him after giving him a nice long scratch on his head and chin. "But I need to get inside and help Jane."

Alice took a quick peek around the inn, hoping maybe to spy Mark and take a few moments to tell him about what she had heard, but he didn't seem to be around.

"Hello, there," said Mr. Langley as he looked up from where he was comfortably reading his newspaper in the parlor. "I felt so good this morning that I decided to get up early and take a little stroll. The wife's still in bed."

"Well, good for you and for her," said Alice. "Isn't it nice to be able to do as you please while you're on vacation?"

"It sure is."

Alice hurried upstairs for a quick shower before she went back down to help Jane. Although it was not even seven o'clock yet, she suspected that Mr. Langley was getting hungry.

"Hey, you," said Jane as Alice came into the kitchen. "You're early this morning."

"I'm not the only one," said Alice as she put on an apron. "Mr. Langley's out there reading the paper and I think he's hungry."

Jane handed Alice a nicely arranged platter of pastries. "Why don't you put this out there along with the coffee pot and invite him to get started."

"Here you go, Mr. Langley," said Alice as she set the items on the dining room table. "There's coffee and pastries, and I'll be back in a minute with some juice."

When she returned with pitchers of orange and apple juice, Mr. Langley had already sat down at the table and was helping himself to a nice plump croissant. "You ladies are going to have me spoiled by the time I go home," he said with a smile. "Not to mention fattened up."

"At least you've been getting some exercise," she said as she set the pitchers down. "Did you have a nice walk?"

"I sure did. And I almost forgot, I saw your friend Dr. Graves as I was leaving, and he asked me to tell you that he and Adam were taking a day trip. He would've told you himself, but you were gone."

"A day trip?"

"He said he was going with Adam to pay his respects to the gravesites of the young man's parents."

She nodded. "I see."

"It's a sad thing to lose your family like that."

"Yes, I feel bad for Adam."

"Anyway, Dr. Graves wanted me to let you know so you wouldn't worry."

"Thank you," said Alice. "I appreciate it." Although she did appreciate it, she felt sad that she had missed the chance to talk to Mark. Perhaps it would work out better this way. Maybe Adam was getting to the place where he would be ready to confide in Mark in the same way he had confided in Laura.

"What are your plans today?" asked Jane as Alice helped her to clean up after breakfast.

"I'm going collecting."

"Collecting?"

Alice grinned. "The prizes for the Easter egg hunt. I sent out the letters to the local businesses about a month ago. Now it's time to go around and see if they are willing to help out."

Jane made a face. "Good luck."

"Yes, I'll probably need it."

"You can put me down for chocolates," said Jane as she rinsed a mixing bowl. "I thought I'd try making some cute decorated eggs that I saw in my cooking magazine. I'll make a batch for the inn, and if they turn out well, I'll do more for the baskets. How many are you going to fill?"

"We're planning on ten," said Alice. "The ANGELs and I will put them together tomorrow night."

"I'm sure they'll think that great fun."

"I hope so. It all depends on what the businesses want to contribute."

"I hope it won't be a bunch of old, useless stuff like last year," teased Jane. "What kid wants a shoe horn in his prize basket?"

"Or a tea ball." Alice chuckled. "Well, I was very specific about contributions this year. I said they must be child-friendly and I even gave them the age categories."

"Well, I can't wait to see what you get," said Jane.

Alice put on her walking shoes again. Just as she was about to head out the door, the phone rang, and she went to pick it up. It was Aunt Ethel asking for help moving her couch. Alice promised to come by later to help her, then she took a sturdy shopping bag and set out on her mission. She decided that she would start at the hardware store. She knew that she could count on Vera's husband Fred to come up with something nice.

"Howdy, Alice," he said as soon as she entered the store. Alice loved the familiar old smell of this store. More than a hundred years old, it was as if the old walls could tell stories of the days gone by. Some of the merchandise probably could too— Alice felt certain that some of these same items had been on the shelves when she was a child. "Hi, Fred." She smiled and stood at the counter. "I've come collecting for the Easter baskets."

He grinned. "I thought maybe that's what the bag was for. Well, you're in luck this year." He stooped down to get something from behind the counter. "I got in far more of these things than I thought I'd ordered." He stood up and placed an assortment of water guns in varying sizes and colors on the counter. "There's ten altogether."

"That's great!" Alice nodded. "I'm sure the children will be delighted with those."

"The parents may not be too thrilled."

Alice began loading them into her bag. "We won't worry about that, will we, Fred?"

He chuckled. "Kind of like being a grandparent."

"Right. You can spoil them and not worry about the results. Any idea what the weather will be like this weekend?" Fred was an amateur meteorologist.

He rubbed his chin. "Well, the news is predicting cloudy, maybe even showers, but I think it'll be all cleared up by the weekend."

"I hope you're right." She put the last squirt gun in her bag. "Thanks so much, Fred. These are great prizes."

The General Store's contribution was not too generous, but at least packs of gum were better than nothing.

She crossed Chapel Road to Nine Lives Bookstore. After entering, she paused to pet one of the shop cats, then went up to the counter.

"Good morning, Alice," said Viola as she lowered her glasses and set aside a thick book.

Alice quickly explained the reason for her visit. "If you haven't got anything, I'll understand."

"Of course, I have something," said Viola with a twinkle in her eye. "I think you'll be impressed too." Then Viola reached down below her counter and pulled out a stack of picture books. "These are hot off the press. Not only that, but they are signed by the author."

"Really?" Alice picked up a book for a closer look.

"These are wonderful. Thank you. They will be a great addition to the baskets," Alice said as she walked toward the exit.

Her next stop was down Berry Lane at Wilhelm Wood's Time for Tea. "Good morning, Wilhelm," she said in a cheerful voice.

"Hello, Alice. I've just brewed some of my new spring blend. Would you like to sample it?"

"Certainly," she told him, waiting as he poured her a small cup.

"It's a green tea," he said, "that I infused with a bit of peppermint."

She took a sip. "Oh, this is lovely. It's very refreshing. I bet it would be good iced too."

He nodded. "Yes, that's what I thought."

Alice picked up a box and set it on the counter. "I'd like this, and I'm also here to see if you'd like to contribute anything to the Easter egg hunt prizes. Did you get my letter?"

"Yes, and do I have something for you. You said there would be ten baskets, right?"

"That's correct."

He went into his backroom and returned with a small basket of what appeared to be tiny fabric teapots. She picked one up. "What is it?"

"Smell," he said.

She took a whiff and was surprised that it smelled faintly of roses.

"They're sachets," he explained, "filled with potpourri." He looked slightly embarrassed now. "Mother makes them. She wants me to carry them in here, but I'm not so sure. What do you think, Alice?"

She studied the small calico teapot trimmed with lace. "This is very sweet. I think someone who loves tea and teapots would like them very much."

Wilhelm smiled. "They are rather cute, aren't they? Sort of a novelty item. Perhaps I should keep a basket of them up by the register."

"Do you have more?"

"Do I have more?" He groaned. "I probably have a hundred by now. Mother just keeps making them."

Alice laughed. "Well, maybe this will be a way to introduce them to the community."

"Yes," he said. "Perhaps you're right."

"Thank you, Wilhelm. And thank your mother too."

"By the way, Alice . . ." Wilhelm had a curious expression on his face. "What's going on with you and the veterinarian? Clara Horn is going around town telling everyone that you two will be married by summer."

Alice tried to laugh. "Oh dear, I better straighten poor Clara out."

Wilhelm frowned. "So, it's not true?"

"Not in the least."

"Dr. Graves seems such a nice fellow."

"Oh yes, he's very nice, and we are good friends." Alice made a movement toward the door.

"But no wedding bells?"

"Not for me."

He shook his head. "Too bad."

Alice just smiled and exited. *Really,* she wondered, *why would he think it was too bad?* Wilhelm himself was not married and, as far as Alice knew, he did not intend to marry anytime soon. While there were several single women who bought far more tea than they could use, Wilhelm did not seem to think of them as anything other than customers. It seemed to Alice that people always wanted someone else to get married. Maybe it was simply for the festivity of a wedding, or something to talk about, or perhaps some people assumed that one could not be happy without the blessed bonds of matrimony.

Alice sighed as she walked back over to Hill Street. The Good Apple bakery donated ten gaily wrapped giant cookies. "What kid doesn't like a cookie?" said Clarissa with a bright smile.

"You're right," said Alice as she slipped them, one by one, into her bag. "Thank you."

Next, Alice went to Nellie's Dress Shop. After she greeted Nellie Carter, she felt somewhat apologetic. "I'll understand if you don't have anything to contribute," Alice told her. "I mean a dress shop —"

"Not at all," said Nellie. "I think I might have something rather fun. Well, at least I think the girls will like them. Maybe the boys can give them to their sisters or mothers." She laid some pairs of brightly colored socks on the counter. "See," she said, "some have Scotty dogs, others have cats, this pair has pigs, and there's even a pair with pink elephants."

"Those are fun," said Alice. "Thank you so much!"

Alice was not too sure about Sylvia's Buttons, the local fabric shop, but since she had sent a letter, she knew she should stop by. "Hi, Sylvia," she called.

"Alice," said Sylvia Songer. "How is the quilt coming?"

"Not as quickly as I hoped."

"Well, you've still got plenty of time before the baby shower."

"I hope so. Easter season is a bit distracting."

Sylvia smiled. "And then, of course, you've got the distraction of Dr. Graves as well . . ."

Alice shrugged. "Oh, that's not so distracting."

"That's not what I hear."

"I'm guessing you've been talking to Jane."

Sylvia leaned forward on the counter. "That Jane has hardly told me a thing. You'd think she'd been sworn to secrecy or something."

Alice laughed. "Well, it's only because there's nothing to tell."

"That's not what the rest of town is saying."

Alice decided not to bite.

Sylvia's eyebrows went up. "Don't you want to know?"

"I can guess."

"Well, your dear aunt has been dropping hints all over the place."

"No one takes Aunt Ethel too seriously."

"Let's just say there's plenty of speculation." Sylvia looked disappointed now. "So, you're really not going to tell me anything."

Alice sighed. "As I said, there's really nothing to tell." Then she forced a smile to her lips. "Now, I'm here on a mission, Sylvia. I know you may not have anything to contribute, but did you get my letter about the Easter egg hunt prizes?"

"I did and I do. I think you'll be pleased. I'll be right back."

While she waited, Alice looked through a pile of new fabric. Then Sylvia returned with all sorts of soft-looking fuzzy critters in her arms.

"They may be a bit young for some of the kids, but aren't they cute?" said Sylvia as she spread them over the counter.

"They're adorable." Alice picked up a soft blue bear.

"I taught a class on recycling chenille bedspreads, and I gave the ladies a nice discount on everything in my shop if they agreed to sew and contribute one item for the Easter basket prize."

"Oh, Sylvia, you're a genius. These are wonderful."

"Aren't they!"

As Sylvia loaded the stuffed toys into another bag since Alice's shopping bag was already rather full, Alice spoke in a lowered voice. "Now, if things should ever change between Mark and me, I promise to give Jane special permission to let you know."

Sylvia smiled. "Why, thank you, Alice."

"Thank you!"

Alice felt as if she had struck it rich in town today. Perhaps it had been a good idea to send out that letter of explanation beforehand after all. Her ANGELs would be thrilled with all the goodies to put in the baskets tomorrow night. These baskets would be so much better than last year.

Chapter Seventeen

O h, Mark called," said Jane that evening as she sifted flour into a large mixing bowl. "He and Adam aren't going to be home in time for dinner tonight. He sends his most sincere apologies."

"How did he sound?" asked Alice. "Could you tell how it was going?"

"Well, to be honest, he sounded a little stressed to me. I think he was disappointed that he wasn't able to speak to you."

Alice started to prepare a salad. "Yes, I wish I'd been here. What time did he call?"

"It was while you were helping Aunt Ethel move her couch. Maybe I should've come over and gotten you."

"That's okay," said Alice. "Although I would've appreciated a rescue."

"Where did she want it moved to anyway?" asked Jane.

Alice laughed. "Good question. First, she wanted it moved over by the window, but it didn't fit quite right.

Then she wanted it in the center of the room, sort of like a room divider."

"In that tiny room?" Jane shook her head.

"Exactly," said Alice. "It looked odd."

"So where did you finally move it?"

"Right back to where it was in the first place."

"Well!"

Alice nodded. "My reaction exactly."

"I should've gone over to help," said Jane. "I would've simply told her that there was only one place for her couch and that's where it already was."

"Oh, I think she probably knows that already. She just enjoys rearranging things every once in a while." Alice transferred the lettuce that she had washed and spun dry into the wooden salad bowl. "Did Mark say anything about their visit to the cemetery?"

"Just that Adam was supposed to be giving the directions and that they got lost a few times. Adam didn't seem to remember where it was. Even when they found the memorial park, it took forever to find the right section."

"That must have been frustrating."

"That Adam," said Jane as she cracked an egg. "He seems to frustrate people even when he's not trying to."

Alice told Jane a bit of the conversation that she had overheard last night. "I know it wasn't much," she said, "but it did give me hope, and I wanted to tell Mark about it."

"Speaking of Adam," said Jane, "I wonder how that poor kitten is doing. Do you think he left it here?"

"Goodness, I don't know," said Alice. "Should I check his room just in case?"

"I think so. That poor creature could be up there starving for all we know. Didn't Mark say it needed to eat every few hours?"

Alice nodded as she set down her knife and wiped her hands. She went to the office, grabbed up the keys and hurried to the second floor. She did not like intruding on Adam's space, but the sisters did go into guest rooms to replace linens and whatnot. As usual, she tapped on the door, although she knew no one was there, then she unlocked the door and let herself in. She was surprised to see that Adam was actually keeping things rather neat.

She glanced around the room, looking for the cat carrier that Mark had bought, but she didn't see it anywhere. Finally, satisfied that the kitten was not there and, consequently not suffering, she started to leave. But something stopped her. She noticed that a Bible, one of the ones that Louise had placed in each room, was sitting on the nightstand, opened up as if Adam had been reading it. Well, that was something, after all.

She quietly closed the door and locked it.

"Who's that?" said a voice.

Alice jumped and turned around to see Laura standing in the open doorway to the guest room she was sharing with her parents.

"Oh," said Alice. "It's just me, Alice. Goodness, you startled me. I didn't realize anyone was up here."

"Why were you in Adam's room?" Laura adjusted her sunglasses in such a way that Alice almost felt that the young woman was studying her, although she knew that couldn't be.

"Well, I just learned that Mark and Adam have been delayed and won't be back until late. Jane and I were worried about Adam's kitten. We thought that poor Boots might be stuck up here without—"

"Adam asked me to watch Boots for him today."

"Oh, good. That's a relief. How's the little guy doing?"

Laura smiled. "I think he's okay. Do you want to come in here and check on him? I mean Adam showed me how to open the can of food and how much to give him and stuff, but my parents have been gone and, well, I just hope I haven't done anything wrong, you know."

"I'd be happy to check on him, but I'm sure he's all right."

Alice followed Laura into the room, watching as Laura felt her way around the bedroom furnishings. "You're getting around much better, Laura."

"Yeah," said Laura when she made it to the roll-away cot and sat down. She leaned over and reached for the cat crate that was right beside it. "I guess I'm trying a little harder."

Alice watched as Laura opened the latch on the cat crate and then carefully extracted the small black and white kitten. She held the kitten up, and Alice reached out and caressed its soft head. "He looks perfectly fine to me, Laura."

"I'm trying not to handle him too much," she said. "My mom told me that kittens could get sick if you hold them too much."

"He looks perfectly fine and happy too."

Laura smiled as she held the kitten against her cheek. "That's what I thought, but I wasn't sure."

"Sometimes I think we can tell things better with our hands than with our eyes," said Alice. "For instance, I sometimes work in the neonatal nursery at the hospital when they're shorthanded, and I've discovered that I can tell as much, and more, by the way a baby feels, breathes and sounds as I can by simply looking at it."

Laura nodded. "Yeah, I guess that kinda makes sense."

"In fact, I think we can be deceived sometimes when we rely only on our eyes. It's as if God gave us these other senses to help us to understand life better, but often we forget to develop them fully."

"You mean until we're forced to?"

"Maybe so."

Laura bent over and put the kitten back into the carrier, gently pushing it back so that she could safely close and then latch the door. "Thanks, Alice," she said as she sat back up.

"You're welcome. I can see that Boots is in very good hands. I'm sure that Adam will be pleased when he gets back."

"Do you know when that'll be?"

"I don't know. It sounds as if they have a long drive ahead."

Laura nodded. "It must be really sad."

"What's that?" asked Alice, although she thought she knew.

"I mean for Adam, being all alone like that, and then going to see his parents' graves today. Well, it just seems really sad."

"Adam's not completely alone," said Alice. "At least he has Mark."

"I don't know if Adam really believes that, I mean deep down, you know."

Alice sighed. "Well, maybe we can all try to help him to understand that there are other people who care for him, people who want to help."

"Yeah, I told him he shouldn't be pushing people away."

"That's good advice, Laura."

"I'm not sure that it did any good though."

"Sometimes it takes awhile for things to sink in. Maybe today's trip with Mark will help."

"I hope so."

"Hello," said Mrs. Winston from the hallway. She looked concerned as she removed her jacket. "Is everything okay in here?"

Alice smiled at her. "Yes, everything's fine. Laura was just letting me have a peek at Boots. She's done a wonderful job of kitty-sitting today."

Mr. Winston frowned. "She refused to go out with us this afternoon, said she had to take care of Adam's cat."

Mrs. Winston gently nudged her husband. "And that was just fine, dear."

"Well, do you think we could talk you into coming out for a bite of dinner now, Laura," he asked in a slightly irritated tone, "or will that be too much inconvenience for our fine furry friend?"

Alice laughed. "Oh, I'm sure Boots will be just fine. In fact, I'll be happy to watch him while you're gone."

Alice suspected that Laura would have preferred staying in and caring for the kitten, but her parents seemed relieved that she agreed to join them for dinner in Potterston.

Alice took the crate downstairs and, with Jane's permission, placed it in a quiet corner in the kitchen and got Boots all settled.

Then the three sisters sat down to a quiet dinner.

"How did your prize collection for the Easter egg hunt go today?" Louise asked Alice.

"Quite well." Then she told about some of the pleasant surprises.

"Speaking of Easter, is Cynthia going to make it here for the holiday?" asked Alice.

"She was unsure when I spoke with her, but that was several days ago. Perhaps things will change by the weekend."

"Maybe I'll have to e-mail that niece of mine," said Jane. "Perhaps toss a little guilt into the message. See if that doesn't make her think twice."

Louise chuckled. "That would be much better coming from an aunt than a mother."

"Speaking of aunts," said Jane. "I heard from Craig Tracy that our dear aunt is telling townsfolk that one of her nieces is hearing wedding bells these days." She looked directly at Alice now.

Alice frowned. "Yes, I heard that in town today too."

"Well, I am sure that people were already making their own assumptions anyway," said Louise. "We can't blame it all on Aunt Ethel."

"I actually tried to set Auntie straight today," said Alice as she buttered a slice of sourdough bread. "When we were, uh, moving furniture."

"Poor Alice," said Jane. She explained to Louise about their aunt's desire to rearrange the carriage house. "This week is supposed to be a vacation for you, but it seems you've been busier than ever."

Alice smiled. "I guess I'll be glad to go back to work next week."

"But what about *this thing?*" asked Louise.

Alice blinked. "What thing?"

"This thing with Mark, of course."

"There is no *thing* with Mark, Louise." Alice looked directly into her older sister's pale blue eyes. "Honestly, if there was a thing, I would tell you. You must know that."

"They haven't even had time to have a thing," added Jane with a twinkle in her eye. "Mark's got his hands full with his young man."

Louise and Jane began discussing Adam. Alice threw in some words in his defense, but finally she just gave up and started clearing the table. Their observations about Adam were not untrue, but it made her uncomfortable to hear them just the same.

"Oh dear," said Louise as she looked at the clock. "I almost forgot that the book group meets tonight. I promised Viola that I would be there early."

"And I'm going to Sylvia's," said Jane. "She invited me over to watch a video with her tonight." Jane looked at Alice. "You're welcome to join us if you like."

"No, thanks," she said as she rinsed a plate. "Why don't you let me finish cleaning things up in here, and you two go ahead and take off."

"Oh, I don't want to leave you with—"

"I insist," said Alice firmly. "I think I'll turn in early tonight, or perhaps I'll work on the baby quilt a bit."

Alice, with the company of the kitten, finished putting things back in order in the kitchen. Just as she finished up, she heard the sound of the Winstons' voices as they returned from dinner.

Alice gave Boots back to Laura and then told them good night. Once in her room, Alice wondered about Mark and Adam. She imagined them driving back toward Acorn Hill in the dark, perhaps having a nice conversation. Maybe Adam was actually opening up to Mark. She could only pray that was happening.

She tried not to think about Louise's questions about her and Mark. Certainly there was nothing to report. Alice was not sure if that was because of her, or Adam, or Mark.

She wondered if things would have gone differently if Adam had not come to the inn. To be perfectly honest, she was not even sure how she would prefer to have had things go. Oh, she did enjoy Mark's friendship, and she was fond of him.

What good does it do to dwell on such things anyway? she thought. She pushed these thoughts from her mind. Then, thankful for the distraction, she focused all her attention into the careful construction of a quilt block.

Chapter Eighteen

*A*lice surprised herself by sewing late into the evening and, consequently, sleeping in later than usual. She got out of bed, hurriedly dressed and practically jogged over to Vera's house. She noticed the gathering of clouds overhead and hoped that Fred's forecast for the bad weather to come and go before Easter was correct.

"I'm sorry I'm late," she called breathlessly when she saw Vera waiting on her front step. "Maybe we can make this a quick walk."

"It's all right," said Vera as she joined her. "Is everything okay?"

"Of course." Alice told her that it was the baby quilt project that had kept her up late. "I can't believe how late I stayed up working on it."

Vera smiled. "So you and Mark obviously didn't have a date?"

Alice shook her head. "He and Adam must have arrived home very late last night. They left early yesterday to visit Adam's parents' graves."

"So you didn't get a chance to talk to him then?"

"No, but I hope to today. I'm praying that things have begun turning around for Adam," she said.

After their walk, Alice and Vera parted, and Alice went home to shower and dress. She knew that she was dressing more carefully than usual, and she admitted to herself that she was hoping to spend some time with Mark that day. As a result, she felt a mixture of nervousness and anticipation.

It was relatively quiet when she went downstairs to join Jane in the kitchen. She was surprised to see Louise already there, washing and stemming strawberries for a fruit platter.

"You're up early," she said to Louise.

"Or perhaps you are late," suggested Louise.

Alice looked at the clock. "I guess you're right. Need any help?"

"Everything's under control," said Jane. "But you could set up the coffee and tea. Is anyone up yet?"

"I didn't see a soul," said Alice as she carried the coffee and tea things out to the dining room.

"Good morning," said Mrs. Winston, coming into the dining room with her husband and Laura trailing behind.

"Good morning," said Alice. "It looks like our weather is changing today."

"I noticed that," said Mrs. Winston as she waited to take Laura's arm to guide her to the table.

Soon the others were coming in, and before long, the dining room was nearly full. Mark and Alice exchanged greetings, and she inquired about his trip the day before.

"A lot of driving," said Mark, glancing uneasily at Adam, who looked as sulky as ever, "but I'm glad I went."

Adam's eyes darted toward Mark, then back down as he silently sipped a cup of coffee.

The guests chatted congenially about things like the weather and some recent news events and, before long, they began finishing their breakfasts and leaving until only Adam and Mark remained at the table. Jane and Louise had quietly slipped off to the kitchen, but not without first eyeing Alice as if to warn her she was not to budge.

Alice suspected that Mark wanted to talk to her. She knew she definitely wanted to talk to him, if only to encourage him about Adam and to relate the hopeful things she had overheard.

Mark set down his coffee cup and cleared his throat. "Adam noticed a place over in Potterston," he began. "It's a recreation center that has a rock climbing wall."

"Oh yes," said Alice. "I've seen that place. It's new, and I've heard it's quite nice."

Mark nodded. "I told him I'd take him over to check it out today."

"That's a good idea." Alice used a positive tone that she hoped covered up her disappointment. "It's a perfect thing to do on a rainy day."

Adam looked curiously at her.

"Would you like to join us?" asked Mark with a smile.

Alice could not tell if that was a genuine invitation or if Mark was simply being polite. She did know that she had absolutely no interest in rock climbing and even less interest in tagging along on this kind of adventure with Adam and Mark. "No, thank you," she said with a smile. "I'm sure you two will have a good time."

"Adam's dad was a rock climber."

"Really?" She glanced at Adam now. "Did you ever get to climb with him?"

He shrugged. "Not much. He mostly did it when he was younger, but he kept promising to teach me . . . someday."

She turned back to Mark. "How about you?" she asked with a bit of concern. "Have you done it before?"

"Oh yeah. Gregory and I climbed occasionally in high school. We did a couple of great trips back then. Of course, that was long before Adam was born. Gregory was actually a lot better at it than I was, but I always had fun. It's a good challenge to stretch yourself."

She sort of laughed. "I think that's more stretching than I would enjoy."

"Well, I'm guessing we'll be back around noon." He smiled at her. "Then perhaps you and I could do something together?"

"That would be nice," she told him.

He looked relieved, and she wondered if he had been worried that she would be offended or hurt by his choice to do something with Adam rather than with her. Surely, he did not think she was that childish. Of course, Mark had been spending a lot of time with a young adult lately, and she hoped that he was not getting her confused with him.

"I hope you both have a wonderful time," she told them as she cleared the last of the breakfast things from the table. "I'll look forward to seeing you this afternoon, Mark."

Alice carried the cups and plates into the kitchen where Jane was loading the dishwasher.

"How'd that go?" asked Jane.

"What do you mean?" Alice rinsed the dishes and handed them to her sister.

"You know," Jane persisted, "with you and Mark and Adam."

"There wasn't much to it really."

Alice paused as Louise and Ethel came in the back door.

"Oh, it's starting to rain cats and dogs out there," said Ethel as she removed her cardigan and gave it a shake. She patted her hair back into place. "I wish I'd thought to grab my umbrella." She smiled at Jane and Alice. "Looks as if I might be stranded here until it lets up."

"Did you come to pick up the truffles for Lloyd?" asked Jane as she set a box on the counter. "They're all ready."

"Yes," said Ethel. "He needs them for his city council meeting at noon."

"Is this some sort of bribe?" asked Jane.

Ethel laughed. "Of course not. Do you think our honorable mayor would resort to such tactics?"

"Well, I heard that the council is giving him a hard time about his proposal to put that four-way stop in."

Ethel waved her hand. "Oh, pish-posh, this is simply Lloyd's little Easter treat for the council."

"Is he going to wear his Easter bunny outfit for the meeting?" asked Jane with a teasing smile.

Ethel firmly shook her head. "No, and for your information, it's a *Mr. Easter Rabbit* suit, and Lloyd only wears it for the Easter egg hunt." She turned to Alice now. "Are we all set for that?"

"Well, other than the egg-dyeing party on Friday. I've collected the prizes and the ANGELs will put together the baskets tonight."

"The order of candy eggs arrived last week," said Louise.

"And I'll be boiling all the real eggs tomorrow," said Jane.

Ethel clapped her hands. "Thank goodness we're all so efficient. Now, how about giving your auntie a cup of coffee?"

Louise nudged Alice as Jane and Ethel headed for the coffee maker. "How did it go with Mark?" she asked in a lowered voice.

Alice shrugged. "Fine."

Ethel turned and looked at them. "Are you talking about your veterinarian, Alice?"

"You can call him Mark, Aunt Ethel."

"Of course, dear. How is it going?"

Alice was getting a bit weary of the inquisition. She felt silly since there was nothing new on this topic. "Mark is doing just fine," she told all three of them. "He and Adam have gone rock climbing this morning."

"Rock climbing?" Louise's eyes grew large. "In this sort of weather?"

"My goodness," said Ethel. "Are those two trying to kill themselves?"

Jane frowned. "That does seem a bit foolish, Alice."

Alice sighed. "They are doing indoor rock-climbing."

"What on earth are you talking about?" demanded Ethel.

Jane's eyes lit up. "Oh, I'll bet I know. They went over to the new recreation center in Potterston."

Alice simply nodded.

Jane explained the concept of an indoor rock-climbing wall to Ethel and Louise. "It's really fun," she finished up. "I did it a few times back in San Francisco. I wish I'd known they were going. I might've tagged along."

"I'm sure they would've enjoyed your company," said Alice.

Jane laughed. "I'm sure they would not. Adam probably would've thrown a fit."

For whatever reason, Alice found that she was tired of speculating over both Mark and Adam. "If you ladies will excuse me," she said, "I thought I might use this free morning to work on the baby quilt."

"Of course," said Ethel. "How's it coming anyway?"

Alice smiled. "It's looking more and more like a quilt."

"It's turning out to be very lovely," said Jane.

"Happy sewing," called Louise as Alice left the kitchen.

Alice paused in the living room to look out the window at the wet and blustery day. Gray and dark, it really was the perfect sort of day to cloister oneself in one's own room and get lost in a quilting project.

Chapter Nineteen

*I*t was nearly one in the afternoon when Alice emerged from her room. She hurried downstairs, worried that perhaps she was keeping Mark waiting.

Mr. and Mrs. Langley greeted her in the foyer. "We're just heading out for a bit of lunch," said Mr. Langley with a bright smile. "Would you like to join us, Alice?"

"Thank you," she told him, "but I already have plans."

"With Dr. Graves?" asked Mrs. Langley with friendly interest.

Alice nodded. "Yes, I was just looking for him."

"I haven't seen him come back," said Mr. Langley. "I've been sitting down here reading the paper for nearly an hour."

"Oh, then I'm sure he'll be here any minute," said Alice with confidence.

"Looks as if the rain's let up some," said Mrs. Langley. "Perhaps we should get going while the going's good."

Alice wished them a pleasant lunch, then went off in search of her sisters. She found Louise dusting in the parlor. "Have you seen Mark?" she asked.

"Not since breakfast." Louise set the pastel-toned porcelain figure of a shepherd girl back on the shelf and turned to Alice. "How is the quilt coming?"

"Nicely," said Alice. "It's such a comforting sort of project, sewing pieces neatly together and making everything line up just so."

"A bit like a jigsaw puzzle."

"Something like that. Nice and neat and orderly." Alice chuckled. "I guess I'm a fussbudget at heart."

"You simply enjoy order," said Louise as she dusted a cloisonné vase. "Nothing wrong with that."

Alice glanced at her watch. "I think I'll ask Jane if she has seen or heard from Mark."

She found Jane in the kitchen, bent over a recipe book wearing a slight scowl. "Is there something the matter?" she asked her younger sister.

Jane looked up. "Oh, I'm fine. I just don't understand this recipe. It somehow doesn't seem right, and I can't find my regular recipe."

Alice laughed. "Well, knowing you, Jane, you'll have created a completely new recipe by the time you're done."

Jane nodded. "That's probably just what I should do." Then she looked up from the book. "Hey, I thought you had a date with Mark this afternoon?"

"Well, it wasn't a date exactly, but I thought we were supposed to be getting together." Alice looked at the kitchen clock, which read one-thirty now. "Maybe I misunderstood. You haven't seen or heard from him, have you?"

"Nope, and I've been in the house all morning. So has Louise."

"I'm sure he and Adam must've just forgotten the time," said Alice. "Perhaps they ran late and decided to stop for lunch."

Jane closed the book and folded her arms across her chest. "Well, that's just wrong, Alice. If Mark keeps this up I will have a hard time liking that man."

"Oh, I'm sure it's—"

"Really, Alice. He can't keep asking you to play second fiddle to that boy. If Mark has feelings for you, he should come right out with it and—"

"Oh, I don't expect him to do that. I just thought it might be nice to have a quiet talk with him. That's all."

Jane rolled her eyes. "Oh, please, Alice. You know that's not all. You've been walking around here on needles and pins ever since Mark arrived. Don't act as if it's no big deal."

"But . . ." Alice stopped, then said slowly, "actually, I'm not sure what it is, Jane."

"What do you want it to be?"

"I'm not sure about that either."

Jane stepped closer, looking into Alice's eyes as if she could see deeper, as if she somehow knew what Alice herself did not know.

Alice grew uncomfortable, blinked and stepped back.

"Come on, Alice," urged Jane. "How do you really feel about him?"

Alice did not want to be dishonest with her sister. "The truth is I'm not sure."

"Not sure?"

Alice nodded.

"Okay, I'll quit pestering you, dear sister." Jane reached out and hugged Alice. "I just don't like seeing you going around with this cloud hanging over you. It's so unlike you."

"Really?" said Alice with interest. "Does it seem to you that I've had a cloud hanging over me?"

Jane nodded. "I've just assumed it's because you are trying to sort things out with Mark and with Adam too. I'm sure it's been frustrating, but I'm so used to you as a cheerful, stable, contented person. And lately, well, you haven't exactly been yourself."

"I know. . . ." Alice sighed.

"Well, I'm sure that everything will fall into place," said Jane.

Alice was not so sure, but she knew that it was useless to keep talking about it. "I think I'll fix a bite of lunch," said Alice, heading toward the refrigerator. "Then perhaps I'll go back to my quilt project. Would you like something?"

"No, thanks. Louise and I already ate."

Alice made a turkey sandwich, which she took back to her room with her. She didn't want to seem unsociable, but she also didn't want to be questioned by her sisters or by her aunt, if she popped in again. Although they had plenty of questions, Alice had no answers.

Alice decided to put Mark out of her mind after she finished her lunch and returned to her sewing. Surely, he and Adam were just fine. Perhaps today was the day when Mark would have that breakthrough with Adam. Wasn't that what she had been praying for? To sit around feeling sorry for herself was not only silly, it was also a waste of time.

It was nearly four o'clock when Jane came upstairs to tell Alice that she had a phone call. "It's someone from your work," said Jane. "If they want you to come in, you better say no."

Alice hurried down to get the phone.

"This is Alice."

"This is Peggy from ER."

"What's up, Peggy?"

"Well, I have a friend of yours here," said Peggy.

"A friend?" Alice felt a chill of alarm run through her. "Who?"

"He's a guest from your inn," said Peggy. "Mark Graves."

"What's wrong?" Alice's heart began to pound.

"It's not serious, Alice. Apparently he and his young friend were climbing a rock wall here in Potterston, and Mark slipped and broke his arm."

"Oh dear."

"Yes, it was a nasty break. He's in surgery with Dr. Tyler right now."

Alice sighed. "At least he's in good hands."

"That's for sure."

"Is there anything I can do?"

"No, he just wanted you to know."

"When will they release him?"

"If all goes well, he should be out by this evening."

"Should I come to pick him up?"

"No, he specifically said to tell you not to worry about that. He said his young friend will drive him back to the inn and that he'll see you later."

"Well, thank you," said Alice. "Do tell him that I'm thinking of him and I hope that he's feeling better after surgery."

"I'm sure he will be."

"Please feel free to call, Peggy, if I can be of any help."

"Of course. By the way, how's your little vacation?"

When Alice heard the word "vacation," she almost laughed. "It's been interesting. Thanks again for calling, Peggy."

"No problem."

After Alice hung up, she told Jane about the bad news.

"Oh, poor Mark," said Jane.

"What happened to Mark?" said Louise as she came down the stairs.

Alice related the story to Louise.

"Goodness, what a bit of bad luck." Louise shook her head.

"I'm beginning to think that *Adam* is a bit of bad luck," said Jane.

"Oh, it's not his fault."

"Don't be so sure," said Jane quickly. "Adam keeps pushing Mark to do things—things that he may be a little too old to be doing."

"That is true," agreed Louise. "I think Adam is not only a bad influence on Laura, but on Mark as well."

"Speaking of Laura," said Jane, "how is she doing?"

"Her mother told me that she's been kitten-sitting again," said Louise. "Mrs. Winston was rather put out that

Adam had not returned yet. I should go and tell her about Mark's accident. At least that gives Adam an excuse."

"It's not really Adam's fault," said Alice as Louise headed back up the stairs.

"Not directly," said Jane, "but think about it, Alice. Mark never would've broken his arm if Adam hadn't challenged him."

"I'm sure that Adam feels bad."

"Maybe." Jane made a sly face. "Or maybe Adam is like that movie from the fifties—*The Bad Seed*. Do you remember watching it on TV?"

"Oh, Jane." Alice just shook her head. "Adam is not a bad seed."

Jane laughed. "No, I don't think he is, but it does make you think."

"Perhaps it would be better to pray."

Jane nodded. "Yes, as usual, I'm sure you're right. Sorry I said that, Alice. It wasn't very nice."

"And, really," said Alice, "Adam can't be feeling too good right now."

"Serves him right." Then Jane winked at Alice and headed to the kitchen.

∞

Mark and Adam didn't get home in time for dinner or before it was time for Alice to head over to the Assembly Room in the chapel to set things up for the ANGELs meeting. Even with Jane helping, it took two trips to take the prizes, baskets and the evening's treats down to the basement room.

"Need any help?" offered Jane.

"I think we'll be fine," said Alice as she set down her last load. "Although you know that you're always more than welcome to join us."

"Thanks, but I think I'll start boiling those eggs," said Jane. "I think I can get about half of them done tonight."

"That sounds like a good idea."

Soon the girls began arriving and, as Alice had suspected, they began to ooh and aah over the prizes.

"These are way better than last year's prizes," said Jenny. "Way to go, Miss Howard."

"Yeah," agreed Ashley as she held up one of the chenille toys. "I wouldn't mind winning one of these baskets for myself."

"You're too old," said Sarah.

The ANGELs put the baskets together with very little help from Alice, laughing and joking as they worked.

"I think they should change the age limit from ten," said Ashley. "I mean, just because we're older doesn't mean we don't like to hunt for eggs."

"It wouldn't be fair," said Jenny. "The older kids would find all the eggs and then how would the little kids feel?"

"Besides," said Sarah, "Who would hide the eggs?"

"That's right," said Jenny. "That's lots more fun anyway."

"Don't forget," added Alice. "You're the ones who have to go around and look for all the missed eggs afterward."

"There were hardly any left over last year," said Ashley.

"Maybe we should hide them better," said Jenny. "Maybe if we started earlier, we could come up with some better places."

"Yeah," said Ashley. "We could make it really hard."

"Not too hard," Alice said. "Remember some of the kids are barely able to toddle. You need some easy ones for them."

"They have their parents to help them," said Jenny. "Did you see how many eggs little Tommy Sanders got last year? His basket was so loaded that the handle actually broke."

"Yeah, my mom said that his dad should've been embarrassed for being so greedy."

Alice laughed. "Don't worry, there are plenty of eggs. Remember it's about having fun."

Soon the gift baskets were filled. The girls wrapped them in colorful cellophane that Jane had found at a craft store and carefully tied large pastel-colored ribbons into big bows on the tops of each one.

"These are beautiful, Miss Howard," said Ashley, her eyes glowing with pride. "Don't you think they're the best ones ever?"

Alice smiled as she recalled the prize baskets from when she had been young. In her mind's eye, they had been even bigger and better than these, but she had been a little girl then. Things look very different when you're young. "You could be right, Ashley," she told her.

When they had finished with the baskets, they had their treat of homemade gingersnaps and punch. Then it was time to review the previous week's memory verses. Alice was pleased that all the ANGELs were well prepared, and she happily gave them prizes, in addition to the chocolate eggs that Jane had made for the girls.

"Wow," said Jenny, "double prizes tonight!"

"Because it's almost Easter," said Alice.

Finally, it was time to clean up and call it a night. Alice finished wiping down the counters and tables after the last ANGEL had left. She was about to turn out the lights, when she suddenly had a realization that filled her with guilt. *Goodness*, she thought, *there Mark is, possibly still recovering from surgery, maybe in pain, and I haven't even thought about him once.* Of course, she told herself that it was like that when she was doing things with the ANGELs. She so enjoyed these girls that she often forgot about the pressures of the day. To make up for her neglect, she said a quick prayer for Mark's recovery as she hurried back toward home.

She saw Mark's Range Rover parked in front of the inn, which under the circumstances, she felt Louise would overlook. After all, the poor man had just been released from the hospital.

She went into the inn, pausing to remove her raincoat, then went off in search of Mark. She found Louise in the living room.

"Hello," said Louise as she looked up from her book. "How was ANGELs tonight?"

"Great," said Alice. "I noticed Mark's car."

Louise nodded and set her book aside. "They got here shortly after you left."

"How is he doing?"

"He has turned in for the night," said Louise. She wore a sober expression that hinted that there was more to her statement than its surface meaning.

Alice sat down in the chair across from her. "Was he feeling okay?"

"He said he was on some pain medication."

Alice nodded. "Probably worn out."

"Actually, he sat here for a bit. He wanted to wait up for you."

"That was sweet, but I'm glad he went to bed if he was tired."

"I think he was more angry than tired."

"Angry?" Alice leaned forward. "What do you mean?"

"I mean he and Adam got into it again."

"Oh dear." Alice glanced toward the open doorway, concerned that someone might overhear them.

"Don't worry, I'm fairly certain that everyone besides Jane, you and me has gone to bed."

"What happened?"

"Apparently, Mark was not impressed by Adam's driving skills or rather lack thereof."

"Oh dear."

"I could tell that he was distraught when they came in. They were barely in the door when Mark mentioned something about Adam's driving and Adam got defensive."

"Hey, you two," said Jane as she entered the room. Then, lowering her voice, "Are you telling Alice about the fireworks?"

Louise frowned. "Yes."

Jane sat down next to Louise. "It was pretty nasty, Alice."

"Well, please, tell me what happened."

"Yes, I will," said Louise. "Adam got irate when Mark told him he needed to drive more safely."

"Adam told Mark to mind his own business," said Jane. "Well, not in those words exactly."

"Worse words," added Louise.

"Mark told Adam that since he was the passenger riding in his own vehicle that it was his business."

"Then Adam proceeded to tell Mark that he should be grateful that Adam was around to drive him from the hospital."

"And Mark told him that he wouldn't have needed to go to the hospital if Adam hadn't insisted on doing the climbing wall for so long."

"Oh dear."

"Yes, it just went from bad to ugly and then got worse." Louise shook her head. "In Mark's defense, he was in pain and under the influence of the medication."

"And he did feel bad when Adam left," added Jane.

"Adam left?"

"Oh yes. Adam went tearing upstairs, got all his belongings and stormed out of here like a cat with his tail on fire."

"Oh no . . ." Alice felt like crying. "Speaking of cats?"

"Adam took the kitten with him," said Jane.

"It doesn't seem that he will be coming back," said Louise.

To Alice's dismay, her older sister seemed relieved. Alice could not really blame Louise, but she did feel sorry for Adam.

"Where did he go?" she asked.

Louise just shrugged.

"Probably to wherever he was before," said Jane. "At least it's not winter. He won't freeze to death."

"But out there in the night?" said Alice. "Living in his car?"

"It's his choice, Alice." Jane stood. "Sorry, I need to go check on the eggs."

"I know it sounds hard," continued Louise. "But perhaps it is for the best."

How could it possibly be for the best? Alice thought. *How could Adam living out on the streets and Mark feeling guilty be for the best?* She kept these thoughts to herself and, thanking Louise for filling her in, she excused herself to go to bed.

Of course, she did not feel a bit like sleeping once she was up there. Instead, she fell to her knees and begged God somehow to undo this horrible mess.

Protect Adam, she prayed. *Please, show him the way home.* Then she said, "Amen," and climbed into bed, trusting that things would be better tomorrow.

Chapter Twenty

"How are you feeling this morning?" Alice asked Mark when she discovered him sitting by himself in the dining room. It was quite early, and no other guests appeared to be up yet. She had been helping in the kitchen but suspected that Jane would excuse her for a few minutes. In fact, knowing Jane, she would probably be unhappy if Alice did not speak with Mark.

He looked up at her and attempted what appeared to be a halfhearted smile. "I've been better."

"Coffee?"

"Please."

She filled a cup and handed it to him. "I heard about the disagreement you and Adam had last night."

"It was more than a disagreement, Alice."

She nodded and sat down. "Yes, I know."

"And although I know that I didn't handle things properly, I think it may have been for the best."

Alice said nothing, just waited for him to continue.

"I feel that I've bent over backward for that kid. I know that he's unhappy, and I understand that he has good reason to be. But, honestly, I've done everything I can think of to get him to—oh, sometimes I don't even know what it is I'm trying to get him to do." Mark pushed his fingers through his beard and sighed loudly.

"To trust you?" she offered.

He looked at her over his coffee cup. "Yes, maybe that's it."

"Good morning," said Mrs. Winston as she and Laura entered the room.

Alice and Mark both turned and greeted them.

"How's your arm?" asked Mrs. Winston.

"Hurts a bit, but that's to be expected."

"Maybe you should take some more of those *wonderful* pain pills," said Laura in a clearly sarcastic tone.

"Laura," said Mrs. Winston in a warning tone.

Alice studied the slender girl's stance and the look of disdain behind today's tangerine-colored sunglasses. It was clear that Laura was angry.

"What, Mother?" Laura snapped. "Do you expect me to just pretend that I don't know what's going on? Act as if I'm *blind?*"

"Laura is feeling concerned for Adam," said Mrs. Winston quickly.

"I'm blind, Mother, not deaf, and I don't need an interpreter."

"Maybe we should go for a walk," said Mrs. Winston, obviously uncomfortable with her daughter's behavior.

"No, that's okay," said Mark. "If Laura has something to say to me, she might as well get it off her chest. It's clear that she's angry with me."

"That's right," said Laura. "I am."

"Why is that?" asked Mark in a tired voice. "Is it because I told Adam the truth? Because I'm tired of playing games with him?"

"You don't even *know* him," said Laura. "You don't understand him at all. And, yes, I may be blind, but I see more than you do."

"Laura!"

"He asked me, Mother."

"But—"

"No, that's all right," said Mark patiently. "I'd like to know, Laura. What exactly is it that you think you can see in Adam? What is it that the rest of us are missing?"

"He's in pain," she told him. "He knew all along that you were going to cut him off like that. He knew that you never really cared."

"I did care," said Mark. "I do care, but how do you reach out to someone who keeps pushing you away?"

She folded her arms tightly across her chest and didn't answer.

"Really, Laura, I'd like to know. Somehow, you seem to have made an impression on Adam. You two seem to understand each other. What would you suggest I do differently?"

"What does it matter now?" She turned away. "I want to go back to our room, Mother."

Mrs. Winston seemed at a loss, but Alice looked her way with what she hoped was an encouraging smile. "It's okay," she told them both. "I think I understand why Laura is upset. You go on along. There's something I need to explain to Mark."

"Like he'll listen to you or anyone for that matter," snapped Laura as she and her mother exited the room.

"Wow." Mark rubbed the cast on his arm with his good hand. "I knew she was upset with me last night, but I had no idea she was this angry. I don't get it."

"That's what parents of teenagers say all the time," said Alice with a rueful smile.

"I wonder if it's possible to straighten this out with her."

"Oh, I'm sure it is, but there's something I'd like to tell you before you try." Alice paused at the sound of footsteps in the living room and realized that the Langleys were about to come into the dining room.

"How would you feel about going out for breakfast so that we can talk?" asked Alice.

"I'd love to."

"Okay," she said quickly. "I'll drive. Let me tell Jane."

"Meet you at the car?" asked Mark as he got up.

"Yes. But do you mind if I have a quick word with Laura first?"

"Not at all. I wish you would."

Alice explained her plans to Jane and Louise, who was helping Jane to prepare breakfast.

"No problem," said Jane. "It's about time you two got together and actually talked."

"Thanks."

"We were not trying to eavesdrop," began Louise in a tentative voice, "but it was impossible not to overhear Laura's outburst."

"It wasn't very nice," said Alice, "but Laura is partially right. Mark doesn't get the whole picture. I want to explain it to him."

"Don't be too hard on the poor guy," said Jane as she washed some blueberries. "He's been through a lot, you know."

"That's right." Louise paused from her stirring. "To be fair, this is mostly Adam's fault. He brought this onto himself."

"I don't think it's really about anyone's fault. It's really a series of misunderstandings," said Alice. "Before I leave, I want to speak with Laura. She was very upset."

"That would be wise," said Louise. "We can't have our guests feeling miserable."

"There goes our little peacemaker," said Jane smiling fondly as she watched Alice leave the room.

Alice tapped gently on the Garden Room door. "It's Alice," she said.

"Oh, Alice," said Mrs. Winston as she opened the door. "I'm so sorry about Laura's—"

"Don't apologize for me, Mother."

"If it's all right, I'd like to speak to Laura for a few minutes," Alice said.

Laura approached the door. "Is Mark with you?" she asked cautiously.

"No," Alice assured her, "it's just me. Do you want to come out in the hallway for a moment?"

Laura reached out and Alice took her by the hand, leading her to the open area at the top of the stairs. "I completely understand how you feel about the trouble between Mark and Adam, Laura."

"You do?"

"I do. I've wanted to explain some things to Mark myself, but I just never had the chance. I realize that Adam's behavior is really his way of protecting himself, of preventing himself from being hurt again."

Laura nodded eagerly. "Yes, that's true. You *do* get it."

"Mark and Adam have been gone so much. Then Mark broke his arm, and I was at my meeting last night. There just hasn't been an opportunity to talk to him." She sighed. "I feel that their disagreement is partly my fault."

"No," said Laura firmly. "It's Mark's fault. If you'd heard him last night, Alice, you'd agree. He never should've talked like that to Adam."

"You know, Mark is generally very even tempered, but he was upset," said Alice, "and I'm sure he was in pain. Then there was the effect of pain pills. Sometimes those pills cause people to let down their guard and say things they normally wouldn't say."

"Yeah, that's what my parents said too, but I still don't think it's an excuse. Adam is in a really fragile place right now."

"What do you mean?"

"He feels like he doesn't have much to live for. And even though he was pushing Mark away, I know that he was really hoping that Mark would somehow prove to him that he wanted to be involved in Adam's life. Kind of like a test. I think Adam was making Mark into his lifeline, but he wouldn't tell him, you know?"

Alice considered this. "You know, Laura, we can't expect another human being to be a lifeline. I mean it's good to have friends and family to lean on, but the only real lifeline is God."

Laura did not say anything.

"Even so," Alice went on quickly, "Adam must know that Mark is really there for him."

"But is he?"

"Of course."

"How do you know that for sure?"

"Well, I guess maybe I don't. But I'm going to spend some time with Mark this morning and I'll try to find out."

Laura sighed. "Well, I hope you knock some sense into that guy."

"Oh, Mark is sensible, Laura. It's just that he's never been a parent. You have to admit that Adam has been a little challenging for everyone."

"Hey, we're kids, ya know. That's what we do." Laura was smiling as she spoke.

"I hope you and your parents will feel comfortable about going down to breakfast now," said Alice. "I know that Jane and Louise are whipping up something special. If it helps to know, Mark and I are going out for breakfast."

"All right then." Laura nodded. "I'll get my parents." She smiled, and then added, "No use starving."

Alice found Mark waiting by her car. She quickly unlocked the doors and started to open the passenger side for him.

"I've still got one good arm," he told her.

"Sorry," she said. "I guess it comes with nursing. I'm just used to taking care of people."

"I didn't mean to growl at you," he said as he slid inside and then smiled sheepishly. "And to be honest, I'll probably need some help with the safety belt."

She reached across to grab the strap and fasten him in. Then, patting him on the head, she said, "Now, that's a good boy."

To her relief, he was actually smiling when she got inside. "You're good medicine, Alice."

"Thanks. I guess I chose the right profession."

Alice turned the radio on to her favorite jazz station. She would not bring up the subject of Adam until they reached the Coffee Shop and were settled. She suspected that Mark welcomed this brief reprieve too.

"Hey there," called Hope Collins, the Coffee Shop's waitress, when they entered the restaurant. "How are you two doing?" Then she saw Mark's arm. "Oh dear, what happened to you, Dr. Graves? Get into an arm wrestling match with a sick polar bear?"

He smiled. "Yeah, something like that."

Alice quickly explained the climbing wall injury, and Hope nodded. "You know, I heard about that place and had actually been thinking about trying that out for myself, but now I might reconsider."

"I think I was just getting overconfident," admitted Mark as she led them to a table in the corner by the window. "I'd scaled it several times and done pretty well. Then Adam got the brilliant idea of timing ourselves to see who was faster."

"Oh dear," said Alice. "And you fell for that challenge?"

"Literally."

This made all three of them laugh. Hope handed them menus and told them about the breakfast special of steak and eggs.

"That sounds great to me," said Mark as he returned the menu.

Alice ordered a bowl of oatmeal with fresh fruit. Hope went back to the counter, but not without discreetly winking at Alice before she did.

Alice decided to get right to the point. She quickly told Mark about the touching scene she had witnessed between Adam and Laura. "It was so sweet, Mark," she said. "He was really sharing his feelings with her, and she told him how much his friendship was helping her. It's as if something amazing was beginning to happen."

"Until I cut it short."

"You can't take all the blame, Mark. Adam was testing you in every way he could."

"All because he didn't think I'd stick by him?"

She nodded. "He said that everyone left him eventually. He blamed himself for it."

"You know, he said something like that to me when we visited his parents' graves. He said that he'd been acting like such a jerk that his parents might still have been angry when they had their accident—or something to that effect. Of course, I told him that was ridiculous and, to be honest, I didn't even take him seriously. But now that I think about it, I wonder if he might actually be carrying a load of guilt about his parents' death. People do that, you know."

"Yes," she agreed. "Guilt is one of the stages of grieving."

"But how long does it last?"

"That depends on the person," she told him. "Some people get stuck in a stage, and it takes a long time for them to move on."

"Well, Adam certainly seems stuck."

Hope brought their order, refilled Mark's coffee cup and refreshed Alice's hot water. "Just holler if you need anything else."

They continued talking as they ate. Their topic was mainly about Adam. When they were finished, Mark seemed encouraged. Yet, at the same time, he seemed troubled.

"Are you feeling okay?" asked Alice after he paid the bill.

He shrugged as he struggled to replace his billfold into his pocket. Alice waited.

"Bye, you two," called Hope as they went out the door.

"Is your arm hurting?" asked Alice when they reached the car.

"A little bit." He frowned. "More than that, I'm feeling bad about Adam now. I really came on strong last night. I'm sure the accident took a toll on his emotions as well. And, if the truth be told, the Range Rover probably presented a big temptation to see what it could do."

"Yes, I'm sure that I would barely keep from challenging other drivers to a race," Alice joked.

Mark managed a smile.

"Seriously, Mark, I think you did what most people would do—especially if you consider your day and that you were under the influence of pain pills."

"Maybe." He opened the door of the car, then climbed in and waited patiently for Alice to buckle him in again.

"There you go," she told him as she closed the door.

"Speaking of pain pills," he said as she started the engine. "I think I'm overdue now. I got up quite early and took one before six."

"Well, that's more than four hours," she noted. "We better get you home."

"Thanks, doctor."

"No problem, doctor." She turned and grinned. "Then I would recommend you have a little rest. There is nothing like rest to help you mend."

"Once again, I think you're right."

Chapter Twenty-One

*M*ark came back downstairs just before noon. "Feeling better?" asked Alice as she straightened the rug in the foyer, then stood up.

"Somewhat. At least I'm rested. But I'm feeling worse and worse about Adam. The idea of him and that kitten out there living in his car . . . well, let's just say it's not a happy thought. I have to go looking for him," said Mark.

"Not with one arm, you can't."

He looked pleadingly at her. "Could I interest you in—"

"You couldn't stop me if you wanted to."

"How about if we take my rig?" said Mark. "I filled it with gas yesterday in Potterston."

"Let me get a jacket," she told him.

By the time Alice came back downstairs, Laura was in conversation with Mark and, to Alice's relief, it seemed much more agreeable than the one earlier that day. Mark was asking if Laura had any idea where they should look for Adam.

"I wish I could be more help," she told him.

"Don't worry. You've already been helpful."

"Do you want me to come too?" asked Laura. "In case I think of something."

"You may if you'd like," said Mark. "If your parents don't mind."

She considered this. "Well, maybe I better not. My mom was in touch with a relative who still lives near Acorn Hill." She made a face. "We're supposed to be going to her house for tea this afternoon. Like that should be fun."

"You never know," said Alice.

Laura turned toward Alice with a hopeful expression. "Dr. Graves said you are going to look for Adam now."

"That's right."

"I wish I had some idea where he might be," said Laura. "But when I went places with him, well, I didn't really pay attention to where we went, you know."

"That's understandable," said Mark.

"Well, good luck," said Laura.

Alice and Mark headed out to his Range Rover. Dark clouds seemed to be gathering quickly, and Alice felt certain that they would be driving through a deluge before long.

"I told Laura that I realized what a complete fool I'd been, and I asked her to forgive me."

"Did she?"

He nodded. "Of course. You know, she's a sweet girl. She's just going through her own hard times, and Adam was actually helping her to work through some things."

"I know. Despite how things may appear, I think she made some real progress this week."

"She said the reason she got angry was because she felt so sorry for Adam, and she is seriously worried about the kitten too. Naturally, she focused her anger on me. Not that I blame her."

They started out looking for Adam's beat-up car around town. "At least it should be easy to spot," said Alice after they checked along the local main roads and parks. "But I'm guessing he's not in Acorn Hill."

"You're right. Why don't we check Potterston?"

It began raining as she got onto the highway. "This really is a nice vehicle," she told Mark. "It feels very safe in the rain."

"Range Rovers are hard to beat," he conceded. "I'll admit they're not cheap, but having been single all these years, well, I always gave myself permission to indulge in the best."

Alice thought about what he had said. She, too, had been single, but she had not embraced that particular philosophy.

"I suppose that sounds selfish to you," said Mark. "To be honest, it sounds a bit selfish to me now that I've verbalized it."

"Oh well . . ."

"You know, the more I think about everything, well, the more I realize that I have led a fairly self-centered and self-indulgent life." He exhaled loudly as he sadly shook his head. "And it's not a very comfortable realization."

"But think about all the animals you've helped."

He laughed. "Yes, all my animal friends, what would they do without me?"

"Your work is important."

He just turned and stared out the side window. "Important to me perhaps, but it was simply doing what I loved. Good grief, Alice, I did what I wanted, when I wanted, without ever considering anyone else."

"Oh, now that's probably an exaggeration."

"I don't think so. Consider that I was barely involved in my best friend's life for the past ten years. And my own godson, Alice, look at the way I ignored that boy all this time."

"But his parents were still alive."

"Yes, but I should've remained a part of their lives."

Alice didn't know how to respond. On one hand, she agreed with Mark. Perhaps he had led a somewhat self-centered life. On the other hand, doing what you like to do in life is a gift and not necessarily selfish. She had devoted much time and energy to her father's ministry and to the church, but the truth was she had done it because it was what she had wanted to do with her life. It was not as if she had given anything up for it. In reality, she had only gained by giving. The people in her community had always respected her for her commitment to her father, and she had to admit that she liked that. In some ways, her lifestyle and choices could be considered just as selfish as Mark's.

But when she tried to explain this to him, he simply laughed.

"Oh, Alice," he said. "Dear, sweet Alice. I don't believe you have a selfish bone in your body."

"Ah, you don't know that, Mark." She turned the windshield wipers up several notches to combat the sheets of rain that were pelting the car. There was a long pause while Alice focused her attention on navigating Mark's Range Rover down the nearly flooded highway.

"Do you ever wonder why neither of us married, Alice?" Mark asked.

Her hands gripped the wheel more tightly, partly because of the weather and partly because of his question. "Well, on occasion . . ." she finally said.

"Well, I've wondered about it a lot," he continued. "The truth is I never really figured it out. Sometimes I believed it was because God was saving us for each other—and for the right timing. Sometimes I believed it was simply because we both prefer not being married."

She nodded. "I've had similar thoughts."

"So which do you think it is, Alice?"

She slowed down as they caught up with a truck that was spewing a wake of water behind it. "I really don't know, Mark."

"I'm sorry," he said suddenly. "Here you are driving through this torrential rainstorm and I'm asking you all these tough questions. I'm sorry, Alice, we'll table this discussion for a better time. For now, we should focus our attention on the road and on finding Adam. Right?"

"You're absolutely right."

The rain let up when they reached Potterston, and after they had scoured the streets of Potterston, they started to feel that their search was useless.

"It's like finding a needle in a haystack," Mark said sadly after they finally turned back toward Acorn Hill.

"It's hard to find someone who doesn't want to be found."

"But maybe he wants to be found," suggested Mark.

"Then, I would think we'd find him."

"Yes, you're probably right."

"Maybe he's back at the inn," said Alice hopefully.

"I guess that's possible." Mark did not sound convinced.

When they got back to the inn, they found that Adam had not returned or called or been seen by anyone. Mark decided to go to his room to rest, and Alice went to help Jane in the kitchen. "You know what's funny," said Jane as Alice stood at the sink, peeling carrots.

"What?"

"Even Laura's parents looked for Adam today."

"Really?"

"Yes. Laura told me. They went all around Acorn Hill looking for him this afternoon after they had tea."

"That's sweet." Alice picked up another carrot.

"Yes, I guess we are all worried about him."

Alice felt a lump form in her throat as she thought about poor Adam and Boots living in a smelly, damp car.

"He'll be okay, Alice."

"I hope so. Mark tried calling Adam's grandmother when we got home, but she said she hasn't seen Adam in ages."

"God knows where he is, Alice."

Alice brightened. "You know, you're right about that."

"Hey," Jane said, observing Alice's smile, "now there's a nice change."

Chapter Twenty-Two

Good Friday dawned cloudy and gray, but according to Jane, the forecast called for clearing later in the day. "The weatherman said we'd have some blue skies by this afternoon," she told Alice as she put a pan of cinnamon rolls into the oven. "And it should be nice for the weekend."

"Oh, good. That's a relief." Alice filled the teapot with hot water.

"Did you have a good walk?"

"Yes, but we cut it short. Vera is preparing for family coming for the weekend. That reminds me, has Louise heard whether Cynthia's coming or not?"

"Yes, she called yesterday and she can't make it, but she promised to come down in a couple of weeks."

Alice slapped her forehead. "Oh my! Jane, I'm so sorry. I forgot to tell you that I invited a guest for dinner tomorrow night."

"That's fine. Who did you invite?"

As Alice stemmed a basket of strawberries, she explained about the unexpected meeting with her old college friend Mattie. "I had not seen her since school," she told Jane. "And she wanted to come over to Acorn Hill for the egg hunt, and well, it just seemed right to invite her to dinner. I hope you don't mind. I'm sorry that I didn't tell you sooner, but so much has been happening it just slipped my mind."

"No problem," said Jane. "I was already planning something special anyway."

"And, of course, I'll help you."

"Tell me about Mattie," said Jane as she sliced a melon in half.

Alice wondered where to begin, and finally decided just to be honest and tell Jane her candid impressions of her old friend.

"Oh my," said Jane. "Four husbands?"

"Well, she did admit to having poor taste in men." Alice pulled the stem off a big strawberry, which she placed into the strainer. "Although she seemed to fully approve of Mark."

"Goodness," said Jane. "I hope you haven't invited trouble along with Mattie."

"Oh, I hardly think so."

"Don't be so naive, Alice. If this Mattie has gone through four husbands, she might think nothing of snatching a nice-looking, successful man from you."

"Oh, Jane." Alice rinsed the stemmed strawberries in cold water. "That's not fair to say. You don't even know her. Besides, do you really think Mark's the sort of man who would go for someone like that?"

"Maybe not, but that probably won't stop her from trying."

Alice really didn't feel concerned. If Mark could be so easily snatched, as Jane put it, then perhaps it would be for the best. Alice knew Mark well enough to believe that Jane's scenario was unlikely.

Breakfast that morning was as somber as the weather, for everyone seemed a bit down. Alice knew her reasons for being quiet had to do with Adam, and she assumed the same was true for Mark and Laura.

Finally, Mr. Langley asked, "Has anyone heard anything from our missing young man?"

Both Mark and Alice looked at the older gentleman with surprise.

"We've been praying for him," explained Mrs. Langley. "We know that he's troubled and, well, we've felt bad for him."

"Thank you for praying for him," said Mark. "Although we've looked for him, we haven't any clues to his whereabouts."

"We looked for him yesterday as well," said Mrs. Winston. "Just around town."

"Yes," said Mark. "I heard about that, and I appreciate it."

"We thought we'd keep an eye out for his car when we head west today," said Mr. Langley. "You never know."

"Thank you," said Alice. "The more people looking for him, the more likely we are to find him."

After the guests had finished their breakfasts and were preparing to leave the table, Louise reminded everyone that they were welcome to color eggs for the egg hunt. "We'll start at around two this afternoon, and we expect to finish before dinnertime."

"That sounds like fun," said Mrs. Winston. "I haven't colored eggs in years." She turned and looked at her daughter. "Do you remember when we used to do that?"

Laura just shrugged, then excused herself.

It was not long before the other guests followed her lead and only Alice, Louise and Mark remained in the dining room.

"Not a very cheerful bunch," observed Louise.

"I feel like I'm to blame," said Mark. "I'm so sorry. If I hadn't asked Adam to meet me here and hadn't then made such a mess of things, well, obviously everyone would be much happier."

"Not necessarily," said Louise. "Laura has been moody since the Winstons arrived last weekend."

"That's true," said Alice.

"I don't know why I thought bringing Adam here would help things," said Mark. "I guess I hoped that he would be as charmed with Acorn Hill as I am and that somehow it would bring him back to his senses. It seems I was wrong."

Jane emerged from the kitchen with a fresh pot of coffee. "More caffeine, anyone?"

Louise and Mark both had another cup, and Alice poured herself a cup of tea, but no one said anything.

"We've got to think of some way to cheer this place up," said Jane. "It's not feeling very festive for Easter weekend."

Alice gave her a warning look. "We were just discussing that, Jane."

"Yes," said Mark. "I've been apologizing for being responsible for the pall of gloom that seems to be hanging over your inn."

Jane frowned. "But, really, what can we do to brighten things up?"

"Well, the egg dyeing should be fun," said Alice.

"And there's the egg hunt," offered Louise.

"I wonder what Father would say if he were here," said Jane.

"It's interesting that you ask that," Alice said. "Father was usually quite somber on Good Friday. He was very quiet and contemplative, spending time in his office, thinking about the Passion and how Jesus suffered on the cross. He usually wrote his Easter sermon on Good Friday."

Jane nodded. "You know, that's just what Pastor Ken was saying to me this morning. I ran into him while jogging, and he was walking along with his head hanging down like he'd lost his best friend."

"He was simply thinking," said Alice.

"So perhaps it's right for us to be a bit more serious on this day," said Louise.

"As true as that may be," said Mark with his eyes on Alice, "I would still like to go looking for Adam again this morning."

"Driving with one arm?" asked Jane.

"I'd be happy to drive for you again," offered Alice.

Mark gave her a grateful smile. "Thanks."

"Will you be back in time for egg coloring?" asked Louise.

"Of course," said Alice.

They decided to try driving north. "Perhaps he's headed for the countryside north of here," said Mark. "He told me that his family vacationed up there."

"Then that's the direction we'll take," said Alice as she headed north on the interstate.

"Perhaps we can just check out camping or rest stops for some miles ahead." Mark sighed and leaned back into the seat. "I suppose it really is useless, isn't it?"

"We might get lucky," Alice said, "or perhaps God will help us."

"I could use some divine help," he admitted. "Sometimes I think I depend on Dr. Mark Graves more than I depend on God." He held up his broken arm. "Then something happens that makes me feel helpless and useless, and suddenly I remember I'm not supposed to do everything on my own."

Alice smiled. "I guess we all need a wake-up call occasionally."

"How about you, Alice?" He turned to watch her as she drove. "Do you ever need a wake-up call? You seem so stable and grounded to me."

She laughed. "Well, don't forget that appearances can be deceiving. As far as stable and grounded? Lately, I've been feeling anything but."

"Is that because of me?"

She shrugged.

"And Adam?"

"Oh, I don't know. I think it's just life in general. And, really, isn't that what life is supposed to be, Mark? Surely, God never intended everything to move in a straight, unwavering line. What would be the point of that?"

"How did you get to be so wise, Alice?"

She smiled. "Well, if that were true, and I'm not sure that it is, I would have to give a lot of the credit to my father. He was the wisest person I have ever known."

He sighed. "I wish I'd gotten to know him better."

"You would've liked him, Mark."

"Yes, I'm sure. I suppose I've actually gotten to know him a bit through you. I'm quite sure that you're very much your father's daughter."

She laughed. "How could I not be?"

They drove for over an hour before they decided to turn back.

"I feel bad for wasting your time like this," said Mark.

"It's not a waste," said Alice. "I love road trips, and your car is wonderful to drive." She smiled. "The company's not bad either."

"Really?" He sounded hopeful now. "I thought perhaps you would be sick of me by now. I feel as if I've brought you nothing but trouble for the past week." Mark pointed to an exit ahead. "Hey, why don't you turn there, Alice. As I recall, there's a pretty good restaurant in this town. Maybe we could get some lunch."

She followed his directions, driving into a small town not unlike Acorn Hill. Soon they were parked in front of what appeared to be an historic inn. "This looks lovely," she told him as she handed him the keys.

"We could take a little stroll," he suggested. "Just to stretch our legs some."

They walked up and down the streets of the quaint little town. Mark told her a bit about his childhood and about the times that his family had stopped in this town while on their way to a lake to the north. "I remember my sister and I used to fight all the way and, once, my father actually threatened to leave us right here in this town."

Alice laughed. "Well, it's not such a bad spot to be abandoned. I'm sure some nice family would've adopted the two of you."

"I think I sometimes forget how important family is," he said. "I mean, I've led such an independent life. As hard as it was spending time with Adam, I really started to get a feeling of what it's like to have family. Even though it was hard, I think I rather liked it too. I mean, it had its moments."

"I'm sure you would've made a good dad, Mark."

"Do you think it's too late? I mean with Adam." He chuckled. "I don't exactly want to have children of my own."

Alice felt herself blushing. "No, I didn't think that's what you meant. But, really, I don't think it's too late with Adam."

"That is, if I ever see him again."

"I'm sure you will, Mark."

By now, they had gone all through town and were back at the inn. The old building was as interesting on the inside as the exterior. With antiques that looked like they had been there for at least a couple hundred years and with waitresses who wore period costumes, Alice felt that she had actually gone back in time. The food was excellent, and by the time they were finished, Alice was not sure she wanted to leave.

"This is a charming place," she told Mark. "I'm so glad you brought me."

"I thought you'd like it." He smiled as he held the door for her with his good hand. "It's not Acorn Hill, but it's got its pluses."

"Oh, I think that this town could give Acorn Hill a run for its money." She glanced down the cobblestone street. "But Acorn Hill has always been and always will be my home."

"I'd hoped to make it my home too," said Mark after they got into the car.

"Yes, I heard that you'd looked at the Olsen house," she said as she started the engine.

"You did, did you?" He chuckled. "Well, I guess it's hard to keep secrets in a town Acorn Hill's size."

"Especially when you have an Aunt Ethel."

He nodded. "An aunt who dates the mayor."

"Yes, you see what I mean."

"Things got so busy with Adam that I never had a chance to get back to the real estate agent."

She made no comment. This was none of her business.

"I rather liked the old house. Oh, I can see it needs lots of work, but I could imagine myself puttering around there, fixing things up. And then there's the carriage house in back that would be perfect for a small animal infirmary."

Part of her wanted to ask him how she fit into this picture, but another part of her was unsure that she wanted to hear that answer just now. So she just drove in silence.

After a bit, Mark turned on his radio. "What is that jazz station you listen to?" he asked as he played with the dial.

"It's 97.4 FM," she told him. "You should be able to get it from here."

He tuned it in to the smooth sounds of Miles Davis. "That's nice," he said. "I'm glad we like the same kind of music."

Alice did not tell him that she liked a variety of music and, occasionally, even listened to country, which Jane could not, for the life of her, understand. Louise didn't even know, thank goodness. But Alice didn't have to reveal everything about herself to Mark or anyone besides God, for that matter. Perhaps it was good to have some secrets.

They got back to the inn just before two. "As much as we'd love your help with the eggs," said Alice as they walked up to the porch, "I'd recommend you have a rest first."

"I won't even argue with you," he said as he opened the door and waited for her to go inside.

Before he went upstairs, Mark asked whether anyone had seen or heard from Adam. Unfortunately, they had not. Alice tried not to notice the distinct slowness to Mark's steps as he went upstairs. She told herself it was simply because he was worn out, but she suspected it had more to do with disappointment.

At least the ANGELs brought some joy and levity to the egg dyeing party, and it was not long before Alice found herself laughing over things like rainbow-colored finger-nails (when Ashley dyed her fingertips various colors) and other childish goings-on. Laura and her mother joined in, and Alice appreciated how the ANGELs gravitated toward the teenaged girl, showing obvious admiration of her age, not to mention her cool, acid-green sunglasses. To every-one's delight, Laura seemed to warm up to the girls too, and didn't even mind them helping her.

Alice had privately informed them that Laura had become blind recently. Of course, this was of huge inter-est to them, and being young, they had no qualms about asking her questions like, "Can you still remember what purple looks like?" and "Do you close your eyes when you get scared?" To everyone's relief and amusement, Laura actually answered them.

"This has been wonderful," said Mrs. Winston as she helped Alice tidy up. "Thank you for including us."

"Thank you for helping," said Alice. "Many hands make light work."

"Your ANGELs are delightful."

"They can get a bit silly sometimes, but I do enjoy them."

By four-thirty, the brightly colored eggs were all carefully placed back into their cartons and stored in the big refrigerator. All the egg dyers were treated to Jane's special Easter egg truffles as a thank you.

Although Mark had not come down yet, Alice saved one for him. She figured he might need something to lift his spirits, and Jane's chocolates were capable of doing just that.

Chapter Twenty-Three

J ust as Alice said good-bye to the last ANGEL, Mark appeared in the kitchen looking tired and downhearted. First, Alice offered him a chocolate egg, and then she invited him to take a walk with her. She could tell that Jane, who had been very patient with the egg dyeing, now wanted her kitchen back to herself, and Alice hoped that some fresh air might cheer up Mark.

"It's turned into a lovely day," she said as their long walk took them to the park where the festivities would take place the next day.

"Should be nice for the big egg hunt tomorrow." He glanced over at the empty bench in the park. "Want to sit for a bit?"

"Sure." She controlled herself from glancing over her shoulder as she and Mark walked across the grass toward the bench. She knew that if she and Mark were spied sitting together in this private but public place, the local tongues would be wagging before dinnertime. Still, she told herself, what did it matter?

Mark sat down and leaned forward in a dejected posture. She reached over and patted his back. "I know you're feeling bad," she said in an understanding voice. "I am too, but I've decided that it won't help anything to go around depressed. Instead, I'm praying for Adam. Every single time I think about him and begin to worry, I just put him in God's hands. As Jane reminded me this morning, we may not know where Adam is right now, but God does."

Mark sat up straighter and looked at her. "I know you're right, but my heart is still heavy."

"Have you been praying for him?"

He nodded.

"Then maybe we just need to believe that God is handling it."

He nodded again. "I'll try."

"Hi, Miss Howard," called a girl's voice from the street.

Alice looked up to see the girl waving wildly from her bicycle. "Hi, Ashley," Alice called back. Now she could be sure that word would get around about her and Mark. If anyone could jump to conclusions, it was Ashley.

"One of your ANGELs?"

Alice smiled. "Yes. They were so helpful today."

"Sorry I didn't make it down."

"It may have been a bit chaotic for you," she told him. "I'm glad you had a good rest."

"You know, Alice," he began, then stopped.

She waited without speaking.

"We need to talk . . . about us . . . you know."

Again, she said nothing.

"I want to, well, make my intentions clear, you know?"

"Intentions?"

"That's probably not the right word, but I feel as if I've been dancing all around this thing. That's partly because of what's been happening with Adam. I guess to be fully honest, I've had a case of chilly toes too."

She laughed. "Chilly toes?"

"Yes, they're not as severe as cold feet. I've been a bachelor my whole life, and I know that I'm self-centered and set in my ways. That's certainly been driven home well enough with my relationship with Adam. Anyway, I want to be perfectly honest with you."

"Yes?"

"Well, I just don't know what's going on in me right now."

She smiled. "Join the club."

"Really?" He peered into her eyes. "You feel like that too?"

She nodded.

"Well, that's a relief." Then he took her hand with his good one. "I do have strong feelings for you, Alice. I'm just not sure of the timing."

"I understand."

"If this thing with Adam hadn't blindsided me, well, maybe it would be different. I don't know."

She patted his hand with her other one. "Perhaps we don't need to be too concerned about these things right now, Mark. I mean, really, we've waited this long. What's the hurry, right?"

He smiled. "Right."

"Now," she slipped her hand away from his, "before we become the talk of the entire town, although I suspect it's already too late, perhaps we should go home."

They reached the inn and were walking up the steps to the front porch when Alice heard a man's excited voice. "Alice and Mark! Over here!"

They looked up to see Mr. and Mrs. Langley sitting together in the porch swing, and Mr. Langley was waving. "Come here," he called. "I have good news."

Alice and Mark went over to join the older couple.

"What is it?" asked Mark as he sat in the wicker rocker.

"It's about Adam," said Mrs. Langley.

"Yes," agreed Mr. Langley, "We're on our way back to

the inn when I pull into a Shell station, and what do you know?"

"There, parked on the side street, was an old car that looked like Adam's," Mrs. Langley said.

"That's right," said Mr. Langley, "so I say to the missus, I say, you wait here while I check into this matter. I go over and sure enough, leaning back in the driver's seat of that rundown little car is a familiar-looking young man. So I knock on the window, giving the poor lad a start. But then he recognizes me and gets out of the car." He sadly shook his head. "And the boy looks worse than ever. But I tell him that everyone at the inn is looking for him."

"That's when I came over," said Mrs. Langley. "And poor Adam didn't believe my husband, so I jumped right in and straightened him out. I told him that we'd all been frantic with worry and that we'd all been looking."

"Well, he is pretty surprised," said Mr. Langley. "And he asks if Mark is looking, and I tell him that Alice has been chauffeuring him all over the state and that, even today, you two are looking up north."

"And did he believe you?" asked Mark hopefully.

"He was still skeptical," said Mrs. Langley. "But we told him that he should come back to the inn and see for himself."

"And will he?" asked Alice.

Mr. Langley held up his hands in that way people do when they are unsure. "I don't really know whether he will or not."

"But we gave him some money," said Mrs. Langley. "His tank was empty, and he was broke."

"And then we begged him to come back to the inn," said Mr. Langley.

"Thank you," said Mark. "I really appreciate it."

"I just hope he does," said Mrs. Langley. "He still has the kitten with him. He said not to worry, that he was taking good care of it."

"Probably better care of it than himself," offered Alice.

"No doubt," said Mrs. Langley.

"I guess all we can do is to pray now," said Mr. Langley.

"Do you think we should drive over?" asked Mark suddenly. "To talk to him?"

"I don't know what more you could say," said Mr. Langley.

"Maybe we should wait," said Alice, "let him come back on his own."

Mark nodded. "Maybe you're right. There's certainly no use forcing him."

"I suspect he's not the kind who likes to be forced," said Mr. Langley.

"Who does?" said Mark.

Dinner was a bit more cheerful that evening. Mark and Alice filled in Jane and Louise on the details as the four of them dined in the comfort of the kitchen. Alice noticed that Mark kept glancing at the clock and out the window, as if he were waiting for someone, and of course, she knew that he was.

After dinner, Louise played piano while Jane and Alice put together a dessert of chocolate-covered cream puffs.

"How are things going with Mark?" asked Jane as she took the pastry shells from the oven.

Alice stirred the custard filling. "Does this look okay?" she asked, ignoring her sister's question.

Jane set the shells on a cooling rack. "That looks perfect," she said. Putting her hands on her hips in that I-mean-business stance, she then turned to Alice and said, "Come on, I've tried to be patient, but you're holding out on me. How's it going with Mark?"

Alice shrugged. "It's fine."

"That's not what I mean and you know it. Tell me what's going on with you guys. Come on, you promised you would."

Alice sighed. "Okay, it's not going anywhere. Does that answer your question?"

"But why?" demanded Jane.

"Oh, it has to do with the whole Adam thing," said Alice, "but there's more to it than that. I think it has to do with us—I just don't think we're ready to make any decisions."

Jane nodded and turned her attention to the chocolate sauce in the double boiler. "Okay," she said as she dipped in a spoon. "That makes sense. I know there's been a lot going on, and I can see that you might not want to make a commitment yet. What about later, when things settle down and Adam gets his life on track? What about then?"

"I honestly don't know."

Jane brought the spoon of chocolate sauce over to Alice. "How's this?"

Alice tasted the sauce, then smiled. "Decadent."

"Okay, then," said Jane, "you will let me know if things change between you and Mark."

Alice nodded. "You'll be the first to know—well, you and Louise both."

"Good." She returned to the stove and turned down the gas.

"Tell me, Jane," said Alice, "why do I feel as if you're pushing me toward Mark? Are you eager to get rid of me?"

Jane turned around wearing a shocked expression. "No, Alice, that's not it at all. You know that I don't want to get rid of you. Selfishly, I'd like everything to stay just as it is, but I want you to be happy too."

"I am happy."

"You really care about Mark, Alice. I can see it."

"Yes, you're right, I do. I care about a lot of people."

"Not like that, Alice. You know what I mean."

"It's just not that simple, and, honestly, sometimes I'm not even sure how I feel."

"Well, as you said, it could be just the timing. There's no harm in waiting."

Alice laughed. "You make it sound as if Mark and I have some big kind of romantic plan to pull off. Really, Jane, trust me, we don't."

"I believe you." Jane set the chocolate pot into cold water to cool. "I just don't want to be out of the loop if you ever do."

Soon they had the cream puffs constructed, and Alice was topping them with dollops of whipped cream. "These are going to disappear before our very eyes," she told Jane. "No one can resist your cream puffs."

She was right. Not only did they disappear, but Mark had more than one. For some reason, that gave Alice hope that his spirits were improving. Still, she prayed long and hard for Adam before she went to bed that night. She prayed for his safety and she prayed for his heart.

Please, let him be like the prodigal son, she prayed. *Let him see that it is time to come home and then help him to humble his heart so he can do it.*

Chapter Twenty-Four

Saturday morning was a flurry of activity at the inn. Alice helped Jane with breakfast and its cleanup, as well as the preparations for the picnic that would follow the egg hunt. She had already made her apologies to Mark, explaining that she would probably be busy until after the egg hunt. They had agreed to meet then.

The ANGELs arrived at the inn and were standing in the foyer when Jenny spotted Laura and her mother in the parlor. "Can Laura help us hide eggs, Miss Howard?" asked Jenny.

Alice glanced at Mrs. Winston, not sure that this plan would work. "Of course," she said. "Laura is welcome to help us if she wants to."

"Oh, I don't think—" Mrs. Winston began.

"Why not, Mother?" said Laura.

"Well, if you'd like to . . ."

Jenny pulled another set of bunny ears from her bag and ran over to take Laura's hand. "You have to wear bunny ears like the rest of us," she said as she reached up and arranged them on Laura's head, careful not to disturb the hot pink sunglasses that Laura was sporting.

"They look cool with your glasses," said Jenny. "The fuzzy white outsides are lined with pink satin on the insides."

Laura reached up and felt the furry ears that were attached to the headband and grinned. "Just call me Peter—no, Mopsy—Cottontail."

"All right, Mopsy," said Ashley. "We better hit the bunny trail."

Sissy gave Laura one of the prize baskets to carry, happily explaining to her what it was and how the ANGELs had put them all together themselves.

"There are ten prize baskets," said Jenny as they all trooped out of the inn wearing bunny ears.

"We'll meet you at the park with the eggs and stuff," called Jane as Alice followed along behind the girls.

The ANGELs started singing as they walked, changing the words of "The Ants Go Marching" to "The Bunnies Go Marching," and to Alice's pleased surprise, Laura sang right along with them.

By the time they reached the park, Jane and Louise were already there. Jane was setting up a table, and Louise was having what seemed to be an intense conversation with Ethel and Lloyd. Alice could tell by their faces that it was some kind of disagreement. Alice decided to pay them no mind. Surely, they would figure out whatever it was in time.

Louise came over to help her sisters. "Good grief," she said under her breath.

"What's up, Louie?" asked Jane as she spread a pretty, pastel print table cloth over the folding table.

"Well, Aunt Ethel has decided that Mr. Easter Rabbit should give the opening words at the beginning of the egg hunt."

"That's always been done by the pastor of Grace Chapel," said Alice. "I already asked Rev. Thompson to do the honors."

"Oh, Ken will understand," said Jane. "I can talk to him."

Louise frowned and shook her head. "Politics."

"Well, the children will probably like it," Alice assured her. "After all, it does seem fitting that a rabbit open the egg hunt. I don't know why we never thought of it before."

"Probably because Mr. Easter Rabbit only got his bunny suit a couple years ago," Louise said with an exasperated shake of her head. "Alice, is that Laura with your ANGELs?"

Alice laughed. "That's Laura. The girls wanted her to help them hide eggs."

Now Louise smiled. "Well, now that is something."

All the pretty prize baskets were lined up on the table, and every last egg was hidden just before ten o'clock, when the festivities were due to begin. Mr. Easter Rabbit gave his opening words, and everyone cheered—even Louise.

"Don't worry," Pastor Ken had assured Jane after she had told him the news. "I'll get my chance to be up front tomorrow."

The children were divided into five different age groups, with the toddlers starting first and with the ten-year-olds ending the hunt. The prize eggs were hidden in areas restricted to the various age groups, with the ANGEL bunnies and Mr. Easter Rabbit paying close attention lest any of the older children try to sneak into one of the younger sections. Alice noticed that Jenny was still holding onto Laura's hand, and it looked as if both of them were having a good time.

While Alice was manning the prize station, she noticed a woman walking across the park toward them. Alice did not recognize her at first, although she felt certain because of the shiny gold suit, that this woman was not a local. It also caught Alice's attention that this woman was not accompanied by a child. As she got closer, Alice realized it was Mattie Singleton.

She waved at Mattie, but her old friend must not have seen her for she suddenly turned and walked toward the spectator area, straight to where Mark and her sisters were seated in the lawn chairs they had brought from home. Well, that was fine. Alice had her hands full for the next hour anyway. They would take care of Mattie.

Eggs were found, a few tears were shed and the much coveted prize baskets awarded. Then it was finally time to move on to the picnic portion of the day's event. Alice was happy to be relieved of her responsibilities as she went over to join her sisters, Mark and Mattie.

"Alice!" Mattie waved to greet her. "I simply adore your little town. The Easter egg hunt was like something out of a Norman Rockwell painting. That funny old Easter Bunny and the little girl bunnies helping the children. Oh, it was just too sweet."

"I'm so glad you came," said Alice as she sat in the empty chair next to Jane. "I see you've met my sisters."

Mattie smiled. "Yes, they've been making me feel right at home."

"I hope you'll join us for lunch, Mattie," said Louise. "We have more than enough."

"I'd love to." Mattie smiled at Mark. "You were absolutely right, Mark. Acorn Hill is a charming, delightful place. I almost feel as if I've been transported back in time. It reminds me of the fifties, back when we were young and life was simple."

Louise handed each person a plate, and Alice poured cups of lemonade while Jane began to arrange the food on a small folding table.

"Let me help you with that, Mark," offered Mattie when Alice attempted to hand him his drink. Mattie scooted her chair closer to Mark and took the drink for him.

"Everything gets a lot trickier when you have only one good arm," he said as Mattie helped him to put his cup in the drink holder.

"I'll get your food for you too," said Mattie as she took his paper plate.

Jane eyed Alice curiously, but Alice simply acted as if she were preoccupied with opening a jar of pickles.

"Hello there," called Ethel as she led Lloyd, or rather Mr. Easter Rabbit, over to where they were sitting. "May we join you?"

"Oh my!" cried Mattie happily. "Do we really get to have lunch with the Easter Bunny?"

"Mr. Easter Rabbit," corrected Ethel.

"Otherwise known as Lloyd Tynan," said Louise in a hushed tone. "The mayor of Acorn Hill." Then she introduced Mattie to them.

"Welcome to our town." Lloyd bowed graciously.

"This is too precious," gushed Mattie. "Mr. Easter Rabbit himself. Oh, I wish I'd brought my camera."

They began loading their plates with fried chicken, potato salad and the other goodies that Jane had packed. Mattie remained on hand to assist Mark, and Alice tried to act as if she didn't mind. Then once her plate was filled, she simply sat back in the chair, focused her attention on the picnic crowd all around them and ate her lunch.

"This potato salad is delicious," said Mattie.

"That's Jane's special recipe," said Louise.

"It's a version of German potato salad," said Jane.

"It's yummy." Mattie turned to Mark. "Can I get you another serving? You seem to have enjoyed it too."

Mark looked uncomfortable. Alice suspected Mattie's attention embarrassed him, but then he admitted he would like more, and Mattie hopped up and got it for him.

Jane turned her head away from them so that only Alice could see and mouthed, "What is going on?"

Alice just shrugged, then said, "There are the Humberts." She waved and called hello, then turning back to Jane, asked, "Where are the Langleys and the Winstons? I thought perhaps they would join us."

Jane pointed across the park. "They're over there. Mrs. Winston's cousin invited them to share a picnic and the Winstons invited the Langleys."

Alice smiled. "How nice."

Jane still looked agitated, but Alice pretended not to notice, and as soon as her plate was empty, she excused herself. "I'm going to go talk to the Humberts," she said. She felt relieved to get away from her little picnic group. It was unsettling to see Mattie cozying up to Mark, but Mark was a grown man. He could surely deal with the situation.

"Alice," said Vera. "Come join us."

"I just thought I'd say hello." Alice said. She chatted for a bit, then went around greeting and visiting with others in the crowd.

"Those prize baskets were wonderful," said Sylvia. "Little Leo Andrews showed me his, and it was very impressive. Good job."

Alice smiled. "I guess it pays off to send out a letter in advance."

Sylvia lowered her voice now. "Where is Dr. Graves?"

"He's over there eating with my sisters and some friends."

"Everything okay?"

Alice nodded. "Of course." She continued making her rounds. By the time she got back, only her sisters were there, packing things up.

"Where have you been?" asked Louise.

"Just visiting," said Alice.

"Well, Aunt Ethel and Lloyd went home. Lloyd had a headache. Then Mattie begged Mark to give her a tour of the town, and he finally gave in and agreed."

"That's nice." Alice forced a smile to her lips.

"That's nice?" Jane stood up and looked at Alice with raised eyebrows. "You think that's nice? Mattie may be determined to make Mark husband number five and you think that's nice?"

Louise blinked. "Husband number five?"

"That's right," said Jane. "Didn't Alice tell you that Mattie goes through men like Kleenex?"

"Well, no . . ." Louise looked at Alice. "Goodness, I don't believe that I have even owned five *cars* in my lifetime. Five husbands?"

"Only four," said Alice.

"That's right," said Jane as she closed the picnic basket. "Mark would be number five."

"Oh, Jane." Alice went over and put her arm around Jane's shoulders. "Don't worry so much. Mark is a grown man. He's able to take care of himself."

"It's not Mark I'm worried about," said Jane. "It's you."

Alice smiled. "I'm fine, Jane. Really." Then she began folding up the chairs and table and helped her sisters to load things back into Louise's car. "You go ahead without me," said Alice. "I'd like to walk home."

"By way of town?" asked Jane hopefully.

Alice shook her head. "I just want to enjoy this lovely day."

Jane gave Alice a look that seemed to question Alice's sanity. Alice decided to pay her no mind. She hummed to herself as she walked back toward the inn. *Really*, she asked herself, *why should I be concerned?*

Chapter Twenty-Five

When Alice reached the inn, she was surprised and delighted to see a familiar car parked not in front, but in back. She knew that beat-up old Nissan had to belong to Adam, and she could barely keep from running as she hurried inside.

"You came back!" she practically cried when she saw him standing in the foyer with Jane and Louise.

Louise smiled at Alice. "Adam was just apologizing for the trouble he caused."

Alice went straight to Adam and threw her arms around him. "I'm so glad you came back, Adam." She hugged him tightly, not caring whether he minded or not, and finally she let him go and stepped back. She could tell he was embarrassed by her display of affection, but at the same time, he seemed to appreciate it.

"I'm sorry I was such a jerk to you, Alice," he told her.

"Never mind about that," said Alice. "I'm so glad that you came back. Do you know how much we all missed you?"

He looked down at the floor. "That's what the Langleys said, but I wasn't really sure."

"Well, be sure," said Alice. "Mark and I looked all over for you. So did the Winstons. Laura's been just sick with worry for you."

"And the kitten," said Jane. "How's Boots?"

"I better go get him," said Adam quickly. "I left him in the car. Just in case . . . you know. I put the window down so he wouldn't get too hot."

"Yes," said Alice. "Do go get him."

"There are leftovers from the picnic," added Jane. "Fried chicken and potato salad. Come in the kitchen when you're ready."

For the first time, Alice thought she almost caught Adam smiling.

"Thanks," he said as he started to head out, then paused. "Where's Mark?"

"Oh, he's showing an old friend the town," said Alice. "He should be back soon."

Adam nodded and went out.

"Isn't it wonderful," said Alice to her sisters.

"I hope so," said Louise with a slightly skeptical expression. "Let's just hope that he's sincere."

"Oh, I'm sure he is," said Alice.

"I think so too," agreed Jane. "Maybe that little stint out on his own helped him to see things differently."

"Let's hope so."

Alice walked Adam up to his room and waited as he got Boots settled in. "That cat is lucky to have you, Adam," she said as they left the room.

"I don't know. . . ." He turned and looked at her. "I mean Mark was kind of right. I can barely take care of myself."

"Maybe you just need some help." She reached over and patted his shoulder. "It's not much fun to be all on your own, is it?"

He shook his head. "You got that right."

"Well, I know we got off to a rocky start, Adam, but I'd really like to be your friend."

"Yeah, I know. I think I was just jealous of you."

"Of me?"

"You know, it's like you were getting Mark's attention, and I was acting like a spoiled brat. Pretty dumb, huh?"

She smiled. "We all make mistakes, Adam. The best thing is to realize what we're doing wrong and try to make it right."

"Yeah, that's what I'm hoping."

Alice felt more hopeful than ever as they went into the kitchen. It really seemed that things had changed, or were changing, with Adam. Why else would he come back here and apologize? Besides, she reminded herself as she filled a plate with picnic leftovers for him, one should always think the best of a person. Of course, she wondered if she could also apply this philosophy to Mattie Singleton.

Adam was just finishing his meal when the Winstons came back to the inn. Alice met Laura at the door with the good news.

"Where is he?" asked Laura.

"Right here," said Adam as he emerged from the dining room. Then he walked right up to the Winstons and apologized for being so disrespectful.

Mr. Winston looked surprised, but he reached out and shook Adam's hand. "Takes a man to say I'm sorry," he said.

Adam nodded, then looked away. Alice felt sorry for him. She knew this couldn't be easy.

"Where's Boots?" asked Laura eagerly.

"I'll go get him," said Adam. "Want to meet me on the porch?"

The afternoon settled into a relaxed pace with Adam and Laura playing with Boots on the front porch, and Mr. Langley and Mr. Winston enjoying a game of chess in the library while their wives visited with Louise in the parlor. Alice went to the kitchen to help Jane get some things ready for dinner.

"Wouldn't you think that Mark and Mattie would be back by now?" asked Jane as she rubbed a leg of lamb with lemon juice, salt and pepper, and began studding it with garlic.

"Depends on how much of the town Mattie wanted to see," said Alice.

"And it doesn't bother you in the least?"

"Oh, Jane." Alice sighed. "Of course, it bothers me."

"Well, that's a relief." Jane smiled. "I thought maybe aliens had snatched you and performed a lobotomy or something. I'm not involved with Mark the way that you are, but it bothers me a lot."

"There's not much I can do about it, Jane. I can't see how it makes anything better to feel unhappy."

"Maybe not, but I think that Mattie has some kind of nerve."

"In all fairness, I told her last week that Mark and I were only just friends."

"Even so."

"And, really, that's all we are, Jane."

"Yeah, but . . ."

"We shouldn't judge Mattie."

"Maybe not, but—"

"Speaking of whom," Alice said, holding a finger to her lips, "I think I hear them now."

"Go and see."

Alice slipped out in time to see Mark and Adam talking in the foyer, and then embracing. She sighed in relief. Well, at least that was over. Then Mark was introducing Adam to Mattie and, despite her earlier words to Jane, Alice felt a small twinge of jealousy. Perhaps she was imagining things, but it seemed as if Mattie had suddenly stepped into the role of Mark's girlfriend.

Alice retreated into the kitchen.

"What's going on?" asked Jane.

Without mentioning her feelings about Mattie, Alice described the reunion of Mark and Adam.

"Oh, that's good," said Jane as she slid the lamb into the oven. "I think we're done in here, at least for the time being, if you'd like to go visit with Mark now."

Alice said nothing.

Jane frowned as she hung up her apron. "Come on, Alice. What's up?"

She just shook her head. "I don't know . . ."

Then Jane took Alice by the shoulders, turned her around so she was facing the door and gave her a gentle shove. "Get out of here, Alice. Go and talk to him."

Feeling like a six-year-old, Alice obeyed. She could hear the voices of Louise and the other women coming from the parlor, and the two men were still playing chess in the library. Looking out the window, she saw that Mark and Mattie had joined Laura and Adam on the porch. Mattie was holding the kitten and the four of them looked so natural and comfortable out there that Alice could not bring herself to interrupt them.

Instead, she went upstairs. She knew, without a doubt, that she had taken the coward's way out. She also knew that she was just plain tired, and so she took a nap.

When she woke, it was time to help Jane with dinner. First, she freshened up and, determined to put on a brave face, she even changed into a festive outfit—a rich-toned paisley skirt and a sage green silk blouse. She even put on a couple pieces of Jane's handmade jewelry.

"There," she said to her image in the mirror. "At least no one will suspect that you're feeling like a wallflower tonight."

"Look at you," said Jane when Alice came into the kitchen. "Very nice outfit."

Alice shrugged and smiled. "You mean this old thing?"

Jane laughed and handed her an apron. "I was with you when you got that old thing, Alice, and it was only a couple months ago."

They worked happily together in the kitchen for a while, and then Jane asked Alice to set the dining room table. Jane had insisted they use the best china and crystal tonight, along with candles and flowers. Alice was just lighting the candles when she heard footsteps.

"Lovely," said a deep voice from behind her.

She jumped and then turned to see Mark. "Oh, you startled me," she said, then blew out the match.

"My apologies."

She smiled. "It does look nice, doesn't it?"

"I wasn't talking about the room, Alice. Although I must admit that it looks lovely too."

She felt herself blushing and was glad that she had already adjusted the dimmer switch on the chandelier so that the lights were low. "Where's Mattie?" she asked as she straightened a napkin.

"Last I saw, she was putting her feet up in the parlor," said Mark. "I think she was a bit worn out."

Suddenly, Alice felt guilty for neglecting her own guest. "Perhaps I should go see if she needs anything."

"I just came in to see what time dinner will be," he said.

Alice glanced at her watch. "Jane said it should be ready around seven. Would you let Adam know?"

"Certainly." He smiled. "Isn't it great that he came back?"

"Yes, I was so glad to see him."

Just then Louise came into the dining room. "This looks very nice," she said after greeting them. Then Mark excused himself.

"I thought I would give Jane a hand," said Louise.

"But I'm already—"

"I think you should see to your guests," said Louise in a firm voice.

Alice sensed that she was referring to Mattie. "Thank you," she told her. "I'll do that."

Of course, Alice was not eager to be with Mattie, but she reminded herself that she was the one who had invited her to dinner.

"Hey, Alice," said Adam as he came down the stairs.

"Hi." She smiled at him, pleased that it appeared he had put a bit of effort into his appearance. Certainly, his shirt could have used a pressing and his trousers still looked to be ready to fall off, but at least his hair was neatly combed. "How's it going, Adam?"

He shrugged. "Okay, I guess."

"How is Boots?"

Adam sighed. "I've been thinking about him."

"What do you mean?"

"I've been thinking that I should give him to Laura."

"Is that what you want to do?"

"It might be the best thing to do."

She nodded, surprised that he was confiding in her like this. "I'm sure Laura would take good care of him."

"That's what I thought too. It's kind of hard having a cat when you live in a car."

"Are you going to keep doing that?"

He shrugged again. "I don't really know."

"You do know that you have friends, Adam. People who are willing to help you." She wanted to say Mark was one of them, but at the same time knew it was not her place.

"Yeah, I guess." Then he frowned at her. "Can I ask you something?"

"Of course."

He glanced over his shoulder as if to check whether anyone else was around. "What's up with this Chatty Mattie lady?"

"Chatty Mattie?" Alice suppressed a giggle.

He nodded. "Yeah, she never stops talking. Anyway, she's like all glommed onto Mark now. I just wondered what was up with it."

"Have you asked Mark?"

He shook his head. "I thought I better not rock his boat."

She quickly explained that they had run into Mattie and that Alice had invited her to visit.

"I don't mean to be rude, but that wasn't such a bright move on your part."

She smiled. "Why's that?"

"Well, I thought you and Mark were like a couple, you know? Now this Chatty Mattie is making the move on him." He sighed. "If it were up to me, I'd get rid of her ASAP."

"That wouldn't be very hospitable."

"Maybe not, but it would be smart."

"I was just going to check on her now," admitted Alice. "The truth is I haven't been very hospitable already."

He grinned. "Way to go."

"See you at dinner," she said, smiling in spite of herself as she headed to the parlor. As odd as that conversation had been, it was strangely comforting.

"Oh, there you are," said Mattie when Alice walked into the parlor. "I thought you'd disappeared off the planet."

"Just took a little rest." Alice sat down in the easy chair across from Mattie. "I hope you didn't feel neglected."

Mattie sat up and patted her hair. "Not at all. Mark took excellent care of me. I just hope I didn't wear the poor man out. I know that his arm is still hurting." She looked toward the doorway. "Where is he anyway?"

"I believe he went upstairs."

Mattie nodded. "I'll just freshen up a bit before dinner. I'm sure I must look a fright."

Alice assured Mattie that she still looked fine, and then showed her to the downstairs bathroom. "Dinner will be at seven," she told her.

"Goodness," said Mattie, clutching her purse. "I hope I can pull myself together by then."

As always, dinner was excellent, but Alice was not so sure about the company. Mattie dominated the conversation, and many of her comments and questions seemed focused directly at Mark. Louise and Jane tried to chime in occasionally, but Alice felt mostly invisible. She noticed that Adam seemed rather quiet too. She hoped he was not slipping back into his moodiness again. Finally, the meal came to an end, and Alice rose and began to clear the table.

"I can help," offered Adam.

She tried not to register surprise as she accepted his offer, telling Jane and Louise just to sit.

"Thanks," she told him as they set the empty dishes on the counter.

"I just wanted to get out of there," he confessed, "away from Chatty Mattie. I was afraid I was going to leap across the table and strangle her or something."

Alice tried not to laugh. "Good that you didn't."

"How can Mark stand her?"

She shrugged. "Maybe he's just being polite."

"Someone should teach her to be polite." Adam studied Alice for a moment. "I know I was mean to you, Alice, and I'm sorry now. I wish you and Mark were still together. I mean, you are way better than Chatty Mattie."

"Thanks." Alice touched his cheek, and Adam smiled shyly.

As they went back out and continued to clear the table, Alice felt a mixture of gratitude and remorse. She appreciated what Adam had said about wishing she and Mark were still a couple, but it bothered her that it appeared that they no longer were a couple.

"Are you okay?" asked Jane when only she and Alice were in the kitchen. "I mean you've been so quiet tonight."

Alice shrugged. "I guess I'm having a lot of mixed feelings."

"About Mark?"

She nodded.

"Jealous?"

"Perhaps a bit, but even more than that, I feel confused."

"You and Mark should talk."

"It's a little hard . . . with Chatty Mattie around."

Jane giggled. "Chatty Mattie?"

"That's what Adam calls her."

"That's perfect."

They had invited all the guests at the inn to join them that evening for music and dessert. Louise had selected some special Easter music to play, and it was a lovely quiet evening. Alice suspected that Mattie would have preferred something more lively, but Alice was relieved that it was subdued. She was also relieved when Mattie, concerned about the drive back to Potterston, finally excused herself from the group.

Alice, playing hostess, got up to walk Mattie to the door.

"Aren't you going to see me out too?" Mattie said to Mark.

Although he looked comfortable, all settled into an easy chair, he quickly rose to his feet and joined them.

"I've had a lovely day," said Mattie directly to Mark. "I so appreciated your little tour of Acorn Hill. I do hope you'll let me know how it goes for you and that sweet little cottage you're considering. You have my number, right?"

"Yes, you gave it to me a couple of times," said Mark as they reached the front door.

Then Mattie reached out and hugged Alice. "Thank you, dear. Let's stay in touch."

"Of course," said Alice as they stepped apart.

Then Mattie hugged Mark. Although Alice didn't time it, she felt certain that Mark's hug was much longer than her own. "You're a dear man, Mark Graves," said Mattie when she finally released him. "Now, you be sure to call me."

He smiled and nodded, then said good-bye.

"Drive safely," called Alice as she closed the front door.

Mark sighed loudly. "Glad that's over."

She studied him. "Really?"

He nodded. "That is the most tiresome woman I have ever met."

Alice couldn't help herself. She laughed aloud.

"I'm afraid I'm completely worn out, Alice. Would you make my apologies to the others?" He rubbed his cast and sighed. "I think I'd like to turn in for the night."

"Yes, that's wise."

"And may I reserve some time to talk with you tomorrow?"

"Of course."

"After church?"

"Certainly."

"Good night, Alice." He smiled warmly.

"Good night, Mark."

Chapter Twenty-Six

The Grace Chapel Easter service was touching and uplifting. Of course, the focus was on the cross, forgiveness, redemption and grace, but for some reason Alice got the feeling that Pastor Ken had prepared his message with Mark and Adam in mind.

"God is truly the great heavenly Father," said the pastor as he finished his sermon. "He was willing to sacrifice His beloved Son in order to adopt us as His very own children. God loved us enough to give up what was incredibly precious in order to make us part of His family. And that, dear friends, is why we have reason to celebrate today."

Not for the first time, Alice thought that her father would have heartily approved of the young pastor who had taken over after his death. Although the two men were different in many ways, they shared spiritually timeless ideals and philosophy.

"That was a great sermon," said Mark as they stood outside the church afterward.

"Do you think Adam liked it?" asked Alice as she watched Adam and Laura quietly conversing.

"I actually saw him wipe a tear from his eye," said Mark.

"He really seems like a changed person," said Alice. "I think God is at work in him."

"I hope so." Mark frowned into the sunlight. "I told Adam that you and I were going to spend some time together this afternoon. Would you like to go have some lunch or do you and your sisters already have plans?"

"Actually, we'd decided to give Jane the day off. She's going to Sylvia's for Easter dinner, and Louise and I were going to join Aunt Ethel and Lloyd. I'm sure they'll excuse me."

"Are you certain?"

"Positive."

"I thought we could go to Potterston," he said. "There's a restaurant that I want to try."

"That sounds good," she said.

"Do you mind driving?"

"Not at all."

They talked as she drove, mostly about Adam and the general happenings at the inn during the past week.

"In some ways, it feels like I've been through the wringer," Mark admitted when Alice finally parked the Range Rover in front of the restaurant.

She nodded and handed him the keys. "I know what you mean."

"I have to ask myself, what was that all about? What was it for?"

They walked in silence into the restaurant, where they were quickly seated at a window that overlooked a garden. Alice took a deep breath, willing herself to relax as she leaned back into the chair.

"How's your arm feeling?" she asked him.

"Better, I think. I didn't even have to take a pain pill today."

"That's good." She turned and looked out the window, spying a young family in their Easter finery, taking pictures among the flowers.

"I've been doing a lot of thinking," he said.

She nodded without saying anything.

"About my life . . . and about you and me . . . and about Adam."

"I can imagine."

"Something just doesn't feel quite right." He sighed. "I have to admit that, at first, I viewed Adam as an intrusion into my life. I resented his expectations of me, or even his lack of them. But somewhere along the way, despite my misgivings, something in me changed. Maybe his change of heart touched me or perhaps even today's sermon. But I suddenly feel different about him."

"I think I know how you mean."

He sighed. "You know, I've led a fairly self-centered life, Alice. I'm sure you have no idea how selfish I am."

She smiled. "I think it's easy to be that way when you're single and without family. I know how much you've sacrificed for your work, Mark. I've heard stories about how you've risen in the middle of the night just to care for an ailing animal or one that's about to give birth. Now, really, that wasn't selfish."

"You're too gracious."

"Besides, I think everyone is selfish in some ways," she continued. "It's just the way we humans are naturally wired."

"I feel that I am ready to quit being so self-centered, Alice." He looked into her eyes. "When I came to Acorn Hill, I planned to ask you to become a bigger part of my life. . . ."

She looked away uncomfortably.

"But now it seems that my life is taking a totally new direction."

She looked back at him, curious.

"When Pastor Thompson spoke about God adopting us as His own children, well, I turned and glanced over at Adam, and it's as if something in me just clicked. Can you understand what I mean?"

She smiled. "I think I do."

"I felt such empathy for him, and I remembered how close I once was to his dad, and I began to care for Adam, well, almost as if he were my own son. It was quite a staggering feeling. Does that make any sense?"

"Of course it does. It's a bit like the way I feel about the girls who are in my ANGELs group. I love them almost as if they were my own."

He nodded. "Yes, but then you're like that, Alice. You are such a fine Christian example that you put the rest of us to shame."

"Oh, please don't say that. I make mistakes all the time. Believe me, I'm just as flawed as the rest."

"So there I was sitting in church and I got this very strong feeling that I was supposed to do something very specific for Adam. Almost as if God himself was speaking to my heart. Have you ever experienced anything like that?"

She nodded. "Yes, I believe I have."

"Well, it was rather amazing. I believe I'm supposed to help Adam."

She smiled. "Yes, I thought maybe that was the case."

"That's not all." He paused as if unsure how to say the next part. "I guess I just need to tell someone, to say these words out loud, Alice."

"Go ahead."

"Well, I believe I need to parent Adam." He looked at her with wide eyes. "Do you think that's strange?"

"Not at all."

He seemed relieved. "You see, all I can think about now is how I can help him, things I can do to get him on his feet again, ways I can encourage him to pull himself up to make something of his life. In the way that a father would help his own son. Do you know what I mean?"

She nodded, eagerly. "Yes, it's as if you've adopted him in your heart, Mark."

"That's how I feel." Mark sighed and looked out the window. "I've already made so many mistakes with him. It's possible that he won't want anything to do with this."

"No, I don't think it's like that," she assured him. "I can tell that Adam really looks up to you. Taking an active part in his life, acting as his guardian, might show him just how committed you really are to him."

"That kid really has potential. He just needs someone to believe in him and to help him get going."

"Yes! That's how I feel about him too. He's really a dear boy, even if he has been a bit confused and hurt by the challenges that life has given him. It was breaking my heart to see him becoming so bitter."

"I haven't spoken to him about any of this yet," continued Mark. "I mean about what I'm thinking, specifically, but what I'd like to do is to move back to Philadelphia with him. I'll help him to get things in line to go to school. At least I hope I will. He mentioned to me that he wants to be a veterinarian. If he's serious about becoming a vet, I'll do whatever it takes to get him there." He looked at Alice. "But I have no idea how much time that will take."

She smiled. "Maybe that's not important."

He reached across the table and took her hand. "But I don't want to lose you, Alice. Or your friendship."

"You don't need to worry about that, Mark."

"So you don't feel bad about this?"

She shook her head. "I feel that you're doing the right thing, Mark. To be honest, I've felt as if something's been off between us all week. I think it's simply that you should be helping Adam right now."

He smiled. "Who knows, maybe Adam will register at a college and perhaps even get situated into a dorm, maybe even by next fall or winter. Perhaps I can still plan to relocate to Acorn Hill sometime after that. Maybe I'll be here as early as next year. Who knows?"

"God knows."

Mark nodded. "You're right, Alice. God does know."

"And it's all in His timing, right?"

"Right."

They had a nice leisurely lunch, enjoying each other's company. By the time they got back to the inn, the other guests were getting ready to leave.

"Oh, I'm so glad you got here in time to say good-bye," Mrs. Winston told Alice as she set her bag by the front door. "I was just telling your sisters how thankful we are that we picked your little inn to visit."

"It's been quite a week," said Alice.

"I think it's just what Laura needed. Even this business with Adam has turned out to be a blessing in disguise. Don't you think?"

"I do," Alice nodded.

"Right after that lovely church service, Laura told me that she's going to start taking charge of her life now."

"Isn't that wonderful."

"She said she's tired of acting like a victim." Mrs. Winston glanced up the stairs, probably to see if the rest of her family was coming yet. "I want you to know, Alice, that even though it wasn't all smooth sailing, I think everything—including Adam and, well, just everything—was absolutely perfect."

Alice squeezed her hand. "I think Laura is going to be just fine."

Mrs. Winston nodded, blinking back tears. "I do too."

"Are you down there, Mom?" called Laura from the top of the stairs.

"Yes, dear."

"Adam wants to know if I can keep Boots for him," she called.

Mrs. Winston smiled. "That'd be just fine, Laura."

Laura made a happy squeal. "It's okay, Adam!"

Soon Mr. Winston, loaded down with luggage, and Laura, holding onto Adam's arm as he carried the cat carrier, were all gathered on the front porch.

"This means you have to stay in touch, Adam," said Laura.

"I know," said Adam. "I plan on it, well, once I get settled, that is. You have to keep your promise to me and learn how to use that special computer program that your dad's been telling you about. That way we can e-mail each other, and you can give me reports on how Boots is doing. That e-mail address I gave you is good until the end of the month."

Mr. Winston winked at Alice. "I'll have the program downloaded and running by tomorrow."

"What does it do?" asked Alice.

"It's specially designed for the vision impaired," he told her, "with an electronic audio voice built right into it and all kinds of other things."

"Yeah, well, it might take me a while to figure it all out," said Laura, "but I'll do my best."

Jane and the Langleys came out onto the porch to join them. Jane had two rather large bags in her hands. "I'm helping Mr. Langley load his car," she said. "Just to prevent him from reinjuring his back."

"Oh, I'm sure I'll be fine," he said.

Alice reached over and took the one bag Mr. Langley was carrying. "Well, just in case, let us help you."

Soon all the guests had their cars loaded, and everyone was saying good-bye, giving hugs all around.

"I feel like I'm going home after a happy time spent at summer camp," said Mrs. Langley, "saying good-bye to all my new friends."

"That's how it is at Grace Chapel Inn," said Mark. "You spend a little time here and, the next thing you know, you want to make it your home."

First, the Langleys, then the Winstons departed, leaving Mark, Adam and the sisters standing on the sidewalk.

"I just told Adam about my idea," said Mark as he set his good hand on Adam's shoulder.

"Yeah, if it's okay with you guys," said Adam, "I'll leave my car parked in the back of the inn for a few days." He made a face. "I know it's an eyesore. Maybe I could throw a tarp over it or—"

"No, no," said Louise. "Don't you worry about that."

Adam nodded. "I'll drive Mark back to Philadelphia today."

"When my arm's better, we'll both drive back here and pick up the Nissan," said Mark. "If that's okay."

"It's fine," Jane reassured him.

"Thanks for everything," said Adam. "I'm sorry I was such a jerk."

Jane gave him a hug. "Hey, you're a kid. It's what you do." He smiled.

"You are always welcome here," said Louise. "Both of you."

Alice nodded. "You're like part of the family now."

They all hugged again, with Mark taking care to hug Alice last. "Thanks for being so understanding," he whispered, "and for being you."

She smiled at him.

"You take it easy on your way home," said Jane.

"Drive carefully, Adam," warned Louise.

"Take care," called Alice as she waved. *Of each other,* she thought.

After the Range Rover drove—slowly—out of sight, the sisters went up to the porch to relax.

Alice sighed as she sank down on the porch swing. "We certainly have a good life, don't we?"

"We do," agreed Jane wholeheartedly.

"And we don't have any guests until next weekend," said Louise.

"Ah . . ." Alice leaned back, pausing from her swinging just long enough for Wendell to pounce into her ready lap.

"A much deserved break," said Jane as she looked out across the yard.

"I made some lemonade after church," said Louise. "Would you two care for some?"

"And there are still some chocolate eggs left over," said Jane.

"I feel like I'm in heaven," said Alice as she happily stroked Wendell's soft coat. While her sisters went off to get their afternoon treat, Alice thanked God for everything, but mostly for His perfect timing.

Ready to Wed

Dedicated to the sweet memory of Jane Orcutt,
dear friend and fellow author
in the Tales from Grace Chapel Inn series.

Chapter One

G ood grief, Jane!" Ethel Buckley exclaimed, wrinkling her nose. "You are covered in dirt."

Jane Howard peeled a sodden garden glove from one hand, then pushed a strand of dark hair from her eyes and sighed. "I've been mulching some fertilizer into the flower beds." Jane peered up at the leaden gray sky. "Not that it's going to do much good if our weather doesn't cooperate a little."

"It's been a strange spring indeed," said Ethel, who was Jane's aunt and neighbor.

"It's hard to believe it's mid-May. It feels more like March to me."

"Yes, my joints have been aching. I hope it's not arthritis." Ethel's tinted eyebrows arched, then she pointed a finger toward her niece's feet. "What on earth are you wearing?"

Jane looked down at her bright orange rubber shoes. "Crocs. They're very popular."

"Well, I can't believe anyone would pay good money for those silly looking things." She shook her head with firm disapproval. "They remind me of duck feet."

Jane held out a foot, pointing a toe upward. "I happen to like them."

"*Tsk-tsk.* It's bad enough you wear those overalls, but why do you want to walk around in duck feet?"

Jane shrugged. "They're comfortable, Auntie."

"You are a strange girl, Jane Howard."

Jane had to control herself to keep from rolling her eyes. "I'm not exactly *a girl,* Auntie."

"You may be fifty years old, but I still think of you as a girl. And you're so pretty, Jane, such an attractive young woman . . . and to be out in public looking like . . . " She held up her hands as if this was a hopeless case. "Like *this.*"

"Working in the garden isn't exactly like being in public." Jane studied Ethel for a moment, taking in her styled and sprayed Titian Dreams red hair, her carefully rouged cheeks and tinted lips, her neatly pressed burgundy wool jacket and knee-length tweed skirt, her faux alligator shoes and matching bag. It wasn't a look that Jane would choose for herself, but it suited her seventy-something aunt. And her aunt was right. Jane hadn't taken much care in her own appearance this morning. She had simply pulled her long, dark hair back in a ponytail and put on her gardening clothes. But one didn't usually dress up to spread fertilizer.

Ethel gave her hair a pat. "I would think you'd want to play up your looks more, Jane." She actually giggled in a coquettish way. "Goodness knows none of us is getting any younger, dear . . . and you just never know when Mr. Right might come ambling along. You might want to consider putting your best foot forward."

Jane stuck out a big orange Croc. "Here it is, Auntie."

"Just my point."

Jane forced a smile for her aunt's sake, then nodded toward the sky. "Those clouds are getting darker. Looks like the weatherman is going to be right about rain again today."

Ethel stood straighter, adjusted her purse and glanced upward. "Yes. And if I'm going to make it to town before it starts pouring, I'd better be on my way."

"Don't let me keep you."

Ethel frowned at her. "I do hope you plan on cleaning yourself up. I'd hate to imagine what your guests might think if they saw the inn's cook going around looking like a farmhand and walking like a duck."

"We won't be having any guests for . . . let's see, this is Wednesday . . . for a couple of days," said Jane. "Not until Friday."

"More cancellations?"

Jane nodded. She and her two older sisters, Louise Howard Smith and Alice Howard, owned and operated Grace Chapel Inn, which they had opened in their family home. The truth was Jane felt somewhat relieved for this lull at the bed-and-breakfast. Of course, at the same time, for her sisters' sakes, she wished they were booked right now. Normally, this was a busy time of year.

"Poor Louise was beside herself when another couple called to cancel last night and the Chandlers went home two days early. It's just not very pleasant to take a vacation with the kind of weather we've been having lately. Everyone seems intent on finding signs of springtime elsewhere."

"Well, signs certainly haven't made an appearance here in Acorn Hill." Ethel waved, finally continuing on her way down the sidewalk. "I'm off to town. See you later."

"You sure you want to go?" Jane called after her. "We might be having a deluge by the time you're ready to walk back."

"Don't worry," she called cheerfully. "Lloyd will bring me home."

Jane tugged on her damp garden glove. Maybe her aunt really didn't mind getting stranded in town if the skies opened up again, and of course, rain would be a good excuse for Ethel to coerce her good friend Mayor Lloyd Tynan to drive her home, but Jane wanted to get her pansies potted before the next downpour. She hurried back to the garden area where two flats of multicolored flowers were waiting. Fortunately, pansies were hardy in this kind of unpredictable weather. It was the heat that could be their undoing.

Jane picked up one of the heavy clay pots that she'd removed from the front of the inn earlier this morning and placed it on her potting table. After all these months of winterlike weather, she'd grown weary of ornamental cabbages. They were a welcome touch of color back in November when she'd first set them out, but it was mid-May and she was ready for something more cheerful. Yet, she'd been hesitant to plant anything else while it was still freezing at night. Just this week, the weatherman had said that this was the coldest May Pennsylvania had experienced in decades. It had snowed on Mother's Day and hailed just a few days ago. Farmers throughout their area were complaining that these unusual freezing temperatures were damaging crops. She glanced around her garden. Even with its freshly prepared soil, it still looked forlorn. In a way, she felt she had acted in faith by applying the fertilizer this morning.

She emptied the partially frozen soil from the clay pot onto her compost pile, then refilled it with some fresh potting mix along with a scoop of the mulch, working the dirt until all was evenly distributed. It was not unlike combining the dry ingredients for a cake. Then she set the flat of pansies that she'd gotten from Craig Tracy's nursery a few weeks ago next to the pot. Craig, who also owned the town's floral shop, Wild Things, had assured her these hardy plants were probably safe to be outside. But Jane, worried about the unpredictable weather, had kept them in her potting shed. Still, she could see that they shared her longing for sunshine. One by one, she began tucking the pansies into the pot. Such pretty colors: purples, yellows, russets and blues. Pansies really did know how to put on happy faces despite the chill in the air.

Jane thought she might learn a thing or two from these little blooms. She, too, could put on a sunny face. She didn't need to let her aunt's criticism about her appearance get to her. But the fact of the matter was Jane *had* been feeling dowdy lately. She wasn't sure if it was the result of this gloomy weather, or just a general weariness, or maybe it was something more. But she definitely had not felt like herself these past few weeks. Even Alice had mentioned it yesterday. Then to be chastised by her elderly aunt about her appearance . . . well, it had stung more than usual. And even that little bit about "Mr. Right ambling along" irritated Jane. Her singleness had rarely bothered her since her marriage fell apart a few years ago, but lately she'd been pestered by thoughts that being unmarried might be a permanent condition.

Certainly, it was some comfort that both of her two older sisters were single as well. Louise, a widow, and Alice, never married, always seemed content with their state. It was only Ethel who carried on about Jane's need for romance. It didn't bother Jane that Ethel put so much focus on her relationship with Lloyd, but Jane felt it was unkind for her aunt to criticize her for being unmarried.

She firmly pushed a yellow pansy plant into the already crowded pot, breaking off a fragile flower stem. She picked up the broken blossom and looked down at its sunny little face. With a sad sigh, she slipped the stem of the sacrificed bloom into the front pocket of her bib overalls, letting the head stick out. Then she carefully used her trowel to gently loosen the soil as she rearranged the plant into a more comfortable position. No sense in taking her angst out on innocent flowers. Finally, she stepped back to admire her pot of pansies. It looked surprisingly cheerful—almost enough to convince her that spring really was around the corner.

She set the finished pot back in the wheelbarrow and took up the second one. As she emptied the old dirt, she thought about her marriage. It wasn't something she normally thought much about—not because it had been so terribly unpleasant, at least not at first. She and Justin had their ups and downs, although toward the end it had mostly been downs. It was something of a relief when the marriage ended. Still, she didn't think she was bitter about the way things had gone with Justin. Really, she had no ill feelings toward him.

Jane used her gloved hand to brush some loose soil off the surface of her potting table, deciding that these thoughts about her ex-husband were probably best swept aside as well. She started on her third pot. And, although the sky was growing darker now, her spirits were actually beginning to lift as a result of her hard work. If the weather wasn't going to cooperate with the season, then at least these flowerpots might help some. And when guests finally arrived, they would be cheerfully greeted by the work of her hands. Her plan was to put the pots in semiprotected places on the front porch just in case the frost didn't let up right away. She'd plant more annuals, and perhaps a few new perennials, along the front walk later.

It was just beginning to sprinkle when she finally had all six pots loaded onto her wheelbarrow and was transporting them to the front yard. One by one, she hoisted them up the steps of the stately Victorian home and arranged them attractively around the front door. She was just settling the last flowerpot into place when she heard a car slowing in front of the inn. She stood and turned to see who it was, but the vehicle was unfamiliar to her. A pink Cadillac convertible with big tail fins that looked straight out of the fifties was parking in front of the inn, just past the front walk. Jane slowly went down the steps, hoping to sneak a glimpse at the driver of this rather unusual car. She spied a youngish-looking blonde woman peering up toward the bed-and-breakfast with a big smile on her face.

"Hey there!" called the woman as she got out of the car and waved over the roof toward Jane. "Is this the hotel?"

"Sort of," Jane called back, pointing to the sign for Grace Chapel Inn the woman obviously missed. "It's a bed-and-breakfast."

The woman clapped her hands together like a little girl. "Oh, goody!"

It was starting to rain harder, but still curious about this woman, Jane went closer to the car. "May I help you?" she asked, noticing that the car's custom license plate, reading *Belle,* was from the state of Georgia.

"Do you work for the bed-and-breakfast?" asked the woman, her heavily made-up big blue eyes widening.

"Uh, yes."

"I'm Belle Bannister," said the woman with a distinctively Southern drawl.

"Belle from Georgia," said Jane, putting two and two together.

"Why, yes!" Belle's finely arched eyebrows lifted with surprise. "That is exactly right. Just like everything else about this place." A raindrop splattered right onto her pink cheek.

"You mean everything but the weather," said Jane with a wry smile.

"Oh my." Belle reached into her car, retrieving a shiny pink purse and a pink overnight bag. "A nice gal in town gave me directions here," she said as she closed the car door. "Do y'all think I can get a room?"

"I'm sure that you can," said Jane, leading the pleasantly plump young woman up the front walk. "I'd offer to help with your bags, but I'm pretty dirty and—"

"Oh, that's okay." She hurried past Jane, trying to escape the raindrops and going so fast she seemed to totter in her pink high-heeled shoes. "I'll just take this little one inside for now and get the rest later when the rain stops." She paused under the cover of the porch to peer up at Jane's family home. "My, what a pretty house. It's absolutely perfect."

"Go right in," said Jane when they came to the door. "I'd go in with you, but I don't want to track mud inside. There's a bell on the desk—"

"A bell for Belle," giggled the woman as she opened the door. "Just perfect."

Jane stood there on the porch, watching as the front door closed behind this strange woman. She actually wished she could go inside and see Louise's reaction to their unexpected, chatty guest with a fondness for pink. Of course, a guest was a guest. And right now, they were running short of them. Besides, this Belle from Georgia seemed like an interesting person. She might even bring some color, albeit pink, into their cloudy gray world. Jane dashed down the porch steps. Grabbing the wheelbarrow, she pushed it through the rain, which was now coming down heavily. By the time she made it to the side door, she was thoroughly drenched. If Ethel could see her now.

Once inside the inn's laundry room, she removed her garden gloves and muddy Crocs and set them in the sink to deal with later. Next she peeled off her soggy, dirty overalls, hung them on a wooden peg, then quickly pulled on a pair of black warm-up pants and slipped her bare feet into a pair of clogs. She did a quick washup and entered the house by way of the kitchen. The warmth of the cheerful kitchen hit her as soon as she entered. She tiptoed through the dining room, curious to see whether Belle had found Louise.

"Oh, there you are again," chirped Belle as Jane came around the corner from the dining room. "Louise just gave me a tour of the first floor."

Jane nodded. "I hope you liked it."

Belle pointed at Jane. "That's the gardener I was telling you about, Louise. She's the one who told me that you had a vacancy here."

Louise gave Jane a sly smile. "Uh, yes, that gardener happens to be my youngest sister, Jane."

Jane came forward and extended her hand. "I'm a little cleaner now."

Belle smiled warmly as they shook hands. She looked from Louise to Jane. "Well, I'll be. I never would've guessed you two were sisters."

Louise was fifteen years Jane's senior, and although she, like Jane, was tall and slender, her hair was silver and her manner and appearance were proper. In her blue-and-beige plaid skirt, pale blue cashmere sweater set and pearls, she looked very much a lady in comparison to Jane's casual attire.

"And we have another sister," said Louise. "Her name is Alice, and she works part-time as a nurse at the hospital."

"And y'all run this inn together?"

"We do," said Louise.

"Well, that's just sweeter than sweet."

"What brings you to Acorn Hill?" asked Louise as Jane began to ascend the stairs.

"A dream," said Belle in a rather wistful voice.

"Indeed?" Louise's tone had a slight note of skepticism in it, and she peered over the top of her reading glasses with a questioning expression.

Jane paused on the stairs to listen to Belle's reply.

"Yes," said Belle, nodding with wide eyes. "God sent me a dream . . . to come here."

"You don't say?"

"And here I am."

"Here you are," said Louise, clearly puzzled.

"Yes," said Belle. "God sent me a dream. And through my dream, God showed me that I was to drive all the way up here, and that I was to relocate my business to your sweet little town, but that's not all."

"No?"

"God also showed me, through my dream, that it was right here that I would meet the man that I am meant to marry."

"Truly?" asked Louise.

"It must sound strange, I know," said Belle, still perfectly serious. "But I know that it's for real. And so, here I am."

"Here you are," said Louise for the second time.

Chapter Two

S he said what?" Alice asked as Jane slid a muffin tin out of the oven. She set the blueberry muffins aside to cool, then turned back to look at her sister. Alice still wore her nurse's uniform as she sat at the kitchen table, enjoying her afternoon cup of tea. Her hair, which was the shade of rusty driftwood, framed her face, and her expression as usual was sweet, although it was now laced with concern.

"Belle said God showed her all this through a dream," Jane said, and then she repeated the strange story about relocating and finding a husband.

Alice chuckled as she refilled her teacup. "*Hmm . . .* I wonder who the lucky man might be."

"I've been going through my mental list of available men," said Jane as she sat across from Alice. "I don't think it could be Kenneth," she said, referring to Rev. Kenneth Thompson, the pastor of Grace Chapel.

"You don't think our pastor is open to matrimony?" asked Alice as she put a modest dab of real butter on her blueberry muffin. The sisters had been watching their cholesterol, but Alice, sixty-two and fit, believed that a bit of butter wouldn't hurt.

"I just don't think that Belle Bannister is Kenneth's type," said Jane. The truth was that Jane felt protective of the pastor, who was her good friend and a widower.

"There's Craig Tracy," said Alice. "And Wilhelm Wood."

"And Jeff Beckett," added Jane.

"I thought you said Belle was youngish?"

"Well, older men have been known to marry younger women. And, for that matter, the other way around."

"Yes, that's true. What about Joshua Bellwood? He's a nice young man."

Jane nodded. "A possibility, I suppose, but Belle Bellwood? That just doesn't sound right. Besides, I don't see Belle as a farm wife." Then she listed off several other unmarried males of varying ages and occupations.

"Goodness," said Alice as Louise joined them in the kitchen. "I suppose I never thought of Acorn Hill as having such a broad selection of available men."

Jane chuckled. "Maybe our Belle came to the right place after all."

"Our Belle is completely worn out from driving," said Louise as she poured herself a cup of tea. "Can you believe that she started out from Georgia yesterday, then drove almost nonstop to get here this morning?"

"Oh my," said Alice. "She must be exhausted."

"What was the big rush?" asked Jane as she slid the basket of muffins toward Louise.

"I can't imagine," murmured Louise.

"Perhaps she was worried that her prospective husband would find someone else," said Alice with a smile.

"Well, I convinced her to take a nap," said Louise. "I told her that the men in Acorn Hill probably were not in any extreme hurry to get married this afternoon. I also invited her to join us for dinner. I hope you don't mind, Jane. I'll help you—"

"That's okay," said Jane. "Although it won't be anything fancy."

"I can help too," offered Alice.

"Really," said Jane. "It's fine. I already got out some ham-and-lentil soup from the freezer. I'll make a salad and some cornbread muffins to go with it."

"How are you feeling, Jane?" asked Alice.

Jane shrugged. "You mean have I quit singing my where-is-springtime blues?"

Alice smiled. "Yes. I noticed the pansies on the porch. Very pretty."

"Well, I'm trying to get over it," said Jane in a falsely

bright voice. "I never thought of myself as being affected by weather. Good grief, I lived in San Francisco for years. And everyone knows that place is famous for its foggy days."

"I wondered if you shouldn't have a physical," said Alice. "I was talking to Dr. Meecham today and he said—"

"I don't need to see a doctor," said Jane firmly. "I had a physical less than a year ago and I was fit as a fiddle. I think I just need to see some sunshine."

"Don't we all," said Louise.

"Yoo-hoo," called Ethel from the back porch.

"Come in," Jane called back as she got up to fetch another teacup. It was amazing how often their aunt popped in on them just as they were having tea and treats. It was as if she had radar.

"Hello, girls," chirped Ethel as she removed her plastic rain bonnet, giving it a shake that managed to splatter poor Wendell, the inn's resident cat, who'd been enjoying a cozy catnap by the warmth of the stove. He stood up, arched his tiger-striped back indignantly, then slowly strutted away.

"Did you get a ride home from town?" asked Jane as she set the extra cup on the table.

"Oh yes. Lloyd drove me home. It was raining cats and dogs."

"We were just discussing the foul weather," said Alice. "Will sunny weather ever come?"

"Lloyd said the forecast for next week looks brighter."

"Good," said the three sisters almost in unison.

"What I must know," said their aunt in a hushed tone, "is whose car is that parked out in front?"

Louise gave her the basic lowdown on their new guest.

"Really? A dream?" asked Ethel with a shake of her head. "How extremely unusual."

"Yes," agreed Alice. "We were just going through Acorn Hill's list of available bachelors."

"And we were surprised to discover it's a rather long list," said Jane.

"Well," said their aunt. "I certainly hope you didn't include *my* Lloyd on it."

Jane laughed. "Well, I think Belle might be young for Lloyd."

"How old is she?"

"I don't know for sure," said Louise, "but I would estimate thirty-something."

"And she's quite a showy dresser," added Jane. "She sort of goes with her car."

"What does she do?" asked Ethel.

"She sells Angel Face cosmetics and she apparently makes a good living at it too. She's already offered to give me a free facial." Louise frowned. "I told her I'd consider it, but I really do not intend to—"

"I think a free facial would be perfectly lovely," said Ethel as she patted her cheek. "Tell your guest I'd be happy to comply."

"Why don't you tell her yourself, Auntie," said Jane. "Join us for dinner tonight and you can meet Belle."

Ethel beamed. "Well, thank you very much, Jane. I'd love to come."

"Speaking of which," said Jane, "I better get started on that cornbread while the oven's still hot." She busied herself getting out a bowl and ingredients.

The sisters and their aunt chatted away pleasantly about the happenings in their small town. Eventually, Louise left to check the inn's e-mail for possible reservations, and Alice went upstairs to change out of her uniform, leaving only Ethel and Jane in the kitchen.

"May I help you with anything?" offered Ethel.

"No thanks," said Jane. "I think it's under control. It's really a simple meal. I hope Belle won't mind."

"I'm sure she'll be grateful," said Ethel. "After all, you girls run a bed-and-breakfast, not a bed-and-three-full-meals." She stood. "The rain seems to have let up. I think I'll head back home."

Alone in her kitchen, Jane tuned the radio to the jazz station, humming along as she made a salad. But when "Smoke Gets in Your Eyes" began to play, she stopped slicing the tomato. She just stood there and listened, and for some reason, those old lyrics just got to her. She found herself thinking about San Francisco; the Blue Fish Grille, where she had been chef; and, finally, about Justin. And, before she knew what hit her, she was crying. She wasn't sobbing, but tears were running down her cheeks. And she had not even sliced an onion.

"Oh, don't be such an emotional basket case," she admonished aloud as she stood in front of the kitchen window, looking out at the gray sky and blotting her tears with a rough paper towel. Maybe Alice was right. Maybe she did need a checkup.

"Hello," a female voice called from behind her.

Jane turned to see Belle standing in the doorway of the kitchen. She tossed the damp paper towel in the trash and forced a smile. "Did you have a good nap?"

Belle nodded. "Indeed I did, but I was afraid to sleep too long. Otherwise I might be awake for half the night." She peered at Jane. "Is something wrong?"

Jane shook her head. "No, no." She pointed to the radio as she turned it off. "I think that song was just getting to me."

"Oh, I understand completely," said Belle, waving her hand. "Music can do that to me too. Sometimes I'll hear an old Patsy Cline song about love gone awry, and just like poor ol' Patsy, I fall to pieces. It can be quite humiliating." She eyed the basket of blueberry muffins still on the kitchen table. "You don't suppose I might beg a muffin, do you? I am absolutely starving. I haven't eaten since breakfast."

"Of course," said Jane. "Help yourself. Would you like some coffee or tea to go with it?"

"Oh, coffee would be divine." Belle sat down at the table. "It might help me to keep my eyes open tonight too." She stifled a yawn. "I'm just totally worn out from driving all night."

"Why on earth did you do that?" asked Jane as she set a mug of coffee in front of Belle.

Belle grinned as she spooned sugar into the mug. "It's sort of hard to explain. I was just so excited after that dream I'd had the night before that I spent the day getting my things in order so that I could leave. And then after it was all taken care of, I thought, why not just go now? So I did."

Jane nodded. "Cream?"

"Yes, please."

Jane set the cream pitcher on the table, then returned to making her salad as Belle chattered away.

"I suppose I was afraid that if I didn't leave right away like that, well, I was worried that I might just chicken out. The dream seemed so very real. Yet I'm sure that most folks must think I'm crazy. My mama is always saying how I'm too impulsive, the way I go around jumping from the frying pan right smack into the fire." She chuckled. "But I think a person needs to grab life by the horns, you know, go for the gusto and make the most of it."

Jane nodded without turning around.

"I wasn't always like that," Belle continued. "I used to be a right careful kind of person. I worked the same old job—as a receptionist at a law office in Atlanta—for ten solid years, straight out of business college." She sighed. "And here I'd grown up in an itty-bitty town, and I started just hating living in the big city, but it was like I was stuck."

"Then what happened?" asked Jane.

"My sister died."

Jane turned and looked at her. "I'm sorry."

Belle nodded. "Thank you. She was my baby sister and the sweetest gal you'd ever meet. But in her senior year of college, she got cancer and went real quick. We were all shocked. And a couple months after she died, it hit me that I wasn't living the life I wanted to live. I didn't like where I lived and I asked myself what I really wanted to do and then I just did it."

"And what was that?"

"Making women look beautiful." She sighed happily. "Nothing else gives me quite the satisfaction of helping a woman to look her very best." Now Belle got up and walked over to where Jane was chopping green onions. "Take you, for instance."

"Me?" asked Jane uneasily.

"You're very pretty for an older woman."

Jane tried not to laugh. Here Ethel had said almost the same thing, only using the term "young" to describe her. It really was a matter of perspective.

"I'm sorry," said Belle quickly. "I don't mean to say you're old. Just older than me. But you're really pretty."

"Thank you," said Jane uncertainly.

"But you don't make the most of your looks."

"Well, I . . . uh, I'm not really—"

"No excuses, Jane." Belle shook her index finger at her. "I'm sure you're busy and all, what with cooking and gardening and whatnot, but like I tell all my clients, you gotta take time out for yourself. If a woman doesn't watch out for her own appearance, no one else will either."

"But I—"

"No buts," said Belle. "This is what I'm going to do for you. Tonight, after dinner, I'm going to give you the complete Super-duper Diva Delight. It's a treatment of my very own invention."

"Super-duper Diva Delight?" Jane echoed, imagining some kind of sweet confection piled high with whipped cream and topped with a cherry.

"That's right. By the time I'm done with you, you won't know what hit you."

Jane nodded cautiously, not knowing what might be in store for her. "But I thought you were going to give Louise a—"

"Oh, I can do you both at the same time." She clapped her hands. "In fact, I can do Alice too. I haven't met her yet, but I'm guessing anyone in the nursing profession could use a little TLC and pampering too. And that's just what I plan to do for all three of you."

"Well, I don't know—"

"I won't take no for an answer, Jane." Belle put her empty coffee cup in the sink. "Now, I'll get some things from the car, do some unpacking and freshen up, and tonight we girls are going to have some fun!"

Jane was about to mention that Ethel was joining them for dinner too, but then Belle was gone, happily humming as she hurried down the hall. Well, at least Belle had one willing volunteer with Ethel. If all else failed, Jane felt certain that her aunt would be thrilled to receive the Super-duper Diva Delight treatment, whatever it turned out to be.

Jane was just putting the finished salad in the fridge when Alice appeared. "I'll set the table," she offered.

"Thanks."

"I just met Belle," said Alice as she counted out set-tings of their everyday dishes. "She seems like an interesting character."

"Did she tell you about the Super-duper Diva Delight?" asked Jane.

"She did mention that she had a surprise for us, an after-dinner treat."

So Jane filled her in.

"Hmm." Alice nodded slowly. "Maybe that'll be nice."

Jane frowned. "I don't know."

"Well, surely it can't hurt us. And who knows, it might even be fun."

After setting the table in the dining room, Alice returned to the kitchen. Jane was stirring the lentil soup, and Alice put a gentle arm around her shoulders, giving her a squeeze. "I'm sorry this dreary weather has been getting to you, Jane," she said. "I hope the forecasters will be right and it'll get sunny and warm soon."

Jane sighed. "And I'll try to be a little sunnier too."

"Oh, I almost forgot," said Alice, "I picked up the mail on my way in this afternoon. There was something for you, Jane. I put it in your room."

Jane continued stirring. "Thanks. I'll get it later."

"I don't mean to seem nosy," Alice continued, "but I noticed it was from San Francisco."

Jane stopped stirring. "Really?"

Alice nodded.

"Did you notice who it was from?"

"I wasn't prying, Jane. But his handwriting is rather bold and easy to read, and then of course, the name Hinton caught my eye."

"It's from Justin?"

"Yes." Alice seemed to avoid eye contact as she took the wooden spoon from Jane. "Do you want me to stir this for you?"

"Thank you. Just turn the flame down to low when it starts to bubble."

"Certainly."

Jane hurried up the two flights of stairs to find a white envelope sitting on her dresser. Sure enough, it was from San Francisco and it was from her ex-husband, Justin Hinton. She slowly opened the envelope, removed and unfolded the one-page handwritten letter, and read.

Dear Jane,

I'm sure you must wonder why I'm writing you so completely out of the blue. But I'm about to start a road trip that will take me across the country. Remember how I always said I wanted to do that before I turned fifty? Well, I'm a little late since I'm nearly fifty-three. But

better late than never, right? Anyway, if all goes well, I plan to be in
Pennsylvania toward the end of May and I hoped you wouldn't mind if
I paid you a visit. I have some things I need to say to you, and it seemed
the only way to do this right (and haven't I done enough wrong?)
would be to do it in person. I hope you don't mind.

    Until then.

Justin

Jane read the letter two more times, trying to decipher the hidden message that seemed tucked between the lines there. Or was she just imagining something? What did this letter mean? Why did Justin have this sudden need to speak to her? Then, realizing it was almost time to serve dinner and the cornbread muffins were surely done by now, she tucked the letter into a drawer and hurried downstairs.

Alice gave her a curious glance as Jane removed the muffins from the oven. Jane busied herself pouring the soup into the warmed tureen and taking the salad from the fridge. Alice helped her carry these things to the dining room, never once questioning her about the letter. But Jane knew that Alice, although too courteous to ask, wondered what was up.

Still, Jane wasn't sure she wanted to discuss Justin's letter with anyone just yet. Not even with sweet Alice. In a way, Jane felt she was in a slight state of shock. The idea of Justin showing up and intruding on her life in Acorn Hill was very unsettling. And yet she was curious. What was it he wanted to tell her?

Chapter Three

*T*hey all bowed their heads, and Louise asked the blessing for their dinner Wednesday evening. Even before the soup was served, Belle was telling Ethel about her plan to give the Howard sisters a special facial treatment.

"And you should join us too," Belle told Ethel with enthusiasm. "The more the merrier."

"I'd love to," said Ethel happily.

"But aren't you worn out, Belle?" Louise asked as she passed the salad bowl to Jane. "After your all-night drive, I would think you might prefer to turn in early tonight. Perhaps we should plan this special facial treatment for some other time?"

"There's no time like the present," declared Belle. "Besides, if I go to bed too early, I'll just wake up in the middle of the night, and before you know it, I'll get my days and nights turned around and everything will be all topsy-turvy."

"Well, I would thoroughly enjoy a little pampering," said Ethel as she slathered butter on a hot cornbread muffin.

"All this nasty, cold weather has wreaked havoc on my complexion. And, being a redhead, I have rather delicate skin."

"You and me both," said Belle. "And I have just the thing for you." She smiled at Louise. "I have something that would be good for your skin too, Louise. Might even do something about those little frown lines between your eyebrows."

Louise touched her forehead, then quickly put her hand back down in her lap. "Well, I imagine it couldn't hurt." She looked at Jane and Alice. "And I suppose if my sisters are willing, I won't be a spoiler."

"I think it sounds like fun," said Alice.

"Jane?" asked Louise. "Are you going to participate?"

Jane suppressed the urge to groan. "I guess so."

"Then it's settled," chirped Belle. "As soon as the dining-room table is cleared, I'll set everything all up. Oh, this will be such fun, ladies. You're all going to get the Super-duper Diva Delight."

"I'll clear the table," offered Alice as they finished their meal.

"Thanks," said Jane. "I think I'll whip us up a little something to go with our Super Diva . . . uh . . . whatever it's called."

"You can call it anything your little ol' heart desires," said Belle as she folded her napkin, "as long as you call it a

real treat." She stood. "Now I'll go get my magical beautify-
ing things."

"Do you need help?" offered Ethel eagerly.

"Well, that would be just dandy," said Belle.

"I didn't mean to rope you girls into this," said Louise
as the three of them congregated in the kitchen. "But I
simply could not see an easy way out."

Jane sighed as she beat two eggs in a bowl. "I guess it's
best to get it over with."

"Who knows?" said Alice as she set plates in the sink. "It
might be just the thing you need to brighten your spirits."

"You know that Belle will try to sell us her magical beauty products," Jane pointed out as she measured
vanilla.

"Well, I could use some moisturizer," admitted
Louise.

"And there's no harm in helping Belle out," said Alice
as she rinsed a plate. "She seems like a nice person."

"Aunt Ethel certainly is taken with her." Louise chuckled
as she put a soup bowl in the dishwasher.

Before long, they were all gathered around the dining-
room table again. Only, this time, the table looked much
different. Laid out on it were pink trays and pink wash-
cloths and mirrors with pink frames and pink packages—
pink, pink, pink.

Belle started with an explanation of the basics of good skin care.

"It seems a little complicated," said Alice.

Belle giggled. "Well, I suppose it might seem that way at first, sugar, but it's really simple." She held up a hand with five fingers extended. "There are five basic steps: cleansing, exfoliation, toning, moisturizing and protection." She grinned. "Now, say it with me, girls." So they all repeated the steps, and soon Belle was helping them to apply varied products to their faces.

"Oh, there goes the oven timer," Jane said after Belle had just lathered some kind of minty cream all over her face. "I better go take out those butterscotch squares."

"Yummy!" said Belle. "I thought I smelled something good."

Ethel pointed at Jane and chuckled. "It's a good thing you don't have any unexpected visitors, dear."

Jane immediately thought of the letter she'd received from Justin. "What do you mean?"

"I mean you'd scare them away with that green face of yours."

Jane laughed as she caught her weird image in the mirror above the sideboard. "Well, yes, I suppose I would."

In the kitchen, Jane removed the hot pan from the oven and filled the teakettle with water, then turned up the flame beneath it. She thought about how nervous she'd felt when Ethel mentioned visitors. Was she worried about Justin and his less-than-welcome visit? What would it matter so much if he showed up here in a week or so? Was she concerned over what her family thought of her ex-husband? He was no longer a part of her life. Why should his visit trouble her in the least? But, the truth was, it *did*. And sooner or later, she'd need to let her family know.

"Come on back in here, Jane," called Belle into the kitchen. "We don't want that mask drying hard as plaster on your face."

Jane returned and sat patiently as Belle carefully removed the mask. And, surprisingly, Jane's face did feel refreshed. "That's nice," said Jane as she patted her cheek.

"You have such lovely skin, Jane," gushed Belle. "You really should take better care of it."

"I'm always telling her that," said Ethel. "She spends a lot of time out in the sun when she's gardening, and half of the time she forgets to wear her hat."

"But surely you wear sunscreen?" asked Belle as she wiped something cool and refreshing across Jane's forehead.

"Uh, sometimes."

"Jane, Jane, Jane," scolded Belle. "You must always wear sunscreen, sugar. You'll be a wrinkled old prune before you turn fifty."

Jane giggled.

"What's so funny?" asked Belle.

"She's already hit that milestone," Alice pointed out.

Belle smiled at Jane. "Well, you could easily pass for much younger than that, especially if you took better care of your skin."

"Belle was telling me more about her dream," said Ethel in a serious voice. "I find it very interesting."

Jane turned to her aunt, whose face now was covered with something that looked like pink frosting, and laughed.

"You find her dream humorous, Jane?" Ethel's voice had a scolding tone as she cocked her head to one side.

"No," said Jane, recovering. "I think you are humorous, Auntie. You look like someone pushed your face into a little girl's birthday cake."

"Oh." Ethel leaned over to peer into the little mirror in front of her. "Well, now I do, don't I?"

"And I wouldn't blame y'all for laughing at my dream," said Belle as she helped Louise to apply her facial mask. "I'm sure it must sound perfectly ridiculous to some folks."

"Not at all," said Ethel. "I think it's rather charming. And I have decided to partner with you in it."

"Really?" Belle stopped wiping the goop on Louise's face. "How do you mean?"

"Well, I know almost everyone in Acorn Hill. I don't know if my nieces mentioned that the mayor and I are on, shall we say, very good terms. And because I am rather well respected in this town, I just thought I'd be the perfect person to introduce you around, Belle. Take you under my wing, so to speak."

"You'd do that for me?" Belle set down the pink tube of white mask she'd been using on Louise, whose face now resembled that of a mime, and rushed over to put her arms around Ethel's shoulders, giving her a big squeeze. "Well, bless your heart. Thank you so much!"

"It'll be my pleasure," said Aunt Ethel. "As well as introducing you to our eligible bachelors, I can also introduce you to some women friends who might be interested in your beauty products." She chuckled. "Besides my three nieces here, there are plenty of ladies in our fair town who could use some professional assistance in the beauty department."

Jane rolled her eyes. Luckily, Ethel missed seeing her, but Alice hid a giggle with a cough and winked at Jane.

"Perhaps you can introduce Belle to Betty Dunkle," Alice suggested.

"Good thinking," said Ethel.

"Betty's a hairdresser," said Alice. "She has a shop called Clip 'n' Curl."

"Oh, I'd love to meet her."

"I think Belle is going to be right at home in our town," said Ethel.

"So what are your plans, exactly?" inquired Louise.

"Well, first of all, I have to meet Mr. Right," said Belle as she helped Alice to apply some toner. "That's my top priority."

"But what if he's not here?" asked Jane.

Belle laughed. "Of course, he's here. Just like in my dream. He has to be."

"But how can you be so sure?" asked Louise.

"Because, so far, everything is happening *just like my dream*. I dreamed I drove into a sweet little town in Pennsylvania, and here I am, just like my dream. I dreamed that I would be helped to find my way. Then I stopped in the Coffee Shop to inquire about a hotel, and a nice waitress named Hope gave me directions. Just like in my dream."

"Hope Collins," said Alice. "She's a lovely person."

"And she could probably use some beauty help," added Ethel. "The last time I spoke to her she was considering dying her hair blonde again. *Tsk-tsk.* Someone should give that girl some advice."

"So, you can see," said Belle. "My dream really does seem to be coming true."

"So, let's say you do meet Mr. Right," said Jane. "What's next?"

"We get married, of course." Belle laughed.

"When?" asked Ethel.

"The first Saturday in June," said Belle dreamily.

"You are planning to be married less than three weeks from now?" asked Louise.

Belle nodded as she helped Ethel to remove her pink mask. "Yes. I have a complete plan."

"My goodness," said Ethel. "That seems rather unrealistic."

"Yes. I hadn't planned to mention that part just yet. But really, I have it all worked out in my head."

"Exactly where will this particular wedding be held?" asked Louise in a tight voice.

Belle grinned. "I sort of hoped that it might be held right here at the inn. The reception anyway. I'd really love to be married in a church."

"Grace Chapel is a very nice church to be married in," offered Alice.

"You can't be serious, Belle," said Jane.

Belle laughed. "You see, I knew I should be careful about saying too much. Just like some of the people in the Bible—you know the ones that God gave dreams to—well, some folks thought they were crazy too. But just you wait, time will tell."

"I guess so," said Jane in a tone that suggested she was unconvinced. She stood, forcing a smile. "I'll get our refreshments." But as she went into the kitchen, she began to think that their guest was more than a little off her rocker. How could Belle possibly imagine that she was going to meet Mr. Right and have a wedding, just like that? It was completely crazy.

After they had all tried many of Belle's beauty products, Jane said, "Thank you, Belle, I really like the way my skin feels—softer and smoother." She refilled their guest's teacup. "I think I'd like to purchase some of these things."

"Oh, goody," said Belle. "But we're not done yet."

"We're not?" asked Louise with a touch of dismay in her voice.

"Of course not." Belle opened up another one of her pink cases, unfolding the sides and back to display a wide array of what appeared to be all sorts of cosmetics. "Now, girls, it's time to get glamorous."

"Oh yes," said Ethel happily. "This should be fun."

Louise cleared her throat. "I don't care much for makeup. A little lipstick in a neutral shade perhaps, but that's more than enough—"

"No, no," scolded Belle. "You have to at least try them, Louise."

And before anyone else could protest, Belle began helping them to apply everything from Wrinkle Away concealer
to Marvelous Mauve eye shadow. They tried out lip colors
and blushes and eyebrow pencils and the works. And when
they were finished, they all looked overdone except for
Ethel, who looked very nice.

"Well, this is too much makeup for me," admitted Alice
as she peered at her image in the mirror. "But it has been
fun, Belle. And I do think I like this lip color."

"Yes," said Belle. "It's lovely with your complexion."

"I'd like to order some," continued Alice, "along with
that moisturizer and facial mask."

"I'm more than happy to help you," said Belle.

"Goodness, it's getting late," said Ethel as she checked
her watch.

Louise looked to be stifling a yawn. "It is, indeed."

"I'll tell you what we can do," said Belle. "I've got lists
of everything you've used tonight, I'll attach those to an
order form for each of you, and you can just sleep on it.
Look everything over tomorrow and let me know if you're
interested in ordering something. More than anything, I
don't like to come across as some high-pressured sales-
person. Beauty should be fun."

They all thanked her, and she reminded them to carefully cleanse their faces before bed. "Now, y'all just go on,"

she called out. "I'll clean up in here so that no one will ever know that I was even here."

Alice and Jane picked up the tea trays and took them to the kitchen, where Jane studied Alice's made-up face.

"Do I look bad?" whispered Alice.

"I really like the lipstick, but the rest of the makeup is a bit heavy for you," Jane said as she directed her sister to a small mirror that hung by the back door.

Alice chuckled quietly. "Can you imagine the reaction I'd get if I showed up at the hospital looking like this?"

"I don't know," Jane said, grinning. "You might catch the attention of one of your available male patients. Maybe you could get yourself engaged by tomorrow and then tie the knot in a week or two. Why, you could beat Belle to the altar."

"Oh, Jane." Alice shook her finger at her. "Don't be such a cynic."

"Well, you have to admit that getting engaged and married in less than three weeks sounds pretty far-fetched."

Alice shrugged. "But don't forget, Jane: God does work in mysterious ways."

Jane felt guilty as she rinsed the china teapot. Maybe Alice was right. She supposed it could be possible that God gave Belle that peculiar dream. Still, it seemed strange. Then again, Jane realized it wasn't her place to second-guess God's ways or to cast judgments on guests.

Chapter Four

*F*or the first time in ages, Jane decided to get up early Thursday morning, lace up her jogging shoes and take a short run before starting breakfast. Going running was a real test of her will because it was still gloomy and chilly out. But she suspected that part of her recent slump was as much a result of a lack of exercise as a lack of sunshine. Still, it was hard to force herself out into the dull gray dawn. Once again, although the temperature seemed warmer, it looked like rain. She was just finishing her run, only a block away from the inn, when she noticed a familiar figure strolling up ahead. Tall and slender, with short dark hair and dressed in casual gray slacks and a navy pullover sweater, the man was easily discernable to Jane as the pastor of Grace Chapel.

"Hello, Kenneth," she called as she slowed her pace to walk beside him.

"Morning, Jane," he said, a smile crinkling his hazel eyes. "Did you have a good run?"

"Yes, thanks," she said breathlessly. "I'm afraid I've gotten out of shape. I haven't run in weeks."

"Well, congratulations to you for getting back to it. That takes discipline."

"What are you doing out this early?"

"Last night, Henry Ley called me. My faithful associate pastor was worried that there might be some water seepage going on at the church." Kenneth chuckled. "Consequently, I woke up in the middle of the night after a bad dream in which I was wearing my hip waders to make my way up to the pulpit to preach on Sunday. The sanctuary was like an indoor swimming pool, and I found myself thigh high in murky water where there were actually a couple of fish swimming around. I should've had my rod handy."

Jane laughed.

"It bothered me enough that I decided to take an early morning walk to investigate."

"I hope it's nothing too serious." Jane glanced toward the chapel, which appeared high and dry to her. "It has been an awfully wet spring."

"Wet and cold," said Kenneth, "but I heard that's going to change soon."

"I sure hope so."

"I also heard this foul weather has hurt your business." They paused in front of the inn. "Louise told me she'd had more cancellations and that it's pretty quiet this week." Then he smiled. "But maybe you ladies need a little break. And I suppose that means you're off the hook for cooking one of your big, delightful breakfasts this morning."

"Not completely off the hook. We got an unexpected guest yesterday. In fact, if you feel hungry after checking out the church—which, I hope, has not converted itself into a swimming pool—stop in and join us."

He grinned. "That's an offer that's hard to resist."

"Good," she called as she jogged up to the house. Then she went upstairs, took a quick shower, dressed and went down to her kitchen to put together a breakfast that was probably more for Kenneth than Belle. She knew how their pastor, being single, appreciated good home cooking. She also knew that if the church was in need of any serious water-damage repairs, he'd probably need a little encouragement as well.

"Good morning," said Alice as she joined Jane in the kitchen.

"You're up early," observed Jane as she stirred waffle batter. "I thought this was your day off."

"There's a staff meeting at the hospital that I need to attend."

Jane shook her head. "That doesn't seem fair, making you come in on your day off."

Alice laughed. "Oh, I don't mind. I don't have to wear my uniform, and I get to come home as soon as it's over. The other nurses will probably wish they were in my shoes."

"The teakettle's hot."

Alice brewed herself a cup of green tea and sat down at the table. Wendell leaped into her lap. "Silly old cat," she said as she petted him.

"Ever since I started the bacon cooking, he's been begging."

"Now, Wendell," warned Alice, "you need to be watching your waistline."

"Exactly what I told him."

"It looks like you're making a rather big breakfast for just one guest," observed Alice.

"Oh, I saw Kenneth a bit ago. I invited him to stop in for some nourishment." Then she told Alice about his nightmare.

Alice chuckled. "You know, I wouldn't be surprised if some water may have leaked in. I remember a time, years ago, when we had the same sort of odd weather with this freezing and raining. Some cracks in the foundation had frozen and thawed, allowing groundwater to seep into the church basement. Father fixed the damage himself, and once the weather cleared up, we never had problems like that again."

"So, no swimming pool in the sanctuary then?"

"Goodness, no."

Jane turned on the waffle iron. "Do you have time for breakfast, Alice?"

"No, I should get going in a few minutes. Besides, they usually bring in all sorts of food for our meetings—sort of an incentive to come, I think." Alice got a curious expression as she peered at Jane over her tea. "You seem to be feeling better, Jane," she said.

Jane shrugged. "Well, I did force myself to run this morning. That probably helps with my somber spirits. They do say that exercise produces endorphins, and endorphins are supposed to make us happier people."

Alice nodded but still looked curious. Jane suspected this was because of the letter Alice put in Jane's room yesterday. Jane wasn't sure she wanted to discuss her dilemma yet. Part of her wanted to believe that it wasn't going to happen, that it was all only her imagination. Or perhaps Justin had changed his mind about coming by now.

"Well, I suppose I should get moving," said Alice as she stood and placed her cup in the sink. "I'll see you in a couple of hours."

Alice had barely left when Jane heard someone tapping on the back door. She was just pouring batter into the hot waffle iron and couldn't go open it. Thinking it was Kenneth, she called out for him to let himself in.

"Jane," called a hoarse-sounding female voice.

Jane closed the waffle iron onto the batter and turned to see who was there. But the puffy red nose poking through the cracked open door looked unfamiliar. She walked over to see more clearly.

"It's me," hissed the voice. "Aunt Ethel. But don't look at me, Jane. I am perfectly hideous."

"What on earth!" exclaimed Jane as she fully opened the door to see Ethel standing there, with a bright purple silk scarf draped over her head and partially covering her face, which was blotchy, red and swollen. "What happened to you, Auntie?"

Ethel pulled her scarf more tightly around her chin, clearly embarrassed by her appearance. "An allergic reaction."

Jane nodded as realization sunk in. "Oh. Was it from last night's facial?"

"I'm afraid so. Anyway, that's what Dr. Bentley suspected."

"You've already been to the doctor?"

"He came to see me. I felt bad calling him so early, but I wasn't sure what had happened to me and I seemed to be having difficulty breathing. I was quite alarmed."

"Oh my!"

"Dr. Bentley gave me a shot and some antihistamine pills. He said I should feel and look better in a day or two." She slowly shook her head, then pulled her scarf over her face a bit more.

"Poor Aunt Ethel." Jane gently patted her aunt's shoulder.

"Believe it or not, my dear, I actually looked worse than this only a few hours ago."

"Good grief," said Jane. "Why didn't you call over here for help?"

"I considered doing that, but I felt it was rather serious and I knew that our good doctor would make a house call. I thought it best to see a physician."

"Yes, it seems you were right about that."

"Anyway, it just hit me a few minutes ago that I had promised to show Belle the town today. I wanted to introduce her around and all. And I'm afraid I won't be able to do that now."

"You could've just called over here to cancel, Auntie. I'm sure Belle will understand."

"Yes, I suppose. But I wanted to ask you a personal favor, Jane. You see, I thought perhaps you could step in for me. Belle is a sweet person, and I do so like her. I really do want to help her, despite my reaction to her beauty products. Anyway, I would like to assist Belle in establishing herself in Acorn Hill. And I thought that you, being not terribly busy since the inn isn't full, well, couldn't you step in for your poor old auntie?"

"Oh, I don't really think that's a good—"

"Please, Jane," pleaded Ethel. "It will only be for a day or two at the most. And, as you know, time is of the essence. Belle needs to get started on her mission right away."

"Her mission?" Jane frowned.

"Of finding a man." She shoved a piece of paper at Jane. "I've made a list of all the people you can begin introducing her to."

"But, Auntie," demanded Jane, "surely you don't expect me to drag poor Belle about the town, introducing her to every available male and making complete fools of both of—"

"I only expect you to use your head, Jane. Of course, you won't let it be known that Belle is, well, on a manhunt. You must be more diplomatic than that. Just casually give Belle a tour of our dear little town and make it seem coincidental when you just happen to run into certain eligible bachelors. It's really quite simple." Ethel sighed heavily, as if this whole business was wearing her out.

"Oh, Auntie, I really don't think—"

"That's just the point, Jane. Don't think. You're always making a mountain out of a molehill, dear. It's really not such a great deal to ask of one's niece. In fact, while you're at it, you might take some notes from Belle because she seems much more likely to wed than you."

Because of Ethel's pitiful condition, Jane decided to control the urge to respond. What good would it do anyway?

"So, you'll do it for me then?" Ethel twisted her swollen and purplish lips into a crooked smile.

"I'll do what I can, Auntie. But no guarantees."

"And I'll give Lloyd a call later this morning. Maybe he can be of some help to us as well. Thank you, Jane." Ethel pulled her scarf closer around her face. "Now I feel the need to go and rest a bit. I think I shall put my feet up, perhaps have a cup of tea."

Jane softened toward her aunt. "And I'll bring you some breakfast in a little bit."

"Oh, you are a dear." Then Ethel went out the back door.

Jane watched as her elderly aunt scurried toward her home in the inn's carriage house. She walked in a hunched-back manner, as if she thought this posture might make her less visible as she quickly returned to the sanctuary of the carriage house. Poor Auntie!

Then, as Jane noticed smoke coming out of the waffle iron, she thought, *Poor Jane!* Not only had her waffles burned, but she had allowed Ethel to rope her into a perfectly silly scheme. *Really, what could I have been thinking?*

"Hello in there?" called Kenneth.

"Come in, come in," she called in a less than welcoming voice as she turned on the range fan and began scraping blackened waffle crumbs from the waffle iron and into the sink.

"Uh-oh," said Kenneth in a teasing tone, "looks like I picked the wrong day to have breakfast at the inn."

"Just a little mishap," she assured him. "I was distracted."

He poured himself a mug of decaf. "Was that your aunt I saw hurrying away from here just now?"

Jane chuckled. "Yes. And *that* was my distraction."

"She was moving pretty fast," he said as he sat down at the kitchen table, planting his elbows and taking a slow sip. "Anything wrong?"

Jane explained that her aunt had suffered an allergic reaction and had been forced to call for medical assistance early this morning.

"God bless small-town doctors who still make house calls."

"My sentiments exactly."

"Are those blueberry muffins?" he asked, nodding to the basket on the counter.

"They are. Help yourself." Jane flipped over the ham slices that she'd been heating on the grill, then began cracking eggs into a heavy ceramic bowl.

"So, what's new with you, Jane?"

"You mean besides the fact that, thanks to the weather, my garden is weeks behind and the inn is having a slump?"

He chuckled as he buttered his muffin. "Yes, besides that. What's up with Jane?"

She avoided his question. Kenneth was a good friend and trustworthy confidant, but even so she just wasn't sure that she was ready to tell him, or anyone, about Justin's impending visit. At least not yet. "Hey, I forgot to ask, how's the church? Will I need to bring my snorkel on Sunday?"

He laughed. "It's not too bad. Just some leaks in the basement. It looks like it may have happened before."

Jane told him about what Alice had said, and he nodded. "Yes, that sounds about right. I'll stop by the hardware store and ask Fred if he has a recommendation."

Then to distract him from any more personal inquiries, Jane told him about Belle's little "beauty treatment" last night and how it may have been the source of Ethel's allergic reaction. "The rest of us seem perfectly fine." She touched her cheek. "In fact, I think my skin genuinely feels better than usual this morning. I was a skeptic, but I may actually buy some of her products myself."

"You say your guest showed up unexpectedly," said Kenneth. "With no reservation? Do you know where she's from?"

"Atlanta. Well, Kenneth, she also mentioned a small town in Georgia. I'm not really sure where she lives now, but she is definitely Southern."

"So what brings her up north?" Kenneth picked up another muffin. She almost warned him not to spoil his appetite, but then she knew how much he was able to eat sometimes. "Certainly not the weather."

"Well, that's a rather interesting question." Jane turned the gas down under the eggs, then checked the temperature of the waffle iron. "Maybe I should let our guest tell you for herself."

"Now you've got me curious."

She poured batter into the waffle iron and closed it again. "Well, it's a curious story."

"Is it supposed to be a secret?"

Jane tossed him a mysterious grin. "Let me just say this: The main thing that brought her to Acorn Hill was a dream. And she believes the dream came from God."

"Oh." He shook his head and his face creased a slight frown.

"Now, don't be a skeptic, Kenneth. As a man well-versed in Scripture, you are well aware that God can give people prophetic dreams."

"I'm thankful the dream I had last night wasn't prophetic."

Jane laughed. "Yes, that is a relief."

"Good morning," Louise cheerfully greeted them both as she entered the kitchen. "Kenneth, it's a pleasure to see you this morning. Are you joining us for breakfast?"

"Yes, I am. Jane kindly invited me."

"Belle is in the dining room," Louise lowered her voice. "She wanted to come in the kitchen, Jane. I explained that we prefer to have the kitchen to ourselves during meal preparation. However, I told her I'd bring her some coffee."

"Breakfast is on the way," said Jane as she checked the waffles, which looked just about perfect.

"Would you care to come out and meet our guest?" Louise asked Kenneth.

"Certainly," he told her as he refilled his cup with decaf.

Jane put the finishing touches on breakfast, setting it on the kitchen table so that she and Louise could transport the warm platters to the dining room table. When they entered the dining room, Kenneth and Belle seemed to be hitting it off, casually chatting about the weather and the church's slight water problem that he'd been investigating. Finally, they were all seated at the table.

"Well, isn't this lovely," said Belle happily. "So homey and sweet and everything smells absolutely delicious." She beamed at Kenneth, who was sitting across from her. "And I'll just bet you're the man to say the blessing too. It's so nice to have a member of the clergy joining us for breakfast."

As Louise bowed her head, a little alarm went off inside of her. Had Belle already set her sights on poor Kenneth? Of course, he didn't have on a wedding ring, but as far as Louise knew, no one had mentioned his marital status just yet. Why would they? But perhaps Belle had radar about such things. Louise wouldn't be a bit surprised.

Chapter Five

S o, I hear you're from a small town in Georgia, Belle." Kenneth passed the platter with eggs and ham across to their guest, and she smiled shyly at him. Carefully made up and dressed in a pale pink pantsuit today, Belle looked very pretty.

"Why, yes, that's right, Rev. Thompson. Warbler, Georgia. It's an itty-bitty town in southwest Georgia. I recently moved back there from Atlanta. I'd been in Atlanta about ten years, but I'm just not a big-city girl. At first, I liked all the things there were to do and all the great shopping, but after a few years, all that traffic and noise and hustle-bustle got to me."

"It must've been a great relief to get back to your hometown." He smiled in a congenial, pastoral way. A completely unsuspecting way, thought Louise as she poured warm maple syrup onto her waffle.

"Oh, I suppose it was something of a relief," said Belle. "But things had changed there. Most of my friends had moved on, and my parents had relocated to Florida a couple years back. So, I guess it wasn't quite what I'd hoped for. Still, it's a sight better than Atlanta. That's for certain."

"Belle is thinking about Acorn Hill for her new residence," said Louise in a way that suggested she was not completely sure about this idea.

"Really." Rev. Thompson nodded with a surprised expression. "That's a pretty big move to make. What motivates you to want to do this? Do you have any friends up here?"

"No. The truth of the matter is, before showing up here, I didn't know a single soul in this sweet little town. Then I met the lovely Howard sisters and their dear aunt Ethel, who has promised to show me around town today."

The pastor nodded, but he looked even more confused. "Yes, they are definitely a delightful family."

"So, I really do think I'm off to a very good start." Belle smiled happily.

"I still don't quite understand how you can be so certain that you want to move up here so soon, Belle. Didn't you only arrive yesterday?" Rev. Thompson asked.

"That's right." She winked at Jane. "Oh, I suppose I might as well just spill the beans. After all, the pastor, being a godly man, should appreciate such things, don't y'all think?"

"Oh yes," said Jane, trying not to chuckle. "I'm sure he should."

"Well, it all started with a dream," she began in a mysterious tone. "A very specific dream that I believe came from God. It was very, very real." She addressed the sisters. "I didn't even tell y'all all the details. In that dream, I moved to a small town in Pennsylvania, a town named after an acorn. I thought the acorn was symbolic at first. You know the old saying about a great oak tree springing from a little acorn—I thought the acorn had to do with faith. But then I got on the Internet and searched the words *acorn* and *Pennsylvania,* and I found Acorn Hill."

"Really?" asked Louise.

"Yes. And God showed me something else in this dream. He showed me that I would move here and that I would meet my Mr. Right and that we would be married on the first Saturday of June."

"*This* June?" Rev. Thompson frowned.

Belle nodded. "In fact, I suppose I should ask you whether the church is available on that day, Rev. Thompson."

"The church?" He studied her as if she was from another planet. "You mean for your wedding?"

"That's right."

"But you don't know who the groom is yet?"

"Oh, I have some ideas." She giggled.

Poor Rev. Thompson actually choked on a bite of waffle. Holding his napkin over his mouth, he coughed several times before he managed to swallow a sip of water.

"I'm sure it must sound a little crazy," Belle continued seriously. "And I guess I'll have to get used to people's reactions. But when God gives you a dream, I believe you should sit up and pay attention. Don't you think so too, Rev. Thompson?"

"Well, yes, when God gives you a dream, of course, you should pay attention. I suppose," said the pastor, "that I'm just unsure as to how you make the determination that a certain dream is from God."

"Faith," said Belle confidently. "I remember from my Sunday school classes: It's the substance of things hoped for, not seen. Just like my dream, Rev. Thompson."

His eyebrows lifted as he picked up his coffee cup and took a slow sip.

"But you never did answer me, Rev. Thompson. Is the church available on the first Saturday of June?"

He slowly cleared his throat. "Actually, it is available. As a matter of fact, it's not booked for the entire month, which is unusual for this time of year."

She clapped her hands, then pressed them to her pink-blushed cheeks. "*Ooh,* that's just wonderful. Now, Rev. Thompson, I'd like you to schedule the wedding ceremony on that day for me. If you don't mind."

"You're sure about this?" He frowned.

"Sure as the sunshine."

Louise laughed. "Well, considering the weather lately, that's not terribly sure, Belle. Not around here anyway."

Belle turned and smiled knowingly at her. "But, darling, you know that the sun is always shining. Even when the clouds are out and it's pouring something awful, the sun is still shining. Even in the darkness of night, it's still shining somewhere. It's just that you can't always see the sun. Sort of like faith, don't you think?"

Louise leaned back in her chair. "Yes, I suppose you're right."

Belle smiled at Kenneth again. Louise thought that he was starting to resemble prey that had been caught in the crosshairs. "And, naturally, I'll expect you to be there too, Rev. Thompson—at the wedding ceremony, I mean."

He sat up straighter, squaring his shoulders and perhaps putting on his pastor's hat. "Of course, I'll be happy to perform the ceremony, Belle. But it's customary for the engaged couple to come in for a premarital counseling session. I could schedule that too, but it might be tricky without a fiancé to bring along with you."

"Oh, don't worry, God is working on that." She nodded her head. "I have no doubt about it."

"Yes, well, I see." Kenneth turned to Jane. "Breakfast, as always, was delicious, Jane. Thank you for having me." Then he turned back to Belle. "Pleasure to meet you, Belle. I hope you enjoy your time in Acorn Hill." Then he stood, excused himself, and left via the back door.

Belle laughed lightly. "Goodness gracious, I certainly hope that I didn't scare the poor man away."

"Oh, I don't think our pastor is too easily scared," said Louise, though her creased brow indicated that she might not be as convinced as she sounded.

"Well, God certainly does work in strange ways," said Belle. "But I believe that He is definitely at work."

Jane began clearing the table.

"He's surely an attractive man." Belle seemed to be speaking to no one in particular as she enjoyed another cup of coffee. "And a godly man too. One could hardly ask for anything more."

"Rev. Thompson is a good and sensible man," said Louise as Jane retreated with a stack of dishes to the kitchen.

Jane set the dishes into the sink and turned on the water, hoping the noise would drown out any more conversation from the dining room. She had no desire to hear another word about Kenneth's fine attributes or Belle's aspirations to lead him to the altar. She chuckled as she rinsed a plate. Poor Kenneth. He thought he'd been simply coming for breakfast, but probably left feeling like he'd been on the menu. She'd have to apologize later.

Louise came in bringing the rest of the dishes from breakfast. "Our guest is inquiring about Aunt Ethel."

Jane clapped a soapy hand over her mouth. "Oh dear, I forgot."

"Forgot what?"

Jane told her about Ethel's condition. "I promised to take her some breakfast, and she also talked me into showing Belle around town today for her." Jane gave an appealing look to her oldest sister. "Unless you'd rather do that, Louise. I'll take Auntie her breakfast and you can go—"

"I'll take Aunt Ethel her breakfast, Jane." Louise gave her a stern look, although it appeared to be hiding mirth. "And you can give Belle the tour."

"Oh, Louie, please."

Louise chuckled. "Not on your life, Jane. I've already had more than enough of that silliness. If you only knew how many times I have held my tongue since Belle arrived. Was it only yesterday? Well, I am sure that even you would be impressed." She started fixing a plate for Ethel. "Besides, I need to work on our accounts and I should be around in case we get some reservations today."

Jane groaned. "So there's no getting out of it?"

"No." Louise nodded toward the dining room. "And you better get out there and inform Belle before she gives our ailing aunt a telephone call. I already wrote down the phone number for her."

Belle had just picked up the office phone when Jane

found her. "You don't need to call my aunt," said Jane quickly. Then she explained about the allergic reaction and how she'd been selected to be Belle's guide today.

"I hope her reaction wasn't from last night's facial." Belle had a horrified look. "I'd hate to think I made that sweet lady sick."

"Aunt Ethel has very sensitive skin." Jane felt like her aunt's parrot as she repeated that line.

Belle actually had tears in her eyes. "Oh my! I've given hundreds of facials, but I've never made anyone sick before. This is terrible."

"Well, Aunt Ethel is special," said Jane wryly. "So, when would you like to have the town tour? I need to finish up some things in the kitchen, but I could be ready to go in, say, an hour."

"That's perfect." Belle nodded, but she was wringing her hands as if she was still quite distraught over Ethel.

"And I'd like to order some of the items you used on me last night," said Jane. "The cleanser and facial mask and moisturizer."

Belle's perfect brow furrowed. "Are you just trying to make me feel better?"

"Not at all," said Jane. "I actually like how my skin feels this morning. I think your products are very nice."

Belle smiled. "Oh, I'm so glad."

"Meet me in the foyer in an hour," said Jane.

"Will do."

Despite the dream business, Jane liked Belle. Maybe it was her southern charm or just her sweet, big-eyed innocence, but it was hard not to like the optimistic woman. Even so, Jane was not the least bit excited about what lay ahead today. She finished up in the kitchen, and then, remembering how fresh and pretty Belle looked in her pale pink pantsuit, Jane decided maybe she should spruce up a little herself. It might make the events of the day easier. So Jane hurried up to her room and changed into a plum-colored corduroy skirt and shirt, topped with a favorite faded denim jacket that always made her feel younger than her fifty years. She added some jewelry and even lip color and blush. Then she pulled her hair back into a fresh pony-tail and tied it with a richly colored scarf in shades of plums and blues. Not bad. Of course, she knew she'd probably look dark and dowdy next to Belle, but it was, at least, an improvement over her breakfast attire.

"Ready to go?" asked Jane when she found Belle at the foot of the stairs, thumbing through a chamber of commerce brochure about Acorn Hill. Louise always made sure the inn was well stocked with local maps and information.

"Ready and waiting," chirped Belle. "For starters, I thought perhaps we could tour the church. I'd like to get an idea of the size and feel of it—for the wedding, you know."

Jane winced inwardly but simply said, "Sure, why not."

As they walked toward the chapel, Jane related the building's history, telling Belle how her father, Daniel Howard, had been the pastor for so many years and had recently passed away.

"Oh, I'm so sorry for your loss."

"Thank you."

"Was it after your father's death that Rev. Thompson came?" asked Belle as they paused outside of the chapel, looking up at the modest yet dignified white clapboard structure.

"Yes, shortly thereafter. There's an associate pastor as well. Henry Ley. He and his wife actually live in the rectory."

"So, where does Rev. Thompson live?"

"In town," said Jane as she pushed open one of the double doors. "Above an antique shop."

"Really?" Belle sounded disappointed. "Being a single man, I suppose a small space would be easier for him to keep up."

"The church is about a hundred years old," said Jane as they entered. She pointed out the stained-glass windows. "My favorite is the one with Jesus holding the little lamb."

"Oh yes," gushed Belle. "That would be mine too." She slowly walked down the center aisle, doing the step, slide, step that some wedding parties still used. Obviously, she was imagining herself as the bride, going down to the altar where she would be met by—

"Hello, ladies," said Rev. Thompson as he popped out from behind the pulpit.

Jane jumped. "Oh, I didn't know anyone was here. Are we interrupting anything?"

"No, not at all." He brushed dust from the knees of his pants as he approached them. Jane could tell that, although he was smiling, something in his eyes suggested he was uncomfortable. "I was just checking on some electrical wiring. We had some shorting out due to the moisture problem downstairs. I wanted to make sure that everything was up and running for Sunday's service."

"Will you be preaching on Sunday?" asked Belle, as if he were an actor and she wanted to know if he had a starring role.

He cleared his throat. "Yes. That's how it usually goes. Unless I'm away or sick, I deliver the main sermon."

"Belle just wanted to see the church," said Jane quickly.

"And it's absolutely perfect," said Belle. "I love it."

"So do we," said Jane. She gave Kenneth an apologetic

look. But it was hard to read his expression in return. Without a doubt, he was unsettled, not his usual cool, calm and reserved self. But whether his reaction was a result of Belle's man-hunting mission or simply the pretty and charming Belle herself, Jane wasn't entirely sure. All she knew was she wanted to get Belle out of there—and fast.

"So, that's about it," she said lightly to Belle. "Our little chapel. Nothing fancy, but near and dear to our hearts." Jane turned around as if to leave.

"Oh, and I can see why," gushed Belle. "It's perfectly lovely in its sweet simplicity. And I'm sure it's going to be near and dear to my heart too. In fact, it already is."

Jane actually took Belle by the arm and gently tugged her back down the aisle and toward the front door. "See you later, Ken—Rev. Thompson. Sorry to disturb you. I hope you get everything squared away by Sunday."

"Me too," called Belle as she nearly tripped over the doormat in her high heels. Jane helped balance her. "See you later, Rev. Thompson."

Then they were outside where, to Jane's surprise the sun was actually beginning to shine. "Well, look at that," she said to Belle. "The sun decided to show its face today."

"A good sign," said Belle. But Jane wasn't so sure.

Chapter Six

*T*he Thursday morning meeting at the hospital had wound up rather quickly, and Alice had barely arrived home when she ran into Jane and Belle. They were just coming back from looking at the chapel.

"Oh, Alice," Jane gushed happily, "you're home!"

"Why, yes," Alice responded with some surprise. It wasn't as if she'd been gone for days. "The meeting was shorter than expected, and now I have a whole day to do whatever I like."

"Would you like to go to town with us?" Jane asked eagerly.

"That sounds nice."

"Wonderful." Jane patted Alice on the back. "And since that's the case, perhaps you won't mind taking Belle around to meet some of the local bachelors while I catch up on some kitchen things."

"I thought Aunt Ethel was in charge of that tour," Alice pointed out, suddenly unsure that she really wanted to go into town.

Then Jane explained about their aunt's mishap.

"But perhaps I should check on her," Alice offered.

"No, Louise has it completely under control," said Jane. "Take as long as you like, Alice. And be sure to stop by and introduce Belle to Lloyd. Auntie called him to say that we would drop in. She thought he might be of assistance." Then Jane simply waved, wished them well, and practically dashed back into the house.

"It looks as if you're stuck with me," said Alice with an apologetic smile.

"Or perhaps you're stuck with me," said Belle.

Alice patted Belle on the arm. "Not at all. I am delighted to be able to get to know you better, Belle. We shall have a wonderful time."

Feeling hopeful about the weather, Alice decided it might be nice to walk to town. Plus, it would give them a chance to chat. However, as they went down Chapel Road, Alice wondered how comfortable Belle would be in her high-heeled pink pumps.

"Do you need to put on walking shoes?" she asked Belle.

"Oh no, these are just fine. I'm used to heels." She chuckled. "I'm so short that I can hardly bear to be seen without them. I suppose that's just my silly vanity, but it's the truth."

As they walked, Alice began to tell Belle a bit of the town's history. Not that it was so extraordinary, but it managed to fill the spaces in their conversation, and it also distracted Alice from the task ahead. Was she really supposed to take Belle around and introduce her to every available bachelor?

"Oh, there's that little coffee shop where I met Hope," said Belle happily as they arrived at Hill Street. "We must stop in for pie later today. She told me that their pie was divine. I believe she said it was worth making the trip to Acorn Hill just for a piece."

Alice laughed. "Well, maybe not all the way from Georgia, but I'll admit their pies are very good. My father loved their blackberry pie. He went in regularly for it."

Belle pointed to the Acorn Hill Antique Shop. "Oh, I simply adore antiques and collectibles. Could we go in there?"

"Of course," said Alice.

Belle paused in front of the store, looking up with interest. "Oh my, is that where Rev. Thompson lives? Jane mentioned an apartment above an antique store."

"Yes. That's right." Alice pushed open the door, at the same time pushing away the image of an eager Belle racing up the stairs to Kenneth's apartment. Alice hoped that Belle wasn't the sort of woman who would be a bother to their pastor.

They looked around for a short time. It seemed that Belle's main interest was in pink carnival glass, and the only pieces in the shop were ones she'd already collected. "Still, it's best to look," she told Alice as they exited. "Leave no stone unturned, my grandma used to say."

Alice wondered if the same theory would apply to Belle's manhunt. "That's our town hall," said Alice, pointing across the street. "And the shop next door, Time for Tea, is owned by one of our town's available bachelors."

"I wouldn't mind picking up some tea," said Belle.

No stone unturned, thought Alice as they crossed the street. The bell jangled as the two of them entered.

"Doesn't it smell good in here?" said Belle.

"Welcome," said Wilhelm Wood, glancing over his shoulder from where he was filling a small canister at the back of the shop. "How are you, Alice?"

"I'm well," said Alice. "Isn't it lovely that the sun is shining?"

"Yes," he agreed as he stepped up to the counter and smiled. "The past few weeks of weather have been depressing." Alice had always felt that Wilhelm was a nice-looking man, tall, and impeccably groomed. Still, she wondered what Belle would think of him.

"I'd like to introduce you to our guest," said Alice.

Wilhelm's blond eyebrows rose expectantly as he smoothed back his already neat, thinning, gray-blond hair.

"Belle, this is our good friend Wilhelm Wood, the owner of Time for Tea. Wilhelm, this is Belle Bannister from Georgia."

He extended his hand. "A pleasure, ma'am."

"Actually, it's *Miss,*" said Alice. "Belle may be relocating to Acorn Hill, Wilhelm."

"And what, may I ask, brings you to our fair town?"

"Well, I suppose it's really a number of things, Mr. Wood," Belle said with an enigmatic smile.

"Please, call me Wilhelm."

"Thank you. Well, you see, I'm just a small-town girl at heart," said Belle. "And I think Acorn Hill might be the perfect place to bring my business to."

"What sort of business is that?"

"I'm a beauty consultant."

"And a fine one at that," added Alice.

Wilhelm chuckled. "Well, I'm sure that our town would welcome a beauty consultant."

"Exactly what Aunt Ethel said."

"Except now the poor woman seems to have had an allergic reaction to one of my products," admitted Belle. "I feel so terrible about it."

"But the rest of us loved your products," Alice reminded her.

"Have you been to the Clip 'n' Curl yet?" asked Wilhelm.

"No," said Alice. "But it's on our list. Aunt Ethel thought that Belle should meet Betty."

Wilhelm nodded. "Betty's shop is just down the way." He straightened his tie. "Is there anything I can help you ladies with while you're here?"

"Oh yes," said Belle. "I just adore a certain peach spice tea. I can't recall the name of it, but it's an herbal tea."

"Hmm." Wilhelm gave her description some thought. "I can't think of anything like that offhand, but I mix some teas myself."

"Oh yes," said Alice. "He's very good at it. Jane says that Wilhelm is a master tea mixer."

Wilhelm waved his hand. "Oh, Jane is very sweet. But I wouldn't call myself a master. I just dabble."

"Well, I can attest that his Asian Orange Spice is legendary in our town," said Alice. "In fact, if I'm not mistaken, I think we could use some for the inn, Wilhelm."

"No problem, Alice." He turned around and picked up a large canister and began to measure some into a small bag. "The usual amount?"

"Yes."

He filled the bag, closed it and handed it to Alice. "On your account?"

"Yes, thank you."

"And now for you, Miss Bannister."

"Oh, please, call me Belle."

"Yes. Indeed. I'm thinking perhaps you ladies could continue on your travels and I will do a little experimental mixing. Stop by here before you head back to the inn, and you can see what you think."

"Oh my," said Belle. "You'd do that for me?"

He smiled. "Certainly."

"Oh, I can't wait to try what you put together," she said.

"We'll see you later then," said Alice.

"Everyone is so nice in this town," said Belle as they continued walking. "I feel so at home already."

"What did you think of Wilhelm?" asked Alice.

"He seemed very nice. And he's a really neat dresser. That jacket looked like Armani to me. Not that I'm an expert when it comes to fashion, but it looked expensive and Italian."

"So, do you think Wilhelm could possibly be the one?" asked Alice.

"Maybe, but I suppose he's older than what I had in mind."

"I think he's about the same age as Rev. Thompson," said Alice.

"Really? Well, that makes me wonder if I may be wrong about the age factor. I don't really think it should matter too much. What should matter is finding the right man, the man that God has chosen for me." She looked up at Alice with big blue eyes. "Don't you think that's what's important?"

"I wouldn't really know," Alice sighed. "I've never been married myself."

"Oh, I know I must seem silly, Alice," said Belle. "You're so smart, a nurse and all. I wish I could be more like you and your sisters. You all seem to have such sensible heads upon your shoulders."

"No, no," Alice firmly shook her head. "It's better to be yourself. If I've learned anything in my sixty years, it's that. But I'll admit that all this dream business and looking for Mr. Right is a little hard for me to grasp. Still, if it works for you, well, I firmly believe God moves in mysterious ways."

"And my dream is rather mysterious."

Alice pointed over to the florist shop. "That's Wild Things," she told Belle. "The owner of that shop is also a bachelor and a good friend of Jane's."

Belle laughed. "It sounds as if Jane is good friends with all the bachelors, Alice. I'm surprised she isn't married. She seems the kind of woman that fellows would admire. I'll bet she's turned most of them down."

"Oh, I wouldn't know about that," said Alice as she pushed open the door, although she did know that part of what Belle said was true. Jane did have a good rapport with a number of the single men in town.

"Oh my," said Belle. "This is a beautiful shop."

"Yes." Alice nodded. "Craig is very talented."

"Do I hear someone singing my praises?" asked Craig as he emerged with an armful of purple irises. He beamed at Alice. "How are you?"

"I'm well, thank you."

"And how is my buddy Jane doing?"

"Much better now that the sun is shining."

"I know what you mean," said Craig as he put the irises into a flower bin. "I was considering a trip to the Bahamas." He pushed back a lock of sandy brown hair that had fallen across his forehead, giving him a boyish look. He smiled warmly at the two women.

"Really?" Craig was more Jane's friend than Alice's, but Alice liked the young man, and she knew he was doing a great job with his business.

"Well, it was an impractical idea, but with this weather I was actually thinking about it." He glanced over at Belle. "Who is your lovely friend, Alice?"

"Forgive my manners," said Alice. "This is Belle Bannister Belle, this is Craig Tracy, owner of Wild Things and the best florist in these parts."

"Pleased to meet you, Belle." Craig politely shook her hand. He was only a few inches taller than Belle, and Alice had to admit, if only to herself, the two would make a cute couple.

"It's a pleasure to meet you too, Craig." Belle looked around the shop and smiled. "And your shop is perfectly lovely. And the aroma in here"—she took in a deep breath—"why, it's like taking a whiff of heaven."

"You like flowers?"

"Oh, I simply adore them."

"I can tell by your accent that you're from the South," he said. "I can't imagine what made you want to come up here for our awful weather."

She laughed. "Well, I didn't think to get a weather report first."

"Belle is considering moving here," said Alice.

"To Acorn Hill?"

"Exactly."

"Well, it is a nice town," he said to Belle. "And to be fair, the weather this time of year is usually much better. Still, what brings you here?"

So Belle gave Craig pretty much the same story she'd given Wilhelm. And Alice supposed it was mostly accurate, except that Belle was leaving out a few details. Still, Alice figured that under the circumstances, discretion was essential. No sense in scaring off these eligible bachelors.

"Well, that sounds interesting," said Craig. "And I am solidly behind anyone who wants to beautify our town, whether it's the flowerbeds or the women." He tapped Alice playfully on the arm.

"Is that a hint?" she teased him.

"No, of course not. You're one of those women who don't need much help in the beauty department. You and your sisters all are naturally good-looking."

She chuckled and turned to Belle. "See, that's why Craig is always welcome around the inn. He has a gift for blarney."

"Oh, sure," he said. "I suppose it has nothing to do with all the starts I give your sister, or how I help her out in times of need."

"Well, we do appreciate that too."

"You know," said Belle, "I'm thinking you would probably do wonderful wedding flowers."

"The best," said Craig. "Or perhaps I should be more modest. Alice, you tell her."

She laughed. "He *is* the best. He recently did a wedding for a friend and it was perfectly lovely."

"So, who's getting married?" asked Craig.

Belle giggled, then shrugged with what seemed embarrassment.

"It's a rather long story," explained Alice, feeling embarrassed herself. If she, or perhaps Jane, could simply take Craig aside and tell him privately, it might not seem so strange, but being forced to explain the dream story with Belle right there was almost more than Alice could bear.

Craig pointed his finger at Belle. "So, you're the one who's getting married?"

"I hope so."

"But do you plan to have the wedding here in Acorn Hill?"

"I do."

"And your husband-to-be doesn't mind moving here?"

"He already lives here."

Craig smiled. "I wonder if I know the lucky fellow." He scratched his head in thought, then started rattling off the same names that Alice and her family had gone over. "Am I even getting warm?" he finally asked Belle.

Alice grimaced. "It might be easier to simply tell him, Belle. Otherwise, he might pester everyone in town to figure it out."

"Yes," said Craig eagerly. "Let's just tell him."

Belle nodded but said nothing. So Alice quickly retold the story of Belle's dream, keeping her account as simple and straightforward as possible. Even so, she still felt silly afterward.

And Craig looked stunned. "No way."

Alice just nodded. Then Belle nodded. And Craig still looked unconvinced. "You girls are pulling my leg, right?"

"No," said Belle firmly. "The dream came from God and, so far, I think it's all right on track. So, seriously, could you schedule me in? I'd love for you to do my floral arrangements."

He still looked incredulous. "For the first Saturday in June?"

"That's right."

Craig glanced uneasily at Alice, and she just nodded with a look that was probably not very reassuring.

"Well, okay. I'll pencil it in. And you be sure to let me know when you find out who the lucky guy is, okay?"

Alice couldn't stop herself, she winked at Craig. "Maybe it's you."

He just nodded, albeit somewhat soberly. "Yeah, as soon as I get a dream from God, I'll get back to you on that."

"Thank you," said Belle politely.

"We better go now," said Alice. Then after Belle had turned around and started heading for the door, Alice turned back and gave him her best apologetic smile.

In response, he rolled his eyes. Then he called out pleasantly, "See you ladies around."

"That's the Clip 'n' Curl over there," Alice pointed out. "Would you like to meet Betty Dunkle now?"

"Yes," said Belle in a weary tone.

"Or, if you'd rather, we could go back to the inn or stop and get some pie?" offered Alice.

"No, no, I'd like to meet Betty."

So they went to the Clip 'n' Curl and without too much ado, introductions were made and Belle offered Betty a free facial. "Just so you can try out my products," she told her. "Then if you see fit, you could perhaps send customers my way."

"Sounds good," said Betty with a hint of impatience. A client was sitting across the room, waiting for Betty to finish her haircut.

The two of them quickly picked a day for the following week, and Belle handed Betty a pink business card. "That's my cell phone," she told her. "Or you might be able to reach me on the inn's phone. I plan to stay there awhile."

"Okay, will do." Betty picked up her scissors, getting ready to return to the interrupted haircut.

"I won't take up any more of your time," said Belle pleasantly. "I can see you're busy in your pretty little shop."

She started to leave, then paused. "But before I go, Betty, I should ask about whether you do hair for weddings."

"Sure," said Betty. "I do hair for just about any occasion."

"Oh, good," said Belle. "Do you think I could get you to schedule me in for the morning of the first Saturday of June?"

Betty frowned. "I might need to move something around, but I think I can do that." She smiled at Belle. "So, you're getting married? Good for you."

"Thank you."

"And you're having the wedding here in Acorn Hill?"

Belle nodded. "Yes. The ceremony will be in Grace Chapel, and the reception will be at the inn."

"Well, isn't that exciting." Betty made note of this in her appointment book. "Let me check on it and I'll get back to you."

"Thank you."

Belle seemed much happier as they exited the shop. Alice wondered if this was because she didn't have to explain all the details to Betty. Still, word was sure to get around before long. And what would people in town think when they discovered that Belle Bannister, guest of Grace Chapel Inn, was planning her wedding while on the lookout for her husband-to-be? Alice knew she was in way over her head. Really, Ethel was the sort of person to handle something like this. Or Jane. She still wondered how her younger sister had talked her into it.

"How about some pie?" asked Alice.

"Sounds heavenly."

As they walked through town toward the Coffee Shop, Alice thought that Belle's pace was slowing some. "How are your feet?" she asked.

"Oh, they're fine."

"How about the rest of you?"

"You want the truth?" Belle stopped walking and turned to look at Alice.

"Certainly."

"Well, the truth is, this is all a lot more trying than I'd expected. Oh, I didn't expect God to just plop Mr. Right straight into my lap. But I did think it would be a little easier. I didn't imagine myself wandering through the streets of Acorn Hill, beating the bushes until every last bachelor poked his head out."

Alice actually laughed. "Maybe that was more my aunt's doing."

"Maybe so. And I'm sure she twisted Jane's arm, and then Jane passed me off on you, and you've been a really good sport."

They started walking again and Alice told her that she didn't mind. "It's actually rather interesting."

"I just thought maybe Mr. Right would be the one to find me," said Belle wistfully. "Sort of like the sleeping princess being found by the prince."

"Yes, I suppose that's every girl's dream at some point in her life," Alice said, "but I don't think life is really like that, Belle."

They stopped in front of the Coffee Shop, and suddenly Belle reached over and grabbed Alice by the arm. "Wait a minute—what am I saying? That was almost exactly what happened this morning. I mean, it wasn't as if I was asleep, but I wasn't out scouring the neighborhood for a man either."

"What?" Alice tried to make sense of Belle's sudden change of mood.

"You see, I was simply minding my own business, coming down to breakfast. And the next thing I know, I am sitting across from the most handsome man, and he is just being charming. Almost as if God Himself had set the whole thing up for me. Don't you think so, Alice?"

"I don't understand. Who do you mean?"

"The pastor, of course." Belle's eyes were wide and bright again, but Alice felt concerned as she thought about Rev. Thompson being pursued by this persistent woman. Even so, Alice just nodded helplessly. "Yes, I suppose that's a possibility."

"And to think I was almost ready to give up." Belle beamed as she pushed open the door and walked confidently into the Coffee Shop.

"To think . . . " Alice mumbled as she trailed her bubbling companion, wondering if she still had as much of an appetite for pie right now as Belle did.

Chapter Seven

"Hey, you're back," said Hope when she saw Belle enter the Coffee Shop.

"I most assuredly am," said Belle happily.

"Hello, Hope," said Alice. "Goodness, isn't this sunshine wonderful?"

Hope grinned. "Absolutely." She waved a menu toward Fred Humbert, who was sitting at the counter with a cup of coffee. Fred was the owner of the town's hardware store and the local weather prognosticator. "Fred was just saying that the weather is going to be seasonal from now on. And he's really glad because he thought he was about to start growing moss on his back."

Alice chuckled. "How about the church basement, Fred? Jane told me there was a moisture problem. Any moss down there?"

He shook his head. "No. It didn't look too bad. I gave Rev. Thompson a couple cans of the best sealer ever made. You can even apply it to damp surfaces. I think he should have it under control before long."

"You're a friend of the pastor?" asked Belle.

Fred looked at Belle curiously, and Alice introduced her, saying she was a guest of the inn. "And Fred is the husband of my best friend Vera," she said in a way that she hoped didn't sound too protective. Surely, Belle wouldn't set her sights on a married man. "He owns the hardware store."

"Pleasure to meet you." He tipped his head politely.

"Any friend of the pastor's is a friend of mine," bubbled Belle.

"You're an old friend of Rev. Thompson?"

"No, no, but, all the same, it's an important little friendship," said Belle with a Scarlett O'Hara smile.

Surprised, Fred looked questioningly at Alice, who shrugged and gave him an uneasy smile.

"We're here for pie, Hope," Alice said as she selected a vacant booth, scooting across the familiar red vinyl seat.

"This is such a fun little place," said Belle as she slid onto the seat across from her, pressing her palms together with happy anticipation. "It reminds me of a café in Warbler, back when I was a kid. But that place went out of business years ago."

"So, what can I get for you two?" asked Hope.

"Tea and pie for me," said Alice. "I'll have the blackberry."

"À la mode?"

"Of course, à la mode," said Belle with enthusiasm. "And this is my treat, Alice. A little thank-you for taking me about town today."

"À la mode then?" Hope directed this to Alice.

"Oh yes, that would be very nice."

"And you, Belle?"

"Oh, that's so sweet, you even remember my name." Belle smiled. "You know what, Hope, I would love to give you a free facial. What do you think?"

"You think I need a facial?" Hope looked distressed. She automatically patted her dark hair, as if to improve her appearance. Hope cared a great deal about her looks, and Alice hoped she wasn't insulted by Belle's offer.

"She's an Angel Face beauty consultant," explained Alice. "She gave my sisters and me facials last night." She purposely didn't mention Ethel.

"Really?" Hope looked interested. "Sure, I'd like that, Belle."

Belle slipped a pink business card to Hope. "Invite a couple of your friends, if you like. It's more fun with a few girls to giggle with."

"That sounds like fun. Now, what kind of pie would you like?"

"Oh my . . . let me think. How about coconut cream? Do you have that?"

"We do."

"Yummy. And a cup of coffee with cream, please."

"Coming right up."

Alice noticed Lloyd Tynan coming through the door. He must've been feeling positive about the weather when he dressed this morning because he looked ready for some May sunshine in his pale blue seersucker suit and jaunty red silk bow tie. Lloyd spoke briefly with Fred Humbert, then waved toward Alice and Belle, making Alice suspect that Ethel had already spoken to him, just as Jane had promised.

"Good day, ladies." He wore his mayoral smile as he approached them. "This must be Miss Belle Bannister." He extended his hand. "I am Lloyd Tynan."

"Oh my," said Belle as she put her hand into his. "I just can't believe that people already know my name. Goodness, I feel almost famous. It's a genuine pleasure to meet you, Mr. Tynan. But how did you know me?"

"My good friend Ethel Buckley told me about the inn's most recent guest. I merely assumed it was you."

Belle looked nervous as she lowered her voice. "And how is dear Ethel doing?"

"A bit under the weather, I'm afraid." He frowned. "Apparently she had an allergic reaction to something yesterday." He looked at Alice. "I understand she had dinner with you folks."

Alice suppressed the urge to set her aunt's beau straight.

"Oh, I'm sure it wasn't anything she ate last night," said Belle quickly. "Jane's cooking is perfectly exquisite."

Lloyd smiled at Belle. "Well, as the mayor of Acorn Hill, I officially welcome you to our fair town."

"Why, thank you ever so much, Mayor Tynan."

"Call me Lloyd," he said amicably.

"Would you like to join us, Lloyd?"

"Don't mind if I do." He slipped in next to Alice, keeping his eyes on Belle. "I understand that you're a Southern belle, Belle."

She giggled. "That's right, sir. Born and raised in Georgia. I'd guess I'm about as southern as they come."

Hope came over with their order. "Anything besides coffee for you, Lloyd?"

He looked at Belle's pie and actually smacked his lips. "Is that coconut-cream pie?"

Belle nodded. "It looks yummy, doesn't it?"

"I'll have a slice of that too, Hope," he said.

"Are you sure?" queried Hope.

"Well, make it a small slice," he said. Then he gave Alice a warning glance. "And you don't need to tell anyone that I cheated on my diet today."

She laughed as she remembered how many times he'd sneaked sweets from Jane's kitchen. "Goodness, Lloyd, if

I'd wanted to tattle on you, I could have done so many times over."

"Yes, I suppose that's true. But just so you know, I had oatmeal with skim milk for breakfast this morning."

"Good for you," said Alice.

Lloyd, as usual, dominated the conversation, directing most of it toward Belle. But Alice was relieved for this reprieve. It wasn't that she didn't enjoy Belle's company, but the idea of the impending wedding was beginning to wear on her.

"I'm pleased to hear you like our town," he said to Belle, "but what about our bachelors? Anyone out there that looks like marriage material?"

Belle waved her hand at Lloyd, feigning, it seemed to Alice, embarrassment. "Well, I've only met a few, mind you, but from what I've seen, there are some good prospects out there."

"You know that our mayor is single too?" asked Alice, then instantly regretted her words. She knew that Ethel considered Lloyd off-limits.

"Why, I can't imagine what's wrong with the good women of Acorn Hill to let a fine specimen of a man like you slip through the matrimonial net."

He chuckled. "It's not for lack of trying, my dear."

Alice had expected him to mention her aunt as part of the reason he was still unmarried. And to her surprise, she felt defensive that he had not.

"Then tell me, Lloyd," said Belle as she fluttered her long eyelashes, "what exactly is it that keeps a good man like you from surrendering to matrimonial bliss?"

"Are you asking out of your own personal interest?" Lloyd cocked his head to one side, using what seemed an almost flirtatious tone. "Or are you simply collecting information to use against a particular male who may be resistant to your obvious charms?"

She waved her hand at him again. "Oh, you are so terribly sweet. I'll bet sugar doesn't even melt in your mouth."

He chuckled. "Well, I suppose if the truth be told—I mean if I were to address the primary reason that I seem unable to surrender to matrimony—it would be that I simply enjoy being a bachelor."

"But don't you get lonely sometimes?" She leaned forward.

"As mayor, I have a rather full life, Belle. I'm included in the major social functions, and I get invited to dinner a lot. I don't really have time to be lonely."

"Lloyd is a very social person," said Alice.

"But what about on a cold winter's evening?" persisted Belle. "When you're home alone, don't you just crave someone warm to cuddle up to?"

Lloyd looked as embarrassed as Alice felt by this rather personal question. He seemed relieved when Hope set a piece of pie before him. "My, my, but doesn't this look good."

"This may be a challenge for you," warned Hope. "I would've given you a smaller piece, but June had already cut up the pie."

Lloyd sunk his fork into the fluffy confection. "Thank you, Hope."

"Did you hear that the church basement suffered some water damage?" Alice attempted to redirect a conversation to a safer topic.

"No," said Lloyd. "Is it serious?"

She explained what little she knew of the situation to him, then turned to Belle. "Lloyd is on the church board of Grace Chapel."

"Oh," said Belle. "I had the pleasure of meeting Rev. Thompson this morning." She sighed. "He seems like a wonderful person."

"He's a very good man," said Lloyd. Then he glanced at Alice with a questioning look. "And he's also a bachelor." The last word came out very slowly.

"Yes," said Belle. "I know."

"Aha," Lloyd nodded knowingly. "Our good pastor is a viable candidate then?"

Belle tipped her head down and smiled shyly. "Well, God did send me that dream, Lloyd. I simply cannot rule out anyone just yet."

"Not even an old mayor?" teased Lloyd as he straightened his bow tie.

"Not even a charming mayor."

Alice had a strong urge to point out that Lloyd was almost old enough to be Belle's grandfather, but she stopped herself. Alice felt certain that Lloyd could never seriously fall for Belle's Southern allure. Although it was interesting: Belle in some ways reminded Alice of Ethel. They were both short and plump. They both enjoyed playing up their feminine charms. But, to be perfectly fair, Belle was softer around the edges than their occasionally sharp-tongued and somewhat bossy aunt. Still, it seemed preposterous to think that Lloyd would be seriously interested. No, Alice was convinced that she was simply witnessing some good-natured, harmless flirting.

She glanced out the window to see that the sun was still shining. "I've given Belle a partial tour of town, Lloyd, but with this wonderful change of weather, I wonder if I shouldn't check in at the inn. It's possible that Louise has booked guests." Even as she said this, Alice felt it was probably unlikely. "I probably should get back to help out."

"I have heard that the nasty weather is supposed to be over for now." Lloyd nodded toward Belle. "Maybe Belle brought this good weather with her from the South."

Belle giggled. "Well, I must admit it was lovely down there when I left."

Alice set down her fork, acting as if she'd just come up with a good solution. "I have an idea. Perhaps you could finish showing Belle around town, Lloyd. If you're not too busy, I mean."

"I'd be pleased to," said Lloyd. "That is, if Belle doesn't mind."

"Mind?" She shook her head. "Of course not. I would be honored to have the mayor as an escort."

"Ethel mentioned some people I might introduce you to," said Lloyd.

"And don't forget to stop by Time for Tea," said Alice. "Wilhelm is mixing a special tea for her."

"Oh yes," said Belle. "That's right. He was such a sweet man. I can't wait to try what he's put together."

"Thanks for the pie, Belle," said Alice, waiting for Lloyd to stand up so she could get out of the booth. "Now, if you two will excuse me, I'll head back to the inn and see if business is brightening up with the weather."

"That reminds me," said Belle. "I completely forgot to ask Louise if she would reserve another room for me for the first weekend of June and perhaps a couple of days prior to that, starting on Wednesday to Sunday or even Monday."

"A room for yourself?" asked Alice, confused.

"No, I already asked Louise to reserve my room until that weekend." She turned to Lloyd. "Oh, I'm staying in the most beautiful room. It's called the Symphony Room with rose wallpaper that's simply lovely."

"Louise picked out that wallpaper," said Alice.

"I want to reserve the second room for my parents," said Belle. "After all, I wouldn't want them to miss my big day."

"Your big day?" asked Lloyd.

"Oh yes," said Belle. "Perhaps Ethel didn't tell you, but my dream came with a date for my wedding. I'm to be married on the first Saturday of June."

"Really?" Lloyd slowly shook his head. "That seems hasty, Belle. Especially considering that you haven't got a specific man lined up just yet."

Alice patted Lloyd on the back and grinned. "I guess that's where you come in, Lloyd. While you're touring the town, you'll have to make sure that Belle continues to meet Acorn Hill's most available bachelors."

Lloyd looked uncertain.

"Oh my," Lloyd nervously adjusted his bow tie, which was already straight.

"I better get on my way," said Alice as she left Lloyd and Belle. She waved from the door. "You have a nice day."

"Bye, Alice," called Hope. "Enjoy the sunshine."

"I will," said Alice as she exited the Coffee Shop. She paused on the sidewalk to take in a long, deep breath of fresh air. As she hurried back to the inn, she felt like a kid who'd just gotten an early release from school. She just hoped that Ethel wouldn't mind her foisting Belle onto Lloyd like that. But Jane had foisted Belle onto Alice. Besides, Ethel had asked Lloyd to help.

By the time Alice reached home, she decided to check on her aunt before going to the inn. Perhaps Ethel needed more medical attention. But to her surprise, Jane was at her aunt's house—probably salving her guilt for having assigned Alice to Belle's tour. She had brought over some leftovers from last night's dinner for their aunt's lunch.

"How are you feeling, Auntie?" asked Alice, seeing that her aunt's face was still quite puffy and red.

"Better, I suppose," said Ethel as Jane set a cup of tea next to her, "but I'm afraid I don't look much better."

"Well, it looks like you've had a serious allergic reaction." Alice bent down to examine the raised hives more closely. "Something this severe might take several days to clear up completely."

"Poor Auntie," said Jane, sitting down on the couch beside Ethel and rearranging the pale peach afghan that covered her aunt's legs.

"Is there anything I can get for you?" offered Alice.

"I only want to know how our Belle is getting along."

"Just fine."

"I would so enjoy showing her around town," said Ethel. "But not looking like this, of course. I do hope that Belle finds her man. I think it would be such fun to have a wedding and see her happily settled in Acorn Hill. Belle even told me that I might be one of her bridesmaids." She chuckled. "Imagine me, a bridesmaid."

Alice tried *not* to imagine it. At least not with her aunt looking like she did at the moment.

"Tea, Alice?" offered Jane.

"No, thanks. I just had pie and tea with Belle." She turned back to her aunt. "In fact, Lloyd joined us at the Coffee Shop."

"Oh, good for him. I asked him to help out. Did he seem to mind terribly?"

"Not at all. In fact, I even coerced him into finishing Belle's tour for me. I thought I might be of more use back at the inn. With this sudden change in weather, I'm hoping that Louise might be getting some bookings. Or perhaps some of the cancellations will reconsider now."

"Yes," agreed Jane. "That does seem likely. By the way, Alice, thanks for covering for me. I owe you one."

Alice chuckled. "Yes, we'll discuss that later."

"I have no worries that Lloyd will do a good job of introducing Belle about," said Ethel. "No one knows Acorn Hill as well as my Lloyd."

"Except for you, Auntie." Alice stood. She felt more tired than if she'd spent a whole day at the hospital. "Since all seems well over here, I think I'll head back to the inn."

Alice paused to look at Jane's garden before going into the inn and remembered the letter that had come for Jane the day before. Perhaps if Jane really did feel she owed Alice a favor, she might be willing to explain what Justin's letter was about.

Chapter Eight

*L*ouise," said Alice as she entered the front hall office area. "Belle asked me to have you reserve another room for her." Then she repeated the dates and for whom the room was intended.

Louise frowned. "Do you think she honestly believes she's going to be married on that date?"

"She seems sincere."

"Oh my." Louise shook her head as she jotted down the reservation. "I'm afraid she is setting herself up for disappointment."

"But what if she's right?" questioned Alice. "I do understand your concern, Louise, and I do think it sounds bizarre, but the more I hear Belle talk, the more I wonder if it might not actually happen. It's possible that God sent Belle that dream."

"I suppose it's possible. It just seems highly unlikely. But suppose Belle did manage to garner the interest of one of Acorn Hill's eligible bachelors, and suppose this fellow did propose marriage and even agreed to her preposterous wedding date: What if the marriage turned out to be an enormous mistake? Wouldn't that be terribly sad?"

Alice nodded. "Yes, of course. On the other hand, well-meaning people get married all the time, often under what seems the best of circumstances, and yet about half the marriages in this country end in divorce. Look at what happened to our own Jane."

"Yes, you make a good point." Louise sighed. "I think I am just very old-fashioned when it comes to marriage. There's a right way to go about things and a wrong way. And I feel she's is going the wrong way."

"Who's going the wrong way?" asked Jane as she entered the hall from the kitchen.

"Belle," said Louise and Alice simultaneously.

"Oh," Jane sighed, "I thought you were talking about me."

"Actually, we were talking about marriage."

"Right." Jane looked curiously at her sisters. There seemed to be something they weren't saying.

"I was simply telling Alice," explained Louise, "that Belle's unconventional attitude toward matrimony might land her in divorce court later on down the line."

"And I said that even marriages that start out on the right foot can end in divorce," added Alice.

"So, it's the luck of the draw?" asked Jane teasingly.

"I wouldn't say that," said Louise. "I'm simply saying that I feel worried for Belle. I hope she's not devastated."

"Or maybe she'll find Mr. Right and live happily ever after," said Jane.

"I guess time will tell," said Alice.

"It always does," said Louise. "Well, I'll go ahead and reserve these dates for Belle's parents. Although I'd be surprised if there's a need for them to come. Goodness, do you think she's told them about her dream? I couldn't imagine how I'd feel if Cynthia informed me of something like this. I'd think she had taken leave of her senses."

"Our niece is far too sensible to do anything like that," said Alice.

Louise frowned. "Of course, to be perfectly honest, I'd love to see Cynthia married. I'd love to have grandchildren. And at the rate she's going, midthirties and not even seriously dating, well, perhaps I'll pray to the good Lord to send her a dream too."

Jane laughed. "Louise, I'm shocked."

"I'm joking, of course."

"Of course," said Alice.

"Oh, by the way, we have guests coming tomorrow. They'll be here through the weekend. I even took it upon myself to call one of the cancellations, just to let them know the weather has improved and the inn is getting busy again, and she said she'd speak to her husband about coming."

"So things are looking up," said Alice.

"Yes. I think our slump is over."

"Well, I hope we're nice and full up for the next few months." Jane had briefly wondered about asking Louise to reserve a room for Justin, but then thought otherwise. The idea of having him under the same roof for even one night was just completely unnerving. For the sake of everyone, she sincerely hoped that all rooms would be occupied when, and if, Justin actually made an appearance.

Jane went to the kitchen and began to putter. First she cleaned out the refrigerator, then she gave the sink a good scrubbing. But cleaning didn't distract her from her thoughts about Justin. Why was he coming? What did he want? When their marriage finally deteriorated, she had purposely blocked out the happy memories from their early married life. Perhaps it had been a form of self-preservation—a way to prevent her aching heart from hurting even more. But now, thanks to that letter, these memories seemed to be coming at her from left and right. Now she found herself reliving their first date, although Justin hadn't called it a date. He'd invited her to dinner, saying that he wanted someone to go with him to the dining room at the Fairmont Hotel so that he could check out the new chef there and try some of the dishes that the reviewers were raving about.

She had dressed carefully in a sapphire jersey dress that the salesgirl said made her blue eyes bluer. She wore strappy patent leather high heels and put on dangling free-form silver earrings. Finally, she swept her hair back in an elegant twist. She could tell he was surprised and pleased by her appearance when he came to pick her up. As cowork-ers, they had only before seen each other in jeans or chefs' uniforms. She was impressed by how handsome and trim he looked in his blue blazer and gray slacks. His curly blond hair was freshly trimmed and his face showed no trace of the five o'clock shadow that he sported every evening at the restaurant. Naturally, they paid great attention to the dishes they ordered, trying to detect which seasoning and herbs were used. And their conversation was easy, filled with friendly banter. By the time their dessert arrived, it was clear they were on a date—a very exciting date.

After that, they went out frequently, visiting many of the finest restaurants in San Francisco, including places like Bix and Chez Spencer and Ana Mandara. They also shared a love of the outdoors and hiked in the hills, explor-ing Monterey, Big Sur and other coastal towns. They took turns making picnic lunches and meals for each other, one trying to surprise and delight the other.

A clear memory of one of those picnics rose in Jane's mind. Justin had told her to dress casually but refused to say much else. They drove up Highway 1 in a borrowed convertible. It was a warm, sunny day, and the view of the coastline was breathtaking. They stopped at times to look at the sea, the breakers crashing on rocks, and occasional groups of surfers waiting for a wave. Eventually, Justin turned off the highway and onto a sandy road along the edge of a cliff, announcing it was time for lunch.

Selecting a smooth sandy area near the cliff's edge, they spread out a red plaid woolen blanket. Then Jane watched with amusement as Justin opened a picnic basket, setting out china, silver and glasses. He had prepared crabmeat sandwiches on thin slices of homemade bread, and a bowl of arugula salad with blue cheese and toasted pine nuts, as well as a cruet of his delicious secret salad dressing. Dessert was a selection of tartlets and cookies served along with peach iced tea. She didn't say so, but Jane felt this was a perfect setup for a marriage proposal. And it was a perfect day—the food, the company, the scenery. The only thing missing was the ring.

Then, suddenly, things changed. The wind picked up, the clouds rolled in, and they hurriedly packed things up. They returned to the car, Justin put the top up, and they quietly drove home. Despite the lovely day, Jane felt let down. She knew she was in love with Justin by then. And she desperately wanted him to feel the same way. Several pleasant but uneventful dates followed, and Jane began to think that marriage was not in Justin's plans.

About a month later, Justin invited her to dinner at the Cliff House. He had reserved a table that overlooked the sea, and midway through the meal they enjoyed a magnificent sunset, watching in awe until the last brilliant shades of orange and red faded into purple. Then, just as they finished a wonderful and filling meal, despite Jane's protests, Justin insisted on ordering dessert for both of them. Minutes later, the waiter set an incredible nest of spun sugar on the table. Jane was just marveling at the pretty confection when she noticed a small blue velvet box inside. Justin feigned surprise but suggested she open it. Inside was an impressive solitaire diamond, exquisitely set in platinum. Then Justin took her hand in his and said the words she had been longing to hear. "Jane Howard, will you marry me?"

"Stop it," Jane scolded herself out loud as she came out of her reverie still holding the sponge and scouring powder above the sink. These memories were not helping her mental state in the least. What she needed right now was a good project, something consuming enough to distract her from obsessing over Justin like this. She took down her mother's old cookbook and sat down at the table to peruse it. There must be something in it that would be a challenge to make. Wendell hopped into her lap and, as she flipped through the pages with one hand, she smoothed his silky coat with the other. It was amazing how calming it was to pet an animal. She felt as if her anxiety diminished with each stroke.

"Hello?" a hushed male voice spoke from the back porch.

She gently set a disappointed Wendell down and went to the door. She was surprised to see Rev. Thompson there. "Come in," she said. "To what do I owe the pleasure of your company three times in one day?"

He glanced over her shoulder. "Belle isn't around, is she?"

Jane laughed. "No, but she should be back in an hour or so. Would you like me to give her a message for you?"

"No, I would not." He gave her a stern look. "Jane Howard, I thought you were my friend. And, suddenly, I feel as if I've been blindsided by you."

"By me?"

"Yes. Inviting me to breakfast, introducing me to Belle, bringing her to the church. What exactly are you up to anyway?"

Her eyes widened in surprise. "I am not up to anything, Kenneth Thompson. Belle just happened to show up at our door without a reservation. And she just happened to have a particular mission as the result of what she honestly believes was a God-given dream. I do not see how you can possibly blame any of that on me."

"*Hmm.*" He glanced over at the coffeemaker. "Got any decaf?"

"I can certainly make some."

"Oh, don't go to any trouble."

"You know it's no trouble." Besides, she thought, she'd been looking for a distraction. Kenneth would work just fine.

"I felt bad when we walked in on you in the sanctuary. I had no idea you were up there, hiding behind the pulpit."

He chuckled. "Yes, you know me, always hiding behind the pulpit."

"I didn't mean it like that."

"No, you meant I was lurking, just waiting to pounce on unsuspecting visitors."

"No. I just meant I didn't plan to pop in on you like that, but Belle wanted to see the inside of the chapel."

"So she could make wedding plans?"

"Well, yes." Jane turned away from him to make the coffee.

"Don't you think that's rather strange?"

"Yes, as a matter of fact, I do think it's strange." She turned to face him. "But, Rev. Thompson, wasn't last Sunday's sermon about not judging?"

He smiled weakly, then nodded. "Yes, Jane. You are right. I guess I should pay better attention."

Jane grinned. "Or maybe God just wanted to press your lesson home. So you'd really have it down well."

"Forgive me, Jane. I have been judgmental."

"If it's any comfort, you're not the only one. In fact, the only one who hasn't judged Belle seems to be Aunt Ethel. Although I think it's simply because she's caught up in the glamour and excitement of having a wedding. And, of course, she does like Belle."

"That doesn't surprise me."

"Hungry?"

He shrugged. "I already sponged one meal off the inn, I shouldn't—"

"Oh, come on, Kenneth. I consider it an honor to feed you. It's like making a church donation."

He made a face. "You do have a way of making a guy feel at home."

"I had a cookie a bit ago," she confessed as she opened the fridge. "But I'm hungry for something healthy. How about a nice Caesar salad with some grilled chicken?"

"*Mmm.* Sounds terrific. Need any help?"

"Just help yourself to some coffee and take a seat. I need company right now." She wished she hadn't said that last line. It seemed an open invitation to an inquiry, and she just was not ready to discuss her concern over Justin's impending visit quite yet. And so she decided to keep the conversation flowing in another direction.

"Due to Aunt Ethel's allergy problems, I was chosen to escort Belle around town." Then, as she got out the ingredients for the salad, she told him about how she'd shoved that pleasure off on poor, unsuspecting Alice.

"You have been naughty," said Kenneth.

"I know," she admitted. "You should've heard Alice a little while ago. She was in here giving me the details. It was seriously funny."

"Sometimes I think you have a warped sense of humor, Jane."

"Well, listen to this," she persisted. "Alice took Belle into Wild Things, where Belle decided to order wedding flowers from Craig. When he discovered that the flowers were for Belle's wedding, but she didn't have a groom, he was flabbergasted. And, can you believe it, our sweet Alice had the nerve to point out that, as an Acorn Hill bachelor, Craig Tracy was also on the list of candidates."

"Alice did that?"

"She did. Naturally, she regretted it right away, but she was a little flustered at the time. And Alice said Craig looked perfectly horrified."

Kenneth laughed loudly. "Oh, you're making me feel much better now."

"So, you see, you are definitely not alone."

"It's really odd, isn't it?"

"Very." Jane flipped some chicken on the grill, then went back to finish tossing the romaine lettuce in the dressing.

"It's not that she doesn't seem to be a nice person," he continued as she sliced some sourdough bread, "and she's attractive enough, but she's a little scary too."

"Especially if you're a bachelor." Then she told him how Alice had felt a little bit guilty for leaving Belle with Lloyd.

"Why is that?"

"She was afraid they were sort of hitting it off."

"Really?"

Jane removed a piece of chicken from the grill and quickly sliced it into strips, neatly arranging these on their individual salads. Then she brought the salads and bread and joined Kenneth at the table, waiting as he said grace.

"You didn't answer me, Jane. Alice didn't really think Lloyd would be interested in Belle, did she?"

She chuckled. "Well, she said that he truly seemed to like her, enough to make Alice uncomfortable. But you know how she's sensitive to people's feelings. I suppose she felt bad for Aunt Ethel."

"Can't say that I blame her."

"Oh, I'm sure it was harmless flirting. Lloyd was probably flattered by the attentions of a young, pretty woman."

"And he was probably just being the congenial mayor."

"Also, to be fair, Aunt Ethel had called Lloyd, asking him to help with Belle. She so wanted to be the one to take Belle around and introduce her to everyone. She's quite taken with Belle."

"Yes, I can imagine that. How is your aunt feeling anyway?"

"She says that she's better, but she still looks rather frightening."

"Poor Ethel. Maybe I should pay her a visit this afternoon."

"Maybe not. I don't think she cares to be seen, not until her face goes back to normal. I know that she doesn't intend to let Lloyd see her like this."

"Understandable. Ethel does care about appearances." He took another bite. "By the way, this is delicious, Jane." He winked at her. "Anytime you want to make a donation to church, you just let me know."

"Okay, now that I've gotten you all relaxed about Belle, I think it's only fair to warn you."

He looked up in mild alarm. "About what?"

"Well, as far as I can see, and Alice confirmed it, Belle has placed a certain Acorn Hill cleric at the top of her eligible-bachelors list."

"Oh my." He shook his head. "Is there any way to get my name off her list?"

Jane shrugged and took another bite.

"Perhaps you could dissuade her, Jane?"

"She's a pretty determined gal. I think if anyone is going to dissuade her, it'll have to be you."

"I was afraid you were going to say that."

"Don't you think straightforward is usually the best approach?"

"Yes. And that is exactly how I would advise someone else in my shoes. Funny how things change when you are the person in an uncomfortable position." He frowned. "I just don't want to hurt her feelings. Despite not wanting to be on her list, I do think she's a sweet and sensitive person. I think she means well. And I'm sure that she believes her dream is from God. And, as you pointed out, who am I to judge?"

"I don't really see that it would hurt her feelings, Kenneth. After all, she wants to marry God's pick for her. Surely, she must understand that there will be some rejection involved. I mean, going about looking for a husband like this is bound to result in a few disappointments. But she shouldn't take it personally."

"You're right." But even as he said this, Jane got the feeling he wasn't convinced.

"But you still don't want to tell her?"

"I don't even know how I'd go about it. What do I do? Simply walk up and say, 'Belle, I have no intention of marrying you'? That seems presumptuous."

"Yes, I see your point. Well, perhaps just let life take its course, and if marriage comes up, which I'm sure it will, be honest and kind to her."

"Most definitely." He grinned. "In the meantime, you'll excuse me if I lay low?"

"That's a long time to lay low, Kenneth. She will probably be on the hunt for a good two weeks."

"Too bad I couldn't go on vacation for a couple of weeks."

"Chicken."

"Certainly," he said, "I'd love some more chicken."

"Oh, you!" But she got up and took another piece off the grill, sliced it and placed it on the remainder of his salad.

"Thank you."

"You know, Louise and Alice were discussing Belle's wedding tactics, and they came to a rather interesting conclusion."

"What's that?"

"Well, there are people who get married for what seem the right reasons, but still many of those marriages end in divorce. Then there are others whom you'd never expect to make it to their first anniversary, and they stay happily married for years. Sometimes there really seems to be no rhyme or reason to marital success. I wonder if it's just the luck of the draw."

"That's a rather cynical view, Jane."

"Perhaps I'm being negative."

"I happen to believe that marriage really was designed by God."

"Yes, of course you would."

"Catherine and I were very happily married before she passed away, and so I have good reason to believe that a godly marriage has a much greater chance of succeeding than a marriage where God is left out."

"So, you think Belle should have a successful marriage?"

"I think if she does indeed marry a godly man, and if they are genuinely in love, well, yes, I would think her chances would be better than average."

"But you don't want to be that man?"

He shook his fork at her. "Jane, Jane, Jane."

"So, do you think that my marriage would've succeeded if Justin had been a godly man? Not that I was such a godly woman when we married. I had rebelled against my roots, you know. Perhaps that in itself destined us to failure."

"Not necessarily. I've known couples who were wed without having God in the picture at the time. Then one comes around, perhaps the other one does too, and they end up being happily married for the rest of their days."

"So what you're saying is that without God, marriage is tricky."

"You do have a way of boiling things down, Jane."

"Just call me a poached philosopher."

They chatted a bit longer and were just finishing up lunch when they heard Belle calling out. "Jane, dear? Are you in there?"

"Excuse me," Kenneth jumped to his feet, dabbed his lips with the napkin, then whispered a thank-you and made a hasty exit.

Jane laughed as she cleared their salad plates. "Coming, Belle," she called as she went through the swinging door to find Belle in the dining room.

Belle held up a little brown bag. "Wilhelm mixed me up the most delicious batch of tea, and I hoped I might beg some hot water from you."

"Of course," said Jane. "Usually we have it out in the dining room, but without many guests, I sort of forgot. Let me get it for you."

"Oh, thank you," gushed Belle.

"I'll be just a few minutes." Jane took the thermos pitcher and retreated to the kitchen. She turned on the tea-kettle and quickly disposed of any evidence that Kenneth had just eaten lunch with her. Of course, she knew that Belle had no idea, but even so, Jane felt guilty.

"Here you go," said Jane as she set the pitcher on the sideboard. "Enough water here for a whole pot if you like. And as you can see, the teapot and cups and sugar and whatnot are right there. Do you need cream?"

"No, I never put cream in tea." Belle opened the bag and held it toward Jane. "Just smell that. Isn't it heavenly?"

Louise came into the dining room. "Did I hear talk of tea?" she asked hopefully.

"Belle has a special blend," said Jane.

"That's right," said Belle. "Would y'all care to join me?" She held out the packet for Louise to sniff.

"It smells like peaches," said Louise, "and spices?"

"That's exactly right," gushed Belle. "It's called Southern Belle. Wilhelm named it after me."

"Wasn't that nice," said Louise, suddenly curious if Wilhelm might be taken with a certain southern Belle. Louise had been telling Wilhelm for years now that he would be quite a catch for the right woman. Was Belle that woman?

"Won't you have some?" asked their guest as she filled the teapot with hot water. "Both of you."

"If you'll excuse me," said Jane. "I've got something I need to tend to in the kitchen."

"I'd love to have some tea," said Louise as she set out two cups.

Soon the tea was brewed, and they both sat down at the table. Louise waited as Belle filled her cup, then she took a cautious sip. It was a bit too flowery for her taste, but refreshing.

"Oh, this is simply wonderful," said Belle. "I'll have to tell Wilhelm to keep it on hand for me."

"And what did you think of Wilhelm?" asked Louise. "Alice mentioned that he seemed to like you. Any possibility that he might be the one?"

"Well, it's hard to say. Although I do think Wilhelm seemed interested in getting better acquainted. He was quite friendly. Then, when Lloyd asked me if I played bridge and I said that I do, Wilhelm seemed pleased. Lloyd even suggested that we might set up a bridge night this weekend. Lloyd and Ethel and Wilhelm and me. I said that sounded nice, and Wilhelm seemed quite agreeable."

"That sounds promising."

"I suppose." Belle frowned. "Except that I don't want to give Rev. Thompson the wrong idea."

"The wrong idea?" Louise's eyebrows lifted.

"I don't want him thinking I've set my sights on Wilhelm."

"Oh, I'm sure no one will think that, Belle. It only makes sense that you should get acquainted with the eligible bachelors of Acorn Hill."

"Yes, I suppose that's true." Belle brightened. "Besides, it might not hurt to make the pastor feel threatened by Wilhelm."

"Threatened?"

"Oh, you know what they say about jealousy. Or maybe I'm thinking of distance, but I do think it makes the heart grow fonder. Sometimes people need a little push to help them realize what they might be missing."

"I see." Louise finished her tea and thanked Belle for it. "Now, if you'll excuse me, I have some office work that I need to tend to." She paused before she left. "Oh, and although we don't normally invite guests staying at the inn to join us for dinner, since you're our only guest at the moment, you're more than welcome to join us again tonight."

"No, but thank you very much." Belle carried her teacup back to the sideboard. "I actually have plans for tonight."

"Really?"

"Yes. Lloyd invited me to join Ethel and him for bingo this evening." She clapped her hands together. "I just adore that game. Oh, Louise, I'm feeling so at home here already. It's just wonderful. And Lloyd mentioned that they'll be serving hot dogs and chili tonight. So I won't need to bother you about dinner. But thanks so much anyway." She picked up her purse and package of tea. "And y'all have a good evening."

Louise wondered if she should make some attempt to stop Belle and tell her that Ethel was most certainly not going to bingo or anywhere else tonight. But it was too late. Belle was already on her way up the stairs. She probably needed to put her feet up after traipsing around the town in those high-heeled shoes all day. Louise couldn't even begin to figure out how she did it.

Louise felt she had a minor dilemma on her hands. Should she tell Ethel that Lloyd had invited Belle to bingo? Or would Ethel even care? After all, it was Ethel who wanted to take Belle under her wing to start with. Surely, Belle had no designs on Lloyd. As Louise checked the inn's e-mail, she decided this really wasn't her problem. Let Lloyd and Aunt Ethel sort it out. Despite everyone's attempts to draw Louise into Belle's strange wedding scheme, this guest was not Louise's personal responsibility.

Chapter Nine

"How is our wedding Belle doing?" asked Alice as the three sisters ate dinner.

"She seemed happy as a clam when I saw her just a few minutes ago," said Jane. "She was on her way to bingo night."

"Bingo night?" Alice blinked. "I'm surprised she figured that one out already."

"Lloyd invited her to go with Aunt Ethel and him," offered Louise as she dished out some salad.

"But Aunt Ethel is home," said Alice.

"I know," said Jane as she passed the platter of pasta to her. "I just took some dinner over to her. She still looks pretty bad."

"Poor Auntie," said Alice. "I suggested aloe vera. It worked wonders for me when I got bee stings. But she wouldn't hear of it. She doesn't want anything to touch her face until the rash clears up, and she's worried that she may be scarred forever."

"She won't be, will she?" asked Louise.

"No, her reaction wasn't that severe," said Alice.

"So, just for clarification," said Jane, "is Lloyd still taking Belle to bingo tonight, without Aunt Ethel?"

"That's my assumption," said Louise.

"Now that you mention it," said Alice. "I do believe his car was in front."

"Don't you think that is a bit odd?" asked Jane.

"Oh, Jane," said Alice. "It's not as if he and Belle are on a date. I'm sure Lloyd was just being friendly and—"

"Going out with a woman who's on a manhunt," added Jane.

"But look at their age difference," said Alice. "Goodness, Lloyd practically could be her grandfather. I'm sure he's simply trying to make Belle feel at home."

"But what about Aunt Ethel?" asked Jane. "How is she going to feel when she finds out?"

"Perhaps she knows," suggested Alice hopefully. "I'll bet she encouraged Lloyd to take her."

Louise looked at Jane. "What do you think? You were just over at our aunt's house. Was she aware of this little development?"

Jane shrugged. "I don't know for sure. She did mention being disappointed that she wasn't going, but I think she said something about Belle's missing out as well. She may have assumed that Belle wouldn't be going either. Or maybe I'm wrong. I couldn't really say."

"Well, I'm worried about this situation," declared Louise. "As soon as Aunt Ethel gets a phone call from one of her friends, inquiring about the young blonde woman accompanying Lloyd, Auntie will be furious."

"Oh, come now, Louise," said Alice. "You make our aunt sound like a shrew. She will probably explain to the curious caller that she's not feeling well and that Lloyd is simply doing her a favor by taking Belle with him tonight."

Jane laughed. "You probably know our aunt better than anyone else, Alice. But the part you left out is that after she hangs up the phone she will begin to fuss and fume, and she will most likely need her ruffled feathers smoothed."

"And I'd be happy to help smooth them," said Alice.

"Speaking of Belle," said Louise. "Did Kenneth recover from his encounter with her at breakfast?"

Jane laughed. "Oh, I think so."

"What happened?" asked Alice.

So they both told her about Belle's happy discovery that Kenneth was single and how she told him about her dream.

"You should've seen his face," said Jane.

"He actually choked on a bite," added Louise. "Poor man."

"But he should be flattered," said Alice. "Belle is a nice young woman. Pretty too. Surely, he didn't take her seriously."

"But she *is* serious," said Jane. "How could he not take her seriously?"

"Because he knows, of course, that he is not Mr. Right. Certainly, not her Mr. Right anyway. At least I don't think he is. Do you?"

"No, not really," said Jane. "Although it was interesting seeing our usual cool, calm and reserved pastor rattled by her and her dream. It did make me wonder, but, no, I really don't think that Belle and Kenneth will tie the knot."

"Of course not," said Louise. "That's ridiculous."

Then Alice changed the subject, asking Louise about how many rooms would be filled during the weekend.

"Oh my, I forgot to tell you. We are going to be full up." Louise's pale blue eyes sparkled happily. "The last call came just before dinner."

"That's wonderful," said Alice.

"And a huge relief," agreed Jane. "Looks like the weather is finally working for us."

Alice glanced at Jane curiously. "So, did today's sunshine put the spring back into your step?"

Jane suspected that Alice's question addressed more than just the weather. Even so, Jane just smiled. "Definitely. Spring has sprung."

As the three of them cleaned up after dinner, Alice began to giggle. "What is so funny?" demanded Louise.

"I'm sorry," said Alice. "I just imagined Lloyd and Belle at bingo, and I realized that you're probably right. Tongues will be wagging."

"Poor Lloyd," said Jane. "I don't envy him having to sort this all out."

"I have an idea," said Louise, eyeing the berry cobbler that Jane had made for their dessert. "Why don't we take dessert over to Auntie and attempt to gently break the news?"

"That's a wonderful idea," said Alice. "It will come much more easily from us than one of her friends."

"Like Florence Simpson?" suggested Jane.

"Oh my," said Louise. "That would be dreadful." Florence was a friend of Ethel's, but friendship would not stop her if she had some gossip to spread. They all knew the way Florence could put a spin on the most innocent tale—not that their own aunt wasn't occasionally guilty of the same thing.

"This is a mission of mercy," said Jane as they gathered the necessities for dessert and traipsed over to Ethel's. They found her snuggled into her couch watching a game show, but she happily turned off her TV in trade for their company.

"We thought you might be in need of a treat," said Louise as she waved the still-warm cobbler under her aunt's nose.

"Oh, my darling nieces," she gushed. "What would I do without you girls?"

"Be lonely?" asked Jane. "Especially since you aren't taking visitors just yet."

Ethel put a hand to her cheek. "I thought the swelling was going down, and then I looked in the mirror and it looked just the same."

"I would prescribe no more mirrors," said Alice. "Not for at least three days."

Soon they were all settled around Ethel's little kitchen table, and the sisters glanced uncomfortably at one another, each wishing one of the others would raise the subject of Belle and Lloyd at bingo. Finally, Jane nudged Louise beneath the table. After all, this was her idea.

Louise cleared her throat. "Too bad you missed bingo tonight, Aunt Ethel."

"Wasn't it though?" She dipped her fork into the berries and sighed.

"I'm sure Belle was disappointed too," added Alice. "She seems to really like you."

"Yes," said Jane. "And I know she was sorry you weren't able to take her around town today."

"As was I."

"It was certainly nice of Lloyd to take Belle to bingo anyway," blurted Jane.

Ethel stiffened. "Oh?"

"Yes. We thought you'd probably encouraged him to take her, since you want to help Belle," Jane said quickly.

"And it turns out that Belle simply adores Bingo," said Alice. "I think those were her very words."

"Yes, that's what she told me," said Jane.

Ethel slowly nodded. "Well, I must admit I'm surprised. But then I did ask Lloyd to help our Belle out. I do want her to find her Mr. Right and get settled."

"That's very generous of you," said Alice.

Ethel set down her fork and leaned back in her chair, folding her arms across her chest. "I hope not too generous." She looked around the table at her nieces, her face still blotchy, red and swollen. "You don't think Belle Bannister will take unfair advantage, do you?"

Jane laughed. "No, of course not. That's silly."

"But Lloyd is one of Acorn Hill's most prominent bachelors."

"But he is also loyal to you," said Alice.

Their aunt nodded. "Yes, you're right. He is."

"And Belle told me that as soon as you're feeling better, Lloyd wants to set up a bridge foursome with you and him and Wilhelm and Belle."

"Oh, do you think that Wilhelm and Belle might be a match?" asked Ethel hopefully.

"You just never know," said Jane.

"Wouldn't they be adorable together? Wilhelm is such a snappy dresser, and Belle with her little outfits and pumps, well, she's quite fashionable too. I can just imagine the two of them strolling through town together. Oh, I realize there's a bit of difference in their ages, but that's not so unusual. And I've been telling Wilhelm for some time that he should stop living with his mother."

"What he needs is for you to get better so that you can help him out," said Alice. "You're such a natural when it comes to these things. I felt completely out of my league today when I showed her around town. I am no good when it comes to matchmaking. I'm sure Belle was greatly relieved when I asked Lloyd to step in to help today."

Ethel patted Alice's hand. "Well, I do appreciate your trying, dear. But I must agree that you are not the most clever person when it comes to romance." She chuckled.

Jane felt bad for Alice. "I don't think I'm much good at it either."

"And you, Jane, goodness gracious." Ethel used a scolding tone. "You could have more romance in your own life if you simply applied yourself."

"I'm sure that's true," said Alice quickly, "but perhaps Jane is not interested in more romance. I know that I'm not."

"Nor am I," said Louise, standing. "Although I am interested in getting home and putting my feet up."

"Thank you, girls, for stopping in," said Ethel. "Your kindness warms my heart."

"I hope you feel much better by morning, Auntie," said Alice as they prepared to leave.

"The truth is I'm feeling just fine," said Ethel. "It's how I'm looking that's upsetting."

"Stay away from those mirrors," Jane reminded her.

"And keep drinking fluids," said Alice.

"That's right," said Louise. "That's exactly what I tell Cynthia with her allergies: Use fluids to flush out the system."

"Yes, yes," said Ethel as she waved. "Thank you again, girls."

Jane patted Louise on the back as they walked back to the house. "You were right, big sister, Auntie did need our help tonight."

"Let's just hope that takes care of it," said Louise as they went up the steps.

"And that Lloyd and Belle haven't run off to Las Vegas to be married tonight?"

"Good grief, Jane," said Louise. "Please keep those ridiculous thoughts to yourself."

"Besides," Alice reminded them. "That would not be in accordance with Belle's dream. It's not the first Saturday of June. And Las Vegas is not Acorn Hill."

"Right." Jane rolled her eyes as they went inside.

"Tomorrow is the beginning of a long weekend," said Louise in a weary tone. "Unless you need me for anything, I think I'll turn in early and get a good night's sleep."

"I'll help Jane in the kitchen," said Alice.

"Oh, that's okay," said Jane.

"No," said Alice firmly. "I want to help."

They were just finishing putting the dinner things away, and Jane had already turned on the dishwasher when Alice broke a congenial silence.

"I really don't mean to pry, Jane," she began in what seemed a cautious tone, "but I just wondered if everything was okay . . . Justin's letter I mean. I keep thinking about how shocked you seemed to receive it. And I wondered if he is having health problems or something."

Jane supposed that was a possibility, although it hadn't occurred to her before. "I don't know, Alice, at least he didn't mention anything like that. But, honestly, I don't know."

"I realize it's none of my business, but if you need to—"

"No, that's okay. And you're right, I probably do need to talk."

"But if this isn't the right time—"

"No, this is as good a time as any." Jane hung up the dish towel. "Why don't we go get more comfortable?"

Alice smiled. "My thoughts exactly."

They situated themselves on the couch in the parlor, and Jane told Alice about the contents of Justin's letter. By now, she had practically memorized the short note, and she didn't hold anything back. Not that there was so much to it.

"So, you see," she said finally, "I don't have the slightest idea why he wants to come all the way here or why he has this urgent need to see me face-to-face. I mean, if he needed to talk, he could easily pick up the phone. Or he could e-mail me. But to have this sudden need to speak to me in person, well, it's unnerving to say the least."

Alice nodded. "Yes, I can imagine."

"Why do you think he's coming?" blurted Jane.

Alice seemed to ponder this. "Well, maybe he regrets losing you, Jane. I know you're my sister and I do tend to be prejudiced in matters of family, but you're a lovely person—so pretty, intelligent, witty, creative—"

"Thank you, thank you." Jane waved her hand in dismissal. "And while my ego is happy to get some strokes, I don't think that's what Justin is thinking."

"How do you know?"

"I suppose I don't know."

"Okay, Jane, here's a question for you. How would you feel if that was the case? What would you do if Justin came here and begged you to take him back?"

"Goodness!" Jane's hand flew up to her mouth. "I have no idea."

"Perhaps that's why he sent the letter, Jane. He wanted to give you time to think. Maybe he wanted you to be mentally prepared for, well, whatever."

"Oh, I don't think so." Jane felt her cheeks grow warm and her heart begin to pound. Just the idea of this was truly unsettling. "I mean we really were over, Alice. We both knew it was for the best to part."

"Perhaps that was true at the time, Jane. But people can change. We can learn from our mistakes. Sometimes we can even repair broken bridges. And, certainly, we've seen you change in the short time that we've all been back together here in Acorn Hill. It may be that this chapter of your life isn't finished yet."

"But I can't imagine going back," said Jane.

"But you were happy in San Francisco. You enjoyed the pace, the art, the music, the restaurants, the theater—all that. You've told me before how you miss it sometimes."

"But not so much that I want to go back. It was never home to me, not the way Acorn Hill is home." Jane felt her eyes getting misty. "Alice, the way you're talking, I almost wonder if you want me to go back."

Now Alice was crying too. "Jane, Jane, you know I love having you here. More than anything, I want you to stay here forever. You and Louise both. I've never been happier than I am now with you two, running this inn."

"So what then? What are you saying?"

"I just want what's best for you, Jane. If somehow things have changed for Justin, if he discovered that he truly loved you and wanted to get back together with you, and if you felt the same way, well, I would want whatever would make you the happiest, even if it meant losing you. You know me well enough to know that I respect the sanctity of marriage. You know that I would never discourage you from doing what you believed was right."

"What if I don't know what's right?"

"God will show you, Jane. I do believe that."

"And do you think God would want me to return to Justin if it made me totally miserable?"

"That doesn't sound like the God I know and serve." Alice smiled as she dabbed at her tears. "I think if it was God's will for you and Justin to reunite, you would be happy about it."

Jane threw her arms around her sister. "Oh, Alice, you are so wise. Sometimes you are just too good to be true. But then I know you are true. And I think I am so lucky to have a sister as good and as kind as you."

"Oh, now you're just trying to feed my ego." Alice patted Jane's back, then released herself from their hug.

"The truth is, I'm not that good. Really, I'm selfish when it comes to family, and if I could have my own way, you would never be allowed to go back with Justin. I would put my foot down so hard that the whole town would think there'd been a small earthquake."

Jane chuckled. "But we both know you would never really do that."

"Maybe not," Alice sighed, "but I do hope that I won't be put to the test."

"Oh, I don't think that will happen—really, I don't, Alice. Honestly, I can't imagine Justin having changed enough to make me seriously consider going back to him. It just seems totally impossible."

"But, Jane," said Alice gently. "With God, all things are possible."

Thursday night, Jane lay in bed thinking about her conversation with Alice. Could Justin really be thinking about reconciling? Jane's memories of the last months of their marriage were not happy ones. But as she stared at the ceiling, she allowed her mind to go back once again to the happy times.

Soon after Jane had said an enthusiastic, "Yes, yes," to Justin's proposal, they began to discuss wedding plans. Jane naturally thought that they would return to Acorn Hill for a ceremony with her family, perhaps even with her father officiating, but Justin reminded her of their busy schedules and lack of funds, convincing her that a simple local wedding made more sense. And so she reluctantly agreed. The restaurant was scheduled to be closed for renovations, and Justin felt this unexpected "vacation" provided a perfect opportunity for their wedding. Unfortunately, it wasn't a perfect opportunity for her family. None of them was able to drop everything and make the cross-country trip to see her wed.

Jane and Justin said their vows in a lovely garden with mutual friends. She wore a gauzy white dress with a circlet of fragrant jasmine blooms in her hair, and Justin wore a charcoal blazer and pale gray pants. The staff from the restaurant where they worked catered a small reception. While all this was nice, sweet and simple, it was nothing like Jane had dreamed of as a girl.

She had always imagined herself walking down the aisle of Grace Chapel on the arm of her father, her sisters in attendance. For years she had made sketches of wedding dresses, of bridesmaids' gowns that would suit her sisters and intricate descriptions of floral arrangements. She felt sad about her family not attending and about the informality of her wedding, but reminded herself that the marriage was the most important, not the extras that surrounded it. And Justin promised that they'd visit Acorn Hill as soon as they had enough time and money to make the trip.

They moved from their single apartments to the top floor of a three-family home. Jane loved it. It had a little enclosed porch on the front of the house, and they were entitled to use the spacious backyard. They had great fun combining their sparse collections of furniture and buying simple accessories to tie everything together. Justin was in awe of Jane's ability to make the apartment homey and distinctive. He loved her artwork and carefully hung her paintings throughout the four rooms. There were windows on all sides, and the golden oak floors glowed with warmth. The combination of modern furnishings, colorful area rugs and Jane's artwork was charming. On days off, they enjoyed entertaining or experimenting with recipes in their tiny but efficient kitchen.

Looking back on those days, Jane recalled how small problems grew increasingly larger. Justin could be impatient and somewhat selfish, and she often deferred to him, thinking that's what a wife should do. But, over time, he took unfair advantage of that deference and eventually became quite controlling. If a culinary experiment at home was successful, Justin would rush to the restaurant and try it there, never giving Jane credit for her input. He might have been generous with his praise of Jane's art and decorating, but he was stingy with compliments when it came to cooking.

He also began treating her as a sous-chef rather than his equal at the restaurant. And because he took credit for all their innovations, he received their boss's praise and eventually a substantial increase in salary. Friction between them increased, and before long, he suggested she leave the restaurant and pursue painting instead. He was not pleased when she told him that cooking, not art, was her main passion. Shortly after that, a friend told Jane that the Blue Fish Grille needed a new chef. Jane hoped that switching to another restaurant might smooth things over with Justin. Not only that, but it would give both of them a much-needed break from being together day in and day out. And for a while, her move to the Blue Fish appeared to resolve their marital problems. At least on the surface.

Chapter Ten

*J*ane took advantage of the continued sunshine on Friday, working happily in her garden for several hours after breakfast. She almost felt like her old self again as she puttered away. It was truly amazing how such a small amount of fair weather had perked up all her plants and flowers, as if they'd simply been waiting for the right moment to pop out and put on a cheerful springtime show.

"Your garden looks lovely, Jane," said Belle as she came over to where Jane was brushing off a metal table and chair set that she planned to place near the flower garden.

"Thank you," said Jane, standing up straight. "Don't you look pretty, Belle." Today, Belle had on a lavender warm-up suit. It looked far too nice for actual athletic activity, and her sneakers, also lavender, did not appear to be designed for running.

"I thought I'd be more casual today," said Belle. "I think sometimes I can intimidate folks, but I'm just one of those girls who like to dress up." She chuckled. "Even when I was itty-bitty, my mama said that I would throw a fit if my clothes weren't coordinated. If I had on a pink dress, my socks and everything else had to be pink too. Isn't that silly?"

Jane smiled. "I guess it's just the way God makes us. We're all wired differently."

"And you must be wired to create beauty," said Belle. "Goodness gracious, Jane, it seems that everything you touch turns out to be pretty. I had no idea that you were the one who did most of the interior decorating for the inn. Louise just informed me. I'm hoping that when I get married and settle down in Acorn Hill, you'll bring some of your expertise my way and help me to set up a beautiful home too."

"I'm happy to give you decorating tips," said Jane cautiously. "But I find that couples need to be in agreement about things like color and style, or decisions can get tricky, especially with newlyweds. Speaking of which, any idea who the lucky guy is yet?"

"No, not really," Belle looked embarrassed as she waved her hand, almost as if the groom were inconsequential. "Although, I must admit, I do have my favorites."

Jane was tempted to ask who, but figured she could probably guess. At least it appeared that Lloyd Tynan was not on the short list. Belle had entertained Jane and her sisters during breakfast, telling them about bingo and how everyone there seemed quite curious as to her relationship with Lloyd, as well as the whereabouts of Ethel. "Why you'd have thought I'd murdered the poor woman and buried her out back in the garden," Belle had told them. Fortunately for Ethel, it sounded as if everything was clarified before the evening ended. Lloyd made it perfectly clear to everyone, including Belle, that his loyalties remained with Ethel. And Alice even made a special point to go over to the carriage house and share this happy news with their aunt following breakfast.

"Are those tulips?" asked Belle, pointing to the rain-beaten blooms that were trying to resurrect themselves.

"Yes. Sadly, they haven't enjoyed the weather much. Usually, they would be over by now, but it's been a cold spring."

"That reminds me," said Belle. "I got to thinking that maybe I could hire you to help with my wedding. I know you're friends with Craig and all, and you have such a knack for decorating. Would you be interested, Jane?"

Jane didn't know how to respond. It seemed ridiculous to plan for a wedding that might not even happen. Still, she didn't want to hurt Belle's feelings. "I suppose I could help," she said weakly.

"Oh, that would be splendid!" Belle clapped her hands. "Now, the main thing is there must be lots of pink."

Jane nodded as if this were a new concept with Belle. "Pink."

"Yes. As long as it's pink and pretty, I know I will love it."

"Well, that's simple enough. However, I think you should know that Craig will need to order your flowers at least a week in advance. And considering that next weekend is Memorial Day weekend, that might be cutting it close, Belle. Are you sure you want to take the risk of ordering expensive flowers before you even know who the groom is going to be?"

"Oh, Jane, it's not a risk, not when God is doing the planning. I simply need to walk in faith. God will provide when the time is right."

"Okay then." Jane turned her attention back to the table, giving it a halfhearted scrub with the brush.

"Well, I know you have things to do, and I wanted to take a little walk through town, so I'll leave you to it."

"Enjoy," called Jane. She couldn't help but shake her head as she returned to her task.

Finally, it was past noon, and Jane knew she should make her way back inside, clean herself up and get busy with other household tasks. She had a lot to do to get ready for the full house that Louise expected for the weekend. Shopping, baking, some flower arrangements

—all things she loved to do. Besides, being busy was a relief to her. It gave her less time to obsess over Justin and why he was coming to see her, a concern that was becoming more and more difficult to push into the recesses of her mind.

"Jane," Louise's voice called from the front hall later that afternoon.

"In the kitchen," called Jane.

"Oh, I'm glad you're back," said Louise.

"Everything okay?" asked Jane as she put a package of butter in the fridge.

"Well, I, uh . . . "

Jane closed the door and turned to look at her sister. She was not accustomed to hearing Louise flustered like this. "What is it, Louise?"

"Well," Louise actually wrung her hands. "I don't know how to say this."

"Please," commanded Jane, "just say it."

"Well, Justin called."

"Oh." Jane felt a strange mixture of relief, curiosity and irritation. She tried to imagine what she thought Louise had been about to say—probably something terrible, like Alice had been in a car wreck. Somehow the news that Justin had called didn't seem quite as catastrophic as Louise's expression suggested.

"You were out, so I asked if I could take a message. When he identified himself, I was quite taken aback."

"Understandably." Jane returned to unloading groceries, a good way to avoid Louise's penetrating gaze.

"He said he'd sent you a letter and wondered if you'd received it."

"I did."

"Indeed. Well, I was unable to confirm that information because you didn't mention it to me."

"I was going to, Louise." Jane heard the trace of irritation in her own voice and regretted it.

"Nonetheless," Louise sighed, "Justin asked if I could reserve a room for him for Memorial Day weekend."

Jane spun around and looked at her sister. "You didn't, did you?"

"Well, I was so surprised, Jane. I really didn't know what to say. Perhaps if you had given me some warning I might have reacted better."

"You gave him a reservation?" asked Jane. "To stay here? In the inn? To sleep under the same roof that I do? To invade my personal—"

"I'm so sorry, Jane. As soon as I hung up the phone I knew it was a mistake."

"Did he leave you a number, so you could call him back?"

"No." Louise sadly shook her head. "He said he was on the road."

"Just great." Jane ran her fingers through her hair in frustration.

"I'm sorry, Jane, but, really, it would have gone much better had I known of this upcoming visit. How long have you been aware of it?"

"Just a few days."

"But you knew he was coming here?"

"I knew he was coming to Acorn Hill. I didn't think he expected to stay at the inn." Jane got an idea. "Hey, maybe I'll be gone that weekend."

"But we need you to cook, Jane. We're booked."

"Why weren't you booked when Justin called?"

"I had two rooms left."

"Why did you give one to him?"

Louise's lips pressed tightly together, and Jane could tell she was getting irate. "I don't tell falsehoods, Jane."

"I know. I'm sorry. I don't expect you to lie, Louise. I just thought perhaps you could have dissuaded him some-how. What about Belle's parents and that whole wedding business?"

"That is the following weekend."

"Oh, right."

"As I said, I'm sorry, Jane. But I was in a difficult position."

"I know, Louise. Actually, I would have told you about his letter last night when I told Alice, but you had gone to bed."

"What's wrong?" asked Alice as she came in through the back door. At this moment, Louise and Jane were standing on opposite sides of the kitchen table, looking tense.

"Justin called," said Jane. "Louise took the call and had no idea what to do."

"Do about what?" asked Alice.

"Justin wanted a room for Memorial Day weekend," explained Louise.

"You didn't give him one, did you?"

Louise let out an exasperated groan. "I'm getting the feeling you two are against me."

Alice went over and put an arm around Louise. "Of course we're not, Louise. I just hoped, for Jane's sake, that Justin might find other lodging during this visit."

"As I informed Jane, I'm not accustomed to telling falsehoods. If someone asks me for a room and a room is available, I book it."

"Poor Louise," said Alice kindly, "you got caught in a tight spot. And anyone in your shoes would've done the same thing."

Jane sighed as she put a carton of cream in the fridge.

"There must be a way to undo this," said Alice. "Can you call Justin back and suggest that other accommodations might be more suitable?"

"He didn't leave a number. He was calling from the road."

Jane stopped her busy work and faced her sisters. "What now?"

"Well, we have a week," said Alice. "Right, Louise?"

"Exactly." She nodded. "Justin said he plans to arrive here next Friday."

"Terrific." Jane rolled her eyes. "I suggested to Louise that I might skip town."

"We need her to cook," said Louise.

"I could do the cooking and prep work ahead of time," said Jane quickly. "Then Alice could take care of serving and whatnot. Right, Alice?"

Alice looked uncertain. "I suppose."

"I got the distinct feeling he was coming here to see you, Jane. Or is there someone else in Acorn Hill that he has an interest in?"

"Perhaps God sent Justin a dream and he is coming here to meet his darling wedding Belle," said Jane.

Alice laughed. "Oh, Jane!"

Louise began to chuckle too. "Nice try, Jane," she said, "but you know good and well Justin is coming here to see you. What I would like to know is, why?"

"That's a very good question, Louise. I wish you had asked him." Jane returned her attention to unloading the pantry items.

"Jane is perplexed over this," Alice said to Louise. "She doesn't know anything more than we do right now. Only that Justin is coming and that he wants to talk to her."

"That's odd," said Louise.

"Yes," agreed Jane with her head still in the pantry. "Very odd."

"But I've come to a conclusion," said Alice. "After Jane told me about Justin last night, I prayed about the whole thing. And although I don't know Justin's purpose in coming to the inn, I do know the purpose of the inn."

The kitchen got quiet. Jane removed her head from the pantry and looked at her sisters. Alice was smiling, and Louise had a thoughtful expression.

"'A place where one can be refreshed and encouraged,'" said Louise, reciting the first line from the plaque that hung by the front door.

Jane nodded, then contributed the second line: "'A place of hope and healing . . .'"

"'And a place where God is at home,'" finished Alice. "And maybe Justin simply needs a sample of those things in his life."

"Maybe." Jane continued putting things away. But what if Justin wanted more than just a sample? What if Justin was coming here for the purpose of reuniting? She wondered if Alice could be right. What if Justin had changed? What if their relationship could be as good as it had been back in the beginning? What would she say to that?

Chapter Eleven

F riday afternoon, Jane was setting out some freshly baked cookies to greet the new guests when Belle made an appearance.

"Good afternoon, Jane. My, those smell just heavenly. I caught a whiff of something delicious clear up in my room."

"You've changed your outfit," said Jane as she arranged the cookies into a pleasing design on the silver platter. Belle now wore a silky pink dress that made her look as if she was going to a party or perhaps planned to be the guest of honor for a wedding shower, although Jane hadn't heard of such plans. "Very pretty," said Jane.

"You've changed too," said Belle with a twinkle in her eye. "I didn't want to say anything, but those were the most curious things you had on your feet, Jane. Whatever do you call them?"

"Crocs," said Jane. "And my aunt Ethel feels the same way about them. She calls them duck feet."

Belle giggled. "Well, I have to admire a girl who goes around looking like that in public. You must have a much better self-image than I do."

Jane chuckled. "Or else I just don't care." Then she pointed down to her more conservative loafers. "But my sister Louise prefers I dress more properly in the house."

"Oh, Jane, did you hear the news?" asked Belle in a lowered voice.

"News?" Jane frowned. "Have you received a proposal of marriage?"

"Oh no, nothing like that. But Louise mentioned that a couple of single men just checked in. They're twins."

"Twins?"

Belle nodded, her eyes wide. "That just increased the percentage of available men in Acorn Hill by, well, I'm not terribly gifted at math, but I would venture to guess about ten percent."

Jane smiled. "Yes, that's probably about right."

Belle clapped her hands. "I can't wait to meet them."

"Perhaps the cookies will lure them down," said Jane. "And since it's nice and warm today, I think I'll go whip up a pitcher of lemonade as well."

Jane was just putting ice into the pitcher when she heard a voice calling, "Hello," from the back porch.

"Come in," Jane called back, wiping her damp hands on a dish towel.

"Hi, Jane," called Sylvia Songer as she let herself in. Sylvia was Jane's best friend in Acorn Hill and the owner of Sylvia's Buttons, a fabric and needlework shop. She was a gifted seamstress and a fabric artist. She held a folded quilt. "I just had to show this to you, Jane. I finished it last night. To celebrate, I had Justine come in to watch the shop for me this afternoon." Then Sylvia unfolded a quilt of intricate sunflowers against a geometric background of varying shades of blue.

"Oh, it's beautiful, Sylvia." Jane fingered the fine craftsmanship. She reached over and hugged her good friend. "It's so great to see you. I've been about to call you dozens of times these past few days and—"

"Why haven't you?"

Jane shook her head. "Something always comes up."

Sylvia pushed a strand of strawberry blonde hair off her forehead and made a funny face. "Like the guest Lloyd brought into my shop yesterday?"

"Belle?" Jane whispered, nodding her head toward the dining room to warn Sylvia that a certain guest might still be in there.

"Want to run out for a cup of coffee?" asked Sylvia as she began to refold the quilt.

"Sure," said Jane. "Just let me put this lemonade out and I think I'm good to go."

Belle was sitting at the dining-room table with a wedding magazine. "Maybe the twins will like some of this," said Jane as she set the pitcher on the sideboard. "You might even want to take it out on the front porch, it's so nice out."

"What a lovely idea."

Jane almost suggested to Belle that she hide the wedding magazine from the twins, but Belle was in command of her campaign, and maybe the magazine was part of it. "I'll see you later, Belle," she called as she went back to the kitchen and rejoined Sylvia. The two of them slipped out the back, and Sylvia put her quilt safely back into her car before they headed toward town on foot.

"So what did you think of Belle?" asked Jane after they were a block from the inn.

"Besides her being odd?"

"She is awfully sweet," said Jane. "It's hard not to like her."

"I suppose. But all that wedding mumbo jumbo, and she doesn't even have a fiancé?" Sylvia shook her head. "What's with that?"

"Did she tell you about the dream?"

"Sort of, but it still didn't make sense."

"No. I don't think it makes sense to anyone," said Jane, "except for Belle."

"Well, I'll tell you one thing, the bachelors in this town are starting to run when they see her coming. The word has spread that she's on a manhunt. Craig Tracy actually ducked into my shop to hide this morning when he saw her walking his way."

Jane laughed. "I can just imagine him crouched between the bolts of calico and baskets of yarn."

"Yes, it was pretty comical. I told him he was being silly and that Belle wasn't going to grab him and drag him down the aisle. But he said she was a formidable force that he'd just as soon avoid."

"I'm worried about her ordering those wedding flowers from him," said Jane. "I mean, what will she do if there's no wedding? Will Craig be stuck with them? Or will Belle have to pay the bill?"

"I say have the girl pay up front. Speaking of which, did you know that Belle asked me if I could make her a wedding gown as well as four bridesmaid dresses and have them all ready for her by the first weekend of June?"

"Are you kidding?" Jane turned to look at Sylvia as they paused at the corner. "Does she think you're some sort of a magician? How could you possibly get all that done in such a short amount of time?"

"I told her it was impossible."

"I wonder who her bridesmaids are supposed to be."

Sylvia chuckled. "She suggested that they were all related to one another, some new female friends that she'd made here in Acorn Hill. Any idea who she might mean?"

Jane gasped. "Ethel did mention that Belle had hinted at including her in the wedding, but I thought that might've been wishful thinking on my aunt's part."

"How is she anyway?"

"Better. But, according to her, still not fit for public viewing."

"Poor Ethel."

"Do you really think Belle is going to ask my sisters and me to be in her wedding?" Jane cringed inwardly, imagining herself and her sisters lining up at the Grace Chapel altar for Belle's pink wedding.

"I'll tell you this much, Jane. After seeing the photo she gave me for the bridesmaid dresses yesterday, well, if I were you, I'd decline the honor." Then Sylvia described a dress with a tiered full skirt trimmed with lace. "And the shade of pink . . ." She shook her head sadly.

"Let me guess?" said Jane. "Pepto-Bismol?"

"Exactly! How did you know?"

"That's the color of her car and, obviously, her favorite."

"Oh my."

Now Jane felt guilty. She hadn't really meant to be mean about Belle. "She really is a sweet person. I don't completely understand her, but she means well."

Sylvia frowned. "Do you think I should help her with her dresses if she persists?"

"Oh, Sylvia, I don't know. You said yourself it's probably not even possible."

"True. But I did give her the name of a bridal shop in Potterston. I told her if she got ready-made dresses, I might be able to do some minor alterations and help her with her veil, just small things."

"Well, I guess it's like Craig and the flowers. As long as Belle pays for everything up front and as long as you have the time and you want to help, well, I suppose it can't hurt."

"Unless it hurts Belle." They paused to let traffic go by.

"But what if she's right? What if her dream was authentic and she really does get married?"

"Get real, Jane."

Jane chuckled as she pointed down the street. Sylvia, as usual, was good medicine. Although a little younger than Jane, they seemed to speak the same language. "How about the Good Apple for coffee?"

"Justine told me they have orange-ginger scones today."

"Sounds good to me."

Once they placed their order and were seated, Jane knew this was her opportunity to ask Sylvia for advice. Now that both her sisters were aware of Justin's impending visit, it seemed right that Sylvia should be in the loop as well.

"Something weird happened this week," said Jane after their coffee and scones were served.

"You mean Belle?"

Jane laughed. "No, no. Let's put the subject of poor Belle to rest for a moment. This was something else, Sylvia. Something from my past."

Sylvia leaned forward with interest. "Ah, tell me more."

"I received a letter from Justin on Wednesday."

"Justin, as in your ex-husband-the-jerk Justin."

"Oh, Sylvia, he's not really a jerk. I think we were both just a little mixed up and misguided. Really, I've put all that behind me. I don't think ill of him. I just don't wish to see him."

"See him?" Sylvia's head cocked to one side. "Is there a chance of that?"

Jane explained his brief letter, followed up by the phone call.

"Oh my," said Sylvia. "What a position to put you in."

"I guess . . ." Jane broke off a piece of scone and examined it. Fluffy, light, yet rich and buttery and, oh, the scent—scrumptious. She took a bite. As Belle would say, it was heavenly.

"Why do you think he's coming, Jane?"

"That's the $64,000 question."

"He didn't give any clues in his letter?"

"No. But it sounded urgent. He mentioned the cross-country road trip that he's been wanting to make since he turned fifty, which was a few years ago."

"Is he having health problems?"

"You know, that's exactly what Alice asked, and I'm beginning to think it's a very good question." She leaned back in the stiff metal chair and mulled over this idea. What if Justin was seriously ill? How would she feel to learn that, say, he was dying? What if this road trip was his last big hurrah and he felt the need to reconnect with his former wife? Naturally, she would be kind and understanding, not to mention terribly sad. After all, he wasn't a monster. She had loved him once. But, on the other hand, what if he was perfectly fine and healthy?

"Feeling conflicted?"

Jane nodded. "Exactly."

"I understand. You love a person and prepare to spend your entire life together, and then everything changes. You have to build a new life and you try to put that person out of your mind, but sometimes you still wonder how it might have been."

"But I'm happy here, Sylvia," protested Jane. "I love my life with my sisters at the inn. I know I was in a slump recently, but that had to do with the weather."

"You're sure?"

Jane shrugged. "I think I'm sure."

"So, you have no problem with Justin making this unexpected visit?"

"I wouldn't go that far." Jane grimaced. "When I heard Louise booked him a room, I threatened to leave home for the weekend."

"Louise booked him a room?" Sylvia looked shocked.

"Well, it wasn't her fault. He caught her off guard, and I hadn't told her he was coming." Jane frowned. "But you know that's like him. He works people sometimes. I went to a counselor once, and he said Justin was passive-aggressive. I've never been certain just what that's supposed to mean."

"*Ooh,* do I sniff a trace of bitterness?"

Jane made a face at her friend. "No, not really. I've just been remembering old stuff. Stuff that's best forgotten. It's funny how you can forgive someone, or at least you think you have, but then a reminder intrudes and you remember something that happened long ago, and it's like you have to do the whole forgiving thing all over again."

"Seventy times seven?"

"Yes, I suppose so."

"Have you thought about the possibility that Justin might regret losing you, Jane?"

"I've tried not to."

"But you know it's possible, don't you?"

"It doesn't seem likely, Sylvia."

"What would you do if that was the case?" Sylvia leaned forward, her eyes wide.

"I don't know. To be honest, I feel pretty conflicted just thinking about it, which is why I have tried to block it out. I mean I'm aware that we made vows."

"Have you told Kenneth about Justin coming?"

"No."

"Will you?"

"I don't know. I'm not really sure why I should trouble him."

"Because he's your friend? Because he's your pastor? Because he has a lot of wisdom about this sort of thing?"

Jane chuckled. "He's also got a lot on his hands with Belle Bannister. Maybe I should leave the poor man alone."

"Belle is chasing after our good pastor?"

"She did admit to me that he was at the top of her list. I foolishly invited him to breakfast the first morning of Belle's stay. I think she thought that was a sign."

"You mean as if God had dropped him from the heavens?"

"Something like that."

"Oh dear."

"Do you need anything else, girls?" asked Clarissa Cottrell, the Good Apple's owner. She stood by their table, rubbing her elbow as if it hurt.

"Clarissa, is your arthritis bothering you?" asked Jane.

"It's been troubling me something fierce," admitted the older woman. "I'm just hoping that this weather change will improve things some." She adjusted her hairnet over her gray bun as she looked down at the table.

"These scones are killer," said Sylvia.

"Killer?" she frowned.

"Meaning really, really good," translated Jane. "They are superb."

Clarissa smiled. "Why, thank you." She paused, looking uncomfortable. "I don't mean to interrupt your conversation, girls," she said, "but could I ask you for advice, Jane?"

"Me?" asked Jane. "Sure."

Clarissa pulled a chair from another table and sat down next to them. "It's that Belle Bannister."

Jane suppressed a groan. "Yes?"

"Lloyd brought her in here yesterday."

"Yes?"

"She expressed an interest in a wedding cake."

"I guess that doesn't surprise me."

"So, she really is getting married?"

"Well, Clarissa, she's booked the inn and the church and ordered the flowers and—"

"And she wants me to make her wedding dress," injected Sylvia, "and her bridesmaids' dresses too."

Clarissa nodded with a curious expression. "So, this is for real then?"

"For real?" queried Jane.

"For real as in should I go ahead and plan to make her wedding cake?"

"I think as long as Belle orders and pays for a wedding cake and you have time and want to make it, then you can go ahead and do it."

Clarissa leaned forward with a puzzled expression. "But is it true there's no fiancé yet?"

Jane nodded soberly.

Clarissa looked from Jane to Sylvia and back to Jane again. "Rather odd, don't you think?"

"Time will tell," said Jane, knowing full well that she was quoting Belle, and it wasn't the first time she'd done so.

Chapter Twelve

As Jane and Sylvia strolled back to the inn, Jane noticed Ethel's good friend Clara Horn walking Daisy, her miniature potbellied pig. Clara was about half a block away and slowly making her way toward them. As Clara recognized them, she waved and smiled, moving a little faster as if to catch them before they crossed the street. She was tugging on the leash attached to Daisy, urging the hefty pig to hurry. No matter how many times Jane saw this elderly woman with her pig, the sight always made her smile. Clara not only treated Daisy like a baby, she dressed her like a baby as well. Today, Daisy sported a pale yellow sweater with buttons shaped like daisies down the back. It really was a sight to see, and Jane couldn't help chuckling.

"Hello, girls," said Clara breathlessly when they finally met.

They both greeted Clara and Daisy.

"Clara, those buttons look wonderful on that sweater," said Sylvia.

"Oh yes. I was so glad you could order them for me. Daisy is so hard on her clothes. I just don't know how she lost three of the original ones."

"Well, there's hardly anything one can't find using the Internet," said Sylvia.

"Yes, well you are so clever about those things, dear," gushed Clara. "Oh, Jane, I'm so glad that I've bumped into you. It's simply providential."

"And why is that?" asked Jane as she reached down to scratch Daisy behind the ear. The pig grunted in appreciation, then flopped down on the sidewalk as if finished with her walk.

"I just had a phone call from my favorite niece, Janet, and it seems that she and her son Calvin who just got home from the Middle East, want to come to Acorn Hill for Memorial Day weekend. Apparently, Calvin has fond memories of visiting here when he was a boy, and it was on his list of things to do when he was released from the service."

"That's nice." But Jane still wasn't quite sure how this news pertained to her. Of course, she also knew that this chatty woman sometimes took a bit of time to get to her point.

"Well, as you know, my house is too small for both Janet and Calvin to stay with me, and since Calvin has been so loyally serving our country these past three years, I thought it would be a nice treat if I put him up at the inn."

"Oh." Jane nodded.

"So, I was so happy to run into you just now. Would you please check to see if you have a room available for Friday through Monday?"

"Wouldn't it be simpler if you called Louise and asked her yourself?" asked Jane. "She's the one who takes care of reservations."

"Oh my." Clara waved her hands as if she were caught in a flurry. "I would do that, Jane. But I am just in a dither. I have so much to do now, and I don't want to lose out on a room, and it's a holiday weekend. By the way, I'm having a barbecue after the Memorial Day ceremony and naturally, you're all invited. Tell your sisters to plan on it," she told Jane. "And right now, I'm on my way to see Lloyd Tynan. I just got the most marvelous idea. It occurred to me as I walked past the cemetery that my grandnephew Calvin would be a perfect candidate to raise the flag at the Memorial Day service. Don't you think so too?"

"That's a lovely idea, Clara."

"And anyway, dear, I would so appreciate it if you could take care of that little detail for me with Louise. I have so much to do right now, I hardly know where to begin."

Jane smiled. "I'll be happy to check with Louise and have her call you to confirm."

"Oh, thank you." Clara looked down at the reclining pig and frowned. "Come on, Daisy, up and at 'em." But the pig just looked at her from one half-shut eye and grunted sleepily. "Come on, Daisy," said Clara more firmly. "There is much to be done, girl."

"Nice seeing you, Clara," said Sylvia. They both stifled giggles as they walked away, glancing back from time to time to see Clara shaking her finger, then tugging on Daisy's leash as she loudly urged her willful pet to get up. Just as Sylvia and Jane were about to return to help Clara, the pig finally lurched up from the sidewalk.

"Can't say that I blame Daisy," said Jane as they turned onto Chapel Road. "I wouldn't mind taking a nap in the sun myself."

"This weather really is divine," said Sylvia. "I think we probably appreciate it even more because it's been so late in coming."

"Now it's feeling as if we went straight from winter to summer," said Jane. "That's not going to be too good for my flowers. All that cold and wet and now hot sun. I hope they don't get sunburned faces today."

"Maybe you can make them little sunbonnets," teased Sylvia as they approached the inn.

"Maybe put up a sun umbrella," said Jane in all seriousness.

"Looks like guests on the front porch," observed Sylvia.

"Yes, it's a full house all weekend." Jane glanced to the porch to see a couple of men and Belle. "Looks like Belle is entertaining the twins."

"Twins?"

"Yes." Jane nudged Sylvia toward the back entrance. "Let's not disturb them. According to Belle, they are two available bachelors who just happen to be passing through town."

"How does anyone happen to pass through this town?" asked Sylvia.

"Well, I did hear Louise mention that a previous guest had referred the Johnsons to us."

"Maybe Belle will find her man right here at the inn," said Sylvia as they paused by the back door. Then she glanced at her watch. "Oh, I better head back to town. It's about time to close shop, and I promised Justine I'd be back in time to go to the bank."

"Thanks for the outing," said Jane. "And for listening."

"Don't you worry about Justin," said Sylvia softly. "Before you know it, he'll have come and gone, and life will be back to normal."

Jane nodded. "Yes, I'm sure you're right." But as she went into the house, she wasn't sure that she was really so sure. Jane pushed thoughts of Justin away as she began getting out things for dinner. She'd decided that she and her sisters might enjoy a spring quiche tonight. And she'd make a couple of spares while she was at it, to use for breakfast tomorrow morning.

"Jane," said Alice, coming into the kitchen, "anything I can help you with?"

"That'd be great," said Jane. "I was about to start dinner." She handed Alice an apron, and soon Alice was grating Swiss cheese, and Jane was rolling out pie crusts. They worked together in a congenial quiet, Jane giving out instructions and Alice following them perfectly. Jane always felt that if she ever wanted to open a restaurant on her own, which she had absolutely no intention of doing anytime soon, she would have to kidnap Alice and employ her as a prep cook.

"Belle and the twins seem to have hit it off," said Alice as she set a bowl of finely chopped onions within Jane's reach.

"Really? Have you met these twins yet?"

Alice chuckled as she began washing the mushrooms. "They're real characters, Jane. Ron and Don Johnson from Bronson."

"Ron and Don Johnson from Bronson," repeated Jane. "It sounds like something you made up. Where is Bronson?"

"A small town in Maine."

"And are they really twins?"

"Yes. And they look and act alike. Apparently, they were redheads, but now their hair color is sort of faded red touched with gray. I honestly can't tell them apart."

"How old are Ron and Don Johnson from Bronson?"

"They're turning forty next week. This is their big birthday trip."

"Where are they going?"

"To Florida."

"Acorn Hill isn't exactly on the direct route to Florida."

"Oh, I think they mentioned that they visited an old college friend and that excursion put them in our area. Ron is a widower, about five years. And Don recently divorced. You'll never guess why."

"Why?"

"His wife was jealous of Ron. The boys were spending too much time together."

"She left him for that?"

"Well, Don said she also found a man she liked better."

"You certainly have learned a lot about Ron and Don."

"Belle lured me out to the porch with her for lemonade, and the next thing I knew, Ron and Don joined us. Belle and the twins hit it off right away."

"It's nice they get along so well," Jane said as she crimped a crust.

"Well, the twins are big car buffs. They'd seen Belle's car and began talking about horsepower and torque and all sorts of things that are meaningless to me."

Jane laughed. "You and me both. Do you think one of the twins might be Belle's intended?"

Alice frowned. "Both Ron and Don seem perfectly happy in Maine. They hunt and fish and know everybody in their town. And, as you know, Belle's dream is for her and her husband to live here in Acorn Hill. Plus, I can't imagine splitting those boys up."

"I see what you mean."

"Need any help?" offered Louise as she joined them.

"Perhaps you can make a green salad," suggested Jane.

"Certainly."

"Oh yes," said Jane as she remembered her conversation with Clara. "I hope the inn isn't full up for next weekend."

"One room left," pronounced Louise. Then Jane told her and Alice about Clara's grandnephew coming home from the Middle East.

"How nice that he wants to visit here in Acorn Hill," said Alice. "You know, I actually do remember Clara's niece Janet. She's about your age, Jane. And I do recall a summer when Janet and her son—what is his name?"

"Calvin."

"That's right. Calvin. He was about ten at the time. And they spent the whole summer at Clara's."

"Well, now that he's a grown man, and Clara's house is so small, she thought he might appreciate more privacy at the inn."

"I will pencil him in and give Clara a call tomorrow."

"I think I hear the bell at the reception desk, Louise," said Jane.

"Yes, I think you're right. I better go see."

"I met some of the other guests too," said Alice.

"Not more eligible men for Belle, I don't suppose."

"No. But they are a nice retired couple from Michigan. The Blankenships. They are both retired tax accountants. They told me how May was always their vacation month, you know, because of finishing up taxes in April. And although they've been retired for more than ten years, they still vacation in May."

Before long, Louise returned. "Well, that was the last of the guests for the weekend. A nice young woman named Shelby. I'm guessing she's about Belle's age. She's a kindergarten teacher in Pittsburgh and she told me that, although school will be out in less than a month, she just needed a little getaway. Poor thing, she said it had been a rough year and if we thought foul weather was hard on running an inn, we should try keeping twenty-some-odd five-year-olds indoors all day for day after day after day."

"Mercy!" said Alice.

"That does sound like torture," agreed Jane.

"So I promised her some peace and quiet," said Louise.

"She's come to the right place," said Alice.

"I hope she'll get it." Louise frowned. "Although I'm not too sure. I was just showing her to her room when Belle popped out and, after I introduced them, Belle immediately tried to talk poor Shelby into checking out the nightlife in Potterston with her and the twins."

"Oh dear," said Jane. "That sounds almost as bad as being stuck inside with a bunch of kindergarten kids."

"Oh, Jane," scolded Alice in a teasing tone.

"I don't know," said Jane. "If it were me, I might be inclined to stick with the five-year-olds."

"I hope Shelby knows how to say no if she's not interested," said Louise as she peeled a cucumber.

"Belle can be awfully persuasive," said Jane. "Goodness, she's got half the town involved in the preparations for her wedding."

"What?" asked Louise. "You must be joking."

"I'm serious." Then Jane told her about her latest conversations with both Sylvia and Clarissa. "And you know she's already booked the church and the inn."

"Well, I can't say I'm taking the booking of the inn too seriously," said Louise. "I will reserve the room for her parents. But as far as that reception goes, well, I'm not holding my breath."

"You never know," said Jane. "It might be that by tomorrow morning, Belle will not only have gotten herself engaged to one of the Johnson brothers, but she may very well convince Shelby and the other Johnson brother to make it a double wedding. And then all four of them can move permanently to Acorn Hill."

"Oh, Jane," said Louise. "You do get carried away with that imagination of yours." Still, the three of them had a good laugh over Jane's vision.

"How's Auntie doing?" asked Jane as she held a small ball of dough in her hand.

"Better," said Alice. "She thinks she'll venture out tomorrow."

"Oh, good. I think I'll use this last bit of dough to make a miniquiche for her. Alice, could you toss two more eggs and a quarter cup of milk into that batter to stretch it a little further?"

"Ethel is on pins and needles in regard to Belle," said Louise. "Goodness knows how those two managed to bond in such a short amount of time, but you'd think Belle was some long-lost relative."

"Well, she's just the sort of fun that Auntie loves," pointed out Alice.

"Much better than her nieces," said Jane dourly.

"Aunt Ethel loves us like daughters," said Louise.

"Yes, but she can be a rather bossy mother. She always wants me to dress more femininely or to do something stylish with my hair."

Alice chuckled. "You're not the only one. Before you two moved back home, I had my go-arounds with Auntie. She was always after me to wear makeup and to try something new with my hair. Fortunately, I had Father to stand up for me."

"I still miss him so," said Jane suddenly. She tried not to think about his passing too much, but she regretted that, of the three sisters, she had probably spent the least amount of adult time with their father.

"Yes, I do too," said Alice. "Especially on days like today. Father really loved the coming of a new season. He would always notice even the tiniest detail, whether it was a new bird's nest in the tree or the first jonquil. A lot like you, Jane. But I like to think that parts of Father are still right here with us." She wiped her damp hands on the front of her apron as she looked from Jane to Louise. "And do you know, more and more, I notice those bits and pieces of Father whenever I spend time with my sisters."

Chapter Thirteen

"Y'all are not going to believe what we did last night," said Belle at breakfast Saturday. She was wearing a hot-pink sweater set and sitting between the twins.

"You went to Potterston, right?" said Jane, noticing that Shelby hadn't made an appearance at breakfast yet. "That narrows it down a bit."

"We went bowling."

"Bowling," said Alice. "Was it fun?"

"I'll say." Belle nodded and poked each of the brothers playfully with her elbows. "And these two cleaned our clocks. We played boys against girls, and the twins just kept getting strike after strike. They neglected to tell Shelby and me that they were the champs of the Bronson bowling league until after the damage was done. But it was such a hoot."

"We got to ride in Belle's car too," said one of the twins. Jane still wasn't sure which twin was which.

"It's a real hot rod," said the other. "I thought for sure Belle was going to get a speeding ticket."

"Oh, I wasn't going that fast," she said. "I barely hit seventy."

"Seventy?" Louise looked shocked. "Goodness, Belle. You are lucky you didn't get a ticket."

"Or in a wreck," said Alice.

"Our son-in-law had a bad wreck this winter," said Mr. Blankenship. "He's still having back problems because of it."

"Oh, now," said Mrs. Blankenship, "let's talk about something more cheerful. No sense in scaring these kids."

"Kids," said one of the twins to the other, his green eyes twinkling. "Here we are almost forty, Ron, and someone just called us kids. You gotta love that."

"Speaking of kids," said Jane. "Do either of you have any?"

"We both do," said Ron. "I have a daughter who just started college last fall."

"Me too," said Don.

"You too?" Alice peered curiously at both of them. "You mean you both have daughters the same age?"

"Born just a week apart," said Ron.

"Both have red hair," added Don.

"Could pass for sisters," said Ron.

"Almost like twins?" ventured Louise.

"Like the Patty Duke show back in the sixties," said Alice. "Remember the look-alike cousins?"

"Both played by Patty Duke," said Louise.

"I read an interesting article about twins," began Alice. "It said they often lead parallel lives. They did a study that included twins separated at birth, and they discovered that twins made similar decisions. Often they chose similar careers, even selected similar mates, frequently marrying persons with the same name."

"Our wives were both brunettes," said Ron. "Linda and Brenda."

"Well, that's close, isn't it?" continued Alice as she refilled Mrs. Blankenship's coffee cup. "Also, the twins in the study had children about the same time, not unlike you two gentlemen. Rather mysteriously interesting, I thought."

"Too bad you didn't have twins yourselves," said Louise. "To carry on the twin tradition."

"Our girls act like they're twins," said Don. "They're at the same university and both want to go into medicine."

"More twins in the family would've been fun," said Ron sadly.

"Yes," agreed Don. "I remember when Linda was pregnant, and we were hoping it was twins."

"Well, you're both young enough to have more children," said Belle. "If you were to marry again, that is."

"Not me," said Ron quickly.

"Not me," echoed his brother.

"Do you mean no to marriage or to more children?" questioned Jane.

"Children," they both said together.

"We're done with that," said Ron. "We both think we started our families too early in life. We got tied down in our early twenties, working hard to care for our families and make ends meet. Consequently, we felt we missed out on some fun."

Don chuckled. "I suppose folks back home think we're having a kind of midlife crisis, taking this trip down to Miami."

"But we just wanted to have a ball," said Ron.

"Thought it was about time," added Don.

"Good for you," said Mr. Blankenship. "You know what they say about all work and no play."

"That's right," said his wife, patting her husband's hand as she addressed the brothers. "You must take time to regenerate your spirits."

"That's what we intend to do down in Miami," said Ron.

"Speaking of regenerating," said Louise, "poor Shelby came to the inn for some rest and recuperation. I'm sure you heard that she teaches kindergarten and that it's been quite stressful these past few months."

"Goodness, I hope we didn't wear her out last night," said Belle. "She did mention being tired and that she might sleep in. I made sure to be real quiet when I came out of my room this morning. I didn't even put on my shoes until I got all the way downstairs."

"That was very thoughtful," said Louise.

"I hope Herb's snoring didn't disturb her," said Mrs. Blankenship.

"I doubt she could hear it all the way from your room," said Louise.

Soon, the guests were finishing up breakfast and discussing plans for the day. The Blankenships planned to take a drive through the countryside, and Ron and Don wanted to go antiquing. To Jane's surprise and relief, it sounded as if Belle and Ethel intended to spend the day together. Apparently, Ethel set it up. But as everyone began heading out in their various different directions, Shelby still hadn't shown up.

"I think I'll set aside some breakfast for her," said Jane as they were cleaning up in the kitchen.

"Yes," said Alice. "That would be nice. I'm glad she felt free to sleep in."

By ten o'clock, the house was quiet. Louise went to town to do some errands. Alice was finishing up in the kitchen, and Jane was just straightening the dining room.

"Coast clear?" asked a quiet voice behind her.

Jane turned to see a young, dark-haired woman tiptoe-ing toward her. "You must be Shelby." Jane smiled and introduced herself. "I'm glad you slept in. Sounds like you had a wild night on the town last night."

"I didn't actually sleep in the whole time," she admit-ted. "I just hoped to avoid Belle and Ron and Don today. I'm in serious need of a day of rest."

"I think the twins were heading out to look for antiques," said Jane as she brushed crumbs from the tablecloth. "And Belle will probably be occupied with my aunt today. I saved you some breakfast, if you're interested."

"You're a saint."

"Go ahead and sit down and I'll get it for you. Coffee or tea?"

"Coffee," she said eagerly. "Black, please."

"You got it."

Jane made the silver tray look pretty, setting a vase with a rosebud in it, before she took it out to Shelby. "I think you should have the inn mostly to yourself," she said as she filled the coffee cup and left the carafe for her guest. "At least for the morning."

"Wonderful." Shelby sighed. "I have a big, fat novel to read, and I thought I might stroll around later on, maybe get some lunch."

Jane made some recommendations for eating in town, then told Shelby to have a peaceful and relaxing day. "And just leave your breakfast things right here when you're done, well take care of them."

"Thank you."

Jane joined Alice in the kitchen. "So, what are your plans today?" she asked.

"Vera and I are going to take a long walk. We've decided to do the walkathon this summer, and we need to get into better shape."

"Is that a fund-raiser for the hospital?" asked Jane as she poured herself another cup of coffee.

"Yes. For a new MRI machine. The hospital really needs it."

"I'd like to participate too," said Jane.

Alice grinned. "I already signed you up. And I suggested to Louise that if she doesn't wish to walk, she can always be a sponsor."

"Good for you."

"Would you like to join Vera and me today?"

"No. I think I'll putter around the yard some more. I still haven't enjoyed enough of this great gardening weather yet."

Alice hung up her dish towel. "Well, enjoy."

"You too."

Jane took her coffee and the newspaper outside and sat down at the table. She had placed it quite near the garden, in a spot where it could get both morning sun and some dappled shade in the afternoon. Without bothering to open the paper, she simply sat there breathing in the scented air of warmed earth and green things growing. Divine.

"Morning, Jane," said a male voice.

She turned and waved. "Come join me, Kenneth. It's lovely out here."

He looked tentative. "Is it safe?"

She chuckled. "Do you refer to a certain guest?"

He nodded.

"She's gone off to Potterston with Aunt Ethel to search for wedding things."

"Seriously?"

"Yes, seriously."

He sat down in the other chair at the table, then suddenly got a hopeful expression. "Does that mean Belle has found her man?"

"I'm not sure what it means. But if you're asking if there is a specific fiancé in the picture yet, well, the answer is no."

"Oh."

"Don't worry, Kenneth. If it's any comfort, Belle's list of potential mates is getting longer." Then she told him about the twins, omitting the part about their being almost inseparable.

"So, you think there's some actual marriage potential there?"

Jane shrugged. "I don't know. I think they had fun bowling last night, but I didn't see either of the brothers leaping at the opportunity to spend time with her today. They seemed happy to go off on their own."

"Someone should tell Belle that most bachelors run the other way when they see a woman with marriage in her eyes. She might try being more subtle."

"Subtle?" Jane laughed. "Somehow that word just doesn't fit our Belle."

"No," he agreed, "I think you're right."

"Everything okay with the church basement now?"

"Yes. The sealer Fred gave me seemed to do the trick. It looked much better this morning." He looked more closely at Jane. "And you seem to be better too. Is that due to the sunshine?"

"Yes, it's definitely good medicine." Then she frowned.

"But something is still troubling you?"

She pressed her lips together as she tried to decide whether she wanted to tell Kenneth about Justin's impending visit.

"I can see that you're worried about something, Jane."

She nodded. "You're right."

"I'd love a cup of decaf if you have any made." He smiled hopefully.

"There is still a full pot left over from breakfast." She slowly stood. "I'll get it for you."

"And, see, that will give you time to decide whether to divulge your troubles to your pastor and friend."

"I'll be right back." As she walked to the house, she wasn't sure that she really wanted to tell Kenneth about her problem. But she wasn't sure that she didn't. Besides, she reminded herself, before long, everyone in Acorn Hill would know. Justin's visit might even replace Belle as the talk of the town, at least briefly, anyway. Wouldn't it be easier to tell Kenneth about this now, rather than to wait until Justin made his appearance? Who knew what Justin might say to people? Goodness, she thought as she filled the thermos pitcher with decaf, how would she introduce Justin to Kenneth and all her other friends?

With her hands full, Jane shoved open the screen door with her foot so forcefully that it slammed against the wall. Oh, why couldn't the past remain just that—the past?

Chapter Fourteen

*B*y the time she returned, carrying the thermos and a cup, she knew she should simply get her disturbing news out into the open. She remembered how her father often said that the best way to do something uncomfortable was to do it quickly. Whether peeling off a Band-Aid, taking foul-tasting medicine or righting a wrong, it was usually best to just get it over with.

"Here you go," she said as she set a cup in front of Kenneth, then filled it.

"I've just been observing Wendell's antics." He nodded over to where the cat was rolling in the dust, enjoying the sunshine as well as a dirt bath.

"Silly kitty," said Jane as she sat and refilled her own cup. "And usually he is so dignified."

"Guess we all need to let down our hair sometimes."

"Even you?"

He chuckled. "Well, I don't think I'll get caught rolling in the dirt, at least not in public, but yes, even me." He held up his cup. "Thank you." Then, as he continued looking at her with an even gaze, she knew this was his gentle hint that now was her time to share.

"I think I'll just get right out with it," she began quickly. "My ex-husband is coming to Acorn Hill."

Kenneth looked momentarily surprised, then, returning to his unflappable pastoral countenance, he simply nodded.

"And the question on my mind, as well as my sisters', is why is Justin coming?"

"You don't know why?"

She shook her head, then took a sip of the hot coffee.

"Obviously, he is coming to see you. Right?"

"Well, yes, I suppose. His letter was quite brief."

"He communicated through a letter?"

She explained the letter, the road trip and the reservation that he had made with Louise.

"He'll be staying here at the inn?"

She frowned. "Yes. I wasn't pleased."

"That could be awkward."

"Louise was caught off guard by his call." Jane gave him a sheepish look. "I hadn't even told her he was coming."

"But he's still staying at the inn?"

"I guess so." Jane made a face. "I'm considering going AWOL."

"But you won't."

She shrugged. "That's probably not the most mature way to handle it."

He smiled. "Probably not."

"So, now you know," said Jane. "That's what's been troubling me the past few days."

"I can imagine that would be unsettling."

"Very."

"How do you feel about your former husband, Jane? What is his name again?"

"Justin."

"Right, how do you feel about Justin?"

"In what way? I mean, if you're asking if I'm still angry with him, the answer is no. I've forgiven him. What's past is past. But are you asking if I still have feelings for him, if I still love him?"

"Do you?"

"I don't think so. I mean I do care about him. How can you not care about a person you were once married to? Alice suggested that perhaps Justin might be ill, and I'll admit the thought of that makes me sad. I really do hope he's okay."

"Naturally."

"Maybe he wants me to donate a kidney or something." She gave a weak smile.

"I'm sure you'd consider it, Jane."

She nodded. "You know, Kenneth, I would."

"So, can you guess why he's coming here?"

"That's just it. I can't."

Kenneth seemed to ponder this for a long moment. Finally, he said, "Maybe he still loves you, Jane."

Jane sat there without responding. She was feeling the warmth of the sun on her head, listening to a bird singing sweetly in a nearby maple tree. She considered what Kenneth had just said to her.

"You have to admit that it's a possibility," he persisted. "Justin might still love you, Jane."

"Yes, that's what Alice said. And Sylvia. Even Louise hinted at it."

He smiled at her. "And it wouldn't be surprising, Jane. You're a wonderful person. I've told you before that I thought he was a fool to let you go."

She felt herself blushing. "Well, I think we were both foolish." She laughed. "We weren't young when we married. I actually thought of myself as rather sophisticated at the time. Now I look back and think I was so naive, so foolish, really."

"Perhaps you've both matured since then."

"That has occurred to me."

"God does give second chances, Jane."

She took a quick sip of coffee, avoiding Kenneth's gaze. In truth, Jane wasn't the least bit convinced she wanted a second chance, even if God was the One offering it to her. Naturally, she could not say this to Kenneth. Not only did it sound irreverent and disrespectful, but she also knew that Kenneth and God were like partners on good speaking terms. Still, it troubled her to feel this way, as if she were being rebellious and willful. She didn't like feeling that she might be putting herself at odds with God. And yet, it troubled her even more to think that God might want her to give Justin a second chance.

"Uh-oh," said Kenneth, glancing out toward the street. "That looks like Belle's car parking. I thought you said she and Ethel were going to Potterston today."

"I thought they were," said Jane. "Now that Auntie is feeling better, she's insistent on helping Belle with the planning."

He took a final sip of coffee. "You'll excuse me if I make a quick retreat, won't you, Jane?"

"Of course." She grinned. "The runaway groom."

He firmly shook his finger at her as he stood. "I am not the groom."

"Not yet, you aren't."

"Jane Howard," he said in a mock warning tone. "You are wicked."

"Later," she called as he hurried off around the back way.

"Hello, Jane," said Ethel as she and Belle made their way toward her.

"Hello, ladies," Jane said as she stood to meet them. "You look like you're doing much better, Auntie."

"Why, yes," Ethel said, patting her smooth cheeks. "Thank you."

"Was that Rev. Thompson?" asked Belle as she eagerly peered over Jane's shoulder in the direction Kenneth had headed.

Jane avoided answering Belle by asking a question of her own. "Why are you back so soon?"

"We need a model," said Ethel.

"A model?" Jane frowned. "What do you mean?"

"We were in town, speaking to Sylvia to get some pointers on wedding gowns, and we were about to head to Potterston when it occurred to me that this would go much more quickly if you could come with us to try on bridesmaid dresses. That way, you can stand next to Belle, and I can stand back and decide which dresses go together best."

Jane wanted to point out that picking out dresses was impractical when no groom had stepped up to the plate. But not only did that sound mean, she would probably get Belle's typical response, "God will provide."

"I really need to stick around the inn today," said Jane.

"Nonsense," said her aunt. "Louise and Alice are both here."

"But I have my garden to—"

"Your garden will wait." Ethel gave Jane a commanding look. "I am your aunt, Jane. And I have been ill. I would think you would show me some cooperation."

"But, Aunt Ethel," tried Jane. "I just don't see the point of—"

"The point is that Belle has a wedding to plan. She came to Acorn Hill because God gave her a dream."

"I know." Jane's exasperation rose to the surface. She turned to Belle. "I don't want to offend you, Belle, but I am having difficulty with this. I mean, if you actually were engaged or at least if there was a particular man involved, it might be—"

"There is a particular man involved," said Ethel.

Jane was surprised. "Who?"

Her aunt glanced about as if to see if anyone was around to listen, which was not the case. "Well, if you must know, Jane. We think it might be Wilhelm."

"Wilhelm?" Jane felt a stab of empathy for the poor man. "And what makes you think it's him?"

Ethel held up one finger. "For one thing, Lloyd thinks that it's possible. He and Wilhelm chatted, and Wilhelm was quite impressed with Belle." Then she held up a second finger. "And tonight, Lloyd, Wilhelm, Belle and I plan to play bridge." Then she held up a third finger. "Finally, Belle and I were just in town and we ran into Wilhelm's mother."

Jane glanced at Belle, who seemed embarrassed. "What did you think of Mrs. Wood?"

"She seemed nice."

Jane turned back to her aunt. "And how did Mrs. Wood react to Belle?"

"She was very kind to Belle." Ethel nodded so firmly that her chins gave a shake. "She seemed to approve, Jane."

Jane thought that unlikely since Wilhelm's mother seemed quite content for her son to remain a bachelor for the rest of his days. Still, several people had noticed the interest Wilhelm seemed to have taken in Belle. Unless he was simply being polite. It was hard to know. Jane turned her attention back to Belle.

"How do you feel about Wilhelm?" she asked.

For the first time, Belle seemed unsure. "I'd like to get to know him better."

Suddenly, Jane felt sorry for Belle. She was getting in over her head with all this wedding nonsense. And with Ethel in charge, Belle might be drowning before long. Still, Jane was not about to let herself be dragged around Potterston, trying on bridesmaid dresses today. She would put her foot down.

"It seems to me," she began, directing this more to Belle than her aunt, "your time might be better spent narrowing down who your groom is going to be rather than running around trying to pick out dresses. After all, a marriage is supposed to last a lifetime, and a wedding dress is just for one day."

Belle's eyes lit up. "You are absolutely right, Jane." She turned to Ethel. "I think I should take your niece's advice, Ethel."

"You don't want to pick out your wedding gown?" asked Ethel.

"Oh, I do," said Belle, "in good time. But at the moment, I think I should focus my attention on my prospective husband."

Ethel was clearly at a loss. She switched her purse to the other arm. "So, then, shall we go pay Wilhelm a little visit? I could use some tea."

"How about if we go visit the pastor first?" suggested Belle.

Aunt Ethel's eyebrows arched, then she glanced uneasily at Jane. "Do you know where he was going?"

"I couldn't say," admitted Jane.

"Well, I would like to get another little peek at the chapel," said Belle as she linked arms with Ethel. "I've been trying to imagine big pink bows at the end of each row, but I'd really like to see it again just to be sure."

"Good idea," said Ethel. "We'll make notes of these details."

And off they headed toward the chapel. Jane hoped that Kenneth would have the good sense to stay out of their way. Or perhaps he should just nicely but firmly let Belle know that he did not wish to be on her list.

Jane briefly toyed with the thought of paying Wilhelm a visit too. She wasn't sure if he was fully aware of Belle's intentions. On the other hand, how could he not be aware? Everyone in Acorn Hill must be aware by now. Finally, she told herself that Wilhelm was a big boy. Goodness, he'd been a bachelor since forever. What were the chances of him accidentally stumbling into marriage now? And certainly his mother would put her foot down if he seemed the least bit inclined to make a mistake. Besides, what if he was seriously interested in Belle? No, she decided, Wilhelm did not need her protection.

Instead, she went inside, then slipped into her overalls and Crocs. She grabbed her garden gloves and her straw hat before she headed back out to lose herself in the sunshine and growing things. She could not imagine a better distraction from disturbing thoughts of marriage, ex-husbands and ill-conceived weddings.

Chapter Fifteen

*S*unday may have been a day of rest for most folks in Acorn Hill, but it was clear that Belle and Ethel had big plans for their day. For starters, Ethel joined Belle for breakfast at the inn, carrying a little notebook full of wedding ideas that she and Belle discussed freely in front of the discreetly amused guests. It also seemed Ethel wished to get a better look at the Johnson twins. Perhaps she thought she might have the power to break up the set and present Belle with the "better" half. But it was clear that the brothers were not interested in matrimony. In fact, Jane thought she detected real fear in their eyes as they finished up breakfast. And when Louise invited them to church, they politely excused themselves by saying that they wanted to get on the road as quickly as possible.

"Florida awaits," proclaimed Don, giving Belle an uneasy glance.

"That's right," agreed Ron. "One more stop in South Carolina to visit our aunt Rae, and then it's straight to Miami."

"By Tuesday, well be hitting the beach."

"After that we'll head out for some fishing and exploring."

The others wished the men well. More than ever, it seemed that Ethel was doggedly determined to find a match for Belle, although Belle seemed unaffected by the twins' hasty departure. Perhaps they had not been to her liking. But as the sisters were cleaning up in the kitchen, they overheard their aunt going over the list of potential targets. It seemed she had broken the list into sections. The sisters had no idea what these sections represented. Perhaps simply their aunt's own personal likes and dislikes.

Later in church, Ethel and Belle sat next to Wilhelm and his mother. After the service, Belle and Ethel monopolized Kenneth's attention.

Finally it was afternoon, and all the guests except Belle had checked out. The inn was quiet, and the sisters gathered on the front porch with iced tea and gingersnaps. Belle was spending the day with Ethel.

"One of the reservations for next weekend is a rather intriguing fellow," said Louise as she refilled her glass with tea.

"You mean someone besides Justin?" asked Jane wryly.

Louise frowned, but she ignored Jane and continued, "Do either of you ever read Clive Fagler in the *Philadelphia Inquirer?*"

"Sure. I read his column all the time." Jane bent down to pick up Wendell, situating him comfortably in her lap. "I like his writing. He's very witty."

"I've read the column a few times myself," said Alice.

"I thought you might be interested to know that he'll be staying here from Wednesday through Memorial Day weekend."

"Really?" Jane brightened as she stroked Wendell's furry coat. "That should be fun."

"Yes. He said that he's looking forward to a restful break from the city."

"He'll find it here." Alice waved her hand toward the quiet street. "I haven't seen a car go by since church."

Louise cleared her throat. "However, it occurs to me that there is a minor problem or at least the potential for one."

"What?" asked Alice as she reached for a cookie.

"Mr. Fagler is a bachelor."

Jane let out a groan. "Belle."

"And Aunt Ethel," said Louise.

"What do we do?" asked Jane.

"I don't want either of them to terrorize the poor man."

"Oh, Louise," said Alice in a good-natured tone. "All you need to do is warn Auntie, and I'm sure she'll respect your wishes. And you know, Belle never terrorizes anyone. She's really very sweet."

"You know what the Bible says about too much honey," said Louise.

"That it can make you sick," Jane finished for her.

"Perhaps if you mentioned our new guest a little ahead of time. Tell Belle that Clive Fagler is coming," suggested Alice. "Simply be up front with her and tell her that Clive is a bachelor, but that he expects to have a restful vacation in Acorn Hill."

"I suppose you're right. Honesty really is the best policy," agreed Louise. "And I do think Belle is a good person. I just feel she is carried away with her unfortunate dream."

"And Aunt Ethel encourages her," said Jane.

"Auntie is simply caught up in the idea of a wedding," said Alice. "You know how she can be, and she felt she missed out on some of the fun while she was cooped up with her rash. Give her a few days, and I'm sure she'll come to her senses."

"Still, I wish we could put a stop to this nonsense." Louise picked up her knitting bag and adjusted her glasses. "I can't tell you how glad I'll be after the first Saturday of June is finally past."

"I was even feeling sorry for our pastor after the service this morning," said Jane. "It seemed that Aunt Ethel and Belle had the poor man cornered."

"Well, if you had been closer, you might have observed that our pastor handled the whole thing quite nicely." Louise's knitting needles began to click together, making a rhythmic sound. "I couldn't help but overhear."

"What?" demanded Jane eagerly. "What did he say?"

"He told Belle that he wished her well. And that, while he respected her wedding dream and that it may very well have come from God, he knew for a fact that he was not meant to be a part in it."

"Except to perform the wedding," added Alice with a smile. "He did promise her he would do that when the time came. Very nicely, I might add."

"It seemed to settle it for her," said Louise. Then she shook her head. "But I noticed Wilhelm observing from a distance, pretending to visit with Clara Horn, but keeping his eyes on Belle the whole time. I do believe he was jealous."

"Really?" Jane chuckled. "Perhaps Wilhelm is interested after all."

"Belle is a charming young woman," said Alice. "Don't you think she'll make a wonderful wife?"

Neither Louise nor Jane responded.

"Anyway," said Louise. "Belle and Wilhelm and Lloyd and Auntie seem to have plans for the evening. After Belle and Aunt Ethel do some things in Potterston, they will meet up with the men to see a matinee, followed by dinner."

"Wouldn't it be wonderful for Wilhelm if Belle really was the woman for him?" asked Alice.

"Despite the age difference?" questioned Louise.

"Age shouldn't matter," said Alice. "Not if they're truly in love."

"And Wilhelm's mother?" ventured Jane.

"I'm sure she'd be happy for Wilhelm."

Louise cleared her throat in a way that suggested she did not agree. And Jane looked dubious.

By Tuesday morning, Belle seemed to have a serious case of the wedding blues. It seemed that Wilhelm was officially off her list. He had made it clear to Belle that, while he found her charming and fun, he had no interest in settling down. Not only that, but Craig Tracy had been forced to take Ethel aside yesterday. He quickly told Jane the whole story when he stopped by to drop off some annuals for her garden Monday afternoon.

"I didn't like being so hard on your aunt," he'd explained, glancing over his shoulder to make sure that neither Belle nor Ethel were about. "But she just kept pestering me."

"She is persistent."

"I'll say. I knew as soon as they entered my shop that I was in for trouble. Naturally, they acted as if they'd come to discuss floral arrangements for this farce of a wedding. But it was obvious something else was going on. So I invited Ethel to come into the back, supposedly to see something I was working on for you and the inn. But in the privacy of the back room, I told her in no uncertain terms that I am not to be considered as a matrimonial candidate. And if they really wanted me to do their flowers, I'd be happy to. But that's where it would end."

Jane had commended him on being so straightforward, then thanked him for the flat of multicolored petunias. He explained that he'd started far more of them than he needed and was surprised when they fared so well in the greenhouse during their extended winter. "Hardy little things."

"Well, they'll really perk up the beds along the front walk. Now, what do I owe you?"

"Just a couple hours of your time this week."

"Doing what?"

"I volunteered to get the planters in front of Town Hall spruced up in time for the Memorial Day celebration.

I'm going with a patriotic color scheme. I thought I might be able to talk you into helping out."

Of course, she agreed, and he promised to pick her up Thursday morning. "That's the soonest I can get to it." Just then, they both noticed Belle strolling their way, probably on her way to Ethel's, and Craig excused himself, making a quick exit. As he left, Jane felt sorry for him. It was a sad day when a good friend like Craig Tracy felt the need to escape the sanctuary of Jane's garden.

But this morning, a day later, she now felt sorry for Belle. Her expression was pitifully sad, and she just didn't look herself. She was wearing a wrinkled white blouse, warm-up pants, and pink fuzzy house slippers. In addition, she had come down to breakfast without a speck of makeup. The poor thing was obviously downhearted.

"More coffee?" Jane offered after Louise excused herself from the table. Alice had already left for work.

"I suppose." Belle sighed. "Might as well drown my sorrows."

"Do you have plans today?" she asked.

"Your aunt said she'd come by around ten for me."

"To do wedding things?" ventured Jane.

"I suppose, although I'm beginning to wonder what the point is. Maybe I should just give up, go home, call it a day."

Jane sat down across from Belle, and using her kindest voice asked, "Do you think it's possible that your dream might have been wrong, Belle?"

She sighed again, more deeply this time.

"I know that God can give people dreams," continued Jane gently. "But sometimes a dream is just a dream, not something you should base a life decision on."

Belle looked at Jane with misty blue eyes. "But it seemed so real. Just as real as you and me sitting here talking right now. And I had such a sense of peace and hope when I woke up. I really do believe it was from God."

As much as Jane wanted to tell Belle to give up and move on, somehow she just couldn't. "Then, if you really believe that, Belle, you should probably keep pursuing it." Even as Jane said this, she wished she hadn't.

"I do believe it, Jane. I really do."

"I don't understand it," admitted Jane. "To be honest, I think it sounds pretty crazy. But if you truly believe it—"

"I do!" exclaimed Belle with what seemed fresh conviction. "And I'm going to see this thing through to the end, no matter which way it goes." She smiled. "Thank you, Jane. Thank you for encouraging me. And when I do get married, I really would like you to be in my wedding party."

Jane controlled herself from rolling her eyes. Then, realizing that a wedding was highly unlikely, she simply nodded. "Thank you, Belle. That's very sweet of you."

Belle stood suddenly. "Well, I better get moving. I need to fix up if I'm going to be running around town with Ethel today."

"Have a good day," said Jane.

"Thank you," Belle beamed at her. "Thanks to you, I think I will."

The irony was that Jane now felt as if she'd switched emotions with Belle. Encouraging Belle to pursue what seemed a hopeless dream left Jane feeling blue. Still, Jane knew that the circumstance wasn't her fault. She'd only been trying to cheer Belle. Besides, there weren't that many bachelors left in Acorn Hill. Jane looked at the calendar— less than two weeks until Belle's big day. Really, it seemed utterly hopeless, not to mention ridiculous. Of course, looking at the calendar also reminded her that Justin was scheduled to arrive in just four days. If only he would change his mind. And yet, she supposed she was getting a little bit curious too. What was it that was bringing him to Acorn Hill? And if, as her family and friends suggested, he was coming to ask her to come back to him, how would she handle the situation?

She sat down with a cup of coffee and pondered the idea. What *would* she say? She had been hurt and disappointed when the marriage ended. She had still loved Justin and wasn't ready to give up. Having been raised in a Christian home with a minister for a father, she had entered into her marriage thinking it was a lifetime commitment. Certainly, she had rebelled against many things in regard to her traditional upbringing, but some values, like the sanctity of marriage, stayed with her. She had assumed that Justin felt the same. Consequently, she felt blindsided by his blithe announcement that their life together was over. At first, she thought he was kidding. But he was not. Then she suggested they get counseling, and he said it was too late. He told her that what they once had together was finished. He said that what was broken could never be fixed. And he suggested that much of it was her fault. That had hurt.

Certainly, she noticed that their fights were becoming more numerous and more emotional. But, usually, they fought about silly things, things that were mostly related to the fact that she'd been offered the prestigious position as head chef at the Blue Fish Grille. Justin, still working at a less impressive restaurant, was just plain jealous. It was food that brought them together, and it seemed ironic that food would ultimately drive them apart. But competition within a marriage, Jane discovered, could be toxic.

Early in their relationship, they had enjoyed what seemed like harmless rivalry. Fellow workers at the restaurant they both worked for seemed to enjoy it too. In fact, their colleagues even encouraged it. The bantering and teasing seemed benign at first. Jane assumed that a little friendly competition made them both better chefs. But in the end, Jane was the one to receive the higher praise in the restaurant world. She was the one who ended up being reviewed in the newspapers. And Justin was the one who ended up being jealous and then underhanded, as he claimed that the recipes Jane was praised for were really his own.

But perhaps Kenneth was right. Perhaps Justin had grown up. Jane knew that she'd matured some since coming back home. What if they both had changed significantly? What if there really was a chance . . . for a *second* chance?

Chapter Sixteen

The beautiful weather continued into the week. Jane's garden seemed to be growing quickly now, as if the flowers knew that they'd been stunted by the previous weather and were doing all they could to make up for it. Jane stood looking out over her plants, knowing that, thanks to the blue sky and sunshine and warm temperature, she should be feeling happy. But, in fact, she felt as if a dark, brooding cloud were overshadowing her. It was Wednesday afternoon, and all she could think about was the dismal countdown leading to Justin's arrival. In two days, her ex would be checking into the inn and wanting to speak to her. It was more than she could bear to think about.

"Yoo-hoo, Jane?" called Ethel as she approached. She had on a stylish suit in a periwinkle blue.

Jane waved. "Hi, Auntie. You look very pretty. Is that a new suit?"

Ethel did a little turnaround to show off her outfit. "As a matter of fact, it is. I found it while shopping in Potterston with Belle. Actually, she picked it out."

"Well, it looks lovely."

"Thank you. Belle really does have fine fashion sense and such an eye for color. Don't you think?"

Jane nodded. "That certainly is a lovely color on you, Auntie."

"Anyway, Jane, I just wanted to tell you that I think you're wonderful for the way you encouraged our Belle the other day. She told me how she'd been feeling so down-hearted about Wilhelm and Craig and even Rev. Thompson, as if she'd used up all her Acorn Hill resources, which is just plain silly. But whatever it was you said to her really lifted her spirits. I thank you for that."

"I only told her that if she really believed in her dream, she shouldn't give up." Jane frowned. "I hope that wasn't bad advice."

"Of course not."

"Is anything new developing?"

Ethel immediately launched into their new hit list, all men that Jane could not imagine someone like Belle being happily married to. Still, she kept her thoughts to herself.

"And," continued Ethel, "I'm taking Belle to see about a house today."

"A house?"

"Yes." She rubbed her hands together with excitement. "Lloyd was talking to Richard Watson yesterday, and it seems that Richard has just listed the McCullough house. Lloyd thinks Belle could get a really good deal on it."

"That cute little bungalow on Oak Street?"

"That's the one."

"What does Belle think of this idea?"

"She doesn't even know yet. I'm on my way to tell her."

"Does she really want to buy a house before she knows if she's actually going—"

"Oh, ye of little faith," Ethel interrupted. "And here I thought you were behind Belle."

Jane held up her hands. "Sorry, Auntie, but it still seems far-fetched to me."

"You'll see," said Ethel, marching toward the house.

"I'm sure I will," muttered Jane. She was afraid that what she was going to see would be disappointing and humiliating for poor Belle. And the idea of her buying real estate in Acorn Hill was too much. Someone really should put a stop to it. She even considered talking to Kenneth. He was a good man to give counsel. But Kenneth, like most of the other bachelors in town, was trying to keep a safe distance from Belle.

Jane watched as Belle's bright pink car, with the top down, drove toward town. Ethel and Belle both had scarves tied around their heads, movie-star style, and both wore sunglasses. They looked quite glamorous, really, especially for Acorn Hill. Jane knew that her aunt had been thoroughly enjoying Belle and her car these past few days. They made quite a pair. Jane felt certain that a stranger might take them for mother and daughter, and she was sure that Ethel would enjoy the mistake. *Really,* Jane thought, *I should be glad for Auntie.* Ethel was certainly making the most of the new friendship. Also, it took her aunt's focus off Jane. Today, despite Jane's wearing her overalls and Crocs, Ethel had barely seemed to notice. Perhaps having Belle as a permanent resident in town wouldn't be such a bad thing.

"Jane," called Louise from the back porch.

"Yes?"

"Can you mind the fort for me for an hour or so?"

Jane set down her hoe and went over to see her sister. "Sure. What's up?"

"Viola just called, and she sounded a little depressed. I thought I might go over to the bookstore and have a cup of tea with her. Tea and sympathy." Louise held up the cordless phone. "I'll just put this here by the back door so you can hear it if it rings. Then you can stay outside and continue in your garden."

"Thanks."

Louise hooked her handbag over her arm and came down the steps toward Jane. "It's such a lovely day."

"Yes. The flowers seem to be enjoying it."

"What a change from last week."

Jane adjusted her straw hat. "So, why is Viola feeling down?"

"It's Gatsby."

Jane tried to recall which one of Viola's many cats was Gatsby. "Is that the black-and-white?"

"Yes. He's quite heavy and he's been having some health problems. He's at the veterinary clinic now for observation. She's worried it might be something serious."

Jane nodded. "Well, tell her I'll be thinking of her . . . and Gatsby."

"Thank you."

"And take your time, Louise. I don't have anyplace to go this afternoon."

Louise nodded. "Perhaps I'll stop by the Good Apple and pick up something to have with our tea. That might cheer Viola up."

"I'm sure she'll appreciate that and your company."

Then Louise waved and headed off toward town.

Jane had just picked up her hoe when the phone began to ring. She dropped the hoe, peeled off her gloves and hurried over to answer it. But just as she was pressing the on button, she had a dreadful feeling that it could be Justin.

"Grace Chapel Inn," she said in a very businesslike manner.

"Hello," said a female voice.

"Hello," said Jane in a much friendlier tone. "How may I help you?"

"Oh, I hope you *can* help me. I spoke to you a week ago about a reservation for our honeymoon, maybe you remember me?"

"Actually, my sister Louise handles the reservations. But if you'll give me a moment, I'll head to the office where I can take a look at the reservation schedule."

"Thank you. You see my husband and I got married last weekend. We had made a reservation to stay at your inn for Memorial Day weekend on our way back from our wedding trip along the eastern seaboard, but the weather report was so nasty for the time of our travel that we just canceled the whole thing."

"You canceled your honeymoon?" asked Jane as she went behind the desk and reached for the reservation book.

"Well, I suppose we mostly postponed it. We just stayed home. But now that the weather has turned so lovely, I thought perhaps we could get our reservation back at your bed-and-breakfast. It was recommended to us by some very dear friends, and we'd been really looking forward to it. Do you think it's possible?"

"When did you want to come?" asked Jane as she thumbed through the pages.

"We had hoped for this weekend." Her voice sounded hopeful.

"Oh." Jane looked down at the schedule for the end of May, noting with dismay that Justin Hinton was written down from Friday through Monday.

"I know it's last-minute," said the woman urgently. "But we did make a reservation way back in February, and I would so love to stay at your bed-and-breakfast. Perhaps our names are still down for those dates. Do you think that's possible? Garth and Gloria Fairview."

"I can see where your reservation used to be," admitted Jane as she saw where their names had been erased and replaced with the name of her ex-husband.

"But you're full up now?" Disappointment oozed from Gloria's voice.

"Well, let me see."

"Oh, I had just so hoped . . . I had actually prayed for a miracle this morning."

"You know," Jane began slowly. "It seems to me that if you made your reservation clear back in February, well, perhaps we should honor your original reservation after all."

"Really?"

Jane erased Justin's name and then wrote down *Mr. and Mrs. Fairview, newlyweds.* "Yes," she said with conviction. "Do you still wish to stay until Monday?"

"Oh yes, that would be wonderful!"

"Okay," said Jane. "I have you down."

"Thank you, thank you," gushed Gloria. "You have no idea how much this means to us."

Jane wanted to tell Gloria that she had no idea how much it meant to her, but she simply said, "You are most welcome. Travel safely." She did feel guilty when she hung up, but then she told herself that the Fairviews had made their reservation prior to Justin. And it was their belated honeymoon. Surely, Louise would have done the same thing.

"Hello?" called a male voice from the foyer.

Jane closed the reservation book and, assuring herself that the voice did not sound the least bit like Justin's, she stepped from behind the desk and greeted a middle-aged man who seemed vaguely familiar. Then it hit her. Clive Fagler, the columnist for the *Philadelphia Inquirer.*

"My name is Clive Fagler. I have a reservation?" he said in a questioning voice, as if perhaps he was in the wrong place.

"Oh yes, Mr. Fagler." Jane looked down at her overalls. "Sorry about my appearance," she said quickly. "I was working in the garden and had to fill in for my sister Louise. She usually handles reservations and guests, but she had to step out."

He grinned. "That's quite okay. I happen to have a pair of old overalls myself."

"You do?" She studied his neatly pressed khakis and yellow button-down shirt topped with a neat navy vest, and wasn't entirely convinced.

He chuckled. "Yes. Actually, I do. A remnant of my former life of attempting to be a hippie back in the late sixties."

She smiled. "My overalls from the old days wore out long ago."

"That's because you, unlike me, must've put them to good use. I was simply a wannabe gardener. Although I've been considering taking it up again."

"Don't you live in the city?"

"Yes, but I have a tiny terrace where I thought I might try some potted herbs. Things I might use in the kitchen."

"That's a super idea. I have an herb garden that I adore. It's so handy to simply step out your door and cut a bit of fresh rosemary or basil to add to a dish."

"So you garden *and* cook?"

She looked shyly down at her Crocs, then back up.

"Actually, I'm a cook by profession, and I do the cooking for the inn."

His eyes lit up. "You and I have some things in common." Then he got a serious look. "Do you write too?"

She laughed. "No. Not unless you count recipes."

"That's a relief." He laughed. "I was starting to get an inferiority complex."

"By the way, I'm Jane Howard. I love your column."

"Thank you."

"My two sisters and I own and run the inn."

"Well, it's a beautiful house, and the town looked charming when I drove through. I'm looking forward to my stay here."

"I hope you have a relaxing and refreshing time. Would you like me to show you to your room?"

"I'll just go get my bags. I left them in the car."

"Need help?"

He grinned. "No, but thanks."

Jane hurried to check out her image in the mirror in the foyer. She'd completely forgotten that she still had on her straw hat. She removed it, shoving it behind the reservation desk, and then she returned to the mirror, where she quickly smoothed her hair and wiped a smudge of dirt from her cheek. At least she had on a pretty, rose, lace-trimmed T-shirt.

"Can you believe this weather?" commented Clive as he came back inside. "One week it's like winter and then we're plunged smack into summer."

"Yes, it has been extremely unpredictable," she said. "But I'll take this warm weather over that nasty stuff anytime."

"It was like the never-ending winter."

"Mr. Fagler, if you'd sign the book there," she said as she pointed to the reception desk, "I'll get your key."

"Please," he said, "call me Clive."

"Certainly, Clive." Louise had given Clive the Sunset Room, Jane's favorite. She took the key and, when he set down the pen, pointed to the stairs. "Your room is on the second floor. Unless you'd like a tour of the inn first?"

"I would love a complete tour of the inn." He looked at her. "And your garden too, if that's okay, Ms. Howard."

"Please, call me Jane. I'll be more than happy to give you a tour, including my garden, not that it's anything fancy. I might even be able to give you some herb-growing tips."

"That sounds great, but I'd like to change into something a little cooler first. This woolen vest seemed a good idea this morning, but I'm baking in it now."

"Right this way," she said as she led him up the stairs. "While you're changing, I'll clean up a bit. I've pretty much promised my sisters that I won't wear my gardening clothes in the house. I think they're worried that I might put off the guests."

He laughed. "Oh, I doubt you could put off anyone, Jane."

"Here is your room." She turned the key in the door, letting it swing open to reveal the terra-cotta-colored walls with the faux finishing that gave it an old-world touch. "It's called the Sunset Room."

He went in, setting his bags on the floor by the bed. "It's lovely."

"Thank you," said Jane. "It's one of my favorites."

He walked around, looking at the interesting styles of painted furniture and finally taking in the various pieces of carefully matted and framed Impressionist prints. "Nice choices of art."

"Thanks," she said.

He turned and peered curiously at her. "Let me guess, Jane, you're a decorator too?"

She shrugged. "I like to dabble. It was fun doing the inn."

"I had a feeling, when I first met you, that you were the creative type."

She was starting to feel self-conscious. "Well, I hope you're comfortable here. If there's anything you need, just let us know."

"We're still on for the tour?"

"Oh, yes," she said, remembering her promise. "Just give me about thirty minutes, and I'll meet you downstairs."

Chapter Seventeen

*J*ane hurried up to the third floor and to her room. She didn't know why she felt nervous. Was it because Clive Fagler was a well-known writer? Or was it because he seemed to be giving her some positive attention? Or, perhaps it wasn't Clive at all. Perhaps her jitters had to do with Justin and that she'd erased his reservation.

She quickly showered and dressed in a pair of cream-colored linen pants topped by a pale blue silk top, then slipped into a pair of sandals. It felt so good to be wearing summer-weight clothing again. She brushed out her hair and put it into a French twist, and even put on a beaded necklace in shades of blue and silver. She added a large silver cuff bracelet and also a light spray of cologne. Then she hurried back downstairs, expecting to find Clive waiting. Instead, she found Louise. And she was frowning.

"Jane?"

"Yes?" Jane glanced toward the dining room.

"Did you take a reservation today?"

Jane swallowed hard. "Uh, yes, let me explain—"

"You canceled Justin's reservation?"

Jane took her sister by the arm and led her back to the kitchen. "We have a guest, Louise. Clive Fagler arrived. I showed him to his room. And he's coming down soon so that I can give him a tour."

Louise looked Jane up and down from head to toe. "You certainly cleaned up nicely, Jane."

Jane stood straighter. "I would think you'd appreciate that."

Louise smiled wryly, then pointed to the reservation book, tapping her forefinger on the spot where Jane had made her little adjustment. "What exactly is going on here, Jane?"

Jane looked at Louise with pleading eyes. "The poor woman was beside herself, Louise. They had planned to stay here for their honeymoon—*their honeymoon*—and she'd actually been praying—"

"They canceled that reservation, Jane."

"I know. But when she told me that they hadn't even gone on their honeymoon because of the weather, and how much they wanted to come to Grace Chapel Inn, and how their friends recommended—"

"That shouldn't matter, Jane."

"It matters to them, Louise." Just then Jane heard the sound of voices out in the foyer. It was impossible to make out the actual words, but it was clearly Belle having a con-versation with Clive.

"Oh no," said Jane, holding a finger in front of her lips.

"What is it?" whispered Louise.

"Belle must've gotten back just in time to make the acquaintance of Clive Fagler."

Louise frowned. "Oh dear."

Jane paused, trying to listen, but it seemed the voices were slowly moving away from them. Perhaps Belle was giving Clive the tour herself. "Maybe I should go rescue him," suggested Jane.

"Not so quickly," said Louise. "What about our little double-booking problem?"

"The Fairviews booked it first."

"But they canceled, Jane."

"And now they have un-canceled."

"But, as you know, I booked that date for Justin."

"And I un-booked it."

"You are making up words, Jane."

"I'm simply being creative. Please, Louise. Let this go."

"But what will I tell—"

"Tell Justin there's been a mistake. Tell him there was a prior booking made clear back in February, Louise. Tell him that there was a mix-up. Tell him that they were new-lyweds on their honeymoon. Tell him that they—"

"Perhaps I should let you tell him"—Louise actually smiled—"since you are so full of wonderful excuses."

"Okay," said Jane. "Give me his phone number and I'll be happy—"

"You know that I don't have a phone number."

"See," said Jane. "That's just another good reason to give up his room. Guests always give you phone numbers, addresses, the works. I'll bet he didn't even secure the room with a credit card, did he?"

"Well, no—"

"And if you've told me once, Louise, you've told me a dozen times, to secure the room with a credit card, right?"

"Yes, but—"

"No buts, Louise. If this reservation had been made properly, it wouldn't have been canceled."

Louise gave Jane a skeptical look. "If this reservation had been made by anyone besides your ex-husband, it never would've been canceled either."

Jane shrugged. "I suppose not. I'm sorry, Louise, really I am. It was a desperate move made by a desperate woman."

Louise chuckled. "Even so, it puts me in a difficult position."

"Blame it on me, Louise. Really, I can take it. Tell Justin that I am the bozo who messed up the reservation. I would much rather have Justin mad at me than you mad at me."

"I'm not mad at you, Jane."

"I know I've frustrated you. And I'm sorry. Really, I am. It's just that I couldn't bear to have Justin staying in our family home, whether or not it's an inn, not for one single night, let alone three. It was simply too much."

Louise pressed her lips tightly together as if she was trying to think of an amicable way to resolve this.

"Even Kenneth was concerned for my well-being," continued Jane quickly. "He was surprised that you'd booked Justin here. He didn't think I should have to stay under the same roof as Justin."

"Kenneth said that?"

"He did."

"*Hmm.*"

"So, please, Louise, can't we just let it go? Really, I'm happy to take the entire blame. And I'm sure Justin will assume it was my doing anyway."

Louise closed her eyes and rubbed her chin. Finally, she nodded. "All right, Jane, we'll do this your way."

Jane hugged her sister.

Then Louise stepped back and looked at Jane. "And I will take the blame, Jane. If Justin asks, I will tell him it was my mistake."

"But you—"

"The truth is, it was my mistake, Jane. Kenneth is right.

You are right. I never should've booked Justin a room here in the first place, at least not without your consent. I'm sorry." Louise's eyes were getting moist.

"Louise?" Jane peered at her. "It's okay. Don't take it so hard. You're not crying, are you?"

"It's just that I, well, I suppose I thought that perhaps Justin was coming to make things right with you." She sniffed. "I know it may sound terribly old-fashioned, Jane, but it has always troubled me that your marriage ended. I've often wondered if I should have done something more . . . as your older sister. Perhaps I neglected something, something that would have made a difference."

"Oh, Louise." Jane firmly shook her head. "You didn't do a thing wrong. You've always been supportive. If anything, you did it all right by having such a strong marriage yourself. I never got to witness Father and Mother's marriage, though I know it was a good one. But seeing you and Eliot in a healthy relationship gave me hope that I could have the same thing. The fact that Justin and I never got there had nothing to do with you."

"You are certain?" Louise dabbed her eyes with a lace-trimmed handkerchief.

"Positive. But it's sweet that you were so concerned."

"It's only because I care about you, Jane. And it's possible that Justin has changed. He could be coming here to make things right with you. What if he wants to win you back? What if he's coming to talk you into returning to San Francisco with him?"

Jane took in a deep breath. "I think that's highly unlikely."

"But don't you think it could be a possibility?"

Jane bit her lip. Maybe it was a slim, very slim, possibility. "I don't know."

Louise took in a deep breath and stood straighter. "I suppose that all we can do is to wait and see."

"Yes." Suddenly Jane remembered Clive . . . in the hands of Belle. "Did you say anything to Belle about Clive, Louise? I mean in regard to her manhunt mission and how he should probably be off-limits?"

"Oh dear!" Louise put her hand to her lips. "I meant to say something. I just never found an opportune moment."

"Well, perhaps Clive will actually find Belle appealing." But, even as Jane said this, she secretly hoped it wouldn't be so. It seemed as if Clive had found Jane appealing. And she had enjoyed his admiration. She would be disappointed if he showed Belle the same sort of attention. Still, she told herself that was silly.

"You should go and find them, Jane," said Louise urgently. "Make sure that Belle is not monopolizing the poor man's time."

"Well, I did promise him a tour of the inn."

"Hurry, Jane. There's no telling what Belle may have told the unsuspecting man by now."

Jane paused in the foyer, listening to determine which direction Belle and Clive had gone. Or perhaps Belle had whisked him away to points unknown in her pink convertible. Jane hoped not. She thought she heard voices and headed toward the library, where she discovered them. She stood in the shadows of the doorway, quietly looking on and trying to decide whether to intrude. Clive had donned a pair of tortoiseshell reading glasses and seemed to be examining the cover of one of her father's old books. Then he carefully opened the leather-bound book and curiously peered inside without speaking. Meanwhile, Belle, less than a foot away, watched with wide-eyed interest and a pleased smile.

"Is it what you thought it was?" she asked.

He nodded. "This is quite a library. I'd like to know the person who collected it."

Jane took this as her cue. "Hello," she said, stepping into the library.

"Clive was just admiring your books," Belle said pleasantly. "Oh, have you two met yet, Jane? Clive just arrived from Phila—"

"We've met, Belle." Clive smiled at Jane. "I thought you'd forgotten your promise to give me the tour."

"It seems you're finding your way without me." Jane returned his smile.

"Belle was doing her best," he said. "But I'm afraid she hasn't been able to get me past the library. It's delightful."

"It was my father's." She waved her hand over the shelves. "He loved books."

"Good books."

"Yes, well, his taste was diverse. He was interested in so many subjects."

"Did you know this was a first edition?" He held out the book.

"I'm not surprised. He was a great one for finding treasures at garage sales and flea markets."

"You don't worry about your guests making off with any of these?"

She laughed. "Well, we don't frisk them at the door, if that's what you mean."

He chuckled. "And I'm sure you must cater to an ethical sort of clientele."

"So far, we've been fortunate." She took out a copy of *Great Expectations* and sighed. "I remember when my father wanted me to read this. I was fourteen and full of myself and I naturally assumed this would be a stuffy and boring old book. But Father promised to take me to dinner, just the two of us, if I read the whole thing."

"Did you?" asked Belle, staring at the thick book with a slight frown.

Jane nodded. "I did. And I absolutely loved it."

"And your father took you to dinner?" asked Clive.

"He did. Just the two of us. And we discussed the book and Dickens the whole time." She sighed. "It's one of my happiest memories."

"Your father must've been quite a man." Clive frowned. "I assume he's not with us anymore?"

"He passed away. And, you're right, he was an amazing man." Then Jane gave Clive a quick history of her father. "He left a rich legacy."

"And you should see the sweet little chapel where he was pastor," gushed Belle. "It's just the most perfect spot for a wedding."

Clive nodded, then turned his full attention on Jane. "Well, you did promise me a tour, Jane. Are you still on?"

"Of course. I just got tied up with my sister and some inn business."

"If you're too busy," said Belle, "I'd be happy to show him around. I feel almost as if I live here now."

"I'm not too busy," said Jane. "But if you'd like to join us, Belle, you are more than welcome."

Belle grinned. "Don't mind if I do. I've heard bits and pieces of history, but I'm always interested in learning more." She turned to Clive. "Did I mention that I am moving to Acorn Hill?"

"How nice," he said in a tone that sounded unenthusiastic.

"Yes. I've only been here a short while, and I feel just completely at home. Why, I've even found a house that I'd like to purchase. It's a lovely little cottage that I plan to paint a soft shade of pink, the same color as the inside of a seashell." She turned to Jane. "Don't you think that would be pretty?"

"It would be a rather unusual color for a bungalow," said Jane as she led them from the library toward the parlor.

"A bungalow?" repeated Belle in alarm. "Why, it's not a bungalow, Jane. It's a cottage."

"Actually it's a bungalow-style cottage," said Jane. "*Bungalow* refers to a type of design that was popular after the turn of the past century. I think bungalows are charming."

"Oh," Belle nodded as if taking this in, and Clive winked at Jane. They continued the tour, and Jane sensed that Clive's opinion of Belle was not entirely positive. Finally, as they were going out to see the garden, Belle, who had been growing increasingly quieter, excused herself.

"What an interesting character," said Clive.

"She most certainly is." Jane led the way along the foot path. "Sometimes she seems a bit much, but she's actually a very sweet person."

"Sort of like a sugared Georgia peach."

Jane chuckled. "Well, you do have a way with words, Mr. Fagler."

"Clive."

She nodded, feeling her cheeks warm as she began to explain the basics of herb gardening. Perhaps it was simply the afternoon sun. Or perhaps it was something more.

Wednesday evening after supper, Jane went to Sylvia's home to watch videos and catch up. Belle was over at the carriage house with Ethel, and Clive was treating himself to a fashionably late dinner at Acorn Hill's fine restaurant, Zachary's.

Louise and Alice sat companionably in the living room, Alice stretched out on the burgundy sofa and Louise seated on the matching overstuffed chair. Alice was engrossed in a new mystery while Louise had just started knitting a tea cozy, using a pattern Jane had found for her on the Internet. The inn didn't really need another cozy, but Louise had some rusty red wool left over from a scarf she had knitted for Alice and decided that the color would go well with the paprika-colored cabinets in the kitchen. Other than the soft classical music wafting from the CD player and the click of knitting needles, the inn was silent.

After a while, Louise put her knitting in her lap and cleared her throat. Alice continued to read, and Louise knew that her sister was deep in a fictional world. Although she hated to bother Alice, Louise could not hold her tongue for another minute.

"Alice, dear, I'm sorry to interrupt, but we really need to talk."

Alice's eyes seemed reluctant to leave the page, but she eventually closed her book and focused on Louise. "Yes?"

"It's about Jane and . . . well . . . Justin."

"Oh, she told me what she did about his reservation." A smile crept onto Alice's lips. "I have to admit that I laughed. Canceling that reservation reminded me of some naughty tricks Jane pulled as a child."

"Yes, well, I didn't find it quite so amusing. However, truth be told, now that the act is done, I'm glad that we could accommodate the honeymoon couple. And I'm pleased for Jane's sake that Justin won't be staying here. That could have been awkward, if not painful, for Jane. But that isn't what I want to discuss right now." Louise let her glasses drop down to hang from the chain around her neck. "I want to talk about Justin's coming East and what it might mean for us."

Alice swung her legs off the couch and onto the floor. "You mean if he wants Jane to give their marriage another chance?"

"Exactly. Although they are divorced, perhaps Justin has changed. Maybe he's realized what was lost and wants to regain it."

"Actually, Louise, when Jane told me he was coming, I broached that idea with her."

"And?"

"I suppose I didn't put it quite right. I was trying to say that if she wanted to go back to San Francisco with him, to sort things out and start over, I thought she should be free to do so. But I did a poor job because she thought I was urging her to leave."

"Oh dear."

"Well, we got over that little misunderstanding and agreed that if it's God's will for them to reunite, then Jane will know it."

"That's precisely it," said Louise, leaning forward and waving a knitting needle for emphasis. "We have to be prepared for that possibility. If Jane feels led to give her marriage another try, we don't want her to be torn. We don't want her thinking that she's deserting us. She must make the decision without feeling we have any claims on her."

"And how do we assure her of this?"

"I've been giving it a lot of thought. I believe that you and I are happy here, and even if Jane left us, we'd want to continue with the inn as best we could."

"Yes, that's what I'd want too. But could we manage? Jane does so much, adds so much."

"We certainly couldn't run the inn the way we do now, but I think if we lowered our standards a bit, we could manage."

"Lower our standards?" Alice's eyebrows rose in surprise.

"Oh, I simply mean in regard to the food we serve. Certainly, neither you nor I will suddenly develop into a chef of Jane's caliber. And we can't afford to hire someone who could fill Jane's shoes. But if we relied on the Good Apple for breakfast breads and pastries, and if we advertised continental rather than full breakfasts, then I think we could make do."

"Yes, breakfast is the biggest hurdle. We could hire help with linens and cleaning during the busy seasons, and I could cut back my work at the hospital. And I suppose we could get help for the grounds and garden as well."

"Exactly. And I, of course, could begin to limit my number of students. Perhaps I'll stop teaching during the summer, our busy season. So many children go on vacation during that time anyway."

"But then we'll need to be extra careful of our budget and expenses. We'll need to tighten our belts to cover paying for outside help and cutting back on our jobs. Not only that, we should send Jane her share of the profits to cover her investment."

"I know, Alice, but I've tentatively worked out most of those considerations." Louise put her glasses back on and reached for a yellow legal pad that was tucked into her knitting bag. She reviewed the numbers and sighed deeply. "I think we can do it. It will be tight, and we won't have much set aside for the unexpected."

"God has always taken care of us," Alice reminded her.

"Yes." Louise firmly nodded. "And even if it's not easy, it might be interesting. We might need to become more creative about filling the inn during off times, but I do believe we could do it, Alice."

"That's good news, I—I guess." Her voice broke just slightly.

Louise looked over at her sister, seeing the tears glistening on her slightly flushed cheeks. "Oh, Alice." Louise got up and sat next to Alice on the sofa. She put her arm around her sister's quivering shoulders. "Oh dear, I know this is hard. I don't want to lose Jane either. But we must be supportive of whatever choice she makes."

"I know." Alice sniffed, searching in her jeans pocket for a tissue. Louise removed a fresh, neatly folded hankie from her sweater sleeve and handed it to Alice.

"Somehow we will get through this," Louise said with confidence she did not feel.

"I do understand," said Alice. "But I'll miss Jane so. It seems we've had her back for such a short time."

Suddenly, Louise's eyes were brimming with tears too. "I know how you feel. She was gone for so long. It seemed she lived at the end of the earth. But I know that we both agree about the sanctity of marriage . . . the solemnity of marriage vows."

Alice nodded sadly, dabbing at her nose.

"And if Jane and Justin can come together again, this time in a happy, healthy and godly union, it is our duty to do all we can to help Jane."

"Y-y-yes," Alice said. "You know you can count on me, Louise. I'll do whatever I can."

"I am certain you will." Louise brushed a tear off her own cheek. "And who knows, perhaps Jane might open a Grace Chapel Inn out in California. Perhaps we could take turns going out there to substitute for her while she returned to Acorn Hill to visit."

Alice responded with a weak laugh. "You know I hate to be selfish, Louise, but I'd insist that you go first. I would want to be here in Acorn Hill with our dear Jane."

Chapter Eighteen

"Jane Howard!" exclaimed Ethel as she burst into the kitchen early Thursday morning without bothering to knock. "I have a bone to pick with you."

"Good morning to you, too, Auntie," said Jane pleasantly.

"I thought you were Belle's friend," snapped her aunt as she pulled out a kitchen chair and sat down with a loud *harrumph*.

"I thought I was too." She continued cracking eggs.

"Belle told me that you snatched a perfectly lovely man right out from under her nose yesterday."

"I did *what?*" Jane turned around and stared at her aunt.

"She said that she and Clive Fagler, that columnist from the *Inquirer*, were getting along famously until you swept in and stole him from her."

Jane tossed an eggshell into the sink. "She said that?"

Ethel shrugged. "Those weren't her exact words."

"Well, if you're going to go around repeating what others have said, you might at least attempt to use their exact words."

Ethel gave her head an impatient shake. "She simply said that she felt she might've had a chance with Mr. Fagler until you entered the picture. And, in Belle's defense, she was very forgiving."

"Forgiving?" Jane frowned. "What would she be forgiving of?"

"Being hurt."

"Well, I'm sorry she was hurt. But when I registered Clive, I told him I'd give him a tour of the inn. I was sidetracked by Louise when Belle made his acquaintance. Then, when I was finished speaking to Louise, I went out and found them. That's when Clive asked me to give him the promised tour."

"Why didn't you suggest that Belle give him a tour?"

"Actually, I think she suggested something like that herself. Clive was not interested."

"Well!"

"I invited Belle to join us, and she did for a while."

"Until she realized it was useless."

Jane held up her hands in a helpless gesture. "Maybe it *was* useless, Auntie. Clive is not her type. Not in the least."

"Perhaps you should've allowed him to figure that out for himself, Jane."

"He did."

Ethel stood. "Well, I thought you were on our side, Jane. I can see I was mistaken."

"This isn't about sides, Aunt Ethel. I like Belle and I hope the best for her. But I know that Clive Fagler would not be the best match for her."

Her aunt's eyebrows shot up. "Why? Do you know something negative about the man?"

"No, of course not. I simply mean that he and Belle would be a bad match."

"In your opinion."

"And his."

"Fine, fine," said her aunt in a weary tone. "I suppose I can't expect any help from you."

Jane leaned forward on the kitchen table between them. "You know, Auntie, it wasn't long ago that you were on my case, trying to get me to have some interest in meeting a man. Now I happen to meet one that I like and you act as if—"

"Oh, Jane!" Ethel slapped her hand over her mouth with a shocked look. "You are absolutely right." Now she leaned forward over the kitchen table, her face just inches from Jane's and a hopeful expression in her eyes. "Are you interested in Clive Fagler?"

Jane shrugged. "He's a nice man. We have a lot in common."

Ethel smiled. "Well, isn't that wonderful, Jane. Please, forgive me for being slow on the uptake. I suppose I can be a little gung ho sometimes. Lloyd says that I tend to think with my heart more than with my head." She rubbed her hands together with enthusiasm. "Goodness, I cannot wait to meet this literary man. He does sound most interesting."

Jane knew she'd made a mistake, but at least Ethel was pacified for the moment. Jane hoped that Ethel wouldn't overwhelm Clive. Perhaps it would be well to warn him that he'd landed in a place where feminine folly was becoming epidemic.

"I'm sorry I can't discuss this further," said Jane, "but Alice has gone to work and Louise is talking to Cynthia on the phone and I need to get busy with breakfast right now."

"Would you like any help?" offered Ethel.

Jane was too busy to accept help from Ethel, who usually slowed things down. "Thanks, Auntie," she said. "I think I have it under control. But if you'd like to join us for breakfast and perhaps play hostess until Louise gets off the phone, you are more than welcome."

"Oh, that would be lovely." She winked at Jane. "And now I can meet Mr. Fagler."

Suddenly, Jane questioned the wisdom of inviting her aunt to breakfast. "Do take it easy on him, Auntie. He is our guest."

Ethel feigned a wounded expression. "Goodness, Jane, you make it sound as if I plan to chew the poor man up and have him for breakfast." She straightened her shoulders and turned toward the swinging door. Taking a deep breath, she pushed the door open and marched into the dining room.

As Jane worked on breakfast, she could hear Clive, Belle and her aunt conversing. She couldn't make out the words, but it sounded congenial. If nothing else, Clive should be amused by the two of them. Perhaps he was gathering humorous material for his writing. Before long, Louise joined her. "Cynthia needed advice," she said as she arranged pastries on a warmed platter.

"What sort of advice?" asked Jane.

"Nothing terribly important," said Louise. "She can't make up her mind where to go on vacation. She wants to go to New Zealand with a friend but can't afford it. And the more we talked, the more it sounded like she can't afford to take that much time off from work either. So she was considering the Bahamas but thinks it will be too hot in July."

"Tell her to come here," suggested Jane.

"I tried that, but she said, 'No offense, but Acorn Hill is not exactly a vacation destination for singles.'"

"Did you tell her about Belle?"

"I did." Louise laughed. "And that's probably what kept us on the phone for so long. Cynthia was so amused, she suggested she might come down for the weekend."

"Did you tell her we were booked?"

"Yes, but she could stay with me in my room," said Louise.

Then Jane filled her in on Ethel's accusation that Jane had snatched an available male from Belle. "I really don't think Belle is Clive's type."

"No, I wouldn't think so." Louise studied Jane with a curious expression. "Although you might be."

"He's an interesting man." Jane picked up the fruit platter she'd just prepared and nodded toward the dining room. "Our guests are waiting."

The five of them visited pleasantly during breakfast. Ethel asked Clive a few personal questions about his marital status and family situation, but in such a way that he was probably not aware of her intent. And the truth was Jane was interested to hear that he had been married for nearly twenty years, but that his wife left him for another man about ten years ago, accusing him of being married to his career instead of her, which he admitted was partially true. He had two grown sons, one just finishing law school and the other working in investment banking.

"Why, you just don't look old enough to have two full-grown sons," said Belle. "You must've started your family when you were a teenager."

"Mandy and I were young by today's standards, but we had just graduated college and thought we were grown-up." He chuckled. "Now I'm not so sure that was the case."

"Funny how our perspectives change with age," said Jane as she refilled his coffee cup.

"Yes," he agreed, "instead of getting wiser in my old age, I realize how little I actually know about almost everything."

"But you do not come across like that in your column," said Louise.

He frowned. "No, I suppose not. Unfortunately, I was still fairly young when I started that column. I set myself up as being much smarter than I really am."

Jane laughed. "Well, it's an act you seem to be pulling off rather convincingly."

"Maybe it's time to change that." He rubbed his chin thoughtfully. "Perhaps I should let my readers know that I'm nearly not as bright as I appear on paper."

"Maybe your readers enjoy the illusion," suggested Louise.

"Sort of like that little man behind the curtain in *The Wizard of Oz*," Belle suggested.

Clive nodded. "Yes, I suppose I'm a bit like that. Although I think the professor at Oz was much smarter than he gets credit for."

"Hello?" called a male voice from the kitchen.

"Who can that be?" asked Louise.

Jane was just getting up when Craig Tracy pushed open the swinging door and grinned in an embarrassed way. "Sorry to interrupt."

"That's okay," said Jane. "We're just finishing up. Want to join us for coffee or a pastry?"

"I came to get you for our planting project at the City Hall," he said, still standing in the doorway. "Remember, I said Thursday morning?"

She slapped her forehead. "I totally forgot."

He nodded. "You still want to help?"

"You go ahead, Jane," said Louise. "I'll take care of the breakfast things."

"Okay." She turned to Craig. "Just let me go put on some jeans and my gardening shoes."

"Please sit down, Craig," said Louise. "I know you have a weakness for Jane's cinnamon rolls."

Then Jane hurried up the stairs to do a quick change. As much as she wanted to help Craig this morning, she was disappointed that this would mean less time to spend with Clive. Not that she expected Clive to spend his time with her, but she had hoped to get to know him a little better today. And who knew what would happen tomorrow, the day when Justin was scheduled to show up?

Sprucing up the town hall planters turned out to be a bigger project than either Craig or Jane had expected. The packed and neglected dirt needed a lot of enrichment, which entailed several trips for bags of potting soil. It was nearly two by the time they finished, and Craig offered to buy her lunch as a thank-you.

"I am starving," Jane admitted as she paused from sweeping spilled soil off the sidewalk. "But I think we better wash up first."

"These planters look wonderful," said Lloyd as he emerged from the building in a crisp blue suit, sparkling white shirt and a gold bow tie. "You two do excellent work."

Jane turned around to admire their efforts. The long cedar boxes were overflowing with cheerful red and white petunias as well as bright blue Lithodora and the silver tones of dusty miller. "It is an improvement."

"And very patriotic," added Craig.

"It is generous citizens like you who keep Acorn Hill the kind of town we all like to call home," said Lloyd.

"Do you mind if we use your restroom to clean up a bit?" asked Jane as she brushed some soil from her jeans.

"Of course not." He smiled. "Make yourselves at home."

Before long, Jane and Craig were seated at the Coffee Shop. They both ordered the lunch special: turkey sandwiches and cream of broccoli soup.

"You didn't tell me that a celebrity was coming to town," said Craig as he sipped his iced tea.

"Oh, you mean Clive?"

He nodded. "I've read his column for years. It was fantastic to meet such a noted writer."

"He seems genuinely nice." Jane picked up the second half of her sandwich. "Not at all stuffy or pretentious."

"Did you expect him to be?"

She shrugged. "He can come across pompous in his column at times. Sort of a know-it-all. I didn't think I'd like him."

He chuckled. "It's obvious that Belle likes him. Does he have any idea what that woman is up to?"

"I haven't warned him, if that's what you mean." Jane felt defensive. She wasn't sure if the feeling was for Belle's benefit or Clive's. "He's a pretty smart guy. I'm sure he'll figure it out."

"I'd say that he's also too old for her, but age doesn't seem to matter to that woman."

"Craig," said Jane. "You don't need to keep calling her 'that woman' like she's some kind of criminal or lowlife or something."

He smiled sheepishly. "Sorry. I suppose that is juvenile on my part." He winked as he nodded toward the door. "Speak of the devil." Then he put his hand over his mouth. "I mean *she* devil."

She gave him a warning look, then glanced up in time to see not only Belle, but also Clive walking toward them.

"Oh, hello, you two," said Belle cheerfully. "I'm giving Clive the tour of the town and I told him he simply had to come to the Coffee Shop for pie."

Clive smiled. "She said the coconut cream is to die for."

Jane smiled. "You can't go wrong with any pie here. The blackberry is a specialty."

He nodded. "That sounds appealing too. With ice cream."

"Would you like to join us?" offered Craig.

"Oh no," said Belle, "we wouldn't dream of intruding, would we, Clive?"

He appeared to be at a loss for words, but Craig assured them that their company would not be an intrusion. Still, Belle tugged on Clive's arm, insisting that they shouldn't interfere with Jane and Craig's "little lunch."

"What'd I say?" said Craig quietly as Belle and Clive took a table against the far wall.

Jane shook her head. "I'm surprised you were so eager to have them join us."

"Not her," said Craig, "Just him. Unfortunately, it was a package deal." He shook his head. "A man like Clive Fagler couldn't possibly be interested in someone like Belle. Could he?"

"They say opposites attract." Jane glanced at their table then away again. "And Belle is a pretty woman."

"In a fluffy sort of way," said Craig. "Kind of like petunias. I don't really like them much, except that they give a lot of instant color and cheer."

"Why, I thought you loved all flowers equally," she teased.

"I appreciate them for their various traits. But I do have my favorites."

"Such as?"

"Columbine."

"Columbine?" She considered his choice. "A nice enough flower, but not exactly splashy or dramatic or exciting."

"No, but somewhat mysterious, alluring and interesting because it's a delicate yet hardy plant."

"*Hmm.*" She took a spoonful of soup. "I can see you've given this careful thought."

"I like peonies too." He laughed.

"Aha!" She pointed her spoon at him. "Now there's diversity for you."

Chapter Nineteen

S omehow, Belle managed to occupy Clive for the remainder of Thursday. Jane told herself that it was of no matter to her, but she experienced a letdown. Also, she was becoming more and more nervous over Justin's impending arrival. As a result, she found herself baking on Thursday night. Louise and Alice kept her company until after nine, but they finally tired and Jane shooed them off to their beds, promising that she'd call it quits before long. Her hope in her frenetic culinary efforts was twofold: that she would wear herself out and fall into bed in an exhausted state of slumber, and that she would have prepared enough muffins, pastries and breads to last throughout the long weekend.

"Hello?"

Jane turned toward the dining room. There was Clive in the doorway. "Oh!"

"I suspect that guests aren't allowed past this hallowed door—"

"No, you're fine." She waved him in.

He smiled. "Thank you." Then he entered, carefully taking in the whole room as he slowly walked around, nodding his head in approval. "Very, very nice."

"Thank you. I like it." She continued washing the muffin tin in the sink.

"Do you always bake late into the night?"

"Not always." She considered confessing to him that she was on pins and needles about Justin's visit tomorrow, but then decided she didn't know Clive well enough to disclose such personal information.

"Mind if I sit down?"

"Go right ahead. Make yourself at home. There's still some decaf over there. It's not the freshest, but—"

"Sounds great." He was up again. "I'll just help myself."

She slipped a cookie sheet into the hot soapy water. "Help yourself to a snack if you like."

"Really?" He looked over to a cooling rack. "Are these oatmeal cookies?"

"Yep. Still warm."

"Groovy."

She laughed. "Now there's a word you don't hear every day."

He sniffed the cookie, then sighed and took a bite, slowly chewing with the sort of expression one might have while sampling a glass of fine wine, trying to discern the bouquet. "Walnuts?"

"Yes." She watched him with amusement.

"Just a touch of cinnamon?"

"Yes."

"Hint of nutmeg?"

"Yes."

"Delicious."

"Thank you."

"Thank *you*."

She chuckled. "So, what have you and Belle been up to this evening?"

"Bingo."

She laughed out loud. "Of course, I totally forgot it was bingo night. Did you win anything?"

"No, but I met a lot of unique people and made some interesting observations." He sat back down at the table. "I almost forgot how charming small-town life can be."

"Have you ever lived in a small town?"

"Not really, but my grandparents did—it was a little one-horse town in Michigan. We'd visit them for holidays and summer vacations. Lots of good memories there. Things I need to be reminded of from time to time." He took another bite, and Jane checked on the breads still in the oven, then returned to washing baking pans.

"So is that what brought you to Acorn Hill?" She glanced over her shoulder. "The need to reconnect with a small town?"

"That and the need for a break from the city. Also, I've been collecting ideas for a book I'm working on. I hoped to use some of my time here to organize them."

"You're writing a book?"

He snickered. "Isn't everyone?"

"I suppose, but you have an advantage because you're already a writer, a published one at that. What sort of book are you writing?"

He frowned. "I'm not really sure. It keeps changing."

"Oh."

"I don't usually talk about my book. It's not something I really want people to know about."

She set the cookie sheet to dry, wiped her hands, then poured herself a half cup of decaf and sat down across from him and smiled. "Well, if it's a secret, it's safe with me."

"Thanks. It's probably more about pride than privacy. I wouldn't want everyone to think I was writing a book and then never have one materialize. That's a little embarrassing."

"I understand."

"Speaking of embarrassing, I'm sure you've heard about Belle's marital plans?"

"It's about all I've heard since Belle showed up at the inn." She looked closely at him. "Don't tell me that you're the man?"

He laughed so loudly that she had to shush him. Then he solemnly shook his head. "Not on your life."

"I didn't think so, but you can never tell."

"She's a sweet gal," he said, "but a little too talkative and cheerful for my taste."

"You go for the silent, grumpy type?"

His eyes crinkled at the corners and he chuckled. "No. I like a woman with some depth to her. A woman who is comfortable with the world and with herself. A woman who's interested and interesting. Is that too much to hope for?"

"Those are the sorts of things I would look for"—she glanced away—"if I were looking."

He nodded. "So, are you involved with the flower man?"

"The flower man?" She suppressed laughter. "You mean Craig?"

"Belle seemed to think you were more than just friends."

"Craig and I are simply friends. Good friends."

"Oh."

The oven timer dinged, and Jane got up to check on the bread, carefully removing it and setting it on racks to cool. "Well, that's the last of my baking tonight," she said as she turned off the oven. She glanced at the clock and untied her apron. "Wow, it's really getting late."

"Time to call it a night?"

"I think so."

"Mind if I peruse the library?"

"Of course not. Feel free to go in there anytime."

"Just don't take the books home?"

She smiled. "That's right. No book snatching allowed."

"Do you have plans tomorrow?"

"No, not really." She tried to pretend that Justin wasn't actually coming. Maybe he wasn't.

"Would you care to spend some time with me?"

She studied his expression and sensed he was uneasy. "Sure," she said. "Did you have anything in mind?"

"I hoped you might have some ideas, since this is your neighborhood. What would you normally do on a sunny Friday in May?"

"Let's see . . . I might go to the nursery and look at plants."

"That sounds good. Maybe I could pick up some things to take back to the city with me. Is there a place to get pots?"

"Yes," she said. "There's a great shop in Potterston and—"

"Okay!" He grinned. "It sounds like we're off to a good start."

"After breakfast then?"

"It's a date." He nodded as he backed out of the kitchen. "Now, I'll get out of your hair."

She smiled, and they exchanged good-nights. Jane put a few more things away in the kitchen before she turned out the lights. As she went upstairs to her room, she wondered if it was selfish to go with Clive tomorrow. Was she simply attempting to escape? Maybe she should cancel the plans with Clive in the morning, but she would only be gone for a few hours. And perhaps Justin wouldn't even arrive until later in the day. He hadn't bothered updating them on his arrival. Besides, she thought as she brushed her hair, she hadn't invited Justin. He wasn't her guest. He had simply notified her that he was coming. Certainly, he didn't expect her to rearrange her life for his sake. For all he knew, she could be in the midst of a serious relationship by now. She could have remarried.

She was so exhausted by the time she got into bed that even these concerns were not sufficient to keep her awake. Before she fell asleep, she placed all her worries in God's hands. As her father used to tell her, "Don't worry about tomorrow. Trust God. Tomorrow will take care of itself."

Jane felt surprisingly refreshed when she woke in the morning. She showered and dressed quickly, then went downstairs to prepare breakfast. She whistled to herself as she made coffee.

"Morning, Jane," said Alice as she came into the kitchen. "You sound happy today. Are you ready to see Justin?"

"Honestly?"

Alice smiled and nodded.

"I'm not ready." Jane took the teakettle to the sink to fill with water. "In fact, I want your opinion on something."

"What?" Alice was getting the teapot ready.

Then Jane told her about Clive's invitation to do something with him this morning. "We won't be long. We'll probably just go check out Craig's nursery and get some planting pots. Clive wants to try some terrace gardening back in the city."

"That's a lovely idea."

"The terrace garden? Or doing something with him?"

"Both."

"So, you think it's okay for me to go with him today?"

"I don't see why not."

"I mean because of Justin."

"Jane, you aren't married to Justin. And, as you said, you don't know when he'll get here. It could be in the afternoon or evening or he might be delayed and not arrive until tomorrow. A getaway for a few hours in the morning

. . . why, I think it would do you good. It might even keep you from fretting about Justin's visit."

Jane hugged her sister. "Thank you, Alice. I knew you'd have sound advice."

"What sort of advice?" asked Louise as she joined them and poured herself a cup of coffee. Jane brought her up to speed, and Louise nodded. "Yes, I agree with Alice. Go out and try not to think about Justin. I know that it's been gnawing at you, Jane."

"Has it been that obvious?"

"Indeed, it has."

"And if you'd like to leave right after breakfast," offered Alice, "I'd be happy to clean up."

"And I will assist," added Louise.

Soon after breakfast, Jane found herself riding through the Pennsylvania countryside with Clive Fagler. The sun was shining, the sky was blue, and it seemed that every green and growing thing had sprung to life.

"I like your SUV," she said. "Lots of room for carrying plants and things."

"I've been feeling guilty for not scaling down. But this actually gets fairly good gas mileage, and it's comfortable.

I don't drive to work, so I figure I'm only using it on the open road where I get the best mileage."

"How do you get to work?"

"Well, sometimes I work at home. And sometimes I ride my bike or take public transit. Driving in the city is a pain, but being completely without a vehicle is a little scary. Sometimes I just need to get behind the wheel and get out of town."

"I can understand that." She told him where to turn.

"This is nice out here," he said as he slowed down on the graveled road that led up to the greenhouses.

"You're going to like Craig's nursery," she said as he parked. "He specializes in native plants, and his herbs are spectacular."

"Uh-oh. That sign says he's closed, Jane."

"Oh, don't mind that. Craig and I have an understanding." She opened the door. "I help him out here sometimes, and he lets me come out and get flowers for the inn and my garden. Sometimes I pay him and sometimes we do an exchange."

"Ah, the small-town life."

She nodded as they walked toward the first greenhouse. "I guess I take it for granted, which is funny considering that I lived in San Francisco all those years and actually thought I was a city girl."

"You're not?"

She shook her head as she paused by the open door to inhale the aroma of damp soil and plants. "Isn't that heavenly?"

"What?"

"The smell."

He took a sniff, then nodded, but she wasn't convinced he liked it as much as she did. "So, how did you find out you weren't a city girl?" he asked as she led him through the greenhouse.

She showed him various plants of interest and told him about her training as a chef and her city life and subsequent marriage, followed by divorce, and then, deciding that she might as well get it into the open, she told him about Justin's coming to Acorn Hill.

"Today?" he said incredulously.

"Yes."

"Do you need to get back to the inn soon?"

"No. I'm not sure what time he's arriving. My sisters thought a break from the inn might do me good."

After about an hour, they had found a nice selection of plants that Jane felt would do well in Clive's terrace garden. "Let's just gather them together over here," she suggested as she began clustering the plants together near a wooden bench. "Then I'll let Craig know that you want these, and he can tally up the cost."

"I can imagine the garden already," said Clive as he stood back and admired the collection of plants.

"Now, we'll go find some interesting pots and get some potting soil and fertilizer, and by the time you head back to the city, you'll be set."

Clive seemed genuinely pleased as they went back to his vehicle. "Now, you're sure you don't need to get back to the inn, Jane?"

She firmly shook her head. "No. I don't even want to think about it right now. I'm having fun."

"Well, good. So am I."

On they went, finding pots and even stopping at a flea market just outside of Potterston, where Jane bought a teapot with yellow rosebuds for Alice and discovered a pair of old Adirondack-style chairs with several layers of peeling paint. "I don't know if you have room for something like this on your terrace, Clive, but I think they'd be lovely." He knelt down to examine them. "I'm not much of a handyman. How would I remove the paint?"

"I actually think the paint layers are charming. There's a technique I can show you that will smooth out the surface, and then you apply a wax finish that makes it more comfortable for sitting."

"I like the sound of that."

She pointed to a small table behind a bookshelf. "Hey, that looks like it might go with the chairs."

He pulled it out and arranged the items together. "So, how do I go about buying these things?" He lowered his voice. "I noticed how you dickered with that last vendor for the teapot, but this is all new to me."

She grinned. "Want me to handle it for you?"

He nodded gratefully, and she stepped in and made an offer for all three items. She and the man in the booth went back and forth a couple of times, but by the time Clive paid him, they were all happy.

"It's a good thing you have your SUV," she said after a couple of workers lugged the chairs back to the parking lot for them. "We can just move the pots around until everything fits."

"I think I have just enough room left for the plants." He closed the hatch.

"For your luggage too?"

"Guess I'll have to put that in the passenger seat." He checked his watch. "Do you have time for lunch? I'd like to treat you to show my appreciation for all the help you're giving me with my garden project."

"Absolutely." She directed him to a nearby restaurant with a patio, where they sat outside in the sunshine and enjoyed a leisurely lunch.

"I suppose I shouldn't keep trying to delay the inevitable," she finally said. "Maybe I should get back to the inn now."

"I'm getting curious to meet this fellow," said Clive. "He must not be the sharpest knife in the drawer to let you go, Jane."

She laughed. "You know what they say: It takes two." As they walked back to the SUV, Jane admitted how she had canceled Justin's reservation and temporarily peeved her oldest sister. "Pretty immature of me, huh?"

Clive laughed. "Who could blame you for that?"

"Louise. Although, to her credit, she did get over it. The problem is that Justin doesn't know he's been canceled yet. Or maybe he does." She pointed to the clock in the dash that showed it was nearly three. "Goodness, I had no idea it was this late."

They both grew quiet as Clive drove back to Acorn Hill. Eventually, he turned on the radio, tuning it to a light classical station, and Jane leaned back in the seat, closed her eyes, and silently prayed that God would give her strength and wisdom for whatever might be waiting at home for her.

Chapter Twenty

There you are," said Louise late Friday afternoon as Jane and Clive entered the inn.

"Sorry, that took longer than I expected," said Jane.

"It's my fault," Clive told Louise. "I enticed Jane into having a late lunch to thank her for all the help she's given me. We discovered all sorts of treasures for my terrace garden." He went into detail then, telling her about their various finds.

Louise smiled. "That's very nice."

"Now, if you two will excuse me"—Clive smiled at Jane—"I think I'll see if I can get some writing done."

"Certainly," said Louise politely. Then when Clive was going up the stairs, she beckoned to Jane and whispered, "He's here."

"Here?"

"Actually, he's not here at the inn right now." Louise was guiding Jane back toward the kitchen, seeking a place where they could talk in private.

"Where is he?"

"Belle took him to town."

Jane tried to imagine this. Belle and Justin, walking through Acorn Hill together. But it was just too weird, like something out of an old *Twilight Zone* episode. "Seriously?"

"Seriously." Louise shook her head as if she too found this rather strange. "As soon as he arrived, I explained to Justin about canceling his room reservation, and he was very understanding. I recommended a nice place to stay in Potterston that he said he'd check out."

"Oh, good." Jane sighed in relief.

"And I told him you'd gone out with a guest and would return soon."

"Yes?"

"And he seemed happy to wait for you. So I told him to make himself at home and got him a cup of coffee. Then he visited with Alice for a bit before she had to leave for a special ANGELs meeting about the Memorial Day service."

"What time did he get here?"

"A bit before noon."

"Oh."

"I had to excuse myself to give Karly Andrews a piano lesson, and that's when I assume Belle made his acquaintance. When I finished the lesson, I found the two of them visiting in the library quite congenially."

"And Justin, uh, he seemed to like her?"

"Well, Jane, you know how Belle can be. She seemed to

be carrying most of the conversation. But I suppose Justin appreciated her company."

"Right." Jane felt a jab of guilt. "I really did lose track of the time."

"Indeed."

"What should I do now?"

Louise held up her hands. "I have no idea, Jane. I imagine that they'll be back soon . . . but then I had thought you would be back soon as well."

"I'm sorry, Louise. I didn't mean to put you in a tough spot again."

Louise patted Jane on the shoulder. "It's all right, dear. But I am tired. I think I'll go put my feet up and read a bit."

"Yes," said Jane eagerly. "Go do that. I'll mind the inn. You just go have a rest."

"Thank you." She paused with her hand on the door. "Oh, by the way, Jane, the newlyweds Garth and Gloria Fairview just checked in. Remember the ones you gave Justin's room to?"

Jane gave her a mischievous smile.

"Well, they seem to be a very nice couple. I am glad they were able to come. I believe you did the right thing."

"Oh, good," said Jane.

"And Clara's greatnephew Calvin should be by anytime now. Clara called, saying that he and his mother have

574 Ready to Wed

arrived, and she's going to bring him over here to settle in."

"Now, you go rest, Louise." Jane gently nudged her toward the hall. "Everything is under control here."

After Louise left, Jane began to putter about the already spotless kitchen. It was bad enough knowing that Justin was in town right now, but the idea of Belle and him doing something together—well, it was just too much. Then, as her nerves and imagination began to get the best of her, she wondered what she would do if Justin turned out to be the man of Belle's dreams. Oh, she knew it was absurd, but how would she react if he actually married Belle, settled here in Acorn Hill, perhaps opened his own restaurant? She was feeling seriously close to a meltdown when she heard the sound of the bell in the reception area. Thank goodness for distractions.

"Hello," she said when she saw Clara and a clean-cut young man carrying a khaki duffle bag.

"Oh, Jane," gushed Clara. "I'd like you to meet my nephew Calvin."

Jane shook his hand, deciding that the tall, blond man was older than she'd first assumed, but not much more than thirty. "It's a pleasure to meet you, Calvin. Welcome to Grace Chapel Inn."

"Thank you, ma'am." He tipped his head politely.

"I hear you're going to raise the flag for our Memorial Day ceremony."

"Yes. It'll be an honor." He smiled shyly.

"Well, it's an honor for us to have a serviceman at the inn. We appreciate what you have done for our country."

Calvin actually blushed and tipped his head in acknowledgment of Jane's words.

"I just took Calvin over to meet Lloyd at Town Hall," said Clara. "And Lloyd showed us the pretty flowers you and Craig Tracy planted. They look so nice by the flagpole. It'll be a real special occasion on Monday."

"I'm looking forward to it."

"Now, I must be off. I told Janet I'd be right back. She's babysitting Daisy for me. You get settled, Calvin, then come on over to the house. I'm making meatloaf and mashed potatoes for dinner." She patted his arm. "I hope that's still your favorite."

"Sounds great, Aunt Clara."

After Jane showed Calvin to his room and left him to get settled, she returned to the kitchen. She glanced at the clock, wondering when Justin and Belle would return. Once again, she tried to imagine what he might have to say to her. And what she would say to him. She considered dashing up to her room to freshen up a bit but remembered her promise to mind the inn. She took out a couple of cookbooks, made herself a cup of tea and sat down at the kitchen table.

"Hello," said Alice as she came through the back door. Jane had just discovered what looked like an interesting recipe for bread pudding.

"Oh, hi," said Jane, marking the page and closing the book. "How were the ANGELs?"

"Well, Ashley and Kate got into a small disagreement, but we smoothed it out and managed to get our Memorial Day project completed." Alice sat down across from Jane with a curious expression. "Have you spoken with him yet?"

Jane shook her head.

Alice looked surprised. "But you've seen him, haven't you?"

"No."

"What happened?"

Jane filled her in.

"Oh dear," said Alice. "That's my fault. I'd been chatting with Justin, but I had to go to my meeting. Belle came in and I introduced them."

"That doesn't make it your fault."

"I suppose not."

"But you said you chatted with him, Alice. What did he say?"

"Not much. He simply told me about his road trip, some of the sights he'd seen."

"How did he seem to you?"

She shrugged. "Oh, I don't know." Alice looked uncomfortable. "I've never known him very well."

"So, you don't have a clue as to why he's here?"

Alice shook her head.

"It's almost six," said Jane. "Should I start dinner?"

"I'm not terribly hungry. I ordered pizza for the girls and probably ate more than I should have myself. And Louise mentioned she was going to Viola's for dinner."

"And I had a late lunch."

"Well, I hate to admit it, but the ANGELs wore me out today," said Alice. "Although it's a good sort of tired. If you'll excuse me, I think I shall go enjoy a little down time."

Jane nodded. "I really do marvel at how you stick with that club year after year, Alice. Middle-school girls can be such holy terrors."

"And that is why I stick to it." Alice smiled as she stood.

Jane thought about going up to her room. Normally, once all the guests were checked in, there wasn't a great need to have someone downstairs, but Justin might return, and Jane figured it was her duty to meet him. So she sat down in the living room with a magazine and waited. At six thirty, Louise came downstairs and stepped into the room.

"I'm heading to Viola's," she told Jane. "Justin isn't back yet?"

"Nope." Jane couldn't mask the irritation in her voice.

"That's odd."

"Maybe he and Belle have really hit it off."

Louise frowned. "That seems doubtful."

"You never know." Jane shrugged. "Tell Viola hello. By the way, how is Gatsby?"

"He came home from the vet, but he is on a restricted diet now."

"Give him my best."

Louise gave her a wry smile.

After Louise left, Jane got up from the chair and began to pace, glancing out the window from time to time. Finally, she was about to give up and go upstairs when Clive came into the room. He glanced around, as if to find Justin, then asked her, "Where is the ex?"

"With Belle," she said.

He chuckled. "Well, I was just heading to the Coffee Shop. I'm not ravenous after that fantastic lunch, but I am hankering after a piece of that blackberry pie. Care to join me?"

"Maybe so. Louise told me that Belle and Justin went to town. Perhaps we'll run into them there. Do I have time to freshen up first?"

"Of course. I'll be right here."

So Jane hurried up the two flights of stairs and quickly changed into a pale blue linen dress that Alice had told her looked lovely with her eyes. Then she slipped on some pretty sandals and tied a lacy white cotton cardigan over her shoulders. She brushed her hair, put on some lipstick and blush and a pair of silver hoop earrings, then went back down.

She found Clive waiting for her in the living room. He stood when she came in, nodding at her with a look of appreciation. "You look lovely, Jane." Then he frowned. "Maybe we should go someplace more festive than the Coffee Shop."

"No," she said quickly. "The Coffee Shop is just fine."

"Would you like to drive or walk?" He looked at her strappy sandals. "Those don't look like the best walking shoes."

"Maybe we should drive. Do you mind?"

"Not at all."

"Maybe we'll see Belle and your ex there," he said as he opened the door for her.

"Maybe."

But they did not see Belle or Justin. Not at the Coffee Shop or anywhere else in town. At Jane's request, Clive had driven slowly through town before parking at the Coffee Shop. Jane wasn't sure whether to be miffed or relieved that Justin seemed to be playing hide-and-seek. She was tempted to ask Hope if Belle had been there with a strange man but decided not to arouse Hope's curiosity. Why should she worry about Justin if he was being so casual about speaking to her? It was rather typical of him, doing things his way, controlling situations.

"Preoccupied?" asked Clive as he started the car.

"Sorry." She sighed. "Just frustrated."

"Do you want to go home now?"

"Did you have something else in mind?"

"I noticed that a film I've wanted to see is playing at the Potterston Theater."

"Really?"

"Interested?"

Then he told her the title, and she realized she was interested. "Sounds perfect."

"And you're not worried about missing your ex?"

"He doesn't seem too concerned about missing me."

"Lucky for me."

So it was that Jane didn't get home until after eleven. To her surprise, both Louise and Alice were waiting for her. Clive excused himself, and she followed her sisters into the kitchen.

"We were worried," said Alice. "We had no idea what happened to you."

"I'm sorry," said Jane, feeling like she was back in high school again.

"You could have called," said Louise.

"I really am sorry." Jane looked at both of them. "I thought I was simply going for pie with Clive. It was nearly seven, and Justin still hadn't shown up here. I thought I might see him in town. When I didn't, I got kind of irritated. I mean what am I supposed to do? Just sit around and wait for him to come? When Clive mentioned a movie, I jumped at the chance."

"I can understand that," said Alice. "I'm sure it's frustrating. Justin and Belle came back a little past seven," said Alice. "You must've just missed them."

"Oh dear."

"Justin said he'd come back tomorrow," Alice told her.

"To see me?" asked Jane. "Or Belle?"

"You, of course," said Louise.

"I really am sorry I worried you both," said Jane. "Please, forgive me."

"It's all right," said Louise as she hugged Jane. "I do realize this is difficult for you. And I hope you and Justin take care of whatever he came here to do as soon as possible. I'm eager to hear why it is that he's come."

"You know how I love mysteries, Jane, but I have to admit that the suspense is killing me," said Alice.

Jane almost laughed as she hugged Alice. "You and me both, sis."

Then the three of them tiptoed up the stairs, said good night and went into their rooms. Jane quietly closed the door and stood wondering what tomorrow would bring.

Chapter Twenty-One

$\mathcal{S}$ aturday morning, Jane overslept. She awoke with a start, pulled on jeans and a sweatshirt and her favorite clogs, and hurried downstairs.

"Good morning," said Alice as Jane burst into the kitchen.

"Sorry I'm late."

"I started coffee and made tea. But that's about all. Put me to work."

Jane tossed out some orders and quickly had things under control. Then Louise joined them after setting the dining-room table, and before long, breakfast was ready. "If you two don't mind serving without me, I'd like to go shower and change into something a little nicer," said Jane as she poured herself a first cup of coffee.

"Not a problem."

"And then you will join our guests for breakfast?" asked Louise.

"Sure."

The truth was, Jane wished that she could lay low today.

She didn't feel the least bit hungry, but that was probably because the idea of seeing Justin was beginning to make her stomach clench. Even so, she went back down to the dining room after showering and dressing.

The only ones still there were Belle and the just-marrieds whom Jane had not yet met. She was surprised that they were older than she'd expected, perhaps close to her age. "You must be the newlyweds," she said to them.

"Yes," said the woman. "I'm Gloria, and this is my husband Garth." She turned and beamed at him. "It feels so good to say that."

"Congratulations on your marriage," said Jane as she sat down and helped herself to a muffin.

"Louise said it was due to you that we got a room this weekend," said Gloria. "We so appreciate that. Thank you."

"Yes, after waiting so long to get married, I was worried we might have to wait that long to have a honeymoon too," said Garth.

Gloria laughed, but Belle seemed sad as she refilled her coffee cup and listened. Jane realized that this banter might be like salt in a wound for Belle. Still, Jane was curious about the Fairviews.

"How long did you wait to get married?" she asked.

"All totaled?" Garth scratched his head as if to think.

"We went together in high school," began Gloria. "Then we lost track of each other in college. We both married other people. Then Garth's wife was killed in a car accident about ten years ago."

"And Gloria's husband passed away after a long bout with cancer, just a couple of years ago." Garth reached for Gloria's hand.

"Both of us were devastated, and neither of us had any idea of marrying again. Then we met at our thirtieth class reunion," said Gloria.

"That was last August," offered Garth.

"And, as you know, we got married a week ago."

Garth nodded toward the window, where the sun was streaming in. "We should get out there and make the most of this wonderful weather, Gloria."

"I hope you have a marvelous day," said Jane as the happy couple exited.

"They are so lucky," said Belle in a dejected tone.

"Yes, but they certainly did wait for their happiness."

"I've been waiting too." Belle sighed. "I keep getting my hopes up, just to get them flattened like a pancake again and again. It's so unfair."

"So how did they get flattened this time?" asked Jane as she reached for the fruit platter.

"You should know," said Belle. "You just keep stealing

all the good men, Jane Howard." Then she smiled. "Sorry, I hope I didn't sound nasty."

"I'm stealing all the good men?" asked Jane as she chose a piece of melon.

"Yes, as a matter of fact, you are." Then Belle began to list off men like Craig Tracy and Kenneth Thompson, acting as if Jane had been seriously involved.

"But they are simply friends," Jane interrupted.

"And what about Clive Fagler?" asked Belle. "He seems to be quite smitten with you, Jane."

"Smitten?"

She nodded. "Yes. Even this morning, I saw the look in his eye when he asked where you were. By the way, he asked your sisters to tell you he would be back down in a few minutes."

"Thank you," said Jane.

"So, you see," said Belle in a teasing tone. "You are hogging all the men in this town, and it's not the least bit fair."

"What about Justin?" asked Jane. "It seems you got to spend some time with him."

"Exactly," said Belle. "But I am fully aware that he is here to see you."

Jane actually rolled her eyes. "You could've fooled me."

She shook her finger at Jane. "You're the one who's been avoiding him, Jane. He just keeps waiting and waiting.

If I had a man interested in me like that, I would not keep him waiting."

Jane tried not to register her shock. "What makes you think he's interested in me?"

"Why else would he make that long trip? Why else would he be parking himself in your house? Of course he's interested in you."

"You do know that we are divorced, don't you?"

"Divorce sha-morse." Belle waved her hand. "People get divorced and remarried all the time. Why, I have an aunt and uncle who are on their fourth go-around, and it wouldn't surprise me in the least if they were thinking about splitting up again even as we speak."

"Yoo-hoo?"

"Ah, Aunt Ethel is here," said Jane, nodding toward the kitchen and ready to change the subject.

"Oh, that's right," said Belle in a hushed tone. "She heard about Justin being here, and she was miffed at you for not telling her about his visit."

"There you are, Jane." Ethel made herself at home at the table, taking a cup and filling it with coffee before Jane had a chance to offer her some. "I'm upset with you."

"I—"

"I cannot believe you kept this news from me, Jane. I had absolutely no idea that your ex-husband was coming to see you."

"Well, I—"

"And in the meantime, you're out cavorting with one of the guests." She addressed Belle, shaking her head. "*Tsk-tsk.* And here I thought Jane was sincerely interested in Mr. Fagler, and I defended her after she stole him from you. I should've known better."

"Aunt Ethel," said Jane in a scolding tone. "You are being outrageous."

"I know that you are playing up to the men in this town."

"Playing up?" Jane tried not to laugh.

"Poor Belle is sincerely searching for a man, and all the while you are out there just—"

"That is enough," said Jane in a stern tone. She stood and, taking her plate, retreated to the kitchen, where Louise and Alice were both standing by the door, obviously aware that Ethel's visit did not bode well. "Did you hear that?" she whispered to them. They both nodded. Then, despite herself, Jane started giggling and, as if it were contagious, her two sisters joined her until all three of them were laughing so hard that tears were streaming down their cheeks.

"I don't even know what is so funny," said Louise as she dabbed her eyes with a lace-trimmed handkerchief.

"I think it was Jane's expression when she caught us eavesdropping," Alice gasped.

Jane just shook her head. "If you don't mind, I'm going to make a quick exit," she said, moving toward the back door. "Call me a big chicken if you like."

"I don't blame you," said Louise, nodding toward the dining room. "It sounds like Auntie is getting her second wind."

"Better run," said Alice.

With her plate and coffee cup still in hand, Jane went outside and sat down at the table by her garden. At last, some peace and quiet.

"Good morning, Jane."

She looked up to see Kenneth approaching and smiled. "Hi, Kenneth. Care to join me?"

He nodded. "Don't mind if I do."

"Although I must make you fetch your own decaf since I'm hiding from my aunt. And if you see her, don't tell her I'm out here, okay?"

He chuckled. "Now you've got me curious, Jane. I'll be back in a jiffy."

Jane had neglected to bring a fork along, so she ate her melon with her fingers, polishing it off just as Kenneth returned with his coffee. "Tell all," he said as he sat down across from her. She quickly related the story, bringing him completely up to date with regard to Clive and Belle and Justin.

"You have been a busy girl."

"Yes, and it seems I am upsetting a number of people."

"Is this thing with Clive serious?"

She waved her hand. "No, of course not. He's an interesting man though. I was simply helping him with his garden plans, and I suppose he was a nice diversion from this whole Justin mystery."

"So, you haven't seen Justin yet?"

"Nope." She glanced out to the street as a sporty red car slowly cruised by, and then she turned her attention back to Kenneth. "Alice said he'll be by today. Naturally, he didn't say when. I hope it's soon. I'd like to get this over with."

"So, you've thought this through, Jane? You know what you're going to say to him"—Kenneth studied her closely—"if he's here to ask for a second chance?"

She shrugged. "I just don't think that's the case."

"But if it is the case?"

"I . . . I guess I don't really know the answer to that."

"I see." He took a slow sip of coffee.

"I wouldn't want to hurt his feelings."

"No, of course not."

"But I can't imagine that I'd leap into his arms and take him back." She sort of laughed. "That doesn't really sound much like me, does it?"

"Not much."

"I suppose I could tell him I would need time to think about it. That's fair, isn't it?"

"Very fair."

She nodded and took a sip from her cup. "And that is just what I will do." She smiled at him. "Thank you, Kenneth, for this impromptu counseling session. It's really amazing how you just pop in right when I need you. Is that something you learned in seminary?"

He laughed. "Yes, Popping-In 101. It's a requirement."

Jane noticed the red car going by again from the opposite direction, moving faster this time. She narrowed her eyes in an attempt to see who was driving, then gasped as she pointed toward the street. "Look at that . . . that car."

Kenneth turned to see the red car driving away. "Yes, I noticed that car here yesterday. It caught my eye because a buddy of mine used to have one like it. If I'm right, that's a 1975 Fiat Spider. Someone has poured a lot of money into restoring it."

"That was Justin driving." Jane took in a deep breath, willing herself to calm down. "I wonder why he just keeps driving by."

"Maybe he's as nervous as you are."

"Maybe."

"Well, unless you're in need of more pop-in counseling, I should probably be on my way. I told Fred I'd meet him at the church to look over some repair suggestions the board has agreed upon." He stood. "Good luck with Justin."

"Thanks." She shook her head. "Ill probably need it."

Then he put a hand on her shoulder. "Ask God to lead you, Jane. You can't go wrong if He's doing the directing."

"Yes. I've been trying to keep that in mind." But as Kenneth walked away, Jane wasn't so sure she wanted to ask God right now. What if God wanted her to get back with Justin? She finished her coffee and thought about going back inside, but didn't want to risk her aunt's wrath again. Besides, the sunshine felt good on the top of her head. Still, she was curious about Justin. Perhaps he was parking, heading to the front door to ask for her. Finally, she decided to simply cut around to the front of the house, where she would wait for him on the front porch. She left her breakfast things on the table, reminding herself to pick them up later. Then, as she went around to the front, she braced herself for this strange meeting. She told herself the best thing would be to simply get it over with.

There was no one in sight when she went up onto the front porch. She sat in the porch swing, then realized she didn't want to chance having Justin sitting down beside her. She moved over to the wicker rocker instead. She wished she could run inside to get a fresh cup of coffee but didn't want to risk having Justin going inside to ask for her. It seemed that it would be much simpler to deal with him out here. After a few minutes, Wendell came wandering across the porch. He stood by her feet, looking up and waiting, she suspected, for an invitation. "Come on, old boy," she said as she patted her lap. In one graceful motion, he was up, making himself comfortable and purring happily as she scratched the top of his head.

"Well, at least one guy is happy to meet me out here on the front porch," she said to Wendell. She looked up and down the quiet street, but did not see a little red sports car or any other car for that matter. After about half an hour, Wendell jumped down and wandered off on his merry way. Jane was about to give up when she heard the front door open, and Clive stepped out.

"Hey, what are you doing out here?" he asked as he came over to join her.

She explained about her spotting Justin, how she'd hoped to head him off at the pass, and how he then disappeared completely. "He's driving a Fiat Spider," she told him. "Kenneth told me that much. I think he said it was a 1975 and completely restored."

Clive sat in the porch swing. "Convertible?"

"Actually, it was. Although the top was up." She considered asking Clive not to sit out here with her because it might complicate things with Justin. But it seemed as if Justin was not coming. She and Clive visited amicably. He complimented her on her gardening skills in the front yard, admiring the pots she'd planted, and asked for some tips for keeping them looking good throughout the heat of summer.

"I wanted to ask you about that refinishing technique you mentioned yesterday too, Jane. Is that a product I can get here in town?"

"Yes. The hardware store carries it." Jane looked at her watch. "I have a feeling that Justin isn't coming, or maybe I didn't really see him earlier. It's probably silly to just sit out here all morning, waiting."

"It's a lovely place to wait."

"Yes." She stood. "But it's also a lovely day for a walk. Do you want me to walk to the hardware store with you? I could show you the product and also some crystals that will hold water in your pots, keeping your plants moist even on the hottest days."

"All right." He stood and smiled. "You are one handy girl to have around, Jane."

Then, just as they were going down the walk, the little red car cruised by again. "That's the car," she whispered to Clive, as if the driver might hear her. This time Jane got a good look at the man behind the wheel, and although he looked away, she had no doubt it was Justin. She even waved, but he didn't see her. He didn't seem to want to see her. What on earth was he up to?

"So, is that your ex driving?"

"Yes. This is infuriating." She watched as the red car kept right on heading toward town.

"Is he nearsighted?"

"No!" she practically shouted. "He is not."

"Well, is he a little eccentric? Unpredictable? Unconventional? Peculiar?"

She sort of laughed. "Maybe so."

"Don't let him get to you, Jane."

She sighed deeply. "I just wish I knew what he was up to."

"I'm sure you'll find out eventually."

Jane decided Justin wasn't worth getting all worked up over. After she and Clive spent a good hour at the hardware store, she told him that she'd like to stop for a cup of coffee.

"Who has the best coffee in town?"

"You mean beside the inn?"

"Yes. And I do think the coffee at the inn is wonderful."

"How about the Good Apple?" suggested Jane. "And, if you don't mind, I'll use the phone there to check in with my sisters."

He reached in his pocket and produced a cell phone. "Here, use my cell."

"Thanks," she said as she pushed the buttons. "My sisters weren't too happy with me for ducking out with you yesterday."

He chuckled. "Yes, I gathered as much last night. Either that or we had missed your curfew."

She rolled her eyes. "Right."

Louise answered, and Jane asked whether Justin had been by.

"Not that I know of."

"And did you notice his car yesterday?"

"I think it was a little red car."

"Yes." Then Jane told her how he'd been driving around town today.

"But he didn't stop to speak to you?"

"No."

"Odd."

"That's what I thought. Anyway, I just wanted to check in with you. Clive and I are getting a coffee at the Good Apple."

"Thank you, Jane. I appreciate you calling."

"If Justin stops by, tell him to wait. Or have him call me here at the Good Apple. Or tell him to come over and meet me here."

"Okay, Jane, I will do my best."

"I appreciate it." She hung up and handed the phone back to Clive. "Thanks."

"You're welcome." He opened the door to the bakery.

But Justin didn't call or show up, and after two cups of coffee, Jane felt she should get back to the inn. "Just in case he's waiting there."

But he was not. No one had seen him. Clive excused himself to work on his book for a couple of hours, and Jane and her sisters gathered in the kitchen.

"So, what am I supposed to do?" Jane asked them impatiently. "Do I simply sit around all day, waiting for Justin to drop in at his leisure?"

They both admitted that they didn't know the answer to that question. Jane decided she would wait, but by one o'clock, she was bored and miffed, and when Clive invited her to give him a tour of the countryside, she eagerly agreed. However, this time she informed her sisters, telling them that he would have his cell phone, and she would ask that he leave it on. "All Justin needs to do is call me," she said as she wrote down the number. "And I'll meet him when he wants. Does that seem fair?"

"More than fair," said Alice. "Have a nice drive."

Chapter Twenty-Two

I can't believe that Justin didn't call yesterday," said Jane as she and her sisters prepared breakfast on Sunday morning.

"It seems rather odd to drive all this way and then avoid you," said Louise.

"Perhaps he thought he would be interrupting something," said Alice.

Jane thought that seemed unlikely but simply nodded as she poured warmed maple syrup into a glass decanter. Surely, Justin wouldn't assume that Jane would have no social life. It wasn't as if he'd made specific plans with her.

"Well, perhaps he will make an appearance today," said Louise.

"If he's still in the area." Jane was beginning to think that maybe he had left town without bothering to speak to her. Maybe he'd lost his nerve. Or maybe he'd seen her and decided that he didn't want to talk to her after all.

"I invited him to church," said Alice quietly.

"What?" Jane turned to stare at her sister.

Alice gave her a weak smile. "On Friday, while we were chatting, I invited him to church, Jane. It just seemed right."

"Do you think he will come?" asked Louise.

"I don't know. He said he'd consider it."

"I seriously doubt that he'll come, Alice," said Jane. "It was sweet of you to ask him, but it seems pretty unlikely."

"It would do him good to come," said Louise as she filled the teapot with hot water.

"I'd be shocked if he did," admitted Jane. "He was never interested in anything even remotely related to church."

"Maybe he's changed," said Alice.

Jane didn't think so. There was something about his turning his head away yesterday, as if ignoring her, and then driving off that made him seem like the same selfish, insensitive Justin. And more and more, she found herself hoping he had already left the state by now. She wished he'd never sent her that letter.

Still, she tried to repress these negative feelings as she, Clive and Alice walked to church together. Louise had gone early to play the organ. And the other guests, including Belle, were walking not far behind them.

"Miss Howard," called a pair of girlish voices from behind. The three of them stopped to see Ashley and Kate running toward them. They each took one of Alice's hands and asked if they could sit with her in church. "We're friends now," said Kate. "Thanks to you, Miss Howard," added Ashley.

Alice winked at Jane, then introduced Clive to the girls, telling them how Mr. Fagler was an important writer for a big Philadelphia newspaper. The girls looked duly impressed, but soon turned their full attention back to Alice, clinging to her hands as they all went into the chapel together. Then, because there wasn't enough room in any pew to seat all five of them, they split up. Alice and the girls sat in front with Jane and Clive behind them. Louise was already playing the organ, and Jane attempted to block the nagging thoughts of Justin from her mind as Kenneth came forward to preach. It was a fine sermon, and Jane knew she should focus on it, but paying attention was a challenge. Still, Jane did get the main theme: forgiveness. By the end of the service, she knew that the only person she needed to forgive—again—was Justin. And so, when Kenneth invited them to bow their heads and to use the quiet moment to forgive someone, Jane forgave Justin. She knew that she might not ever get a chance to tell him. Perhaps it didn't even matter. Most importantly, she forgave Justin.

But as Jane and Clive walked down the aisle toward the exit, she sucked in a quick breath. Justin was standing at the back of the church near the entrance. He had on a tan sports coat and jeans, and he was staring at her. Their eyes locked. Then his gaze shifted to Clive, and he frowned. Jane continued toward him, but before she could reach him, he turned and went out the door, followed by Florence and Ronald Simpson.

"That's Justin," she said quietly to Clive. "Will you excuse me while I attempt to catch him?"

"Of course."

Jane tried to press past members of the congregation as they happily greeted one another, clogging the aisle and blocking her way. It seemed to take forever before she finally made her way out the door. She stood for a moment, using a church bulletin to shield her eyes from the sun as she searched the church grounds, but Justin was nowhere to be seen.

"Everything okay?" asked Kenneth. He was getting into position to greet church members as they exited from the chapel.

"Justin was in church this morning," she told him quietly. She was still looking to the left and the right as if she expected Justin to hop out from behind the bushes at any moment.

"Good for him," said Kenneth. "I hope he enjoyed the sermon."

"Yes, so do I. But he seems to have disappeared. I don't see him anywhere."

"He certainly is an evasive person."

"Yes. You're probably beginning to think I've imagined he was in town."

Kenneth laughed. "I rather doubt that. Besides, didn't I see him yesterday? The red Fiat Spider?"

"Yes, that's right. Anyway, thanks for a wonderful sermon today." She shook his hand and stepped aside as she realized that others were waiting behind her now. She slowly walked out into the churchyard, looking out toward the street and thinking that she might still spot Justin or his sporty red car, but he had vanished.

"No luck?" asked Clive as he joined her.

"No. He must've been in a huge hurry to get away."

"I don't think he liked seeing you with me, Jane."

She nodded. "Yes, that crossed my mind."

"I'm sorry."

"Oh, it's not your fault, Clive. There's not much we can do if he wants to jump to conclusions. He's the one who took off running."

"Well, I hope he hasn't left for good."

Jane nodded. "And just when I'd forgiven him—again."

"That was a good message," said Clive as they began walking back toward the inn. "I don't normally attend church, and I certainly don't think of myself as a religious person, but I like your minister and he gives an excellent sermon."

"I'll let him know you said that."

"And something he said this morning has inspired me in regard to my book, Jane."

"Really?"

"Yes. I don't want to talk about it right now. But I think I will spend some time working on it today. While it's still fresh in my mind."

"Good for you."

Once again, Jane found herself waiting for Justin. After church, she and her sisters ate lunch, then Jane tried to stay busy, puttering in the kitchen, checking e-mail, reading a book. By late afternoon, she was fed up. What sort of game was he playing anyway? And who said she had to play along?

Jane was back in the kitchen again, pouring herself a glass of iced tea and thinking about calling Sylvia. She had missed seeing her friend at church this morning and hoped that nothing was wrong.

"Yoo-hoo?"

She knew it was Ethel at the back door, probably ready to lecture Jane again. She was tempted to make a run for it, but decided not to act like Justin. She would take the high road instead. "Hello, Auntie," she said cheerfully as she opened the door. "Care for some iced tea?"

Ethel looked surprised. "Well, yes, dear, that sounds nice."

Jane busied herself fixing another glass, even garnishing it with a sprig of mint. "Here you go, Auntie."

"Thank you, Jane." She took a sip and nodded in approval. "Now, Jane, what is going on with you and Justin? Belle told me that he's been here several times, but that you keep disappearing."

Jane shrugged. "I'm here now, Auntie. And I was here yesterday. I've spotted Justin a couple of times, and he's the one who keeps disappearing."

Ethel frowned. "That's odd."

"I agree."

"Belle thought Justin was very nice."

Jane felt her curiosity growing. "And did she say what Justin thought of her?"

"Belle told me they had an enjoyable time together, but she knew that he was here to see you." She set down her glass with a loud clunk. "The question is *why*, Jane. Why has he come? And why is he acting so mysteriously? What is going on?"

"I don't know, Auntie. The truth is I'm in the dark."

"Well, I'd like to have a chat with that young man."

Jane grinned. "If you can catch him, I'd say go for it." She set her empty glass in the sink. "But I'm getting tired of sitting around waiting for him to show up. He hasn't even called."

"Strange."

"Very."

"My guess is that he's here to get you back, Jane. He is feeling nervous and insecure, and you keep flitting about and—"

"Speaking of flitting about, I think I'll take a walk."

"Where are your sisters?"

Jane nodded her head in the direction of comforting tones of classical piano music coming from the open door of the parlor. "Louise, as you can hear, is playing, and Alice is at the Humberts' helping Vera with something or other."

"How about Belle? Is she here?"

"I don't know, Auntie. Why don't you look around?"

"Don't mind if I do."

"Would you tell Louise that I'm stepping out for a bit?" Jane reached for her purse. "I just need some fresh air."

"Certainly, dear. I will let her know. I do hope you and Justin can sit down and discuss this thing like civilized adults."

Jane suppressed the urge to scream as she simply nodded and made a quick exit. It was a relief to be away from the inn. Jane walked quickly toward town. She wasn't entirely sure where she was going, but it felt good to go. Perhaps she would pop in on Sylvia's Buttons to see if Sylvia was in the shop, as she sometimes was on Sundays, working on a personal project or catching up on paperwork. Maybe she could entice Sylvia to join her on her walk.

But Sylvia wasn't there. "She went to an estate sale in Lancaster early this morning," said Justine. "She just learned about it. She asked me to do inventory for her while the shop is closed."

"Would you tell Sylvia I stopped by?" asked Jane.

"Of course. Have a good day now," said Justine.

Jane went back outside.

"Jane?" called a female voice. Jane turned to see Belle, still dressed in her pink suit, which she'd worn to church. She was clicking toward Jane on her spike heels and waving with enthusiasm. "Oh, you are just the person I need."

"I am?" Jane waited for Belle.

"Yes. Are you busy right now?"

"Not particularly."

"Well, you have such a good eye for things like houses and gardens and kitchens and whatnot, and I just ran into Richard Watson, you know the real-estate agent, and he told me that another buyer is interested in that same little cottage that I've had my eye on. He told me that if I was serious, I should make an offer as soon as possible." Belle held up her hands in a helpless gesture. "And I just don't know what to do. It's a big decision, Jane. Would you be willing to walk through the house with me? I went through it once with Ethel, but I can't even remember if it had a bathtub or not. Imagine buying a house and not knowing something like that. I am a bubble-bath girl and I would simply perish without a bathtub."

Jane suppressed the urge to laugh. It was clear that Belle was perfectly serious. "I'd be happy to look at it with you."

Belle reached over and grabbed Jane's hand. "Oh, thank you, thank you. And, please, forgive me for being a bit upset with you the other day. I know you aren't trying to hog all the men on purpose, Jane. They just like you."

Jane laughed. "Perhaps it seems that way to you."

"Well, come along. Let's go to Richard's office and see if he's still there."

Soon, Jane and Belle were carefully going through the McCullough house, which was quite nice. And it did have a bathtub, an old-fashioned claw-foot that Belle simply adored. Jane tried to point out things that might require work, as well as things that added value to the house. "All in all," said Jane, "I think this is a sweet little bungalow, and if I were looking for a home to invest in, I would consider it myself."

"Oh, thank you, Jane," gushed Belle. "I do like it."

"Still . . ." Jane studied Belle's bright eyes. "Do you really think it's wise to buy a house here in Acorn Hill? I mean you haven't met Mr. Right yet and—"

"I know you think I'm crazy, Jane. Almost everyone in town does too. But it's like you said that time. It's my dream and I have to follow it."

"But buying a house, Belle?"

"You said yourself it was a good investment, Jane."

"Yes, but—"

"No buts." Belle firmly nodded. "I am going to make my offer."

"You're sure that's a good idea?"

"Yes. I'm going to speak to Richard about it right now. Do you want to come too?"

"I should probably get back to the inn."

"Have you talked to Justin yet?" asked Belle.

Jane shook her head.

Belle reached over and put a hand on Jane's arm. "I just do not understand you, Jane Howard. If ever there was a single woman who could get a man to marry her, I do believe it is you. And yet you seem to have absolutely no interest in doing so. What's up with that?"

Jane laughed. "I have no idea."

"Yes," said Belle as she locked the front door and slipped the house key into her purse. "I do believe that's a fact. And it's all I can do not to be pea green with envy."

Chapter Twenty-Three

*J*ane thought about what Belle had said as she walked back toward the inn. Of course, Belle's perspective had to be somewhat skewed by her own wedding hopes, but the truth was, Jane had no interest in being married right now. Not to anyone. It was a huge relief to admit this to herself, so much so that when she saw Justin's car parked in front of the inn, she was ready to express these feelings to him as well.

She walked up the porch steps and was about to enter the house when she heard the familiar squeak of the porch swing. She turned, and sitting there in the shadows was her ex-husband.

"Justin!" she exclaimed. "You startled me."

"Sorry about that." Justin slowly stood. "But we seem to be passing like two ships in the night."

"Or else you've been trying to avoid me."

"I thought you were trying to avoid me, Jane." He stepped closer, looking carefully at her. "You're looking well."

"You too."

"Do you have time to talk?"

Jane looked around the porch, wondering how private this would actually be, especially if guests decided to come out to enjoy some fresh air. "Here?"

"Maybe not." He pointed toward his car. "Want to take a ride?"

Just then, Jane noticed Louise and Ethel peeking out the front window. She wiggled her fingers in a little wave, and both women stepped back simultaneously. "Yes," she told him. "Too many observers here."

"They all seem quite curious," he said as they walked to his car. "Your aunt could probably get a job with the CIA."

Jane chuckled. "She can be inquisitive."

"I'll say."

"Nice car, Justin."

He opened the passenger door, smiling proudly as he helped her in. "Thanks. I've always wanted one of these. Just before Christmas last year, a customer at the restaurant mentioned he was selling his, and I thought, why not?"

She tried to focus on the attractive interior as he walked around to the other side. She forced herself to take in a slow, deep breath to settle her nerves. She could do this. She could.

"Want me to put the top down?" he offered when he was in the car.

"It's your call."

He shrugged, then started the engine, which purred. "Maybe later." As he drove through town, neither of them said a word, and the tension between them was palpable.

"So how have you been, Justin?" asked Jane, pretending that she was speaking to an old friend and not the man who had promised to stay with her until death would part them. "Are you at the same restaurant?"

"Yes." He told her about some mutual restaurant friends, which ones were still in San Francisco and which ones had moved on. "This is pretty countryside," he said. "I can see why you like it here, Jane."

"Yes." She gazed absently out the window, wondering why this had to be so difficult. "I saw you in church this morning, Justin," she began cautiously. "I tried to catch up with you, but you disappeared."

"Yes . . . I don't know what came over me. Sorry about that."

"It's okay. Did you enjoy the sermon?"

"Forgiveness?"

"Yes." She nodded.

"Do you mind if I pull over up there?"

"Not at all."

After stopping the car, he got out and put down the top.

"The fresh air is nice," she told him when he got back in.

He turned in the driver's seat, facing her. "Jane, I need to talk to you."

She smiled. "Here I am."

"Yes." He took in a deep breath. "This isn't easy."

She wanted to appear calm, but on the inside, she was in turmoil. She wished that whatever it was, he would get it over with.

"The reason I came to see you, Jane, is to tell you something."

She nodded. "Yes?"

"I know you've moved on with your life, Jane."

"Yes, I have."

"And you might even be involved seriously with someone by now. I've noticed you seem to have some men in your life."

"I wouldn't say I was serious about anyone, Justin. I don't think I'm ready for anything like that."

"Right."

"And just for the record, Justin . . ." She figured she might as well get this out into the open. "I have forgiven you for, well, everything. I thought I took care of forgiving you some time ago, but I was touched by today's sermon, and I realized that I was still carrying some baggage. So, if it's any comfort, you should know that I have forgiven you. And I hope that you've forgiven me."

"You?" He looked confused. "Why would I need to forgive you, Jane?"

"Oh, it takes two to mess things up. I knew how competitive you were about cooking, and still I didn't step back. I suppose I might have put my career second to yours. Our failed marriage was partially my fault too."

Now he firmly shook his head. "No, Jane. And that is what I came to tell you."

"What do you mean?" She studied his face, trying to understand what he was up to. Was this a trick? A way to get her to come back to him?

"I mean that I came to ask your forgiveness. It was my fault the marriage failed."

"But why bring this up now?"

"Because I've been suffering from a guilty conscience, and it's beginning to affect my health."

"Are you ill?"

He waved his hand. "Not seriously. Just an ulcer. Still, I knew I needed to make things right between us. I've been going to a counselor, and he suggested that I speak to you."

Jane simply nodded.

"Anyway, I know I made you believe that you were responsible for our marriage falling apart. I told you that you were competitive and that you made my life miserable. I said all sorts of horrible things to you, Jane. But the truth is that I have always been a jealous person. I never could stand anyone besting me. When we married, I thought that I would be the one to shine and that you would be the 'good cook' while I'd be the 'well-known chef.' Instead, things turned out just the opposite. You got rave reviews, and the Blue Fish was booked weeks in advance, while I was just plugging along as I always had. I couldn't stand it. I did some terrible things. . . ."

"You mean claiming my recipes were yours?"

He took in a quick breath. "Not just that. I hinted to reviewers that you got all your ideas from other people. That you couldn't create, that you could only present the work of others as your own."

Jane felt indignant. "I knew that you were trying to undermine me, but I never knew that you went so far."

He nodded with a guilty expression. "After I did it, I felt terrible. But the funny thing was the rumors never hurt you. I suspect no one believed me. The reviewers still raved about you, and the customers still called weeks in advance for reservations. I guess that made me even more determined to end our marriage. I just couldn't stand your success. Recently, I've thought a lot about what I did, the harm I caused you, and, well, I knew I needed to clear the air. For both our sakes."

So many emotions were rushing through her. She wasn't sure how to react.

"Say something," said Justin.

"I'm stunned."

"I'm sorry, Jane. I know I hurt you."

She sighed. "Yes, you did." She slowly shook her head as she tried to make sense of this. "And here I thought I had completely forgiven you."

"Now you're not so sure? Are you taking it back?"

"No, I just need to forgive you all over again."

"Can you?"

She hesitated, then said, "I don't think I can afford *not* to forgive you, Justin. Not according to what Kenneth said in church, or what the Bible says." She studied his sad face and felt a trace of sympathy for him. "You really have an ulcer?"

He nodded. "And high blood pressure too."

"Justin?"

"Yes?"

"I do forgive you. Okay?"

He brightened. "Okay."

"But I do think we're over. Don't you?"

His brow creased, and he nodded. "The fact is, I'm involved with someone else."

"Really?" Jane felt hopeful . . . and curious . . . and a teeny, tiny bit jealous.

"Her name is Lenore. She's a little older than me. She teaches accounting at a community college."

"Well, you won't have any professional jealousy between you then," said Jane with a smile.

"The truth is, I began to question my relationship with Lenore when I saw you again, Jane."

"Oh?"

"Yes." He let out an exasperated sigh. "I know I must seem flaky."

She didn't say anything, just watched him, trying to read his expression. Mostly, she thought he looked older.

"But yesterday, when I saw you, Jane, sitting outside with that guy, I felt so jealous."

"That was our minister. The one who preached today. He's simply a good friend, Justin."

"The point is that I felt jealous of him."

She didn't know what to say.

"And then when I saw you with that other fellow today, the one that Belle said was some hotshot journalist from Philadelphia, well, I got even more jealous."

"Oh, Justin."

"I know, it's crazy. I'm the one who let you go, and now I'm feeling like you've done me wrong."

"Do you really feel that way?"

"No, I suppose not. But even seeing you now, Jane . . ." He reached over and touched her cheek and, before she could stop herself, she jerked her head back, moving away from him. "I'm sorry," he said as he put his hand down.

"I'm sorry too, Justin." She felt confused. And, she hated to admit it, but she was inclined to agree with Justin. He was a little flaky.

"I asked Lenore to marry me, Jane. Right before I left on this trip."

She felt an enormous sense of relief. But she also felt concerned. "Do you love her, Justin? I mean I hope you have found someone special. I'd hate to see you make a mistake."

"I'm not sure if I really understand love," he admitted. "As you know, I'm a pretty selfish guy. Maybe I'm incapable of loving someone."

She couldn't completely disagree with him on that account. Even his unnecessary confession seemed self-serving. He'd been having health problems. He thought a clear conscience might improve his ulcer problem, lower his blood pressure, improve his quality of life, perhaps even help with his next marriage. Well, for his sake, she hoped it would.

"I suppose you want to go home now?" he asked.

"Actually, I do. It's been a long day."

"Thanks for listening," he said as he turned the car back toward town.

"You won't believe this," she said suddenly, hoping to change to a more lighthearted subject, "but I actually thought maybe you and Belle were going to hit it off, Justin. She is looking for a marrying man, you know."

He laughed. "I know. She told me all about her dream."

"So, you're not interested?"

"She's very sweet and pretty, but she's not my type." He turned and gazed longingly at her. "Not like you at all, Jane."

Finally, they were back at the inn. "Would you like to come in?" she asked in a way she knew must have sounded halfhearted.

"No, thanks. I think I'll be on my way."

"Back across the country?"

"Yes. This time I'll take the northern route and see some new sights."

"I wish you well, Justin."

"Thanks. You too." His eyes were sad, and she felt a lump in her throat as she told him, "Take care."

When she reached the steps to the inn, he tooted his horn and she turned and waved. She stood there and watched as his little red car drove slowly away. There was a sense of finality in this good-bye. She felt certain that Justin would not be back.

Chapter Twenty-Four

*T*he Memorial Day celebration went off without a hitch the following morning. Almost. The high school band played patriotic songs that were nearly on key. Calvin Horn raised the flag to the top of the pole, then slowly lowered it to half-staff in honor of those who had given their lives for their country. After that, Lloyd Tynan performed his mayoral role by giving a speech that was long-winded but heartfelt. Meanwhile, while no one was paying attention to her, Clara Horn's pet pig Daisy had a free-for-all in the recently restored planters as she uprooted and ate dozens of petunias that Jane and Craig had just put in.

"Oh my goodness," said Clara as they examined the destruction afterward. "I do hope poor Daisy doesn't get sick from eating all those blooms." She turned to Jane with concerned eyes. "Do you think the flowers are poisonous, dear?"

Jane reassured Clara that petunias were actually quite edible. "In moderation," she added, "although Daisy did make a pig of herself."

Alice giggled as she attempted to replant a ravaged petunia into one of the planters.

"We'll have these planters back to normal in no time," Craig told the flustered mayor as he winked at Jane.

"And the city will reimburse you for everything," Lloyd said to Craig. "Such a shame." He shook his finger at Daisy, who was now tied to the flagpole and looked a tiny bit guilty. "Bad girl!"

"Maybe we'll plant something different this time," Craig told Jane, assuming that she would be joining him. "As you know, I'm not a huge petunia fan anyway."

"Don't forget you all are invited to my house for a celebration barbecue," said Clara Horn to the inn crowd as well as Craig and Lloyd. "It's in honor of my greatnephew Calvin and his distinguished service to our country. I hope you'll all come."

"I know I'm going," said Belle happily. She was standing right next to Calvin, who looked quite handsome in his uniform. Jane wondered if perhaps he was the one, but judging by his deer-caught-in-the-headlights expression, that was probably not the case.

"How about you, Jane?" asked Clive. "Are you going?"

She stepped over the mess Daisy had made all over the sidewalk. "I might go if I thought Clara was planning to barbecue a certain *porker*."

"Oh, Jane," said Alice. "You like Daisy."

"I think I'd like her even better with a nice sweet-and-sour sauce."

Clive laughed loudly, but Louise gave Jane a warning glance suggesting that Clara might be in earshot.

"Just kidding," said Jane quickly. Then she turned back to Clive. "How about you, are you going to go catch a little more local color?"

He grinned. "I am getting a lot of inspiration for my book," he said quietly to her. "But I'm thinking I should get back to the city before the holiday traffic picks up. I have a column that's due tomorrow morning. Besides, I can't wait to see how my new terrace garden turns out."

"Don't forget that you promised to e-mail me photos," said Jane.

"And you promised to let me take you to lunch next time you're in town," he reminded her. "As a thank-you."

She shook his hand. "It's a deal."

"Then if you good ladies will accept my sincere gratitude for a lovely few days at your delightful inn, I think I will bid you all good-bye." He shook hands with all of them, pausing longer with Jane. "And I plan to come back to Grace Chapel Inn again, perhaps next fall."

Then Jane and her sisters walked over to Clara's house, where not a speck of barbecued pork was to be found, though the burgers were tasty and abundant.

"Belle seems to have latched onto poor Calvin," said Sylvia as she and Jane observed from the sidelines. "Do you think he's the one?"

"I don't know," said Jane. "But you should see all the wedding goodies that Belle has collected for the big event. I was putting fresh linens in her room this morning, and it looked like a mini bridal boutique in there."

"Oh my." Sylvia sighed. "I hope she's not too devastated next weekend."

Then Jane told Sylvia about yesterday's conversation with Justin. It was a relief to tell more of the details, and Sylvia, as usual, was an eager and sympathetic listener. Jane had told her sisters about how it had gone with Justin, but the inn was busy and then Clive requested some of her time. The plan was to fill them in more fully after things settled down.

"Get a look at that," whispered Sylvia as she nodded over to where Clara and Belle seemed to be having a private conversation behind the lilac bush. "Do you think Clara is asking Belle whether her intentions are honorable?"

Jane chuckled. "She's probably giving Belle romantic advice. Or perhaps she's setting up an appointment for a beauty consultation."

Unfortunately, for Belle's sake, they were both wrong. According to Ethel, who was always in the know, Clara was simply informing Belle that Calvin had a serious girlfriend back home. He had even been thinking about proposing to her. Consequently, on Tuesday morning, it appeared that Belle's last hopes of getting a man were completely dashed. And, as much as the sisters tried to cheer her, it seemed to be of no use. Not only that, but Wednesday afternoon, Belle learned that her offer to buy the McCullough house had been turned down. It seemed that someone had outbid her.

"It doesn't matter anyway," she told them all on Thursday morning. "I might as well give up and go home. I know when I've been beaten."

"You might not want to be stuck in a town with so many disappointing memories. Perhaps it's a blessing," said Alice as she refilled Belle's coffee cup.

Belle nodded sadly. She had come to breakfast wearing warm-ups and not a speck of makeup. Even her hair was not perfectly done as it usually was. Belle seemed so un-Belle-like that the sisters felt very sorry for her. The poor woman was clearly depressed.

"I don't know about that," said Ethel, mustering a positive tone. She had come by this morning to offer her condolences as much as to partake in Jane's cinnamon rolls. "I think we need Belle in Acorn Hill. I know plenty of women who were looking forward to trying out your beauty products, Belle. You can't let them down just because you haven't found the right man yet. You can't give up so easily."

"But the wedding," said Belle. "It was supposed to be this weekend."

"Maybe you had the date wrong," suggested Louise.

"Y'all are so sweet trying to cheer me up," said Belle. "But can't you see it's hopeless? I already called my folks and told them there would be no wedding." She let out a little sob. "No wedding."

"What about the flowers?" asked Jane as she suddenly imagined Wild Things buried in pink carnations and roses. "Did Craig already place an—"

"I called and canceled yesterday. He said it was okay."

"And the cake?" asked Jane.

Belle nodded. "I called the Good Apple too. It's all taken care of." Belle was really starting to cry. "It was going to be such a . . . such a pretty cake too."

Alice handed Belle a tissue, and Ethel stood and checked her watch. She patted Belle on the shoulder. "I'm sorry that I can't stay and commiserate with you, dear, but I did promise to meet Lloyd for coffee."

"It's okay," sniffed Belle. "I appreciate you coming by."

Ethel looked sternly at her nieces. "Since I have to go, it's up to you girls to make our Belle feel better."

"I'm sorry," said Alice. "I would be happy to stay with Belle, but I must go to work. It's my half day."

"Oh, don't y'all worry about me." Belle blew her nose loudly.

"And I must do books this morning," said Louise.

Jane looked at their unhappy guest. Belle's face was damp and pink from crying, and she reminded Jane of a wilted pink rose. "Maybe you'd like to join me in the kitchen, Belle," suggested Jane. "We can visit while I clean up."

Belle took in a quick, choppy breath and muttered a meek thanks as she followed Jane into the kitchen and sat down at the table with her coffee. Jane was trying to think of something, anything, to say that might cheer her up, but her mind was blank.

"I know I must seem like a shallow little fool to you, Jane. The way I've carried on, obsessing over every silly little detail of my wedding, my wedding that is never going to be. I'm sure y'all have enjoyed some good laughs at my expense. And I'll be the first one to admit that I deserve it."

"No, not at all." Jane felt really bad.

"But I have come to at least one conclusion."

"Yes?" Jane stopped rinsing a pot and looked at Belle.

"I know I was wrong to be so focused on all the trappings and trimmings of having the picture-perfect wedding. I can only blame that on the fact that I have dreamed of that day since I was just a little gal."

"That's understandable, Belle. Most little girls have similar dreams."

"But I think now that if I really did have a wedding, I would do it differently . . . not so much hoopla. Do you know what I mean?"

Jane nodded.

"And I think I would focus my energy on my husband instead of playing the role of queen for a day."

"I think that sounds very sensible," said Jane.

"That's Belle for you. I figure it all out after the party's over. I'm always a day late and a dollar short."

"Oh, I don't think—"

"I just feel so sorry that I've dragged all you good folks in Acorn Hill through my little drama. I think I should just pack up and head South."

At that moment the phone rang, and Jane was thankful for the distraction. Without waiting for Louise, she ran and picked it up. "Grace Chapel Inn," she said formally.

"This is Richard Watson," said a male voice. "Is Miss Bannister there?"

Jane handed Belle the phone. "It's for you," she said, quietly identifying the caller. Jane hoped that it wasn't more bad news.

Belle mustered a congenial hello, then listened quietly, her face completely devoid of expression. Finally, she said,

"Well, I suppose I could do that. If you really think— Okay, I'll be down in a little bit." Then she hung up.

"What is it?" asked Jane.

"Richard wanted me to know that I could make another offer on the house. He said that I could go higher than the other bid and maybe get the house. Of course, the other buyer could go higher than my second offer."

"Do you really want that house?" asked Jane. "I mean still?"

Belle shrugged.

"Do you want to remain in Acorn Hill even if you don't get married?" asked Jane. Despite Ethel's desire to keep her here, Jane was not convinced this was in Belle's best interest. And, as much as Jane had first been uneasy about this woman, she sincerely cared about her now.

"I do like it here, Jane. Acorn Hill feels like home to me. More so than the place I grew up."

"But do you like it well enough to reside here as a single woman?"

With tears still glistening in her eyes, Belle took in a deep breath then answered. "Yes. I do feel at home here, Jane. I really, truly do."

"You are absolutely certain?"

"I am certain." She gave a very firm nod. "Naturally, I would feel even more at home here if I were a married woman, but I will not let that stop me now."

Jane smiled at her. "Well, that's honest."

"And I really do believe I want that adorable cottage, Jane. I just love every little thing about it. Even if I take your advice and don't paint it pink. Do you think I'm crazy?"

"No, I don't. I think it's a darling little house—pink or otherwise. Do you want me to go down to the real-estate office with you?"

Belle's eyes lit up. "Yes. Yes, I do, Jane. Just give me a few minutes to clean up a bit. Not the whole nine yards, mind you, but I can at least put on some lipstick and run a comb through my hair."

Chapter Twenty-Five

To Jane's surprise, Belle was back downstairs in less than ten minutes. Her hair was combed and fluffed. She'd put on some makeup and changed into jeans topped with a crisp pink oxford shirt.

"Ready?" asked Jane as she reached for her car keys.

"Ready." Belle seemed to be returning to her old cheerful self as they drove toward the real-estate office. Her optimism and hopefulness were returning. But, to Jane's relief, there was no mention of weddings, husbands or dreams. Belle's primary focus seemed to be fixed on getting that bungalow. And Jane was ready to back her all the way.

Richard, an energetic man in his forties, greeted them both warmly, escorting them to his private office and explaining about making a new offer in meticulous detail. Belle decided on her terms and signed the necessary papers. She and Jane were in the reception area saying good-bye to Richard when the phone in his office rang, and he excused himself to get it. As he left the room, a middle-aged woman and a lanky middle-aged, balding man walked into the office. Jane recognized the woman from church but didn't know the gentleman.

"Hi, Mrs. Wren," said Jane, introducing her to Belle.

"You ladies have not met my cousin Larry Mitchell," said Mrs. Wren. "He just retired from the post office in Pittsburgh and plans to open a small business here in Acorn Hill."

"What sort of business?" Jane asked Larry politely.

He gave her a shy half smile, and his big brown eyes, which reminded her of a puppy's, lit up. "A shoe store actually."

"Oh, I simply adore shoes," said Belle. "If there's one thing a girl can never have too many of, it's shoes. Now what sort of shoes do you plan to carry in your shoe store, Mr. Mitchell?"

"You can call me Larry." He stood straighter. "I plan to sell sensible shoes. Comfortable shoes . . . shoes that are good for your feet."

Belle frowned. "Well, I suppose that could catch on, with some people anyway."

"After spending more than twenty years on my feet delivering mail," he continued in an earnest tone, looking directly at Belle, "I believe that people can only be as happy as their feet."

Belle's eyebrow creased as she thought about what he had said, and then she nodded. "You know, Larry, as much

as I hate to admit it, that does make sense. Goodness gracious, my tootsies can be wailing something awful by the
time I kick off a pretty pair of pumps."

"You see?"

"I certainly do. I never really thought about it before, but I
can get terribly grumpy after wearing high heels all day long."

"I don't think I've ever seen you grumpy," said Jane.

"That's only because I hide it."

Larry laughed. "Perhaps I'll have a customer in you
after all."

Richard joined them. "I see you've all met."

"Yes," said Belle. "Larry was just telling us about his
plans for a shoe store."

"Is that why you're here?" Jane asked Larry. "Are you
looking at business property in town?"

Richard cleared his throat. "This is awkward," he said,
"but I might as well get it out into the open. Larry is the
other party bidding on the McCullough house."

"My house?" asked Belle with wide eyes.

"It's not your house yet," said Mrs. Wren indignantly.

"You're the other bidder, Belle?" asked Larry. "Well,
I'm sorry. Perhaps I should—"

"You don't need to be sorry," said Mrs. Wren sharply.
"It's called free enterprise, Larry. You can bid on a house
if you want to."

"And if you really want it," began Belle. "I could always cancel my off—"

"No," said Larry quickly. "I can't ask you to do that, Belle. Maybe I should cancel my—"

"Maybe no one wants the house," said Mrs. Wren irritably. She turned to Richard. "This is certainly quite a fine kettle of fish."

"I'm sure we can work this all out amicably," he said. "This is awkward. I didn't anticipate your coming in this morning."

"Well, I think this was highly irregular," said Mrs. Wren.

Richard tried to explain to Mrs. Wren that his obligation was to the seller, whom he represented. He had the duty to get the seller the best price he could. As Mrs. Wren began to go on about business ethics and business etiquette, Jane noticed that Larry and Belle were standing about a foot apart, talking quietly while staring into each other's eyes in an infatuated manner.

"I have an idea," said Jane. "Why don't we let Belle and Larry settle this?" She nudged Richard. "Do you have someplace where they can sit down and talk about this alone?"

"Well, I suppose they could use my office."

"Come on, you two," said Jane as she led them toward Richard's private office. "You can go right in there, make yourselves at home, and discuss the situation." She smiled at Larry, whose expression was a mixture of bewilderment and happy anticipation. "I'm sure you'll discover that Belle is a kind and good-hearted young woman who wouldn't take advantage of a soul." Then she closed the door behind them.

"What on earth are you doing?" demanded Mrs. Wren.

"Oh, it's okay." Jane winked at the woman. "I have a feeling they can work this out on their own."

Belle and Larry did work it out. After a few minutes in Richard's office, the couple came out and announced that Larry would purchase the house. Then Larry said he was taking Belle for a ride and to dinner.

When the sisters tried to ask Belle about the decision on Friday morning at breakfast, she simply said that she felt it was the right thing to do. Then she excused herself from the table and rushed upstairs to get ready for her date with Larry.

The next evening, they went out again, and over dinner at Zachary's, Belle received Larry's wedding proposal. As it turned out, Larry popped the big question on the first Saturday of June, and Belle joyfully accepted.

"You see," she told Jane and her sisters at breakfast the following morning. "I just got my dates a little mixed up. That's all."

"So when *is* the big day?" asked Ethel who had joined them.

"We haven't set the actual date yet," said Belle with a happy sigh. "I think I'll be leaving that up to Larry. He needs to get his business plans worked out, and, really, I'm in no hurry now."

Jane refilled Belle's coffee cup and smiled. "That sounds wise."

"Besides," said Belle, "this gives me more time to work out all the details." She unfolded and smoothed out a wrinkly magazine page that showed a model wearing a ghastly pink bridesmaid's gown and showed it to them. "I would still love to have the four of you in my wedding. Oh, I can just see y'all standing up there in the chapel waiting for me to come down the aisle, wearing these delectable dresses and looking like a pretty row of pink tulips. Oh my, it's going to be simply divine."

Before the sisters could respond, Larry arrived and stopped at the dining room door. "I know I'm a little early," he said to Belle eagerly. "But maybe we can take a little stroll before we go to church?"

"Ready when you are," she said cheerfully. "See you girls later."

"And ready to wed," said Jane after the two had left. "Now if we can only think of a way to talk her out of those horrid pink dresses."

Later in the day, after all the guests had checked out except for Belle, who had taken Larry for a drive in her pink convertible, Jane fixed a tray with a pitcher of lemonade—not pink—and plate of sugar cookies and took them out to the porch. There, she and her sisters sat back and relaxed, enjoying the refreshments and peaceful quiet.

"It is impossible not to be happy for Belle," said Louise. "Despite all my earlier misgivings about her dream, I must admit that she seems to have made a good match in Larry Mitchell."

"I'm so glad she didn't give up." Alice smiled at Jane. "And you had much to do with that, Jane. I have a feeling Belle will want you for her maid of honor."

Jane groaned. "Oh, those awful pink dresses!"

"Speaking of marriages and weddings," said Louise, "we've been so busy that we never heard the details of your conversation with Justin, Jane. I don't want to seem intrusive, but Ethel continues to pester me with questions."

"I must admit that I've been curious too," admitted Alice. "I hate being nosy, but we are your sisters, Jane."

Jane patted Alice's hand. "You are the least nosy person I know, Alice. Neither you nor Louise ever pry into people's personal affairs."

"You should know, Jane," said Alice, "that Aunt Ethel has been speculating that you and Justin are secretly planning to remarry, despite our assurances to the contrary."

Louise nodded. "I would not be surprised if she has shared that idea with others."

"Oh dear, I'd better get that cleared up right away." Jane shared her conversation with Justin. "Mostly he just wanted to apologize," she said finally. "There is absolutely no chance that we would reunite. In fact, he has a fiancée."

"Jane, you have no idea what a relief this is for us," added Louise.

"Yes," agreed Alice. "We were getting nervous, Jane. Aunt Ethel kept saying how it was right for you to reunite with him and that we should be supportive if this were the case. She actually predicted that the two of you would remarry before summer ended."

"And that you would return to San Francisco where you would open a new world-class restaurant," added Louise.

"She certainly has an imagination," said Jane.

"And you know how much she loves a wedding," said Alice. "She's over the moon about Belle."

"She would be even more ecstatic if the wedding involved a member of the family." Louise nodded toward Jane. "Particularly a niece."

"Not this niece." Jane firmly shook her head. "I guess I should be extra thankful that our Belle has come through."

"I was so glad to hear that she made the decision to settle in Acorn Hill whether or not she got married," said Alice.

"Yes, it was the first time she wasn't completely obsessed with wedding bells," said Jane.

"Isn't that how God works?" said Alice. "He allowed Belle to reach the place where she accepted being single, and then He brought in the groom."

"However, there is nothing wrong with being single," said Louise firmly.

"Being single can be very freeing," said Alice. "Even though Vera is happily married, she reminds me of this fact at least once a week."

They all three chuckled.

"Freeing and satisfying." Jane sighed happily as she leaned back into the porch swing. What she had just said was absolutely and refreshingly true. "You know," she continued, "I wasn't so sure of that a few weeks ago. I was in such a slump because of the weather that I began to question my life choices."

"I think we all question such things at times," admitted Louise. "It's only natural."

"Human," added Alice.

"Yes. But now, after going through this stress with Justin and even the craziness with Belle, I can honestly say that I am truly content with my life." She smiled. "And that feels good."

"And you know what the Bible says in 1 Timothy 6:6," said Alice. "'Godliness with contentment is great gain.'"

"Yes," agreed Jane. "I think that should be my mantra: godliness with contentment *is* great gain."

"Amen," said Louise.

About the Author

*M*elody Carlson is the author of numerous books for children, teens and adults—with sales totaling more than two million copies. She has two grown sons and lives in central Oregon with her husband and a chocolate Labrador retriever.